ISAAC ASIMOV

PRESENTS THE BEST FANTASY OF THE 19TH CENTURY

Also edited by Isaac Asimov,
Charles G. Waugh,
and Martin H. Greenberg

Isaac Asimov Presents the Best Science Fiction of the 19th Century
The Science Fiction Solar System
The Thirteen Crimes of Science Fiction
TV: 2000

ISAAC ASIMOV
PRESENTS THE BEST FANTASY OF THE 19TH CENTURY

Edited by Isaac Asimov,
Charles G. Waugh,
and Martin H. Greenberg

BEAUFORT BOOKS, INC.
New York / Toronto

No character in this book is intended to represent any actual person; all the incidents of the stories are entirely fictional in nature.

Library of Congress Cataloging in Publication Data
Main entry under title:

Isaac Asimov presents the best fantasy of the 19th century.

1. Fantastic fiction. 2. Fiction—19th century.
I. Asimov, Isaac, 1920–
II. Waugh, Charles. III. Greenberg, Martin Harry.
PN6120.95.F25I8 808.83'876 82-4480
ISBN 0-8253-0099-1 AACR2

Published in the United States by Beaufort Books, Inc., New York.
Published simultaneously in Canada by General Publishing Co. Limited.

Printed in the U.S.A. First Edition
10 9 8 7 6 5 4 3 2 1

CONTENTS

Introduction: WHEN FANTASY BECAME FANTASY

Isaac Asimov

In some ways, all fiction writing is fantasy. If a tale is truly fiction, it never happened; and if it never happened, it is fantasy; it is a creation of the mind, the imagination. For that matter, if we want to be very strict about it, much supposed ''non-fiction'' is fantasy, too.

The fact is, though, we *don't* want to be very strict about it. If we define fantasy in such a way as to include almost everything, then the word loses its force and it comes to mean no more than ''writing.''

Let us look for a different definition. Fantasy should mean not only something that is not so and therefore exists only as an idea, but also something that *could not possibly be so* and therefore can exist *in no other way* than as an idea.

Thus, Charles Dickens's *Nicholas Nickleby* is not a fantasy. Though its characters never existed and its events never took place, those characters and events could have existed without upsetting the accepted order of the universe.

On the other hand, Dickens's ''A Christmas Carol'' is clearly a fantasy, for it deals with ghosts and with abstractions such as ''Christmas Past,'' which have been made concrete. The accepted order of the universe does not include ghosts and concretized abstractions.

In fact, we can be stricter still and insist that fantasy must deal not only with matters that we conceive as not capable of existence in our universe, but which we insist are incapable of existence even in a universe modified by reasonable scientific advance. If reasonable scientific advance *could* make them possible, then we would have science fiction. (To be sure, an ingenious person can manipulate the possibilities of scientific advance in such a way that what we would casually think of as fantasy can be made into a kind of science fiction. Usually, however, the manipulation is not bothered with, so that fantasy and science fiction remain distinct.)

And now that we have an idea as to what we mean by fantasy as a restricted branch of literature, we have a right to ask how old it is. It might seem a fair guess that fantasy is forever; that it is as old as language; as old as the human imagination.

It would seem that over the Stone Age campfires, our uncivilized ancestors froze each other's blood with tales of monsters, and ghosts, and demons of all sorts.

We'll never know that for sure, of course, so if we prefer to cling to greater certainties, we have to turn to the oldest surviving scraps of literature, and these, we find, are quite likely to deal with fantasy.

The Epic of Gilgamesh, written by nameless Sumerians about 2700 B.C., is, I believe, the oldest surviving work of fiction, and it contains elements of fantasy—gods, monsters, plants that confer immortality, and so on. The *Iliad* and *Odyssey* are to some extent fantasies, especially the latter. The tales of Polyphemus the Cyclops and of Circe the Witch remain, to this day, among the most popular fantasies in existence.

Folk tales are almost invariably fantasies; *The Arabian Nights* are fantasies, for instance, as are *Snow White* and *Cinderella*. Every age has its fantasies and even the twentieth century has developed some that rival those of the past in skill and popularity. Consider *Mary Poppins*, *The Hobbit*, and *Watership Down*.

And yet—when is a fantasy not a fantasy?

The answer, surely, is this: When its events are not accepted as running contrary to the accepted order of the universe. Even more so, when its events, however fantastic they may seem, are accepted as literal truth.

Thus, the Bible is filled with wonder tales—the speaking serpent in the Garden of Eden; the speaking ass that Balaam bestrode; the parting of the Red Sea; the deeds of Elijah and Elisha; the activities of Jesus as a healer. If these were encountered by some well-educated Chinese scientist who had never heard of the Bible before, he would have no hesitation in labeling the book a fantasy collection. Naturally, pious Jews and Christians would reject such a view with horror and would consider it blasphemous.

In the same way, unsophisticated people of the past who believed in the Olympian gods and goddesses and who had no doubt that strange monsters existed in the misty regions beyond the small patch of ground they knew well, would accept Homer's tales as accurate history in all its details.

And, in later times, those who believed in ghosts, or afreets, or ghouls, or fairies, or elves would accept tales involving them as at least true in concept, if not necessarily in detail, and they would not be thought of as fantasies at all.

How far into the present does this notion of fantasies that are not fantasies extend? Obviously, right into the present and, probably, into the future as far as the mind can see. Every religion seems like a fantasy to outsiders, but as holy truth to those of the faith. There are always people who are unsophisticated, because of youth or lack of modern secular and scientific education, who believe in Santa Claus, in zombies and voodoo, in the tooth fairy and the Easter bunny, and so on.

There are even adults who, to all appearances, are intelligent, educated, and sophisticated, who are nevertheless believers in astrology, spiritualism, creation-science, or other irrationalities that seem like nonsensical fantasy to those of us who are untainted by such things.

In that case, when, if ever, did we start thinking of fantasy as *fantasy*?

No doubt there were always some sceptics, some people we would view today as hard-headed realists, in even the most superstitious and faith-ridden times. These people scorned anything not based on observational and rational evidence, and were firm in the belief that what most people accepted without question was, in actuality, mere fantasy.

This is, however, not enough. The occasional skeptic can barely make a mark on society. Did there come a time, however, when such rationalism became an accepted part of a secular society and when people in reasonably large numbers were educated into the belief that the universe could be understood only by reason, so that anything beyond that was fantasy?

Such a state of affairs began to arrive in the western world after the end of the period of the religious wars and the coming of the Age of Reason. The latter half of the seventeenth century, the time of the Royal Society and of Isaac Newton, marks the dividing line.

Even then, however, rationality was confined to a rather thin layer of the educated. It was not till the nineteenth century that, in the western world, there gradually arose the notion of mass-education under the control of a secular state. For the first time, there were extensive regions in which large percentages of the population were educated in school systems that were not run by some religious group or other. And then, for the first time, there arose large numbers of individuals who could tell what fantasy was and who enjoyed it all the more because they recognized it as pure exercises of untrammeled imagination.

In introducing *Isaac Asimov Presents the Best Science Fiction of the 19th Century* (the companion volume to this), I said that the nineteenth century was the first century of science fiction. I believe, for the reasons I have presented, that it was the first century of true fantasy as well, and the stories represented in this book are the prize examples of that first century.

Washington Irving (1783–1859)

Essayist, short-story writer, biographer, humorist, and historian, Washington Irving is a good illustration of the problems involved in evaluating pioneers. Critics are bitterly divided about the quality of his writing and the worth of his work, though most would agree upon his credentials as the father of American literature, one of the fathers of the short story, and the first American writer to achieve international fame.

Born in New York City, the last of eleven children, Irving grew up the beloved favorite of his brothers and sisters. He constantly perused his father's library even though his formal schooling was sketchy, so that when, at the age of sixteen, delicate health prevented him from attending Columbia University, he turned to reading law. At the time, his brother Peter ran a newspaper, *The Morning Chronicle*, and Irving began submitting humorous sketches. They became his first book, *The Letters of Jonathan Oldstyle, Gent*. (1802–1803).

Ill health forced him to travel abroad for two years, but when he returned, he was admitted to the bar, and published his first major success, Knickerbocker's *A History of New York* (1809).

In 1810, to help subsidize his literary activities, two of his brothers included him as a partner in an importing firm they had founded. Five years later he left to manage the Liverpool, England, office, but the company failed in 1818 and Irving was forced to depend entirely on his literary skills. He responded with his best work, *The Sketch Book of Geoffrey Crayon* (1819–1820), which brought him fame and wealth.

As his money started running low six years later, he received an offer to translate some papers about Christopher Columbus. He traveled to Madrid and ended up producing four original books including *A*

History of the Life and Voyages of Columbus (1828) and *The Legends of the Alhambra* (1832).

By now his reputation was so great that he returned home to adulation in 1832. Journeying out West, he wrote a book on the subject, and then bought an estate near Tarrytown. He left to serve as Minister to Spain for four years (1842–1846), but returned to begin a number of projects, including a five volume *Life of Washington* that ruined his health and probably quickened his death.

Personally, Irving was a magnetic charmer whose good looks in youth and diplomatic nature in later life helped insure many of his successes. His twenty-five fantastic stories were based mainly on folktales and legends, and set mostly in Spain or elsewhere in Europe. But the story we chose for this collection, ''The Legend of Sleepy Hollow,'' has been referred to as uniquely American[1] and ''an inseparable part of our national heritage.'' One of his two most famous works, it foreshadows regional conflicts and features charming prose and picturesque characters.

---

[1]It is, however, based on Bürger's *Der Wilde Jäger* and one of the Rübezahl tales.

THE LEGEND OF SLEEPY HOLLOW

Found among the Papers of the Late Diedrich Knickerbocker

A pleasing land of drowsy head it was,
Of dreams that wave before the half-shut eye;
And of gay castles in the clouds that pass,
For ever flushing round a summer sky.

CASTLE OF INDOLENCE

In the bosom of one of those spacious coves which indent the eastern shore of the Hudson, at that broad expansion of the river denominated by the ancient Dutch navigators the Tappan Zee, and where they always prudently shortened sail, and implored the protection of Saint Nicholas when they crossed, there lies a small market-town or rural port, which by some is called Greensburgh, but which is more generally and properly known by the name of Tarry Town. This name was given, we are told, in former days, by the good housewives of the adjacent country, from the inveterate propensity of their husbands to linger about the village tavern on market days. Be that as it may, I do not vouch for the fact, but merely advert to it, for the sake of being precise and authentic. Not far from this village, perhaps about two miles, there is a little valley, or rather lap of land, among high hills, which is one of the quietest places in the whole world. A small brook glides through it, with just murmur enough to lull one to repose; and the occasional whistle of a quail, or tapping of a woodpecker, is almost the only sound that ever breaks in upon the uniform tranquility.

I recollect that, when a stripling, my first exploit in squirrel-shooting was in a grove of tall walnut trees that shades one side of the valley. I had wandered into it at noontime, when all nature is peculiarly quiet, and was startled by the roar of my own gun, as it broke the Sabbath stillness around, and was prolonged and reverberated by the angry echoes. If every I should wish for a retreat, whither I might steal from the world and its distractions, and dream quietly away the remnant of a troubled life, I know of none more promising that this little valley.

From the listless repose of the place, and the peculiar character of its inhabitants, who are descendants from the original Dutch settlers, this sequestered glen has long been known by the name of Sleepy Hollow, and its rustic lads are called the Sleepy Hollow Boys throughout all the neighboring country. A drowsy, dreamy influence seems to hang over the land, and to pervade the very atmosphere. Some say that the place was bewitched by a high German doctor, during the early days of the settlement; others, that an old Indian chief, the prophet or wizard of his tribe, held his powwows there before the country was discovered by Master Hendrick Hudson. Certain it is, the place still continues under the sway of some witching power, that holds a spell over the minds of the good people, causing them to walk in a continual reverie. They are given to all kinds of marvellous beliefs; are subject to trances and visions; and frequently see strange sights, and hear music and voices in the air. The whole neighborhood abounds with local tales, haunted spots, and twilight superstitions; stars shoot and meteors glare oftener across the valley than in any other part of the country, and the nightmare, with her whole nine fold, seems to make it the favorite scene of her gambols.

The dominant spirit, however, that haunts this enchanted region, and seems to be commander-in-chief of all the powers of the air, is the apparition of a figure on horseback without a head. It is said by some to be the ghost of a Hessian trooper, whose head had been carried away by a cannonball, in some nameless battle during the Revolutionary War; and who is ever and anon seen by the country folk, hurrying along in the gloom of night, as if on the wings of the wind. His haunts are not confined to the valley, but extend at times to the adjacent roads, and especially to the vicinity of a church at no great distance. Indeed, certain of the most authentic historians of those parts, who have been careful in collecting and collating the floating facts concerning this spectre, allege that the body of the trooper, having been buried in the churchyard, the ghost rides forth to the scene of battle in nightly quest of his head; and that the rushing speed with which he sometimes passes along the Hollow, like a midnight blast, is owing to his being belated, and in a hurry to get back to the churchyard before daybreak.

Such is the general purport of this legendary superstition, which has furnished materials for many a wild story in that region of shadows; and the spectre is known, at all the country firesides, by the name of the Headless Horseman of Sleepy Hollow.

It is remarkable that the visionary propensity I have mentioned is not confined to the native inhabitants of the valley, but is unconsciously imbibed by everyone who resides there for a time. However wide awake they may have been before they entered that sleepy region, they are sure, in a little time, to inhale the witching influence of the air, and begin to grow imaginative—to dream dreams, and see apparitions.

I mention this peaceful spot with all possible laud; for it is in such little retired Dutch valleys, found here and there embosomed in the great state of New York, that population, manners, and customs, remain fixed; while the great torrent of migration and improvement, which is making such incessant changes in other parts of this restless country, sweeps by them unobserved. They are like those little nooks of still water which border a rapid stream; where we may see the straw and bubble riding quietly at anchor, or slowly revolving in their mimic harbor, undisturbed by the rush of the passing current. Though many years have elapsed since I trod the drowsy shades of Sleepy Hollow, yet I question whether I should not still find the same trees and the same families vegetating in its sheltered bosom.

In this by-place of nature, there abode, in a remote period of American history, that is to say, some thirty years since, a worthy wight of the name of Ichabod Crane; who sojourned, or, as he expressed it, "tarried," in Sleepy Hollow, for the purpose of instructing the children of the vicinity. He was a native of Connecticut; a state which supplies the Union with pioneers for the mind as well as for the forest, and sends forth yearly its legions of frontier woodsmen and country schoolmasters. The cognomen of Crane was not inapplicable to his person. He was tall, but exceedingly lank, with narrow shoulders, long arms and legs, hands that dangled a mile out of his sleeves, feet that might have served for shovels, and his whole frame most loosely hung together. His head was small, and flat at top, with huge ears, large green glassy eyes, and a long snipe nose, so that it looked like a weathercock, perched upon his spindle neck, to tell which way the wind blew. To see him striding along the profile of a hill on a windy day, with his clothes bagging and fluttering about him, one might have mistaken him for the genius of famine descending upon the earth, or some scarecrow eloped from a cornfield.

His schoolhouse was a low building of one large room, rudely constructed of logs; the windows partly glazed, and partly patched with leaves of old copybooks. It was most ingeniously secured at vacant hours, by a withe twisted in the handle of the door, and stakes set against the window shutters; so that, though a thief might get in with perfect ease, he would find some embarrassment in getting out; an idea most probably borrowed by the architect, Yost Van Houten, from the mystery of an eel-pot. The schoolhouse stood in a rather lonely but pleasant situation, just at the foot of a woody hill, with a brook running close by, and a formidable birch tree growing at one end of it. From hence the low murmur of his pupils' voices, conning over their lessons, might be heard in a drowsy summer's day, like the hum of a beehive; interrupted now and then by the authoritative voice of the master, in the tone of menace or command; or, peradventure, by the appalling sound of the birch, as he urged some tardy loiterer along the flowery path of knowledge. Truth to say, he was a conscientious man, and ever bore in mind the golden maxim, "Spare the rod and spoil the child."—Ichabod Crane's scholars certainly were not spoiled.

I would not have it imagined, however, that he was one of those cruel potentates of the school, who joy in the smart of their subjects; on the contrary, he administered justice with discrimination rather than severity; taking the burthen off the backs of the weak, and laying it on those of the strong. Your mere puny stripling, that winced at the least flourish of the rod, was passed by with indulgence; but the claims of justice were satisfied by inflicting a double portion on some little, tough, wrongheaded, broad-skirted Dutch urchin, who sulked and swelled and grew dogged and sullen beneath the birch. All this he called "doing his duty by their parents"; and he never inflicted a chastisement without following it by the assurance, so consolatory to the smarting urchin, that "he would remember it, and thank him for it the longest day he had to live."

When school hours were over, he was even the companion and playmate of the larger boys; and on holiday afternoons would convoy some of the smaller ones home, who happened to have pretty sisters, or good housewives for mothers, noted for the comforts of the cupboard. Indeed it behooved him to keep on good terms with his pupils. The revenue arising from his school was small, and would have been scarcely sufficient to furnish him with daily bread, for he was a huge feeder, and though lank, had the dilating powers of an anaconda; but to help out his maintenance, he was, according to country custom in those parts, boarded and lodged at the houses of the farmers, whose children he instructed. With these he lived successively a week at a time; thus going the rounds of the neighborhood, with all his worldly effects tied up in a cotton handkerchief.

That all this might not be too onerous on the purses of his rustic patrons, who are apt to consider the costs of schooling a grievous burden, and schoolmasters as mere drones, he had various ways of rendering himself both useful and agreeable. He assisted the farmers occasionally in the lighter labors of their farms; helped to make hay; mended the fences; took the horses to water; drove the cows from pasture; and cut wood for the winter fire. He laid aside, too, all the dominant dignity and absolute sway with which he lorded it in his little empire, the school, and became wonderfully gentle and ingratiating. He found favor in the eyes of the mothers, by petting the children, particularly the youngest; and like the lion bold, which whilom so magnanimously the lamb did hold, he would sit with a child on one knee, and rock a cradle with his foot for whole hours together.

In addition to his other vocations, he was the singing master of the neighborhood, and picked up many bright shillings by instructing the young folks in psalmody. It was a matter of no little vanity to him, on Sundays, to take his station in front of the church gallery, with a band of chosen singers; where, in his own mind, he completely carried away the palm from the parson. Certain it is, his voice resounded far above all the rest of the congregation; and there are peculiar quavers still to be heard in that church, and which may even be heard half a mile off, quite to the opposite side of the millpond, on a still Sunday morning, which are said to be legitimately descended from the nose of Ichabod Crane. Thus, by divers little makeshifts in that ingenious way which is commonly denominated "by hook and by crook," the worthy pedagogue got on tolerably enough, and was thought, by all who understood nothing of the labor of headwork, to have a wonderfully easy life of it.

The schoolmaster is generally a man of some importance in the female circle of a rural neighborhood; being considered a kind of idle gentlemanlike personage, of vastly superior taste and accomplishments to the rough country swains, and, indeed, inferior in learning only to the parson. His appearance, therefore, is apt to occasion some little stir at the tea-table of a farmhouse, and the addition of a supernumerary dish of cakes or sweetmeats, or, peradventure, the parade of a silver teapot. Our man of letters, therefore, was peculiarly happy in the smiles of all the country damsels. How he would figure among them in the churchyard, between services on Sundays! gathering grapes for them from the wild vines that overrun the surrounding trees; reciting for their amusement all the epitaphs on the tombstones; or sauntering, with a whole bevy of them, along the banks of the adjacent millpond; while the more bashful country bumpkins hung sheepishly back, envying his superior elegance and address.

From his half itinerant life, also, he was a kind of travelling gazette, carrying the whole budget of local gossip from house to house; so that his appearance was always greeted with satisfaction. He was, morever, esteemed by the women as a man of great erudition, for he had read several books quite through, and was a perfect master of Cotton Mather's *History of New England Witchcraft*, in which, by the way, he most firmly and potently believed.

He was, in fact, an odd mixture of small shrewdness and simple credulity. His appetite for the marvellous, and his powers of digesting it, were equally extraordinary; and both had been increased by his residence in this spellbound region. No tale was too gross or monstrous for his capacious swallow. It was often his delight, after his school was dismissed in the afternoon, to stretch himself on the rich bed of clover, bordering the little brook that whimpered by his schoolhouse, and there con over old Mather's direful tales, until the gathering dusk of the evening made the printed page a mere mist before his eyes. Then, as he wended his way, by swamp and stream and awful woodland, to the farmhouse where he happened to be quartered, every sound of nature, at that witching hour, fluttered his excited imagination: the moan of the whippoorwill from the hillside; the boding cry of the treetoad, that harbinger of a storm; the dreary hooting of the screech owl, or the sudden rustling in the thicket of birds frightened from their roost. The fireflies, too, which sparkled most vividly in the darkest places, now and then startled him, as one of uncommon brightness would stream across his path; and if, by chance, a huge blockhead of a beetle came winging his blundering flight against him, the poor varlet was ready to give up the ghost, with the idea that he was struck with a witch's token. His only resource on such occasions, either to drown thought, or drive away evil spirits, was to sing psalm tunes;—and the good people of Sleepy Hollow, as they sat by their doors of an evening, were often filled with awe, at hearing his nasal melody, "in linked sweetness long drawn out," floating from the distant hill, or along the dusky road.

Another of his sources of fearful pleasure was to pass long winter evenings with the old Dutch wives as they sat spinning by the fire, with a row of apples roasting and spluttering along the hearth, and listen to their marvellous tales of ghosts and goblins, and haunted fields, and haunted brooks, and haunted bridges, and haunted houses, and particularly of the headless horseman, or Galloping Hessian of the Hollow, as they sometimes called him. He would delight them equally by his anecdotes of witchcraft, and of the direful omens and portentous sights and sounds in the air, which prevailed in the earlier times of Connecticut; and would frighten them woefully with speculations upon comets and shooting stars; and with the alarming fact that the world did absolutely turn round, and that they were half the time topsy-turvy!

But if there was a pleasure in all this, while snugly cuddling in the chimney corner of a chamber that was all of a ruddy glow from the crackling wood fire, and where, of course, no spectre dared to show his face, it was dearly purchased by the terrors of his subsequent walk homewards. What fearful shapes and shadows beset his path amidst the dim and ghastly glare of a snowy night!—With what wistful look did he eye every trembling ray of light streaming across the waste fields from some distant window!—How often was he appalled by some shrub covered with snow, which, like a sheeted spectre, beset his very path!—How often did he shrink with curdling awe at the sound of his own steps on the frosty crust beneath his feet; and dread to look over his shoulder, lest he should behold some uncouth being tramping close behind him!—and how often was he thrown into complete dismay by some rushing blast, howling among the trees, in the idea that it was the Galloping Hessian on one of his nightly scourings!

All these, however, were mere terrors of the night, phantoms of the mind that walk in darkness; and though he had seen many spectres in his time, and been more than once beset by Satan in divers shapes in his lonely perambulations, yet day light put an end to all these evils; and he would have passed a pleasant life of it, in despite of the Devil and all his works, if his path had not been crossed by a being that causes more perplexity to mortal man than ghosts, goblins, and the whole race of witches put together, and that was—a woman.

Among the musical disciples who assembled, one evening in each week, to receive his instructions in psalmody, was Katrina Van Tassel, the daughter and only child of a subtantial Dutch farmer. She was a blooming lass of fresh eighteen; plump as a partridge; ripe and melting and rosy cheeked as one of her father's peaches, and universally famed, not merely for her beauty, but her vast expectations. She was withal a little of a coquette, as might be perceived even in her dress, which was a mixture of ancient and modern fashions, as most suited to set off her charms. She wore the ornaments of pure yellow gold, which her great-great-grandmother had brought over from Saardam; the tempting stomacher of the olden time; and withal a provokingly short petticoat, to display the prettiest foot and ankle in the country round.

Ichabod Crane had a soft and foolish heart toward the sex; and it is not to be wondered at, that so tempting a morsel soon found favor in his eyes; more especially after he had visited her in her paternal mansion. Old Baltus Van Tassel was a perfect picture of a thriving, contented, liberal-hearted farmer. He seldom, it is true, sent either his eyes or his thoughts beyond the boundaries of his own farm; but within those everything was snug, happy, and well-conditioned. He was satisfied with his wealth, but not proud of it; and piqued himself upon the hearty abundance, rather than the style in which he lived. His stronghold was situated on the banks of the Hudson, in one of those green, sheltered, fertile nooks, in which the Dutch farmers are so fond of nestling. A great elm tree spread its broad branches over it; at the foot of which bubbled up a spring of the softest and sweetest water, in a little well, formed of a barrel; and then stole sparkling away through the grass, to a neighboring brook, that bubbled along among alders and dwarf willows. Hard by the farmhouse was a vast barn, that might have served for a church; every window and crevice of which seemed bursting forth with the treasures of the farm; the flail was busily resounding within it from morning to night; swallows and martins skimmed twittering about the eaves; and rows of pigeons, some with one eye turned up, as if watching the weather, some with their heads under their winds, or buried in their bosoms, and others swelling, and cooing, and bowing about their dames, were enjoying the sunshine on the roof. Sleek unwieldy porkers were grunting in the repose and abundance of their pens; whence sallied forth, now and then, troops of sucking pigs, as it to snuff the air. A stately squadron of snowy geese were riding in an adjoining pond, convoying whole fleets of ducks; regiments of turkeys were gobbling through the farmyard, and guinea fowls fretting about it, like ill-tempered housewives, with their peevish discontented cry. Before the barn door strutted the gallant cock, that pattern of a husband, a warrior, and a fine gentleman, clapping his burnished wings, and crowing in the pride and gladness of his heart—sometimes tearing up the earth with his feet, and then generously calling his ever-hungry family of wives and children to enjoy the rich morsel which he had discovered.

The pedagogue's mouth watered, as he looked upon this sumptuous promise of luxurious winter fare. In his devouring mind's eye, he pictured to himself every roasting-pig running about with a pudding in his belly, and an apple in his mouth; the pigeons were snugly put to bed in a comfortable pie, and tucked in with a coverlet of crust; the geese were swimming in their own gravy; and the ducks pairing cosily in dishes, like snug married couples, with a decent competency of onion sauce. In the porkers he saw carved out the future sleek side of bacon, and juicy relishing ham; not a turkey but he beheld daintily trussed up, with its gizzard under its wing, and peradventure, a necklace of savory sausages; and even bright chanticleer himself lay sprawling on his back, in a side dish, with uplifted claws, as if craving that quarter which his chivalrous spirit disdained to ask while living.

As the enraptured Ichabod fancied all this and as he rolled his great green eyes over the fat meadowlands, the rich fields of wheat, of rye, of buckwheat, and Indian corn, and the orchards burthened with ruddy fruit, which surrounded the warm tenement of Van Tassel, his heart yearned after the damsel who was to inherit these domains, and his imagination expanded with the idea, how they might be readily turned into cash, and the money invested in immense tracts of wild land, and shingle palaces in the wilderness. Nay, his busy fancy already realized his hopes, and presented to him the blooming Katrina, with a whole family of children, mounted on the top of a wagon loaded with household trumpery, with pots and kettles dangling beneath; and he beheld himself bestriding a pacing mare, with a colt at her heels, setting out for Kentucky, Tennessee, or the Lord knows where.

When he entered the house the conquest of his heart was complete. It was one of those spacious farmhouses, with high-ridged, but lowly sloping roofs, built in the style handed down from the first Dutch settlers; the low projecting eaves forming a piazza along the front, capable of being closed up in bad weather. Under this were hung flails, harness, various utensils of husbandry, and nets for fishing in the neighboring river. Benches were built along the sides for summer use; and a great spinning wheel at one end, and a churn at the other, showed the various uses to which this important porch might be devoted. From this piazza the wondering Ichabod entered the hall, which formed the centre of the mansion and the place of usual residence. Here, rows of resplendent pewter, ranged on a long dresser, dazzled his eyes. In one corner stood a huge bag of wool ready to be spun; in another a quantity of linsey-wooley just from the loom; ears of Indian corn, and strings of dried apples and peaches, hung in gay festoons along the walls, mingled with the gaud of red peppers; and a door left ajar gave him a peep into the best parlor, where the claw-footed chairs, and dark mahogany tables, shone like mirrors; and irons, with their accompanying shovel and tongs, glistened from their covert of asparagus tops; mock oranges and conch shells decorated the mantelpiece; strings of various colored birds' eggs were suspended above it: a great ostrich egg was hung from the centre of the room, and a corner cupboard, knowingly left open, displayed immense treasures of old silver and well-mended china.

From the moment Ichabod laid his eyes upon these regions of delight, the peace of his mind was at an end, and his only study was how to gain the affections of the peerless daughter of Van Tassel. In this enterprise, however, he had more real difficulties than generally fell to the lot of a knight-errant of yore, who seldom had any thing but giants, enchanters, fiery dragons, and such like easily-conquered adversaries, to contend with; and had to make his way merely through gates of iron and brass, and walls of adamant, to the castle keep, where the lady of his heart was confined; all which he achieved as easily as a man would carve his way to the center of a Christmas pie; and then the lady gave him her hand as a matter of course. Ichabod, on the contrary, had to win his way to the heart of a country coquette, beset with a labyrinth of whims and caprices, which were forever presenting new difficulties and impediments; and he had to encounter a host of fearful adversaries of real flesh and blood, the numerous rustic admirers, who beset every portal to her heart; keeping a watchful and angry eye upon each other, but ready to fly out in the common cause against any new competitor.

Among these the most formidable was a burly, roaring, roystering blade, of the name of Abraham or, according to the Dutch abbreviation, Brom Van Brunt, the hero of the country round, which rang with his feats of strength and hardihood. He was broad shouldered and double-jointed, with short curly black hair, and a bluff, but not unpleasant countenance, having a mingled air of fun and arrogance. From his Herculean frame and great powers of limb, he had received the nickname of "Brom Bones," by which he was universally known. He was famed for great knowledge and skill in horsemanship, being as dexterous on horseback as a Tartar. He was foremost at all races and cockfights; and, with the ascendency which bodily strength acquires in rustic life, was the umpire in all disputes, setting his hat on one side, and giving his decisions with an air and tone admitting of no gainsay or appeal. He was always ready for either a fight or a frolic; but had more mischief than ill will in his composition; and, with all his overbearing roughness, there was a strong dash of waggish good humor at bottom. He had three or four boon companions, who regarded him as their model, and at the head of whom he scoured the country, attending every scene of feud or merriment for miles round. In cold weather he was distinguished by a fur cap, surmounted with a flaunting fox's tail; and when the folks at a country gathering descried this well-known crest at a distance, whisking about among a squad of hard riders, they always stood by for a squall. Sometimes his crew would be heard dashing along past the farmhouses at midnight, with whoop and halloo, like a troop of Don Cossacks; and the old dames, startled out of their sleep, would listen for a moment till the hurry-scurry had clattered by, and then exclaim, "Ay, there goes Brom Bones and his gang!" The neighbors looked upon him with a mixture of awe, admiration, and good will; and when any madcap prank, or rustic brawl, occurred in the vicinity, always shook their heads, and warranted Brom Bones was at the bottom of it.

This rantipole hero had for some time singled out the blooming Katrina for the object of his uncouth gallantries, and though his amorous toyings were something like the gentle caresses and endearments of a bear, yet it was whispered that she did not altogether discourage his hopes. Certain it is, his advances were signals for rival candidates to retire, who felt no inclination to cross a lion in his amours; insomuch, that when his horse was seen tied to Van Tassel's paling, on a Sunday night, a sure sign that his master was courting, or, as it is termed, "sparking," within all other suitors passed by in despair, and carried the war into other quarters.

Such was the formidable rival with whom Ichabod Crane had to contend, and, considering all things, a stouter man than he would have shrunk from the competition, and a wiser man would have despaired. He had, however, a happy mixture of pliability and perseverance in his nature; he was in form and spirit like a supplejack—yielding, but tough; though he bent, he never broke; and though he bowed beneath the slightest pressure, yet, the moment it was away—jerk! he was erect, and carried his head as high as ever.

To have taken the field openly against his rival would have been madness; for he was not a man to be thwarted in his amours, any more than that stormy lover Achilles. Ichabod, therefore, made his advances in a quiet and gently-insinuating manner. Under cover of his character of singing master, he made frequent visits at the farmhouse; not that he had anything to apprehend from the meddlesome interference of parents, which is so often a stumbling block in the path of lovers. Balt Van Tassel was an easy indulgent soul; he loved his daughter better even than his pipe, and, like a reasonable man and an excellent father, let her have her way in everything. His notable little wife, too, had enough to do to attend to her housekeeping and manage her poultry; for, as she sagely observed, ducks and geese are foolish things, and must be looked after, but girls can take care of themselves. Thus while the busy dame bustled about the house, or plied her spinning wheel at one end of the piazza, honest Balt would sit smoking his evening pipe at the other, watching the achievements of a little wooden warrior, who, armed with a sword in each hand, was most valiantly fighting the wind on the pinnacle of the barn. In the meantime, Ichabod would carry on his suit with the daughter by the side of the spring under the great elm, or sauntering along in the twilight, that hour so favorable to the lover's eloquence.

I profess not to know how women's hearts are wooed and won. To me they have always been matters of riddle and admiration. Some seem to have but one vulnerable point, or door of access; while others have a thousand avenues, and may be captured in a thousand different ways. It is a great triumph of skill to gain the former, but a still greater proof of generalship to maintain possession of the latter, for the man must battle for his fortress at every door and window. He who wins a thousand common hearts is therefore entitled to some renown; but he who keeps undisputed sway over the heart of a coquette, is indeed a hero. Certain it is, this was not the case with the redoubtable Brom Bones; and from the moment Ichabod Crane made his advances, the interests of the former evidently declined; his horse was no longer seen tied at the palings on Sunday nights, and a deadly feud gradually arose between him and the preceptor of Sleepy Hollow.

Brom, who had a degree of rough chivalry in his nature, would fain have carried matters to open warfare, and have settled their pretensions to the lady, according to the mode of those most concise and simple reasons, the knights-errant of yore—by single combat; but Ichabod was too conscious of the superior might of his adversary to enter the lists against him: he had overheard a boast of Bones, that he would "double the schoolmaster up, and lay him on a shelf of his own schoolhouse"; and he was too wary to give him an opportunity. There was something extremely provoking in this obstinately pacific system; it left Brom no alternative but to draw upon the funds of rustic waggery in his disposition, and to play off boorish practical jokes upon his rival. Ichabod became the object of whimsical persecution to Bones, and his gang of rough riders. They harried his hitherto peaceful domains; smoked out his singing school, by stopping up the chimney; broke into the schoolhouse at night, in spite of its formidable fastenings of withe and window stakes, and turned every thing topsy-turvy: so that the poor schoolmaster began to think all the witches in the country held their meetings there. But what was still more annoying, Brom took all opportunities of turning him into ridicule in presence of his mistress, and had a scoundrel dog whom he taught to whine in the most ludicrous manner, and introduced as a rival of Ichabod's to instruct her in psalmody.

In this way matters went on for some time, without producing any material effect on the relative situation of the contending powers. On a fine autumnal afternoon, Ichabod, in pensive mood, sat enthroned on a lofty stool whence he usually watched all the concerns of his little literary realm. In his hand he swayed a ferule, that sceptre of despotic power; the birch of justice reposed on three nails, behind the throne, a constant terror to evil doers; while on the desk before him might be seen sundry contraband articles and prohibited weapons, detected upon the persons of idle urchins; such as half-munched apples, popguns, whirligigs, fly cages, and whole legions of rampant little paper gamecocks. Apparently there had been some appalling act of justice recently inflicted, for his scholars were all busily intent upon their books, or slyly whispering behind them with one eye kept upon the master; and a kind of buzzing stillness reigned throughout the schoolroom. It was suddenly interrupted by the appearance of a Negro, in tow-cloth jacket and trowsers, a round-crowned fragment of a hat like the cap of Mercury, and mounted on the back of a ragged, wild, half-broken colt, which he managed with a rope by way of halter. He came clattering up to the school door with an invitation to Ichabod to attend a merrymaking or ''quilting frolic,'' to be held that evening at Mynheer Van Tassel's; and having delivered his message with that air of importance, and effort at fine language, which a Negro is apt to display on petty embassies of the kind, he dashed over the brook, and was seen scampering away up the hollow, full of the importance and hurry of his mission.

All was now bustle and hubbub in the late quiet schoolroom. The scholars were hurried through their lessons, without stopping at trifles; those who were nimble skipped over half with impunity, and those who were tardy, had a smart application now and then in the rear, to quicken their speed, or help them over a tall word. Books were flung aside without being put away on the shelves, inkstands were overturned, benches thrown down, and the whole school was turned loose an hour before the usual time; bursting forth like a legion of young imps, yelping and racketing about the green, in joy at their early emancipation.

The gallant Ichabod now spent at least an extra half-hour at his toilet, brushing and furbishing up his best, and indeed only suit of rusty black; and arranging his looks by a bit of broken looking-glass, that hung up in the schoolhouse. That he might make his appearance before his mistress in the true style of a cavalier, he borrowed a horse from the farmer with whom he was domiciliated, a choleric old Dutchman, of the name of Hans Van Ripper, and, thus gallantly mounted, issued forth, like a knight-errant in quest of adventures. But it is meet I should, in the true spirit of romantic story, give some account of the looks and equipments of my hero and his steed. The animal he bestrode was a broken-down plough horse, that had outlived almost everything but his viciousness. He was gaunt and shagged, with a ewe neck and a head like a hammer; his rusty mane and tail were tangled and knotted with burrs; one eye had lost its pupil, and was glaring and spectral; but the other had the gleam of a genuine devil in it. Still he must have had fire and mettle in his day, if we may judge from the name he bore of Gunpowder. He had, in fact, been a favorite steed of his master's, the choleric Van Ripper, who was a furious rider, and had infused, very probably, some of his own spirit into the animal; for, old and broken-down as he looked, there was more of the lurking devil in him than in any young filly in the country.

Ichabod was a suitable figure for such a steed. He rode with short stirrups, which brought his knees nearly up to the pommel of the saddle; his sharp elbows stuck out like grasshoppers'; he carried his whip perpendicularly in his hand, like a sceptre, and, as his horse jogged on, the motion of his arms was not unlike the flapping of a pair of wings. A small wool hat rested on the top of his nose, for so his scanty strip of forehead might be called; and the skirts of his black coat fluttered out almost to the horse's tail. Such was the appearance of Ichabod and his steed, as they shambled out of the gate of Hans Van Ripper, and it was altogether such an apparition as is seldom to be met with in broad daylight.

It was, as I have said, a fine autumnal day, the sky was clear and serene, and nature wore that rich and golden livery which we always associate with the idea of abundance. The forests had put on their sober brown and yellow, while some trees of the tenderer kind had been nipped by the frosts into brilliant dyes of orange, purple, and scarlet. Streaming files of wild ducks began to make their appearance high in the air; the bark of the squirrel might be heard from the groves of beech and hickory nuts, and the pensive whistle of the quail at intervals from the neighboring stubble-field.

The small birds were taking their farewell banquets. In the fullness of their revelry, they fluttered, chirping and frolicking, from bush to bush, and tree to tree, capricious from the very profusion and variety around them. There was the honest cock-robin, the favorite game of stripling sportsmen, with its loud querulous note; and the twittering blackbirds flying in sable clouds; and the golden-winged woodpecker, with his crimson crest, his broad black gorget, and splendid plumage; and the cedar bird, with its red-tipt wings and yellow-tipt tail, and its little monteiro cap of feathers; and the blue jay, that noisy coxscomb, in his gay light-blue coat and white underclothes; screaming and chattering, nodding and bobbing and bowing, and pretending to be on good terms with every songster of the grove.

As Ichabod jogged slowly on his way, his eye, ever open to every symptom of culinary abundance, ranged with delight over the treasures of jolly autumn. On all sides he beheld vast store of apples; some hanging in oppressive opulence on the trees; some gathered into baskets and barrels for the market; others heaped up in rich piles for the cider press. Farther on he beheld great fields of Indian corn, with its golden ears peeping from their leafy coverts, and holding out the promise of cakes and hasty pudding; and the yellow pumpkins lying beneath them, turning up their fair round bellies to the sun, and giving ample prospects of the most luxurious of pies; and anon he passed the fragrant buckwheat fields, breathing the odor of the beehive, and as he beheld them, soft anticipation stole over his mind of dainty slapjacks, well buttered, and garnished with honey or treacle, by the delicate little dimpled hand of Katrina Van Tassel.

Thus feeding his mind with many sweet thoughts and "sugar suppositions," he journeyed along the sides of a range of hills which look out upon some of the goodliest scenes of the mighty Hudson. The sun gradually wheeled his broad disk down into the west. The wide bosom of the Tappan Zee lay motionless and glassy, excepting that here and there a gentle undulation waved and prolonged the blue shadow of the distant mountain. A few amber clouds floated in the sky, without a breath of air to move them. The horizon was of a fine golden tint, changing gradually into a pure apple green, and from that into the deep blue of the midheaven. A slanting ray lingered on the woody crests of the precipices that overhung some parts of the river, giving greater depth to the dark gray and purple of their rocky sides. A sloop was loitering in the distance, dropping slowly down with the tide, her sail hanging uselessly against the mast; and as the reflection of the sky gleamed along the still water, it seemed as if the vessel was suspended in the air.

It was toward evening that Ichabod arrived at the castle of the Heer Van Tassel, which he found thronged with the pride and flower of the adjacent country. Old farmers, a spare leathern-faced race, in homespun coats and breeches, blue stockings, huge shoes, and magnificent pewter buckles. Their brisk withered little dames, in close crimped caps, long-waisted short gowns, homespun petticoats, with scissors and pincushions, and gay calico pockets hanging on the outside. Buxom lasses, almost as antiquated as their mothers, excepting where a straw hat, a fine ribbon or perhaps a white frock, gave symptoms of city innovation. The sons, in short square-skirted coats with rows of stupendous brass buttons, and their hair generally queued in the fashion of the times, especially if they could procure an eel-skin for the purpose, it being esteemed, throughout the country, as a potent nourisher and strengthener of the hair.

Brom Bones, however, was the hero of the scene, having come to the gathering on his favorite steed Daredevil, a creature, like himself, full of mettle and mischief, and which no one but himself could manage. He was, in fact, noted for preferring vicious animals, given to all kinds of tricks, which kept the rider in constant risk of his neck, for he held a tractable well-broken horse as unworthy of a lad of spirit.

Fain would I pause to dwell upon the world of charms that burst upon the enraptured gaze of my hero, as he entered the state parlor of Van Tassel's mansion. Not those of the bevy of buxom lasses, with their luxurious display of red and white: but the ample charms of a genuine Dutch country tea table, in the sumptuous time of autumn. Such heaped-up platters of cakes of various and almost indescribable kinds, known only to experienced Dutch housewives! There was the doughty doughnut, the tenderer *oly koek,* and the crisp and crumbling cruller; sweet cakes and shortcakes, ginger cakes and honey cakes, and the whole family of cakes. And then there were apple pies and peach pies and pumpkin pies; besides slices of ham and smoked beef; and moreover delectable dishes of preserved plums, and peaches, and pears, and quinces; not to mention broiled shad and roasted chickens; together with bowls of milk and cream, all mingled higgledy-piggledy, pretty much as I have enumerated them, with the motherly teapot sending up its clouds of vapor from the midst!—Heaven bless the mark! I want breath and time to discuss this banquet as it deserves, and am too eager to get on with my story. Happily, Ichabod Crane was not in so great a hurry as his historian, but did ample justice to every dainty.

He was a kind and thankful creature, whose heart dilated in proportion as his skin was filled with good cheer; and whose spirits rose with eating as some men's do with drink. He could not help, too, rolling his large eyes round him as he ate, and chuckling with the possibility that he might one day be lord of all this scene of almost unimaginable luxury and splendor. Then, he thought, how soon he'd turn his back upon the old schoolhouse; snap his fingers in the face of Hans Van Ripper, and every other niggardly patron, and kick any itinerant pedagogue out of doors that should dare to call him comrade!

Old Baltus Van Tassel moved about among his guests with a face dilated with content and good humor, round and jolly as the harvest moon. His hospitable attentions were brief, but expressive, being confined to a shake of the hand, a slap on the shoulder, a loud laugh, and a pressing invitation to ''fall to, and help themselves.''

And now the sound of the music from the common room, or hall, summoned to the dance. The musician was an old gray-headed Negro who had been the itinerant orchestra of the neighborhood for more than half a century. His instrument was as old and battered as himself. The greater part of the time he scraped on two or three strings, accompanying every movement of the bow with a motion of the head; bowing almost to the ground, and stamping with his foot whenever a fresh couple were to start.

Ichabod prided himself upon his dancing as much as upon his vocal powers. Not a limb, not a fiber about him was idle; and to have seen his loosely hung frame in full motion, and clattering about the room, you would have thought Saint Vitus himself, that blessed patron of the dance, was figuring before you in person. He was the admiration of all the Negroes; who having gathered, of all ages and sizes, from the farm and the neighborhood, stood forming a pyramid of shining black faces at every door and window, gazing with delight at the scene, rolling their white eyeballs, and showing grinning rows of ivory from ear to ear. How could the flogger of urchins be otherwise than animated and joyous? the lady of his heart was his partner in the dance, and smiling graciously in reply to all his amorous oglings; while Brom Bones, sorely smitten with love and jealousy, sat brooding by himself in one corner.

When the dance was at an end, Ichabod was attracted to a knot of the sager folks, who, with old Van Tassel, sat smoking at one end of the piazza, gossiping over former times, and drawing out long stories about the war.

This neighborhood, at the time of which I am speaking, was one of those highly favored places which abound with chronicle and great men. The British and American line had run near it during the war; it had, therefore, been the scene of marauding, and infested with refugees, cowboys, and all kinds of border chivalry. Just sufficient time had elapsed to enable each storyteller to dress up his tale with a little becoming fiction, and, in the indistinctness of his recollection, to make himself the hero of every exploit.

There was the story of Doffue Martling, a large blue-bearded Dutchman, who had nearly taken a British frigate with an old iron nine-pounder from a mud breastwork, only that his gun burst at the sixth discharge. And there was an old gentleman who shall be nameless, being too rich a mynheer to be lightly mentioned, who, in the battle of Whiteplains, being an excellent master of defense, parried a musket ball with a small sword, insomuch that he absolutely felt it whiz round the blade, and glance off at the hilt: in proof of which, he was ready at any time to show the sword, with the hilt a little bent. There were several more that had been equally great in the field, not one of whom but was persuaded that he had a considerable hand in bringing the war to a happy termination.

But all these were nothing to the tales of ghosts and apparitions that succeeded. The neighborhood is rich in legendary treasures of the kind. Local tales and superstitions thrive best in these sheltered long-settled retreats; but are trampled under foot by the shifting throng that forms the population of most of our country places. Besides, there is no encouragement for ghosts in most of our villages, for they have scarcely had time to finish their first nap, and turn themselves in their graves, before their surviving friends have travelled away from the neighborhood; so that when they turn out at night to walk their rounds, they have no acquaintance left to call upon. This is perhaps the reason why we so seldom hear of ghosts except in our long-established Dutch communities.

The immediate cause, however, of the prevalence of supernatural stories in these parts, was doubtless owing to the vicinity of Sleepy Hollow. There was a contagion in the very air that blew from that haunted region; it breathed forth an atmosphere of dreams and fancies infecting all the land. Several of the Sleepy Hollow people were present at Van Tassel's and, as usual, were doling out their wild and wonderful legends. Many dismal tales were told about funeral trains, and mourning cries and wailings heard and seen about the great tree where the unfortunate Major André was taken, and which stood in the neighborhood. Some mention was made also of the woman in white, that haunted the dark glen at Raven Rock, and was often heard to shriek on winter nights before a storm, having perished there in the snow. The chief part of the stories, however, turned upon the favorite spectre of Sleepy Hollow, the headless horseman, who had been heard several times of late, patrolling the country; and, it was said, tethered his horse nightly among the graves in the churchyard.

The sequestered situation of this church seems always to have made it a favorite haunt of troubled spirits. It stands on a knoll, surrounded by locust trees and lofty elms, from among which its decent, whitewashed walls shine modestly forth, like Christian purity beaming through the shades of retirment. A gentle slope descends from it to a silver sheet of water, bordered by high trees, between which peeps may be caught at the blue hills of the Hudson. To look upon its grass-grown yard, where the sunbeams seem to sleep so quietly, one would think that there at least the dead might rest in peace. On one side of the church extends a wide woody dell, along which raves a large brook among broken rocks and trunks of fallen trees. Over a deep black part of the stream, not far from the church, was formerly thrown a wooden bridge; the road that led to it, and the bridge itself, were thickly shaded by overhanging trees, which cast a gloom about it, even in the daytime; but occasioned a fearful darkness at night. This was one of the favorite haunts of the headless horseman; and the place where he was most frequently encountered. The tale was told of old Brouwer, a most heretical disbeliever in ghosts, how he met the horseman returning from his foray into Sleepy Hollow, and was obliged to get up behind him; how they galloped over bush and brake, over hill and swamp, until they reached the bridge; when the horseman suddenly turned into a skeleton, threw old Brouwer into the brook, and sprang away over the treetops with a clap of thunder.

This story was immediately matched by a thrice-marvellous adventure of Brom Bones, who made light of the Galloping Hessian as an arrant jockey. He affirmed that, on returning one night from the neighboring village of Sing Sing, he had been overtaken by this midnight trooper; that he had offered to race with him for a bowl of punch, and should have won it too, for Daredevil beat the goblin horse all hollow, but, just as they came to the church bridge, the Hessian bolted, and vanished in a flash of fire.

All these tales, told in that drowsy undertone with which men talk in the dark, the countenances of the listeners only now and then receiving a casual gleam from the glare of a pipe, sank deep in the mind of Ichabod. He repaid them in kind with large extracts from his invaluable author,

Cotton Mather, and added many marvellous events that had taken place in his native state of Connecticut, and fearful sights which he had seen in his nightly walks about Sleepy Hollow.

The revel now gradually broke up. The old farmers gathered together their families in their wagons, and were heard for some time rattling along the hollow roads, and over the distant hills. Some of the damsels mounted on pillions behind their favorite swains, and their lighthearted laughter, mingling with the clatter of hoofs, echoed along the silent woodlands, sounding fainter and fainter until they gradually died away—and the late scene of noise and frolic was all silent and deserted. Ichabod only lingered behind, according to the custom of country lovers, to have a tête-à-tête with the heiress; fully convinced that he was now on the high road to success. What passed at this interview I will not pretend to say, for in fact I do not know. Something, however, I fear me, must have gone wrong, for he certainly sallied forth, after no very great interval, with an air quite desolate and chopfallen. Oh these women! these women! Could that girl have been playing off any of her coquettish tricks?—Was her encouragement of the poor pedagogue all a mere sham to secure her conquest of his rival?—Heaven only knows, not I!—Let it suffice to say, Ichabod stole forth with the air of one who had been sacking a hen-roost, rather than a fair lady's heart. Without looking to the right or left to notice the scene of rural wealth, on which he had so often gloated, he went straight to the stable, and with several hearty cuffs and kicks, roused his steed most uncourteously from the comfortable quarters in which he was soundly sleeping, dreaming of mountains of corn and oats, and whole valleys of timothy and clover.

It was the very witching time of night that Ichabod, heavyhearted and crestfallen, pursued his travel homewards, along the sides of the lofty hills which rise above Tarry Town, and which he had traversed so cheerily in the afternoon. The hour was as dismal as himself. Far below him, the Tappan Zee spread its dusky and indistinct waste of waters, with here and there the tall mast of a sloop, riding quietly at anchor under the land. In the dead hush of midnight, he could even hear the barking of the watch dog from the opposite shore of the Hudson; but it was so vague and faint as only to give an idea of his distance from this faithful companion of man. Now and then, too, the long-drawn crowing of a cock, accidentally awakened, would sound far, far off, from some farmhouse away among the hills—but it was like a dreaming sound in his ear. No signs of life occurred near him, but occasionally the melancholy chirp of a cricket, or perhaps the guttural twang of a bullfrog, from a neighboring marsh, as if sleeping uncomfortably, and turning suddenly in his bed.

All the stories of ghosts and goblins that he had heard in the afternoon, now came crowding upon his recollection. The night grew darker and darker; the stars seemed to sink deeper in the sky, and driving clouds occasionally hid them from his sight. He had never felt so lonely and dismal. He was, moreover, approaching the very place where many of the scenes of the ghost stories had been laid. In the center of the road stood an enormous tulip tree, which towered like a giant above all the other trees of the neighborhood, and formed a kind of landmark. Its limbs were gnarled, and fantastic, large enough to form trunks for ordinary trees, twisting down almost to the earth, and rising again into the air. It was connected with the tragical story of the unfortunate André, who had been taken prisoner hard by; and was universally known by the name of Major André's tree. The common people regarded it with a mixture of respect and superstition, partly out of sympathy for the fate of its ill-starred namesake, and partly from the tales of strange sights and doleful lamentations told concerning it.

As Ichabod approached this fearful tree, he began to whistle; he thought his whistle was answered—it was but a blast sweeping sharply through the dry branches. As he approached a little nearer, he thought he saw something white, hanging in the midst of the tree—he paused and ceased whistling; but on looking more narrowly, perceived that it was a place where the tree had been scathed by lightning, and the white wood laid bare. Suddenly he heard a groan—his teeth chattered and his knees smote against the saddle: it was but the rubbing of one huge bough upon another, as they were swayed about by the breeze. He passed the tree in safety, but new perils lay before him.

About two hundred yards from the tree a small brook crossed the road, and ran into a marshy and thickly wooded glen, known by the name of Wiley's swamp. A few rough logs, laid side by side, served for a bridge over this stream. On that side of the road where the brook entered the wood, a group of oaks and chestnuts, matted thick with wild grapevines, threw a cavernous gloom over it. To pass this bridge was the severest trial. It was at this identical spot that the unfortunate André was captured, and under the covert of those chestnuts and vines were the sturdy yeomen concealed who surprised him. This has ever since been considered a haunted stream, and fearful are the feelings of the schoolboy who has to pass it alone after dark.

As he approached the stream, his heart began to thump; he summoned up, however, all his resolution, gave his horse half a score of kicks in the ribs, and attempted to dash briskly across the bridge; but instead of starting forward, the perverse old animal made a lateral movement, and ran broadside against the fence. Ichabod, whose fears increased with the delay, jerked the reins on the other side, and kicked lustily with the contrary foot: it was all in vain; his steed started, it is true, but it was only to plunge to the opposite side of the road into a thicket of brambles and alder bushes. The schoolmaster now bestowed both whip and heel upon the starveling ribs of old Gunpowder, who dashed forward, snuffling and snorting, but came to a stand just by the bridge, with a suddenness that had nearly sent his rider sprawling over his head. Just at this moment a plashy tramp by the side of the bridge caught the sensitive ear of Ichabod. In the dark shadow of the grove, on the margin of the brook, he beheld something huge, misshapen, black and towering. It stirred not, but seemed gathered up in the gloom, like some gigantic monster ready to spring upon the traveller.

The hair of the affrighted pedagogue rose upon his head with terror. What was to be done? To turn and fly was now too late; and besides, what chance was there of escaping ghost or goblin, if such it was, which could ride upon the wings of the wind? Summoning up, therefore, a show of courage, he demanded in stammering accents—"Who are you?" He received no reply. He repeated his demand in a still more agitated voice. Still there was no answer. Once more he cudgelled the sides of the inflexible Gunpowder, and, shutting his eyes, broke forth with involuntary fervor into a psalm tune. Just then the shadowy object of alarm put itself in motion, and, with a scramble and a bound, stood at once in the middle of the road. Though the night was dark and dismal, yet the form of the unknown might now in some degree be ascertained. He appeared to be a horseman of large dimensions, and mounted on a black horse of powerful frame. He made no offer of molestation or sociability, but kept aloof on one side of the road, jogging along on the blind side of old Gunpowder, who had now got over his fright and waywardness.

Ichabod, who had no relish for this strange midnight companion, and bethought himself of the adventure of Brom Bones with the Galloping Hessian, now quickened his steed, in hopes of leaving him behind.

The stranger, however, quickened his horse to an equal pace. Ichabod pulled up, and fell into a walk, thinking to lag behind—the other did the same. His heart began to sink within him; he endeavoured to resume his psalm tune, but his parched tongue clove to the roof of his mouth, and he could not utter a stave. There was something in the moody and dogged silence of this pertinacious companion, that was mysterious and appalling. It was soon fearfully accounted for. On mounting a rising ground, which brought the figure of his fellow traveller in relief against the sky, gigantic in height, and muffled in a cloak, Ichabod was horror-struck, on perceiving that he was headless! But his horror was still more increased, on observing that the head, which should have rested on his shoulders, was carried before him on the pommel of the saddle: his terror rose to desperation; he rained a shower of kicks and blows upon Gunpowder, hoping, by a sudden movement, to give his companion the slip—but the spectre started full jump with him. Away then they dashed, through thick and thin; stones flying, and sparks flashing at every bound. Ichabod's flimsy garments fluttering in the air, as he stretched his long lank body away over his horse's head, in the eagerness of his flight.

They had now reached the road which turns off to Sleepy Hollow; but Gunpowder, who seemed possessed with a demon, instead of keeping up it, made an opposite turn, and plunged headlong down hill to the left. This road leads through a sandy hollow, shaded by trees for about a quarter of a mile, where it crosses the bridge famous in goblin story, and just beyond swells the green knoll on which stands the whitewashed church.

As yet the panic of the steed had given his unskillful rider an apparent advantage in the chase; but just as he had got halfway through the hollow, the girths of the saddle gave way, and he felt it slipping from under him. He seized it by the pommel, and endeavored to hold it firm, but in vain; and had just time to save himself by clasping old Gunpowder round the neck, when the saddle fell to the earth, and he heard it trampled under foot by his pursuer. For a moment the terror of Hans Van Ripper's wrath passed across his mind—for it was his Sunday saddle; but this was no time for petty fears; the goblin was hard on his haunches; and (unskillful rider that he was!) he had much ado to maintain his seat; sometimes slipping on one side, sometimes on another, and sometimes jolted in the high ridge of his horse's backbone, with a violence that he verily feared would cleave him asunder.

An opening in the trees now cheered him with the hopes that the church bridge was at hand. The wavering reflection of a silver star in the bosom of the brook told him that he was not mistaken. He saw the walls of the church dimly glaring under the trees beyond. He recollected the place where Brom Bone's ghostly competitor had disappeared. "If I can but reach that bridge," thought Ichabod, "I am safe." Just then he heard the black steed panting and blowing close behind him; he even fancied that he felt his hot breath. Another convulsive kick in the ribs, and old Gunpowder sprang upon the bridge; he thundered over the resounding planks; he gained the opposite side; and now Ichabod cast a look behind to see if his pursuer should vanish, according to rule, in a flash of fire and brimstone. Just then he saw the goblin rising in his stirrups, and in the very act of hurling his head at him. Ichabod endeavored to dodge the horrible missile, but too late. It encountered his cranium with a tremendous crash—he was tumbled headlong into the dust, and Gunpowder, the black steed, and the goblin rider, passed by like a whirlwind.

The next morning the old horse was found without his saddle, and with the bridle under his feet, soberly cropping the grass at his master's gate. Ichabod did not make his appearance at breakfast—dinner hour came, but no Ichabod. The boys assembled at the schoolhouse, and strolled idly about the banks of the brook; but no schoolmaster. Hans Van Ripper now began to feel some uneasiness about the fate of poor Ichabod, and his saddle. An inquiry was set on foot, and after diligent investigation they came upon his traces. In one part of the road leading to the church was found the saddle trampled in the dirt; the tracks of horses' hoofs deeply dented in the road, and evidently at furious speed, were traced to the bridge, beyond which, on the bank of a broad part of the brook, where the water ran deep and black, was found the hat of the unfortunate Ichabod, and close beside it a shattered pumpkin.

The brook was searched, but the body of the schoolmaster was not to be discovered. Hans Van Ripper, as executor of his estate, examined the bundle which contained all his wordly effects. They consisted of two shirts and a half; two stocks for the neck; a pair or two of worsted stockings; an old pair of corduroy small-clothes; a rusty razor; a book of psalm tunes, full of dogs' ears; and a broken pitch-pipe. As to the books and furniture of the schoolhouse, they belonged to the community, excepting Cotton Mather's *History of New England Witchcraft*, a New England Almanac, and a book of dreams and fortunetelling; in which last was a foolscap much scribbled and blotted in several fruitless attempts to make a copy of verses in honor of the heiress of Van Tassel. These magic books and the poetic scrawl were forthwith consigned to the flames by Hans Van Ripper; who from that time forward determined to send his children no more to school; observing, that he never knew any good come of this same reading and writing. Whatever money the schoolmaster possessed, and he had received his quarter's pay but a day or two before, he must have had about his person at the time of his disappearance.

The mysterious event caused much speculation at the church on the following Sunday. Knots of gazers and gossips were collected in the churchyard, at the bridge, and at the spot where the hat and pumpkin had been found. The stories of Brouwer, of Bones, and a whole budget of others, were called to mind; and when they had diligently considered them all, and compared them with the symptoms of the present case, they shook their heads, and came to the conclusion that Ichabod had been carried off by the Galloping Hessian. As he was a bachelor, and in nobody's debt, nobody troubled his head any more about him. The school was removed to a different quarter of the hollow, and another pedagogue reigned in his stead.

It is true, an old farmer, who had been down to New York on a visit several years after, and from whom this account of the ghostly adventure was received, brought home the intelligence that Ichabod Crane was still alive; that he had left the neighborhood, partly through fear of the goblin and Hans Van Ripper, and partly in mortification at having been suddenly dismissed by the heiress; that he had changed his quarters to a distant part of the country; had kept school and studied law at the same time, had been admitted to the bar, turned politician, electioneered, written for the newspapers, and finally had been made a justice of the Ten Pound Court. Brom Bones too, who, shortly after his rival's disappearance, conducted the blooming Katrina in triumph to the altar, was observed to look exceedingly knowing whenever the story of Ichabod was related, and always burst into a hearty laugh at the mention of the pumpkin; which led some to suspect that he knew more about the matter than he chose to tell.

The old country wives, however, who are the best judges of these matters, maintain to this day that Ichabod was spirited away by supernatural means; and it is a favorite story often told about the neighborhood round the winter evening fire. The bridge became more than ever an object of superstitious awe, and that may be the reason why the road has been altered of late years, so as to approach the church by the border of the millpond. The schoolhouse being deserted, soon fell to decay, and was reported to be haunted by the ghost of the unfortunate pedagogue; and the plough boy, loitering homeward of a still summer evening, has often fancied his voice at a distance, chanting a melancholy psalm tune among the tranquil solitudes of Sleepy Hollow.

Postscript, found in the handwriting of Mr. Knickerbocker

The preceding Tale is given, almost in the precise words in which I heard it related at a corporation meeting of the ancient city of Manhattoes, at which were present many of its sagest and most illustrious burghers. The narrator was a pleasant, shabby, gentlemanly old fellow, in pepper-and-salt clothes, with a sadly humorous face; and one whom I strongly suspected of being poor—he made such efforts to be entertaining. When his story was concluded, there was much laughter and approbation, particularly from two or three deputy aldermen, who had been asleep the greater part of the time. There was, however, one tall, dry-looking old gentleman, with beetling eyebrows, who maintained a grave and rather severe face throughout: now and then folding his arms, inclining his head, and looking down upon the floor, as if turning a doubt over in his mind. He was one of your wary men, who never laugh, but upon good grounds—when they have reason and the law on their side. When the mirth of the rest of the company had subsided, and silence was restored, he leaned one arm on the elbow of his chair, and sticking the other akimbo, demanded, with a slight, but exceedingly sage motion of the head, and contraction of the brow, what was the moral of the story, and what it went to prove?

The storyteller, who was just putting a glass of wine to his lips, as a refreshment after his toils, paused for a moment, looked at his inquirer with an air of infinite deference, and, lowering the glass slowly to the table, observed, that the story was intended most logically to prove:

"That there is no situation in life but has its advantages and pleasures—provided we will but take a joke as we find it.

"That, therefore, he that runs races with goblin troopers is likely to have rough riding of it.

"Ergo, for a country schoolmaster to be refused the hand of a Dutch heiress, is a certain step to high preferment, in the state."

The cautious old gentleman knit his brows tenfold closer after this explanation, being sorely puzzled by the ratiocination of the syllogism; while, methought, the one in pepper-and-salt eyed him with something of a triumphant leer. At length he observed, that all this was very well, but still he thought the story a little on the extravagant—there were one or two points on which he had his doubts.

"Faith, sir," replied the storyteller, "as to that matter, I don't believe one half of it myself."

Prosper Mérimée (1803–1870)

One of the pioneers of the short story, Prosper Mérimée was born and educated in Paris. But, after completing his legal studies in 1823, he decided to pursue a literary career.

La Théâtre de Clara Gazul (1825) and *La Guzla* (1827), his first two successes, were both hoaxes. The first purported to be translations of six short plays written by a Spanish actress, while the second (which fooled several experts), was supposed to be a compilation of Illyrian national songs and poems.

By 1830, however, his work as a civil servant began to take precedence over his fiction. In 1834, he was appointed Inspector General of Historical Monuments, a job demanding extensive travel throughout France which he held for the next eighteen years. When Napoleon III took over the government in 1852, Mérimée (a good friend of the emperor's wife) became a senator, functioning as an influential, though unofficial, advisor. In his later years, ill health forced him to slow down and winter at Cannes, where he died shortly after the start of the Franco-German War.

About two-thirds of Mérimée's writing consists of correspondence or official work such as reports, essays, and short historical sketches. But his fame rests on the score of stories and novelettes he wrote primarily between 1829 and 1850. They include classics like "The Taking of the Redoubt" (1829), *Colomba* (1840), and "Carmen" (1845). The last turned into the famous opera by Georges Bizet.

Personally, Mérimée was tender-hearted and affectionate as well as a devoted friend. Once he got himself tossed into jail for too vigorously defending a friend charged with stealing library books. But he was terrified of being thought soft, lest someone try to dupe or exploit him, a condition was probably brought about by his mother, since she tried to get him to accept "trust no one" as a motto. So he cultivated a proud, cynical, and indifferent manner, repressing any outward sign of emotional weakness.

Certainly this personal struggle had a profound influence on his stories: coupling together as they did, melodramatic themes of primitive passion with a detached, cynical, and understated style. Eventually, however, he destroyed his creativity by attempting to put down his own work, as in the rewrite of "Carmen," so that others could not claim he was serious about his inventions.

Mérimée was fascinated by, and wrote about, the supernatural throughout his entire career, though he did not believe in it. His two most famous examples are "The Venus of Ille" (1837), about a statue coming to life, and "Loki, the Manuscript of Professor Wittembach" (1869), about a werewolf.

For this volume, though, we have chosen, "Federigo," among his earliest and least known works. It is a delightful deal with the deity story that inverts Mérimée's usual theme that the passion of love, in whatever form, inevitably ruins and destroys. Indeed, it seems so revelatory of Mérimée's hidden nature, that that is probably why he subsequently repressed it.

FEDERIGO

(Translated by Emily Mary Waller and Mary Helena Dey)

Once upon a time there was a young nobleman named Federigo. He was handsome, well-built, courteous and easy tempered, but of exceedingly dissolute habits, for he was inordinately fond of wine, women, and gaming, especially gaming. He never went to confession, and he frequented the churches only to find chances for indulging in sinful pleasures.

Now Federigo ruined at the gambling-table twelve young men who afterward became brigands and perished unshriven in a fierce battle with the *condottieri* of the King. And it befell that he himself, in less time than it takes in the telling, lost all that he had won, and in addition his whole patrimony, save a little manor whither he retired to hide his poverty behind the hills of Cava.

For three years he had been living in seclusion, hunting by day and in the evening playing his game of *hombre* with his steward. One evening when he had just come home after the best day's hunting he had had, Jesus Christ, followed by the twelve apostles, knocked at his door and asked for shelter. Federigo, who was a generous soul, was delighted to see the guests come at a time when he had the wherewithal to feast them well. So he welcomed the pilgrims into his cottage, invited them with all possible cordiality to his board, and begged them to excuse him if he could not offer them what was befitting them, as they found him at a moment when his larder was exceedingly bare. Our Lord, who knew what to believe concerning the opportunities of this visit, forgave Federigo this little display of vanity, since he showed himself so hospitably inclined.

"We shall be well satisfied with what you have," He said to him:

''but pray have supper served as speedily as you may: for my friend here is very hungry,'' he added, pointing to Saint Peter.

Federigo did not wait to be asked a second time, and wishing to offer his guests something besides what he had got in the hunt, he ordered his steward to lay hands on his last kid, which was straightway put on the spit.

When supper was ready and the company seated at the table, Federigo had only one regret, which was that his wine was not better.

''Sire,'' he said to Jesus Christ, ''I wish very much that my wine were better; nevertheless, such as it is, I offer it with sincere hospitality.''

Whereupon our Lord, having tasted the wine, said to Federigo, ''Why do you complain? Your wine is perfect. Just ask my friend here what he thinks about it'' (pointing to Saint Peter).

Saint Peter, having quaffed it with relish, declared it excellent (*proprio stupendo*) and begged his host to drink it with him.

Federigo, who looked upon all this as mere civilities, nevertheless acceded to the apostle's request; but what was his surprise to find that this wine was more delicious than any he had ever tasted in the days of his affluence! Becoming aware, from this miracle, of the presence of the Saviour, he at once arose from his seat as being unworthy to sit at table with that holy company. But our Lord commanded him to be seated; which order he obeyed without any great protest. After the supper, during which they were waited upon by the steward and his wife, Jesus retired with the apostles into the room which had been prepared for them. Federigo, being left alone with the steward, played his game of *hombre*, as usual, and drank what was left of the miraculous wine.

The next day when the holy travellers were gathered together in the parlour with the master of the house, Jesus Christ said to Federigo:

''We are greatly pleased with the reception which thou hast accorded us, and we wish to recompense thee. Ask any three favors and they will be granted thee; for all power has been given to us in Heaven, and upon earth, and in Hades.''

Then Federigo drew from his pocket a pack of cards which he always carried with him and said: ''Master, grant that I may always win when I play with these cards.''

''So be it!'' said Jesus Christ.

But Saint Peter, who was near Federigo, whispered to him, ''Of what art thou thinking, miserable sinner? Thou shouldst pray the Master for the salvation of thy soul."

"Oh, I don't worry much about that," answered Federigo.

"Thou hast yet two favors to receive," said Jesus Christ.

"Master," continued the host, "since Thou art so gracious, grant, I pray you, that whosoever climbs into the orange tree that shades my door shall be unable to come down again without my permission."

"So be it," said Jesus Christ.

At these words the apostle Saint Peter, nudging his neighbor violently, said, "Miserable sinner, dost thou not fear the hellfire which awaits thy sins? Ask the Master to accord thee a place in Paradise; there is still time. . . ."

"There is no hurry," replied Federigo, drawing away from the apostle. And our Lord said: "What dost thou ask as a third favor?"

"I beg," he answered, "that whosoever may seat himself upon this bench shall be unable to rise without my permission."

Our Lord having granted this prayer as well as the other two, departed with his disciples.

The last apostle was no more than out of the house, when Federigo, wishing to prove the virtue of his cards, called his steward, and played a game of *hombre* with him without looking at his hand. He won the game in a trice; as well as a second and a third. So being quite confirmed in his confidence, he set out for town, lodged at the best inn, where he took the finest apartment. The news of his arrival spread very quickly and his old dissolute companions crowded to see him.

"We thought that you were lost for good and all," cried Don Giuseppe. "We were assured that you had become a hermit."

"That was quite true," answered Federigo.

"How the deuce have you been spending your time these last three years that we have not been seeing you?" the others asked all at once.

"In praying, my dear brethren," answered Federigo in a most pious voice. "Here is my prayer book," he added, drawing from his pocket his pack of cards which he had most carefully preserved.

This answer created an outburst of laughing, and everyone was convinced that Federigo had repaired his shattered fortunes in foreign parts at the expense of less skillful players than those with whom he then was, and they were all keen to ruin him a second time. Some wished without any further delay to drag him over to a gambling table. But

Federigo, after begging them to defer the game until evening, invited the company into a room, where according to his orders a dainty repast had been served. It was hailed with enthusiasm, needless to say.

This dinner was somewhat more lively than the apostles'; it is true nothing was drunk but Malvoisie and Lacryma, but the merrymakers with one exception knew no better wine.

Before the arrival of his guests Federigo had provided himself with a pack of cards exactly like the first, in order that he might at will substitute it for the other, and by losing one or two games avoid suspicion on the part of his adversaries. One he carrried in his right pocket and the other in his left.

When the dinner was over and the noble band seated around a baize-covered table Federigo placed the unblessed cards first on the table and limited the stakes to a moderate sum for the whole séance. Wishing then to interest himself in the game and gauge his own ability, he played his best for the first two games, and lost them one after the other, not without a certain amount of inward annoyance. Then he called for wine and taking advantage of the moment when the winners were drinking to their past and future successes, he took away the unblessed cards and replaced them with the pack that had been blessed. When the third game was begun, as Federigo paid no attention to his own hand whatever, he had leisure to watch the others—and he found they were not playing fairly. This discovery delighted him greatly, as he felt that he could with a perfectly clear conscience empty his adversaries' pockets. He had been ruined, he now saw, by their dishonesty, not by their skill in playing, nor their good fortune. He could then have a better opinion on his own relative force, an opinion justified by previous successes. Self-esteem, to what will it not attach itself? The certainty of revenge and of gain are sentiments that are very sweet to the human heart. Federigo experienced them one and all at the same time. But thinking of the twelve young men at whose expense he had grown rich, and feeling persuaded that they were the only honest players with whom he had ever had to do, he repented for the first time his victory over them. A slight shadow clouded his face which had been shining with joy, and he sighed deeply as he won the third game.

This game was succeeded by several others, and Federigo arranged to win the greater number of them, so that he raked in, that first evening, enough to pay for his dinner, and the rent of his apartments for a month.

That was all he wished for the first day. His companions withdrew greatly disappointed, but promising to return the following day.

The next day and succeeding days Federigo arranged to win and lose so aptly that in a short time he acquired a considerable fortune, without anyone's suspecting the real cause. Then he left his hotel and went to live in a large palace, where he gave, from time to time, most magnificent entertainments. The loveliest women disputed his most passing glance. His table was covered every day with the most exquisite wines, and the palace of Federigo became renowned as the center of pleasure.

At the end of a year's discreet gambling he resolved to make his revenge complete by draining the pockets of the foremost noblemen of the country. To this end, having converted the greater part of his money into precious stones, he invited those gentlemen eight days beforehand to an unusually splendid feast, for which he had called into requisition the best musicians, dancers, etc. This entertainment was to end with a game with fat stakes. Those who had no money squeezed it out of the Jews. The others brought what they had, and all was swept away. Federigo departed in the night with his gold and his diamonds.

From that moment he never used the magic cards except with dishonest gamblers, finding that he could play a strong enough game himself to win from the others. So he went through all the cities in the world, playing everywhere, always winning, and at every halt feasting upon the fat of the land.

Nevertheless, the memory of his twelve victims was ever present in his mind, and poisoned all his joys. At last he decided one fine day either to deliver them, or to perish with them.

Having so resolved he set out for hell with a staff in his hand and a sack on his back, and with no escort save his favorite hound Marchesella. When he reached Sicily he climbed Mount Gibel, then went down into the volcano as far below the foot of the mountain as the mountain itself rises above Piedmont. Thence, in order to go to Pluto's abode, you must cross a court which is guarded by Cerberus. Federigo got across without any difficulty, while Cerberus was playing with the hound, and knocked on Pluto's door.

When he had been led into the monarch's presence:

"Who art thou?" demanded the king of the infernal abyss.

"I am Federigo, the gambler."

''What in the devil's name dost thou here?''

''Pluto, if thou deemest the best gambler on earth worthy to play a game of *hombre* with thee, here is what I would propose: we shall play as many games as thou wilt. If I lose by a single game then my soul will rightfully belong to thee, as well as all those that people thy realm. But if I win, I shall have the right to choose from among thy subjects one soul for every game I win, and I shall be entitled to carry them off with me.''

''So be it,'' said Pluto.

And he called for a pack of cards.

''Here is one,'' said Federigo, immediately drawing from his pocket the miraculous pack, and they began to play.

Federigo won the first game, and asked for the soul of Stephen Pagani, one of the twelve whom he wished to save. It was at once handed over, and having received it, he put it in his bag. In the same way he won a second game, then a third up to the twelfth game, each time asking for and putting into his sack one of the souls in which he was interested. When he finished the dozen he offered to continue playing.

''Very gladly,'' said Pluto (who however was annoyed at losing), ''but let us go out a moment; some very disagreeable odor seems to pervade this apartment.''

Now he was trying to find a pretext for getting rid of Federigo, for scarcely was the latter outside with his sack and his souls, when Pluto shouted with all his might to close the door upon him.

Federigo having again traversed the courtyard of Hades without Cerberus's noticing it, so charmed was he with the hound, once more reached the summit of Mount Gibel. Then he called Marchesella, who speedily rejoined him, and went down again toward Messina more elated over this spiritual success then he had ever been over any wordly success. When he reached Messina he set sail to return to *terra firma* and end his days in his old manor house.

A few months later Marchesella gave birth to a litter of little monsters, some of which had as many as three heads. They were all drowned.

At the end of thirty years (Federigo was then seventy) Death came to his door and told him to put his affairs in order, for his hour was come.

''I am ready,'' said the dying man; ''but before you carry me off, O

Death, give me, I pray you, some of the fruit from the tree that shades my door. Just this one little pleasure and I shall die happy."

"If that is all you need," said Death, "I am quite willing to satisfy you."

He got into the orange tree to gather an orange; but when he tried to get down he could not: Federigo would not allow it.

"Ah! Federigo! You have deceived me," cried he: "I am now in your power: but give me back my liberty and I will promise you ten more years of life."

"Ten years! That is not much!" exclaimed Federigo. "If you wish to come down, my friend, you must be more liberal than that."

"I'll give you twenty."

"Come! Be serious!"

"I'll give you thirty."

"That is not even one-third enough."

"Do you wish then to live for a century?"

"Just exactly, my dear."

"Federigo, you are unreasonable."

"What would you have? I like to live."

"Well, then, take a hundred years," said Death; "it will have to come to that."

And at once he was able to get down. As soon as Death departed, Federigo arose in perfect health, and began a new life with all the strength of a young man and the experience of an old one. All that is known of this new existence is that he continued to satisfy every craving of his carnal appetite, doing a little good when occasion arose, but giving no more attention to his soul's salvation than in his first life.

The hundred years rolled around and Death came again to knock at his door, and found him in bed.

"Are you ready?" he said.

"I have just sent for my confessor," said Federigo; "sit down by the fire until he comes. I am just waiting to be absolved and then I will fly with you into eternity."

Death, who was a kindly person, went and sat down on the bench in the inglenook, and waited for a whole hour without seeing any priest appear. Beginning at last to lose patience he said to his host:

"Old man, once again, have you not had time to put your affairs in order during the whole century that has passed since I saw you before?"

“My word, I had something else to do,” answered the old man with a mocking smile.

“Well,” answered Death, indignant at his impiousness, “you have only one minute longer to live.”

“Bah!” said Federigo, while Death tried in vain to get up. “I know by experience that you are too obliging to refuse to grant me a few years of respite.”

“A few years, wretched man!” and he made vain efforts to leave the inglenook.

“Yes, certainly, but this time I shall not require so much, and as I am not very fond of old age I shall be satisfied with eighty years for the third round.”

Death saw that he was held to the bench, as he had been once before to the orange tree, by some supernatural power; but in his rage he was unwilling to grant anything.

“I know how I can bring you to reason,” said Federigo.

And he had three fagots thrown on the fire. In a moment the flames filled the whole fireplace so that Death was horribly tortured.

“Spare me! Spare me!” he cried as he felt the flames burning him to the bone. “I'll promise you eighty years of health.”

Upon hearing these words Federigo broke the charm, and Death fled half-roasted.

At the end of the time agreed upon he came back to wait for his man, who was awaiting him with his sack on his back.

“Your hour has come this time and no mistake,” said Death, entering brusquely; “no drawing back now. But what do you mean to do with this sack?”

“It contains the souls of twelve gambler friends of mine whom I once delivered from hell.”

“Let them return with you!” said Death, and seizing Federigo by the hair, he flew away toward the south and with his prey plunged down into the abyss of Mount Gibel. When he reached the gate of hell, he knocked three times.

“Who is there?” said Pluto.

“Federigo, the gambler,” answered Death.

“Don't open the door,” cried Pluto, who at once remembered the twelve games which he had lost; “that rogue would depopulate my realm.”

As Pluto refused to open, Death carried his prisoner off to Purgatory; but the angel at the door refused him admission seeing that he was in a state of mortal sin. It was necessary then at all cost and to the great regret of Death, who bore Federigo a grudge, to wing his way to the celestial regions.

"Who art thou?" said Saint Peter to Federigo, when Death had set him down at the gate of Paradise.

"Your old host," he answered, "the one who regaled you with the game he himself had hunted."

"Dost thou dare present thyself here in the state in which I see thee?" cried St. Peter. "Dost thou not know that Heaven is closed to such as thee? What! Thous art not even fit for Purgatory and thou desirest a place in Paradise!"

"Saint Peter," said Federigo, "is it thus that I received thee when thou camest with thy Divine Master, some hundred and eighty years ago, to ask hospitality from me?"

"That is all very well," replied Saint Peter in a reproving voice, though somewhat touched by the reference. "But I can not take upon myself to let you in. I will go and tell Jesus Christ about your arrival. We shall see what He will say about it."

Our Lord hearing the news came to the gate of Paradise, where He found Federigo kneeling at the gate with his twelve souls, six on each side. Then allowing Himself to be moved with compassion:

"Thou mayest pass," he said to Federigo, "but these twelve souls whom hell claims, I could not in all conscience allow them to pass."

"What, my Lord," said Federigo, "when I had the honor of receiving Thee in my house wert Thou not accompanied by twelve travellers whom I received with Thee, with all the hospitality that I could show."

"Really, one cannot resist this man," said Jesus Christ. "Come in, then, since ye are all here: but boast not of this favor I have shown. It would really be too bad a precedent."

Nathaniel Hawthorne (1804–1864)

One of the best known American writers of the nineteenth century, Nathaniel Hawthorne was a major producer of fantasy and science fiction short stories—many of which can be found in *Twice-Told Tales* (1837) and *Mosses from an Old Manse* (1846). He believed truth that mattered was inner and that the artist, therefore, had the right to change the world to strengthen his point. Consequently, much of his work, is strongly allegorical: cautioning against pride, particularly the intellectual pride of standing alone, taking merely speculative or scientific interest in others.

Born in Salem, Massachussetts, Hawthorne was descended from an old colonial family which had seen better days before being cursed by a victim of the Salem Witch Trials. A handsome, reticent, and somewhat brooding man, he developed avid reading habits during a three-year recuperation from a severe foot injury, a preference which may have influenced his decision to become an author.

At the time, however, the lack of international copyright laws made it very difficult for a young American to succeed as a writer. American publishers found it more profitable to reprint British authors, to whom no royalties were paid, than to try cultivating the more costly local talent. Nevertheless, Hawthorne was determined. So, after majoring in literature at Bowdoin College (where he made some extremely valuable contacts), he moved back into his mother's house and started to work.

In 1828 he completed *Fanshawe,* a vanity novel, which caught the attention of Boston publisher Samuel Goodrich. Goodrich edited an annual short story collection, *The Token,* and during the next eleven years he was to publish more than twenty-five of Hawthorne's works.

However, to insure that several could be used in the same issue, Goodrich never listed an author. Indeed, Hawthorne's authorship only became known because Horatio Bridge, an old Bowdoin chum, paid Goodrich two hundred and fifty dollars to publish a collection of his friend's tales (*Twice-Told Tales*, 1837).

Hawthorne's income from *The Token* totaled less than three hundred and fifty dollars, so when he began contemplating marriage in 1839, he secured a political appointment which he held for two years until resigning to follow his love to Brook Farm. In 1842, he married and obtained another political appointment only to be ousted when his side lost the next election.

Subsequent attempts to support his family by writing faltered until Boston publisher James T. Fields stumbled across the first draft of *The Scarlet Letter*. This novel made its triumphant appearance in 1850 and was followed a year later by the Poe-like masterpiece, *The House of the Seven Gables* (1851). When old college friend Franklin Pierce became President in 1853, Hawthorne was rewarded with a consulship in Liverpool, England. Increasing royalties, plus five years of lucrative service, finally provided financial security. So he retired, and after a two year sojourn in Italy, returned home to continue writing, rather unsuccessfully, until his death four years later.

Our selection, ''Dr. Heidegger's Experiment,'' is one of his cleverest stories, a humorously pessimistic look at how people might behave when attempting to relive their lives.

DR. HEIDEGGER'S EXPERIMENT

That very singular man, old Dr. Heidegger, once invited four venerable friends to meet him in his study. There were three white-bearded gentlemen, Mr. Medbourne, Colonel Killigrew, and Mr. Gascoigne, and a withered gentlewoman, whose name was the Widow Wycherly. They were all melancholy old creatures, who had been unfortunate in life, and whose greatest misfortune it was that they were not long ago in their graves. Mr. Medbourne, in the vigor of his age, had been a prosperous merchant, but had lost his all by a frantic speculation, and was now little better than a mendicant. Colonel Killigrew had wasted his best years, and his health and substance, in the pursuit of sinful pleasures which had given birth to a brood of pains, such as the gout, and divers other torments of soul and body. Mr. Gascoigne was a ruined politician, a man of evil fame, or at least had been so, till time had buried him from the knowledge of the present generation, and made him obscure instead of infamous. As for the Widow Wycherly, tradition tells us that she was a great beauty in her day; but, for a long while past, she had lived in deep seclusion, on account of certain scandalous stories which had prejudiced the gentry of the town against her. It is a circumstance worth mentioning, that each of these three old gentlemen, Mr. Medbourne, Colonel Killigrew, and Mr. Gascoigne, were early lovers of the Widow Wycherly, and had once been on the point of cutting each other's throats for her sake. And before proceeding farther, I will merely hint that Dr. Heidegger and all his four guests were sometimes thought to be a little beside themselves; as is not unfrequently the case with old people, when worried either by present troubles or woeful recollections.

"My dear old friends," said Dr. Heidegger, motioning them to be seated, "I am desirous of your assistance in one of those little experiments with which I amuse myself here in my study."

If all stories were true, Dr. Heidegger's study must have been a very curious place. It was a dim, old-fashioned chamber, festooned with cobwebs, and besprinkled with antique dust. Around the walls stood several oaken bookcases, the lower shelves of which were filled with rows of gigantic folios and black-letter quartos, and the upper with little parchment-covered duodecimos. Over the central bookcase was a bronze bust of Hippocrates, with which, according to some authorities, Dr. Heidegger was accustomed to hold consultations in all difficult cases of his practice. In the obscurest corner of the room stood a tall and narrow oaken closet, with its door ajar, within which doubtfully appeared a skeleton. Between two of the bookcases hung a looking glass, presenting its high and dusty plate within a tarnished gilt frame. Among many wonderful stories related of this mirror, it was fabled that the spirits of all the doctor's deceased patients dwelt within its verge, and would stare him in the face whenever he looked thitherward. The opposite side of the chamber was ornamented with the full-length portrait of a young lady, arrayed in the faded magnificence of silk, satin, and brocade, and with a visage as faded as her dress. Above half a century ago, Dr. Heidegger had been on the point of marriage with this young lady; but, being affected with some slight disorder, she had swallowed one of her lover's prescriptions, and died on the bridal evening. The greatest curiosity of the study remains to be mentioned; it was a ponderous folio volume, bound in black leather, with massive silver clasps. There were no letters on the back, and nobody could tell the title of the book. But it was well known to be a book of magic; and once, when a chambermaid had lifted it, merely to brush away the dust, the skeleton had rattled in its closet, the picture of the young lady had stepped one foot upon the floor, and several ghastly faces had peeped forth from the mirror; while the brazen head of Hippocrates frowned, and said—"Forbear!"

Such was Dr. Heidegger's study. On the summer afternoon of our tale, a small round table, as black as ebony, stood in the center of the room, sustaining a cut-glass vase of beautiful form and elaborate workmanship. The sunshine came through the window, between the heavy festoons of two faded damask curtains, and fell directly across this vase; so that a mild splendor was reflected from it on the ashen visages of the five old people who sat around. Four champagne glasses were also on the table.

"My dear old friends," repeated Dr. Heidegger, "may I reckon on your aid in performing an exceedingly curious experiment?"

Now Dr. Heidegger was a very strange old gentleman, whose eccentricity had become the nucleus for a thousand fantastic stories. Some of these fables, to my shame be it spoken, might possibly be traced back to mine own veracious self; and if any passages of the present tale should startle the reader's faith, I must be content to bear the stigma of a fictionmonger.

When the doctor's four guests heard him talk of his proposed experiment, they anticipated nothing more wonderful than the murder of a mouse in an air pump, or the examination of a cobweb by the microscope, or some similar nonsense, with which he was constantly in the habit of pestering his intimates. But without waiting for a reply, Dr. Heidegger hobbled across the chamber, and returned with the same ponderous folio, bound in black leather, which common report affirmed to be a book of magic. Undoing the silver clasps, he opened the volume, and took from among its black-letter pages a rose, or what was once a rose, though now the green leaves and crimson petals had assumed one brownish hue, and the ancient flower seemed ready to crumble to dust in the doctor's hands.

"This rose," said Dr. Heidegger, with a sigh, "this same withered and crumbling flower, blossomed five-and-fifty years ago. It was given me by Sylvia Ward, whose portrait hangs yonder; and I meant to wear it in my bosom at our wedding. Five-and-fifty years it has been treasured between the leaves of this old volume. Now, would you deem it possible that this rose of half a century could ever bloom again?"

"Nonsense!" said the Widow Wycherly, with a peevish toss of her head. "You might as well ask whether an old women's wrinkled face could ever bloom again."

"See!" answered Dr. Heidegger.

He uncovered the vase, and threw the faded rose into the water which it contained. At first it lay lightly on the surface of the fluid, appearing to imbibe none of its moisture. Soon, however, a singular change began to be visible. The crushed and dried petals stirred, and assumed a deepening tinge of crimson, as if the flower were reviving from a deathlike slumber; the slender stalk and twigs of foliage became green; and there was the rose of half a century, looking as fresh as when Sylvia Ward had first given it to her lover. It was scarcely full blown; for some of its delicate red leaves curled modestly around its moist bosom, within which two or three dewdrops were sparkling.

"That is certainly a very pretty deception," said the doctor's friends; carelessly, however, for they had witnessed greater miracles at a conjurer's show; "pray how was it effected?"

"Did you never hear of the 'Fountain of Youth'?" asked Dr. Heidegger, "which Ponce de Leon, the Spanish adventurer, went in search of, two or three centuries ago?"

"But did Ponce de Leon ever find it?" said the Widow Wycherly.

"No," answered Dr. Heidegger, "for he never sought it in the right place. The famous Fountain of Youth, if I am rightly informed, is situated in the southern part of the Floridian peninsula, not far from Lake Macaco. Its source is overshadowed by several gigantic magnolias, which, though numberless centuries old, have been kept as fresh as violets by the virtues of this wonderful water. An acquaintance of mine, knowing my curiosity in such matters, had sent me what you see in the vase."

"Ahem!" said Colonel Killigrew, who believed not a word of the doctor's story; "and what may be the effect of this fluid on the human frame?"

"You shall judge for yourself, my dear colonel," replied Dr. Heidegger; "and all of you, my respected friends, are welcome to so much of this admirable fluid as may restore to you the bloom of youth. For my own part, having had much trouble in growing old, I am in no hurry to grow young again. With your permission, therefore, I will merely watch the progress of the experiment."

While he spoke, Dr. Heidegger had been filling the four champagne glasses with the water of the Fountain of Youth. It was apparently impregnated with an effervescent gas, for little bubbles were continually ascending from the depths of the glasses, and bursting in silvery spray at the surface. As the liquor diffused a pleasant perfume, the old people doubted not that it possessed cordial and comfortable properties; and, though utter skeptics as to its rejuvenescent power, they were inclined to swallow it at once. But Dr. Heidegger besought them to stay a moment.

"Before you drink, my respectable old friends," said he, "it would be well that, with the experience of a lifetime to direct you, you should draw up a few general rules for your guidance, in passing a second time through the perils of youth. Think what a sin and a shame it would be, if with your peculiar advantages, you should not become patterns of virtue and wisdom to all the young people of the age!''

The doctor's four venerable friends made him no answer, except by a feeble and tremulous laugh; so very ridiculous was the idea, that, knowing how closely repentance treads behind the steps of error, they should ever go astray again.

''Drink then,'' said the doctor, bowing; ''I rejoice that I have so well selected the subjects of my experiment.''

With palsied hands they raised the glasses to their lips. The liquor, if it really possessed such virtues as Dr. Heidegger imputed to it, could not have been bestowed on four human beings who needed it more woefully. They looked as if they had never known what youth or pleasure was, but had been the offspring of Nature's dotage, and always the gray, decrepit, sapless, miserable creatures, who now sat stooping round the doctor's table, without life enough in their souls or bodies to be animated even by the prospect of growing young again. They drank off the water, and replaced their glasses on the table.

Assuredly, there was an almost immediate improvement in the aspect of the party, not unlike what might have been produced by a glass of generous wine, together with a sudden glow of cheerful sunshine, brightening over all their visages at once. There was a healthful suffusion on their cheeks, instead of the ashen hue that had made them look so corpselike. They gazed at one another, and fancied that some magic power had really begun to smooth away the deep and sad inscription which Father Time had been so long engraving on their brows. The Widow Wycherly adjusted her cap, for she felt almost like a woman again.

''Give us more of this wondrous water!'' cried they eagerly. ''We are younger—but we are still too old! Quick—give us more!''

''Patience, patience!'' quoth Dr. Heidegger, who sat watching the experiment with philosophic coolness. ''You have been a long time growing old. Surely you might be content to grow young in half an hour! But the water is at your service.''

Again he filled the glasses with the liquor of youth, enough of which still remained in the vase to turn half the old people in the city to the age of their own grandchildren. While the bubbles were yet sparkling on the brim, the doctor's four guests snatched their glasses from the table, and swallowed the contents of a single gulp. Was it delusion? Even while the draught was passing down their throats, it seemed to have wrought a change on their whole systems. Their eyes grew clear and bright; a dark shade deepened among their silvery locks; they sat around the table, three gentlemen of middle age, and a woman hardly beyond her buxom prime.

"My dear widow, you are charming!" cried Colonel Killigrew, whose eyes had been fixed upon her face, while the shadows of age were flitting from it like darkness from the crimson daybreak.

The fair widow knew, of old, that Colonel Killigrew's compliments were not always measured by sober truth; so she started up and ran to the mirror, still dreading that the ugly visage of an old woman would meet her gaze. Meanwhile, the three gentlemen behaved in such a manner as proved that the water of the Fountain of Youth possessed some intoxicating qualities; unless, indeed, their exhilaration of spirits were merely a lightsome dizziness, caused by the sudden removal of the weight of years. Mr. Gascoigne's mind seemed to run on political topics, but whether relating to the past, present, or future, could not easily be determined, since the same ideas and phrases have been in vogue these fifty years. Now he rattled forth full-throated sentences about patriotism, national glory, and the people's rights; now he muttered some perilous stuff or other, in a sly and doubtful whisper, so cautiously that even his own conscience could scarcely catch the secret; and now again he spoke in measured accents, and a deeply deferential tone, as if a royal ear were listening to his well-turned periods. Colonel Killigrew all this time had been trolling forth a jolly bottle song, and ringing his glass in symphony with the chorus, while his eyes wandered towards the buxom figure of the Widow Whycherly. On the other side of the table, Mr. Medbourne was involved in a calculation of dollars and cents, with which was strangely intermingled a project for supplying the East Indies with ice, by harnessing a team of whales to the polar icebergs.

As for the Widow Wycherly, she stood before the mirror curtsying and simpering to her own image, and greeting it as the friend whom she loved better than all the world beside. She thrust her face close to the glass, to see whether some long-remembered wrinkle or crow's-foot had indeed vanished. She examined whether the snow had so entirely melted from her hair, that the venerable cap could be safely thrown aside. At last, turning briskly away, she came with a sort of dancing step to the table.

"My dear old doctor," cried she, "pray favor me with another glass!"

"Certainly, my dear madam, certainly!" replied the complaisant doctor; "see! I have already filled the glasses."

There, in fact, stood the four glasses, brimful of this wonderful water, the delicate spray of which, as it effervesced from the surface, resembled the tremulous glitter of diamonds. It was now so nearly sunset that the chamber had grown duskier than ever; but a mild and moonlike splendor gleamed from within the vase, and rested alike on the four guests, and on the doctor's venerable figure. He sat in a high-backed, elaborately carved, oaken armchair, with a gray dignity of aspect that might have well befitted that very Father Time whose power had never been disputed save by this fortunate company. Even while quaffing the third draught of the Fountain of Youth, they were almost awed by the expression of his mysterious visage.

But, the next moment, the exhilarating gush of young life shot through their veins. They were now in the happy prime of youth. Age, with its miserable train of cares, and sorrows, and diseases, was remembered only as the trouble of a dream from which they had joyously awoke. The fresh gloss of the soul, so early lost, and without which the world's successive scenes had been but a gallery of faded pictures, again threw its enchantment over all their prospects. They felt like new-created beings, in a new-created universe.

"We are young! We are young!" they cried, exultingly.

Youth, like the extremity of age, had effaced the strongly marked characteristics of middle life, and mutually assimilated them all. They were a group of merry youngsters, almost maddened with the exuberant frolicsomeness of their years. The most singular effect of their gaiety was an impulse to mock the infirmity and decrepitude of which they had so lately been the victims. They laughed loudly at their old-fashioned attire, the wide-skirted coats and flapped waistcoats of the young men, and the ancient cap and gown of the blooming girl. One limped across the floor, like a gouty grandfather; one set a pair of spectacles astride of his nose, and pretended to pore over the black-letter pages of the book of magic; a third seated himself in an armchair, and strove to imitate the venerable dignity of Dr. Heidegger. Then all shouted mirthfully, and leaped about the room. The Widow Wycherly—if so fresh a damsel could be called a widow—tripped up to the doctor's chair, with a mischievous merriment in her rosy face.

"Doctor, you dear old soul," cried she, "get up and dance with me!" And then the four young people laughed louder than ever, to think what a queer figure the poor old doctor would cut.

"Pray excuse me," answered the doctor quietly. "I am old and rheumatic, and my dancing days were over long ago. But either of these gay young gentlemen will be glad of so pretty a partner."

"Dance with me, Clara!" cried Colonel Killigrew.

"No, no, I will be her partner!" shouted Mr. Gascoigne.

"She promised me her hand, fifty years ago!" exclaimed Mr. Medbourne.

They all gathered round her. One caught both her hands in his passionate grasp—another threw his arm about her waist—the third buried his hand among the glossy curls that clustered beneath the widow's cap. Blushing, panting, struggling, chiding, laughing, her warm breath fanning each of their faces by turns, she strove to disengage herself, yet still remained in their triple embrace. Never was there a livelier picture of youthful rivalship, with bewitching beauty for the prize. Yet, by a strange deception, owing to the duskiness of the chamber, and the antique dresses which they still wore, the tall mirror is said to have reflected the figures of the three old, gray, withered grandsires, ridiculously contending for the skinny ugliness of a shriveled grandam.

But they were young: their burning passions proved them so. Inflamed to madness by the coquetry of the girl-widow, who neither granted nor quite withheld her favors, the three rivals began to interchange threatening glances. Still keeping hold of the fair prize, they grappled fiercely at one another's throats. As they struggled to and fro, the table was overturned, and the vase dashed into a thousand fragments. The precious Water of Youth flowed in a bright stream across the floor, moistening the wings of a butterfly, which, grown old in the decline of summer, had alighted there to die. The insect fluttered lightly through the chamber, and settled on the snowy head of Dr. Heidegger.

"Come, come, gentlemen!—come, Madam Wycherly," exclaimed the doctor, "I really must protest against this riot."

They stood still, and shivered; for it seemed as if gray Time were calling them back from their sunny youth, far down into the chill and darksome vale of years. They looked at old Dr. Heidegger, who sat in his carved armchair, holding the rose of half a century, which he had rescued from among the fragments of the shattered vase. At the motion of his hand, the four rioters resumed their seats; the more readily, because their violent exertions had wearied them, youthful though they were.

"My poor Sylvia's rose!" ejaculated Dr. Heidegger, holding it in the light of the sunset clouds; "it appears to be fading again."

And so it was. Even while the party were looking at it, the flower continued to shrivel up, till it became as dry and fragile as when the doctor had first thrown it into the vase. He shook off the few drops of moisture which clung to its petals.

"I love it as well thus as in its dewy freshness," observed he, pressing the withered rose to his withered lips. While he spoke, the butterfly fluttered down from the doctor's snowy head, and fell upon the floor.

His guests shivered again. A strange chillness, whether of the body or spirit they could not tell, was creeping gradually over them all. They gazed at one another, and fancied that each fleeting moment snatched away a charm, and left a deepening furrow where none had been before. Was it an illusion? Had the changes of a lifetime been crowded into so brief a space, and were they now four aged people, sitting with their old friend, Dr. Heidegger?

"Are we grown old again, so soon?" cried they dolefully.

In truth, they had. The Water of Youth possessed merely a virtue more transient than that of wine. The delirium which it created had effervesced away. Yes! they were old again. With a shuddering impulse that showed her a woman still, the widow clasped her skinny hands before her face, and wished that the coffin lid were over it, since it could be no longer beautiful.

"Yes, friends, ye are old again," said Dr. Heidegger; "and lo! the Water of Youth is all lavished on the ground. Well—I bemoan it not; for if the fountain gushed at my very doorstep, I would not stoop to bathe my lips in it—no, though its delirium were for years instead of moments. Such is the lesson ye have taught me!"

But the doctor's four friends had taught no such lesson to themselves. They resolved forthwith to make a pilgrimage to Florida, and quaff at morning, noon, and night, from the Fountain of Youth.

Nikolai Gogol (1809–1852)

One of Russia's greatest writers, Nikolai Gogol was born at Sorochintsy in the Ukraine, an area rich in legend and folklore. In high school at Nezhin, Gogol participated in theatrics and contributed prose and poetry to the school magazine. He moved to St. Petersburg in 1828 to seek a civil service job, but found only scorn for a vanity poem (1829) he published. Always sensitive to criticism, he attempted emigration to the United States. However, he ran out of money in Germany and returned to St. Petersburg, eventually securing an ill-paying government position. To escape his dreary life, he began writing about the fantastic creatures and demons of his native province. These works were published in 1831–1832 as *Evenings on a Farm Near Dikanka*. They met with widespread acclaim and led to his appointment as an assistant professor of history at St. Petersburg University in 1834.

He left a year later because he felt inadequate for the work. But by then he had published two more books (*Mirgorod* and *Arabesques,* 1835) containing some of his best work. "Vii" told a vivid story of demonology; "The Diary of a Madman" foreshadowed and encouraged surrealism; and "The Portrait" examined the evil influence of a painting.

His successes continued in 1836 with "The Nose" and *The Inspector General* (a play). The first was a satirical account of a man's nose leaving in quest of a better life, the latter a caustic, biting indictment of government corruption which was peformed only after being personally approved by the Tsar. Public controversy over his play greatly disturbed Gogol and he left the country for Rome, where he subsequently published his two greatest works (*Dead Souls* and "The Overcoat") in 1842.

Influenced by E.T.A. Hoffmann, Gogol's style was a rich mixture of stark realism and fantasy. His ''ornate and agitated'' prose, his concern with moral issues, and his psychological portrayals had a tremendous impact on Dostoevski and many other Russian writers. Indeed, Dostoevski claimed that all Russian realists came ''from under Gogol's greatcoat.'' And Vladimir Nabokov called Gogol's tale of the ''Overcoat,'' ''Greatcoat,'' or ''Cloak'' the greatest Russian short story ever written.

Unfortunately, however, Gogol was a complex and tormented personality, riddled with anxieties, obsessions, and feelings of guilt and insufficiency. The poet Aleksander Pushkin acted as a much needed stabilizing influence—offering criticism, judgments about taste, and even ideas (for *Dead Souls* and *The Inspector General*). But Pushkin died in a duel while Gogol hid in Italy, and left to his own devices, Gogol fell apart. He became fascinated with religion: coming to believe his success demonstrated he was God's spokesman and that it was his duty to lead Russia into righteous ways of living.

His attempts to defend Russian society in *Selected Passages from Correspondence with My Friends* (1847) led to denunciation by Belinsky and the radicals. His ten year labor to turn *Dead Souls* into a prose *Divine Comedy* proved prosaic, probably because he had few ideas to offer.

Believing God had deserted him, he tried pilgrimages, prayers, and abasement. When they failed to bring solace, he burned his completed sequel to *Dead Souls* in despair, dying, near madness, ten days later.

THE OVERCOAT

In the department of . . . but I had better not mention in what department. There is nothing in the world more readily moved to wrath than a department, a regiment, a government office, and in fact any sort of official body. Nowadays every private individual considers all society insulted in his person. I have been told that very lately a petition was handed in from a police captain of what town I don't recollect, and that in this petition he set forth clearly that the institutions of the State were in danger and that its sacred name was being taken in vain; and, in proof thereof, he appended to his petition an enormously long volume of some work of romance in which a police captain appeared on every tenth page, occasionally, indeed, in an intoxicated condition. And so, to avoid any unpleasantness, we had better call the department of which we are speaking a certain department.

And so, in a certain department there was a government clerk; a clerk of whom it cannot be said that he was very remarkable; he was short, somewhat pockmarked, with rather reddish hair and rather dim, bleary eyes, with a small bald patch on the top of his head, with wrinkles on both sides of his cheeks and the sort of complexion which is usually associated with hæmorrhoids . . . no help for that, it is the Petersburg climate. As for his grade in the service (for among us the grade is what must be put first), he was what is called a perpetual titular counsellor, a class at which, as we all know, various writers who indulge in the praiseworthy habit of attacking those who cannot defend themselves jeer and jibe to their hearts' content. This clerk's surname was Bashmatchkin. From the very name it is clear that it must have been derived from a shoe (*bashmak*); but when and under what circumstances it was derived from a shoe, it is impossible to say. Both his father and his grandfather and even his brother-in-law, and all the Bashmatchkins without exception wore boots, which they simply resoled two or three times a year. His name was Akaky Akakyevitch. Perhaps it may strike the reader as a rather strange and farfetched name, but I can assure him that it was not farfetched at all, that the circumstances were such that it was quite out of the question to give him any other name. Akaky Akakyevitch was born toward nighfall, if my memory does not deceive me, on the twenty-third of March. His mother, the wife of a government clerk, a very good woman, made arrangements in due course to christen the child. She was still lying in bed, facing the door, while on her right hand stood the godfather, an excellent man called Ivan Ivanovitch Yeroshkin, one of the head clerks in the Senate, and the godmother, the wife of a police official, and a woman of rare qualities, Arina Semyonovna Byelobryushkov. Three names were offered to the happy mother for selection —Moky, Sossy, or the name of the martyr Hozdazat. "No," thought the poor lady, "they are all such names!" To satisfy her, they opened the calendar at another place, and the names which turned up were: Trifily, Dula, Varahasy. "What an infliction!" said the mother. "What names they all are! I really never heard such names. Varadat or Varuh would be bad enough, but Trifily and Varahasy!" They turned over another page and the names were: Pavsikahy and Vahtisy. "Well, I see," said the mother, "it is clear that it is his fate. Since that is how it is, he had better be called after his father, his father is Akaky, let the son be Akaky, too." This was how he came to be Akaky Akakyevitch. The baby was christened and cried and made wry faces during the ceremony, as though he foresaw that he would be a titular counsellor. So that was how it all came to pass. We have recalled it here so that the reader may see for himself that it happened quite inevitably and that to give him any other name was out of the question. No one has been able to remember when and how long ago he entered the department, nor who gave him the job. However many directors and higher officials of all sorts came and went, he was always seen in the same place, in the same position, and at the very same duty, precisely the same copying clerk, so that they used to declare that he must have been born a copying clerk, in uniform all complete and with a bald patch on his head. No respect at all was shown him in the department. The porters, far from getting up from their seats when he came in, took no more notice of him than if a simple fly had flown across the vestibule. His superiors treated him with a sort of domineering chilliness. The head clerk's assistant used to throw papers under his nose without even saying: "Copy this," or "Here is an interesting, nice little case," or some agreeable remark of the sort, as is usually done in well-behaved offices. And he would take it, gazing only at the paper without looking to see who had put it there and whether he had the right to do so; he would take it and at once set to work to copy it. The young clerks jeered and made jokes at him to the best of their clerkly wit, and told before his face all sorts of stories of their own invention about him; they would say of his landlady, an old woman of seventy, that she beat him, would enquire when the wedding was to take place, and would scatter bits of paper on his head, calling them snow. Akaky Akakyevitch never answered a word, however, but behaved as though there were no one there. It had no influence on his work even; in the midst of all this teasing, he never made a single mistake in his copying. Only when the jokes were too unbearable, when they jolted his arm and prevented him from going on with his work, he would bring out: "Leave me alone! Why do you insult me?" and there was something strange in the words and in the voice in which they were uttered. There was a note in it of something that aroused compassion, so that one young man, new to the office, who, following the example of the rest, had allowed himself to mock at him, suddenly stopped as though cut to the heart, and from that time forth, everything was, as it were, changed and appeared in a different light to him. Some unnatural force seemed to thrust him away from the companions with whom he had become acquainted, accepting them as well-bred, polished people. And long afterward, at moments of the greatest gaiety, the figure of the humble little clerk with a bald patch on his head rose before him with his heartrending words: "Leave me alone! Why do you insult me?" and in those heartrending words he heard others: "I am your brother." And the poor young man hid his face in his hands, and many times afterwards in his life he shuddered, seeing how much inhumanity there is in man, how much savage brutality lies hidden under refined, cultured politeness, and my God! even in a man whom the world accepts as a gentleman and a man of honor. . . .

It would be hard to find a man who lived in his work as did Akaky Akakyevitch. To say that he was zealous in his work is not enough; no, he loved his work. In it, in that copying, he found a varied and agreeable world of his own. There was a look of enjoyment on his face; certain letters were favorites with him, and when he came to them he was delighted; he chuckled to himself and winked and moved his lips, so that it seemed as though every letter his pen was forming could be read in his face. If rewards had been given according to the measure of zeal in the service, he might to his amazement have even found himself a civil counsellor; but all he gained in the service, as the wits, his fellow clerks, expressed it, was a buckle in his buttonhole and a pain in his back. It cannot be said, however, that no notice had ever been taken of him. One director, being a good-natured man and anxious to reward him for his long service, sent him something a little more important than his ordinary copying; he was instructed from a finished document to make some sort of report for another office; the work consisted only of altering the headings and in places changing the first person into the third. This cost him such an effort that it threw him into a regular perspiration: he mopped his brow and said at last, "No, better let me copy something."

From that time forth they left him to go on copying forever. It seemed as though nothing in the world existed for him outside his copying. He gave no thought at all to his clothes; his uniform was—well, not green but some sort of rusty, muddy color. His collar was very short and narrow, so that, although his neck was not particularly long, yet, standing out of the collar, it looked as immensely long as those of the plaster kittens that wag their heads and are carried about on trays on the heads of dozens of foreigners living in Russia. And there were always things sticking to his uniform, either bits of hay or threads; moreover, he had a special art of passing under a window at the very moment when various rubbish was being flung out into the street, and so was continually carrying off bits of melon rind and similar litter on his hat. He had never once in his life noticed what was being done and going on in the streets, all those things at which, as we all know, his colleagues, the young clerks, always stare, carrying their sharp sight so far even as to notice any one on the other side of the pavement with a trouser strap hanging loose—a detail which always calls forth a sly grin. Whatever Akaky Akakyevitch looked at, he saw nothing anywhere but his clear, evenly written lines, and only perhaps when a horse's head suddenly appeared from nowhere just on his shoulder, and its nostrils blew a perfect gale upon his cheek, did he notice that he was not in the middle of his writing, but rather in the middle of the street.

On reaching home, he would sit down at once to the table, hurriedly sup his soup and eat a piece of beef with an onion; he did not notice the taste at all, but ate it all up together with the flies and anything else that Providence chanced to send him. When he felt that his stomach was beginning to be full, he would rise up from the table, get out a bottle of ink and set to copying the papers he had brought home with him. When he had none to do, he would make a copy expressly for his own pleasure, particularly if the document were remarkable not for the beauty of its style but for the fact of its being addresed to some new or important personage.

Even at those hours when the grey Petersburg sky is completely overcast and the whole population of clerks have dined and eaten their fill, each as best he can, according to the salary he receives and his personal tastes; when they are all resting after the scratching of pens and bustle of the office, their own necessary work and other people's, and all the tasks that an over-zealous man voluntarily sets himself even beyond what is necessary; when the clerks are hastening to devote what is left of their time to pleasure; some more enterprising are flying to the theater, others to the street to spend their leisure, staring at women's hats, some to spend the evening paying compliments to some attractive girl, the star of a little official circle, while some—and this is the most frequent of all—go simply to a fellow clerk's flat on the third or fourth story, two little rooms with an entry or a kitchen, with some pretentions to style, with a lamp or some such article that has cost many sacrifices of dinners and excursions—at the time when all the clerks are scattered about the little flats of their friends, playing a tempestuous game of whist, sipping tea out of glasses to the accompaniment of farthing rusks, sucking in smoke from long pipes, telling, as the cards are dealt, some scandal that has floated down from higher circles, a pleasure which the Russian can never by any possibility deny himself, or, when there is nothing better to talk about, repeating the everlasting anecdote of the comanding officer who was told that the tail had been cut off the horse on the Falconet monument—in short, even when every one was eagerly seeking entertainment, Akaky Akakyevitch did not give himself up to any amusement. No one could say that they had ever seen him at an evening party. After working to his heart's content, he would go to bed, smiling at the thought of the next day and wondering what God would send him to copy. So flowed on the peaceful life of a man who knew how to be content with his fate on a salary of four hundred rubles, and so perhaps it would have flowed on to extreme old age, had it not been for the various calamities that bestrew the path through life, not only of titular, but even of privy, actual court, and all other counsellors, even those who neither give council to others nor accept it themselves.

There is in Petersburg a mighty foe for all who receive a salary of four hundred rubles or about that sum. That foe is none other than our northern frost, although it is said to be very good for the health. Between eight and nine in the morning, precisely at the hour when the streets are full of clerks going to their departments, the frost begins giving such sharp and stinging flips at all their noses indiscriminately that the poor fellows don't know what to do with them. At that time, when even those in the higher grade have a pain in their brows and tears in their eyes from the frost, the poor titular counsellors are sometimes almost defenseless. Their only protection lies in running as fast as they can through five or six streets in a wretched, thin little overcoat and then warming their feet thoroughly in the porter's room, till all their faculties and qualifications for their various duties thaw again after being frozen on the way. Akaky Akakyevitch had for some time been feeling that his back and shoulders were particularly nipped by the cold, although he did try to run the regular distance as fast as he could. He wondered at last whether there were any defects in his overcoat. After examining it thoroughly in the privacy of his home, he discovered that in two or three places, to wit on the back and the shoulders, it had become a regular sieve; the cloth was so worn that you could see through it and the lining was coming out. I must observe that Akaky Akakyevitch's overcoat had also served as a butt for the jibes of the clerks. It had even been deprived of the honorable name of overcoat and had been referred to as the "dressing jacket." It was indeed of rather a strange make. Its collar had been growing smaller year by year as it served to patch the other parts. The patches were not good specimens of the tailor's art, and they certainly looked clumsy and ugly. On seeing what was wrong, Akaky Akakyevitch decided that he would have to take the overcoat to Petrovitch, a tailor who lived on a fourth story up a back staircase, and, in spite of having only one eye and being pockmarked all over his face, was rather successful in repairing the trousers and coats of clerks and others—that is, when he was sober, be it understood, and had no other enterprise in his mind. Of this tailor I ought not, of course, to say much, but since it is now the rule that the character of every person in a novel must be completely drawn, well, there is no help for it, here is Petrovitch too. At first he was called simply Grigory, and was a serf belonging to some gentleman or other. He began to be called Petrovitch from the time that he got his freedom and began to drink rather heavily on every holiday, at first only on the chief holidays, but afterwards on all church holidays indiscriminately, wherever there is a cross in the calendar. On that side he was true to the customs of his forefathers, and when he quarrelled with his wife used to call her "a worldly woman and a German." Since we have now mentioned the wife, it will be necessary to say a few words about her too, but unfortunately not much is known about her, except indeed that Petrovitch had a wife and that she wore a cap and not a kerchief, but apparently she could not boast of beauty; anyway, none but soliders of the Guards peeped under her cap when they met her, and they twitched their moustaches and gave vent to a rather peculiar sound.

As he climbed the stairs, leading to Petrovitch's—which, to do them justice, were all soaked with water and slops and saturated through and through with that smell of spirits which makes the eye smart, and is, as we all know, inseparable from the backstairs of Petersburg houses—Akaky Akakyevitch was already wondering how much Petrovitch would ask for the job, and inwardly resolving not to give more than two rubles. The door was open, for Petrovitch's wife was frying some fish and had so filled the kitchen with smoke that you could not even see the black beetles. Akaky Akakyevitch crossed the kitchen unnoticed by the good woman, and walked at last into a room where he saw Petrovitch sitting on a big, wooden, unpainted table with his legs tucked under him like a Turkish pasha. The feet, as is usual with tailors when they sit at work, were bare; and the first object that caught Akaky Akakyevitch's eye was the big toe, with which he was already familiar, with a misshapen nail as thick and strong as the shell of a tortoise. Round Petrovitch's neck hung a skein of silk and another of thread and on his knees was a rag of some sort. He had for the last three minutes been trying to thread his needle, but could not get the thread into the eye and so was very angry with the darkness and indeed with the thread itself, muttering in an undertone "It won't go in, the savage! You wear me out, you rascal." Akaky Akakyevitch was vexed that he had come just at the minute when Petrovitch was in a bad humor; he liked to give him an order when he was a little "elevated," or, as his wife expressed it, "had fortified himself with fizz, the one-eyed devil." In such circumstances Petrovitch was as a rule very ready to give way and agree, and invariably bowed and thanked him, indeed. Afterwards, it is true, his wife would come wailing that her husband had been drunk and so had asked too little, but adding a single ten kopeck piece would settle that. But on this occasion Petrovitch was apparently sober and consequently curt, unwilling to bargain, and the devil knows what price he would be ready to lay on. Akaky Akakyevitch perceived this, and was, as the saying is, beating a retreat, but things had gone too far, for Petrovitch was screwing up his solitary eye very attentively at him and Akaky Akakyevitch involuntarily brought out: "Good day, Petrovitch!" "I wish you a good day, sir," said Petrovitch, and squinted at Akaky Akakyevitch's hands, trying to discover what sort of goods he had brought.

"Here I have come to you, Petrovitch, do you see . . . !"

It must be noticed that Akaky Akakyevitch for the most part explained himself by apologies, vague phrases, and particles which have absolutely no significance whatever. If the subject were a very difficult one, it was his habit indeed to leave his sentences quite unfinished, so that very often after a sentence had begun with the words, "It really is, don't you know . . ." nothing at all would follow and he himself would be quite oblivious, supposing he had said all that was necessary.

"What is it?" said Petrovitch, and at the same time with his solitary eye he scrutinized his whole uniform from the collar to the sleeves, the back, the skirts, the buttonholes—with all of which he was very familiar, they were all his own work. Such scrutiny is habitual with tailors, it is the first thing they do on meeting one.

"It's like this, Petrovitch . . . the overcoat, the cloth . . . you see everywhere else it is quite strong; it's a little dusty and looks as though it were old, but it is new and it is only in one place just a little . . .on the back, and just a little worn on one shoulder and on this shoulder, too, a little . . . do you see? that's all, and it's not much work. . . ."

Petrovitch took the "dressing jacket," first spread it out over the table, examined it for a long time, shook his head and put his hand out to the window for a round snuffbox with a portrait on the lid of some general—which precisely I can't say, for a finger had been thrust through the spot where a face should have been, and the hole had been pasted up with a square bit of paper. After taking a pinch of snuff, Petrovitch held the "dressing jacket" up in his hands and looked at it against the light, and again he shook his head; then he turned it with the lining upwards and once more shook his head; again he took off the lid with the general pasted up with paper and stuffed a pinch into his nose, shut the box, put it away and at last said: "No, it can't be repaired; a wretched garment!"

"Why can't it, Petrovitch?" he said, almost in the imploring voice of a child. "Why, the only thing is it is a bit worn on the shoulders; why, you have got some little pieces. . . ."

"Yes, the pieces will be found all right," said Petrovitch, "but it can't be patched, the stuff is quite rotten; if you put a needle in it, it would give way."

"Let it give way, but you just put a patch on it."

"There is nothing to put a patch on. There is nothing for it to hold on to; there is a great strain on it, it is not worth calling cloth, it would fly away at a breath of wind."

"Well, then, strengthen it with something—upon my word, really, this is . . . !

"No," said Petrovitch resolutely, "there is nothing to be done, the thing is no good at all. You had far better, when the cold winter weather comes, make yourself leg wrappings out of it, for there is no warmth in stockings, the Germans invented them just to make money." (Petrovitch was fond of a dig at the Germans occasionally.) "And as for the overcoat, it is clear that you will have to have a new one."

At the word "new" there was a mist before Akaky Akakyevitch's eyes, and everything in the room seemed blurred. He could see nothing clearly but the general with the piece of paper over his face on the lid of Petrovitch's snuffbox.

"A new one?" he said, still feeling as though he were in a dream; "why, I haven't the money for it."

"Yes, a new one," Petrovitch repeated with barbarous composure.

"Well, and if I did have a new one, how much would it . . .?"

"You mean what will it cost?"

"Yes."

"Well, three fifty-ruble notes or more," said Petrovitch, and he compressed his lips significantly. He was very fond of making an effect, he was fond of suddenly disconcerting a man completely and then squinting sideways to see what sort of a face he made.

"A hundred and fifty rubles for an overcoat," screamed poor Akaky Akakyevitch—it was perhaps the first time he had screamed in his life, for he was always distinguished by the softness of his voice.

"Yes," said Petrovitch, "and even then it's according to the coat. If I were to put marten on the collar, and add a hood with silk linings, it would come to two hundred."

"Petrovitch, please," said Akaky Akakyevitch in an imploring voice, not hearing and not trying to hear what Petrovitch said, and missing all his effects, "do repair it somehow, so that it will serve a little longer."

"No, that would be wasting work and spending money for nothing," said Petrovitch, and after that Akaky Akakyevitch went away completely crushed, and when he had gone Petrovitch remained standing for a long time with his lips pursed up significantly before he took up his work again, feeling pleased that he had not demeaned himself nor lowered the dignity of the tailor's art.

When he got into the street, Akaky Akakyevitch was as though in a dream. "So that is how it is," he said to himself. "I really did not think it would be so . . ." and then after a pause he added, "So there it is! so that's how it is at last! and I really could never have supposed it would have been so. And there . . ." There followed another long silence, after which he brought out: "So there it is! well, it really is so utterly unexpected . . . who would have thought . . . what a circumstance. . . ." Saying this, instead of going home he walked off in quite the opposite direction without suspecting what he was doing. On the way a clumsy sweep brushed the whole of his sooty side against him and blackened all his shoulder; a regular hatful of plaster scattered upon him from the top of a house that was being built. He noticed nothing of this, and only after he had jostled against a sentry who had set his halberd down beside him and was shaking some snuff out of his horn into his rough fist, he came to himself a little and then only because the sentry said "Why are you poking yourself right in one's face, haven't you the pavement to yourself?" This made him look round and turn homeward; only there he began to collect his thoughts, to see his position in a clear and true light and began talking to himself no longer incoherently but reasonably and openly as with a sensible friend with whom one can discuss the most intimate and vital matters. "No, indeed," said Akaky Akakyevitch, "it is no use talking to Petrovitch now; just now he really is . . . his wife must have been giving it to him. I had better go to him on Sunday morning; after the Saturday evening he will be squinting and sleepy, so he'll want a little drink to carry it off and his wife won't give him a penny. I'll slip ten kopecks into his hand and then he will be more accommodating and maybe take the overcoat. . . .''

So reasoning with himself, Akaky Akakyevitch cheered up and waited until the next Sunday; then, seeing from a distance Petrovitch's wife leaving the house, he went straight in. Petrovitch certainly was very tipsy after the Saturday. He could hardly hold his head up and was very drowsy: but, for all that, as soon as he heard what he was speaking about, it seemed as though the devil had nudged him. ''I can't,'' he said, ''you must kindly order a new one.'' Akaky Akakyevitch at once slipped a ten-kopeck piece into his hand. ''I thank you, sir, I will have just a drop to your health, but don't trouble yourself about the overcoat; it is not a bit of good for anything. I'll make you a fine new coat, you can trust me for that.''

Akaky Akakyevitch would have said more about repairs, but Petrovitch, without listening, said: ''A new one now I'll make you without fail; you can rely upon that, I'll do my best. It could even be like the fashion that has come in with the collar to button with silver claws under appliqué.''

Then Akaky Akakyevitch saw that there was no escape from a new overcoat and he was utterly depressed. How indeed, for what, with what money could he get it? Of course he could to some extent rely on the bonus for the coming holiday, but that money had long ago been appropriated and its use determined beforehand. It was needed for new trousers and to pay the cobbler an old debt for putting some new tops to some old boot-legs, and he had to order three shirts from a seamstress as well as two specimens of an undergarment which it is improper to mention in print; in short, all that money absolutely must be spent, and even if the director were to be so gracious as to assign him a gratuity of forty-five or even fifty, instead of forty rubles, there would be still left a mere trifle, which would be but as a drop in the ocean beside the fortune needed for an overcoat. Though, of course, he knew that Petrovitch had a strange craze for suddenly puttting on the devil knows what enormous price, so that at times his own wife could not help cryng out: ''Why, you are out of your wits, you idiot! Another time he'll undertake a job for nothing, and here the devil has bewitched him to ask more than he is worth himself.'' Though, of course, he knew that Petrovitch would undertake to make it for eighty rubles, still where would he get those eighty rubles? He might manage half of that sum; half of it could be found, perhaps even a little more; but where could he get the other half? . . . But, first of all, the reader ought to know where that first half was to be found. Akaky Akakyevitch had the habit every time he spend a ruble of putting aside two kopecks in a little locked-up box with a slit in the lid for slipping the money in. At the end of every half-year he would inspect the pile of coppers there and change them for small silver. He had done this for a long time, and in the course of many years the sum had mounted up to forty rubles and so he had half the money in his hands, but where was he to get the other half, where was he to get another forty rubles? Akaky Akakyevitch pondered and pondered and decided at last that he would have to diminish his ordinary expenses, at least for a year; give up burning candles in the evening, and if he had to do anything he must go into the landlady's room and work by her candle; that as he walked along the streets he must walk as lightly and carefully as possible, almost on tiptoe, on the cobbles and flagstones, so that his soles might last a little longer than usual; that he must send his linen to the wash less frequently, and that, to preserve it from being worn, he must take it off every day when he came home and sit in a thin cotton-shoddy dressing-gown, a very ancient garment which Time itself had spared. To tell the truth, he found it at first rather hard to get used to these privations, but after a while it became a habit and went smoothly enough—he even became quite accustomed to being hungry in the evening; on the other hand, he had spiritual nourishment, for he carried ever in his thoughts the idea of his future overcoat. His whole existence had in a sense become fuller, as though he had married, as though some other person was present with him, as though he were no longer alone, but an agreeable companion had consented to walk the path of life hand in hand with him, and that companion was no other than the new overcoat with its thick wadding and its strong, durable lining. He became, as it were, more alive, even more strong-willed, like a man who has set before himself a definite aim. Uncertainty, indecision, in fact all the hesitating and vague characteristics vanished from his face and his manners. At time there was a gleam in his eyes, indeed, the most bold and audacious ideas flashed through hs mind. Why not really have marten on the collar? Meditation on the subject always made him absentminded. On one occasion when he was copying a document, he very nearly made a mistake, so that he almost cried out ''ough'' aloud and crossed himself.

At least once every month he went to Petrovitch to talk about the overcoat, where it would be best to buy the cloth, and what color it should be, and what price, and, though he returned home a little anxious, he was always pleased at the thought that at last the time as at hand when everything would be bought and the overcoat would be made. Things moved even faster than he had anticipated. Contrary to all expectations, the director bestowed on Akaky Akakyevitch a gratuity of no less than sixty rubles. Whether it was that he had an inkling that Akaky Akakyevitch needed a greatcoat, or whether it happened so by chance, owing to this he found he had twenty rubles extra. This circumstance hastened the course of affairs. Another two or three months of partial fasting and Akaky Akakyevitch had actually saved up nearly eighty rubles. His heart, as a rule very tranquil, began to throb. The very first day he set off in company with Petrovitch to the shops. They bought some very good cloth, and no wonder, since they had been thinking of it for more than six months before, and scarcely a month had passed without their going to the shop to compare prices; now Petrovitch himself declared that there was no better cloth to be had. For the lining they chose calico, but of a stout quality, which in Petrovich's words was even better than silk, and actually as strong and handsome to look at. Marten they did not buy, because it certainly was dear, but instead they chose cat fur, the best to be found in the shop—cat which in the distance might almost be taken for marten. Petrovitch was busy over the coat for a whole fortnight, because there were a great many buttonholes, otherwise it would have been ready sooner. Petrovitch asked twelve rubles for the work; less than that it hardly could have been, everything was sewn with silk, with fine double seams, and Petrovitch went over every seam afterwards with his own teeth imprinting various figures with them. It was . . . it is hard to say precisely on what day, but probably on the most triumphant day of the life of Akaky Akakyevitch that Petrovitch at last brought the overcoat. He brought it in the morning, just before it was time to set off for the department. The overcoat could not have arrived more in the nick of time, for rather sharp frosts were just beginning and seemed threatening to be even more severe. Petrovitch brought the greatcoat himself as a good tailor should. There was an expression of importance on his face, such as Akaky Akakyevitch had never seen there before. He seemed fully conscious of having completed a work of no little moment and of having shown in his own person the gulf that separates tailors who only put in linings and do repairs from those who make up new materials. He took the greatcoat out of the bandana in which he had brought it (the bandana had just come home from the wash), he then folded it up and put it in his pocket for future use. After taking out the overcoat, he looked at it with much pride and, holding it in both hands, threw it very deftly over Akaky Akakyevitch's shoulders, then pulled it down and smoothed it out behind with his hands; then draped it about Akaky Akakyevitch with somewhat jaunty carelessness. The latter, as a man advanced in years, wished to try it with his arms in the sleeves. Petrovitch helped him to put it on, and it appeared that it looked splendid too with his arms in the sleeves. In fact it turned out that the overcoat was completely and entirely successful. Petrovitch did not let slip the occasion for observing that it was only because he lived in a small street and had no signboard, and because he had known Akaky Akakyevitch so long, that he had done it so cheaply, but on the Nevsky Prospect they would have asked him seventy-five rubles for the work alone. Akaky Akakyevitch had no inclination to discuss this with Petrovitch, besides he was frightened of the big sums that Petrovitch was fond of flinging airily about in conversation. He paid him, thanked him, and went off on the spot, with his new overcoat on, to the department. Petrovitch followed him out and stopped in the street, staring for a good time at the coat from a distance and then purposely turned off and, taking a short cut by a side street, came back into the street and got another view of the coat from the other side, that is, from the front.

Meanwhile Akaky Akakyevitch walked along with every emotion in its most holiday mood. He felt every second that he had a new overcoat on his shoulders, and several times he actually laughed from inward satisfaction. Indeed, it had two advantages, one that it was warm and the other that it was good. He did not notice the way at all and found himself all at once at the department; in the porter's room he took off the overcoat, looked it over and put it in the porter's special care. I cannot tell how it happened, but all at once every one in the department learned that Akaky Akakyevitch had a new overcoat and that the "dressing jacket" no longer existed. They all ran out at once into the porter's room to look at Akaky Akakyevitch's new overcoat, they began welcoming him and congratulating him so that at first he could do nothing but smile and afterwards felt positively abashed. When, coming up to him, they all began saying that he must "sprinkle" the new overcoat and that he ought at least to stand them all a supper. Akaky Akakyevitch lost his head completely and did not know what to do, how to get out of it, nor what to answer. A few minutes later, flushing crimson, he even began assuring them with great simplicity that it was not a new overcoat at all, that it was just nothing, that it was an old overcoat. At last one of the clerks, indeed the assistant of the head clerk of the room, probably in order to show that he was not proud and was able to get on with those beneath him, said, "So be it, I'll give a party instead of Akaky Akakyevitch and invite you all to tea with me this evening; as luck would have it, it is my name day." The clerks naturally congratulated the assistant head clerk and eagerly accepted the invitation. Akaky Akakyevitch was beginning to make excuses, but they all declared that it was uncivil of him, that it was simply a shame and a disgrace and that he could not possibly refuse. However, he felt pleased about it afterwards when he remembered that through this he would have the opportunity of going out in the evening, too, in his new overcoat. That whole day was for Akaky Akakyevitch the most triumphant and festive day in his life. He returned home in the happiest frame of mind, took off the overcoat and hung it carefully on the wall, admiring the cloth and lining once more, and then pulled out his old "dressing jacket," now completely coming to pieces, on purpose to compare them. He glanced at it and positively laughed, the difference was so immense! And long afterwards he went on laughing at dinner, as the position in which the "dressing jacket" was placed recurred to his mind. He dined in excellent spirits and after dinner wrote nothing, no papers at all, but just took his ease for a little while on his bed, till it got dark, then, without putting things off, he dressed, put on his overcoat, and went out into the street. Where precisely the clerk who had invited him lived we regret to say that we cannot tell; our memory is beginning to fail sadly, and everything there is in Petersburg, all the streets and houses, are so blurred and muddled in our head that it is a very difficult business to put anything in orderly fashion. However that may have been, there is no doubt that the clerk lived in the better part of the town and consequently a very long distance from Akaky Akakyevitch. At first the latter had to walk through deserted streets, scantily lighted, but as he approached his destination the streets became more lively, more full of people, and more brightly lighted; passersby began to be more frequent; ladies began to appear, here and there, beautifully dressed; beaver collars were to be seen on the men. Cabmen with wooden trelliswork sledges, studded with gilt nails, were less frequently to be met; on the other hand, jaunty drivers in raspberry colored velvet caps with varnished sledges and bearskin rugs appeared, and carriages with decorated boxes dashed along the streets, their wheels crunching through the snow.

Akaky Akakyevitch looked at all this as a novelty; for several years he had not gone out into the streets in the evening. He stopped with curiosity before a lighted shop-window to look at a picture in which a beautiful woman was represented in the act of taking off her shoe and displaying as she did so the whole of a very shapely leg, while behind her back a gentleman with whiskers and a handsome imperial on his chin was putting his head in at the door. Akaky Akakyevitch shook his head and smiled and then went on his way. Why did he smile? Was it because he had come across something quite unfamiliar to him, though every man retains some instinctive feeling on the subject, or was it that he reflected, like many other clerks, as follows: "Well, upon my soul, those Frenchmen! it's beyond anything! if they try anything of the sort, it really is . . . !" Though possibly he did not even think that; there is no creeping into a man's soul and finding out all that he thinks. At last he reached the house in which the assistant head clerk lived in fine style; there was a lamp burning on the stairs, and the flat was on the second floor. As he went into the entry Akaky Akakyevitch saw whole rows of galoshes. Amongst them in the middle of the room stood a samovar hissing and letting off clouds of steam. On the walls hung coats and cloaks, among which some actually had beaver collars or velvet revers. The other side of the wall there was noise and talk, which suddenly became clear and loud when the door opened and the footman came out with a tray full of empty glasses, a jug of cream, and a basket of biscuits. It was evident that the clerks had arrived long before and had already drunk their first glass of tea. Akaky Akakyevitch, after hanging up his coat with his own hands, went into the room, and at the same moment there flashed before his eyes a vision of candles, clerks, pipes, and card tables, together with the confused sounds of conversation rising up on all sides and the noise of moving chairs. He stopped very awkwardly in the middle of the room, looking about and trying to think what to do, but he was observed and received with a shout and they all went at once into the entry and again took a look at his overcoat. Though Akaky Akakyevitch was somewhat embarrassed, yet, being a simple-hearted man, he could not help being pleased at seeing how they all admired his coat. Then of course they all abandoned him and his coat, and turned their attention as usual to the tables set for whist. All this—the noise, the talk, and the crowd of people—was strange and wonderful to Akaky Akakyevitch. He simply did not know how to behave, what to do with his arms and legs and his whole figure; at last he sat down beside the players, looked at the cards, stared first at one and then at another of the faces, and in a little while began to yawn and felt that he was bored—especially as it was long past the time at which he usually went to bed. He tried to take leave of his hosts, but they would not let him go, saying that he absolutely must have a glass of champagne in honor of the new coat. An hour later supper was served, consisting of salad, cold veal, a pasty, pies and tarts from the confectioner's, and champagne. They made Akaky Akakyevitch drink two glasses, after which he felt that things were much more cheerful, though he could not forget that it was twelve o'clock and that he ought to have been home long ago. That his host might not take it into his head to detain him, he slipped out of the room, hunted in the entry for his greatcoat, which he found, not without regret, lying on the floor, shook it, removed some fluff from it, put it on, and went down the stairs into the street. It was still light in the streets. Some little general shops, those perpetual clubs for house-serfs and all sorts of people, were open; others which were closed showed, however, a long streak of light at every crack of the door, proving that they were not yet deserted, and probably maids and men-servants were still finishing their conversation and discussion, driving their masters to utter perplexity as to their whereabouts. Akaky Akakyevitch walked along in a cheerful state of mind; he was even on the point of running, goodness knows why, after a lady of some sort who passed by like lightning with every part of her frame in violent motion. He checked himself at once, however, and again walked along very gently, feeling positively surprised himself at the inexplicable impulse that had seized him. Soon the deserted streets, which are not particularly cheerful by day and even less so in the evening, stretched before him. Now they were still more dead and deserted; the light of street lamps was scantier, the oil was evidently running low; then came wooden houses and fences; not a soul anywhere; only the snow gleamed on the streets and the low-pitched slumbering hovels looked black and gloomy with their closed shutters. He approached the spot where the street was intersected by an endless square, which looked like a fearful desert with its houses scarcely visible on the further side.

In the distance, goodness knows where, there was a gleam of light from some sentry box which seemed to be standing at the end of the world. Akaky Akakyevitch's light-heartedness grew somehow sensibly less at this place. He stepped into the square, not without an involuntary uneasiness, as though his heart had a foreboding of evil. He looked behind him and to both sides—it was as though the sea were all round him. "No, better not look," he thought, and walked on, shutting his eyes, and when he opened them to see whether the end of the square were near, he suddenly saw standing before him, almost under his very nose, some men with moustaches; just what they were like he could not even distinguish. There was a mist before his eyes and a throbbing in his chest. "I say the overcoat is mine!" said one of them in a voice like a clap of thunder, seizing him by the collar. Akaky Akakyevitch was on the point of shouting "Help" when another put a fist the size of a clerk's head against his very lips, saying, "You just shout now." Akaky Akakyevitch felt only that they took the overcoat off, and gave him a kick with their knees, and he fell on his face in the snow and was conscious of nothing more. A few minutes later he came to himself and got on to his feet, but there was no one there. He felt that it was cold on the ground and that he had no overcoat, and began screaming, but it seemed as though his voice could not carry to the end of the square. Overwhelmed with despair and continuing to scream, he ran across the square straight to the sentry box, beside which stood a sentry leaning on his halberd and, so it seemed, looking with curiosity to see who the devil the man was who was screaming and running towards him from the distance. As Akaky Akakyevitch reached him, he began breathlessly shouting that he was asleep and not looking after his duty not to see that a man was being robbed. The sentry answered that he had seen nothing, that he had only seen him stopped in the middle of the square by two men, and supposed that they were his friends, and that, instead of abusing him for nothing, he had better go the next day to the superintendent and that he would find out who had taken the overcoat. Akaky Akakyevitch ran home in a terrible state: his hair, which was still comparatively abundant on his temples and the back of his head, was completely dishevelled; his sides and chest and his trousers were all covered with snow. When his old landlady heard a fearful knock at the door she jumped hurriedly out of bed and, with only one slipper on, ran to open it, modestly holding her shift across her bosom; but when she opened it she stepped back, seeing what a state Akaky Akakyevitch was in. When he told her what had happened, she clasped her hands in horror and said that he must go straight to the superintendent, that the police constable of the quarter would deceive him, make promises and lead him a dance; that it would be best of all to go to the superintendent, and that she knew him indeed, because Anna the Finnish girl who was once her cook was now in service as a nurse at the superintendent's; and that she often saw him himself when he passed by their house, and that he used to be every Sunday at church too, saying his prayers and at the same time looking good-humoredly at every one, and that therefore by every token he must be a kind-hearted man. After listening to this advice, Akaky Akakyevitch made his way very gloomily to his room, and how he spent that night I leave to the imagination of those who are in the least able to picture the position of others. Early in the morning he set off to the police superintendent's, but was told that he was asleep. He came at ten o'clock, he was told again that he was asleep; he came at eleven and was told that the superintendent was not at home; he came at dinnertime, but the clerks in the anteroom would not let him in, and insisted on knowing what was the matter and what business had brought him and exactly what had happened; so that at last Akaky Akakyevitch for the first time in his life tried to show the strength of his character and said curtly that he must see the superintendent himself, that they dare not refuse to admit him, that he had come from the department on government business, and that if he made complaint of them they would see. The clerks dared say nothing to this, and one of them went to summon the superintendent. The latter received his story of being robbed of his overcoat in an extremely strange way. Instead of attending to the main point, he began asking Akaky Akakyevitch questions. Why had he been coming home so late? Wasn't he going, or hadn't he been, to some house of ill-fame? Akaky Akakyevitch was overwhelmed with confusion, and went away without knowing whether or not the proper measures would be taken in regard to his overcoat. He was absent from the office all that day (the only time that it had happened in his life). Next day he appeared with a pale face, wearing his old "dressing jacket" which had become a still more pitiful sight. The tidings of the theft of the overcoat—though there were clerks who did not let even this chance slip of jeering at Akaky Akakyevitch—touched many of them. They decided on the spot to get up a subscription for him, but collected only a very trifling sum, because the clerks had already spent a good deal on subscribing to the director's portrait and on the purchase of a book, at the suggestion of the head of their department, who was a friend of the author, and so the total realized was very insignificant. One of the clerks, moved by compassion, ventured at any rate to assist Akaky Akakyevitch with good advice, telling him not to go to the district police inspector, because, though it might happen that the latter might be sufficiently zealous of gaining the approval of his superiors to succeed in finding the overcoat, it would remain in the possession of the police unless he presented legal proofs that it belonged to him; he urged that far the best thing would be to appeal to a Person of Consequence; that the Person of Consequence, by writing and getting into communication with the proper authorities, could push the matter through more successfully. There was nothing else for it. Akaky Akakyevitch made up his mind to go to the Person of Consequence. What precisely was the nature of the functions of the Person of Consequence has remained a matter of uncertainty. It must be noted that this Person of Consequence had only lately become a person of consequence, and until recently had been a person of no consequence. Though, indeed, his position even now was not reckoned of consequence in comparison with others of still greater consequence. But there is always to be found a circle of persons to whom a person of little consequence in the eyes of others is a person of consequence. It is true that he did his utmost to increase the consequence of his position in various ways, for instance by insisting that his subordinates should come out on to the stairs to meet him when he arrived at his office; that no one should venture to approach him directly but all proceedings should be by the strictest order of precedence, that a collegiate registration clerk should report the matter to the provincial secretary, and the provincial secretary to the titular counsellor or whomsoever it might be, and that business should only reach him by this channel. Everyone in Holy Russia has a craze for imitation, everyone apes and mimics his superiors. I have actually been told that a titular counsellor who was put in charge of a small separate office, immediately partitioned off a special room for himself, calling it the head office, and set special porters at the door with red collars and gold lace, who took hold of the handle of the door and opened it for everyone who went in, though the "head office" was so tiny that it was with difficulty that an ordinary writing table could be put into it. The manners and habits of the Person of Consequence were dignified and majestic, but not complex. The chief foundation of his system was strictness, "strictness, strictness, and—strictness!" he used to say, and at the last word he would look very significantly at the person he was addressing, though, indeed, he had no reason to do so, for the dozen clerks who made up the whole administrative mechanism of his office stood in befitting awe of him; any clerk who saw him in the distance would leave his work and remain standing at attention till his superior had left the room. His conversation with his subordinates was usually marked by severity and almost confined to three phrases: "How dare you? Do you know to whom you are speaking? Do you understand who I am?" He was, however, at heart a good-natured man, pleasant and obliging with his colleagues; but the grade of general had completely turned his head. When he received it, he was perplexed, thrown off his balance, and quite at a loss how to behave. If he chanced to be with his equals, he was still quite a decent man, a very gentlemanly man, in fact, and in many ways even an intelligent man, but as soon as he was in company with men who were even one grade below him, there was simply no doing anything with him: he sat silent and his position excited compassion, the more so as he himself felt that he might have been spending his time to incomparably more advantage. At times there could be seen in his eyes an intense desire to join in some interesting conversation, but he was restrained by the doubt whether it would not be too much on his part, whether it would not be too great a familiarity and lowering of his dignity, and in consequence of these reflections he remained everlastingly in the same mute condition, only uttering from time to time monosyllabic sounds, and in this way he gained the reputation of being a very tiresome man.

So this was the Person of Consequence to whom our friend Akaky Akakyevitch appealed, and he appealed to him at a most unpropitious moment, very unfortunate for himself, though fortunate, indeed, for the Person of Consequence. The latter happened to be in his study, talking in the very best of spirits with an old friend of his childhood who had only just arrived and whom he had not seen for several years. It was at this moment that he was informed that a man called Bashmatchkin was asking to see him. He asked abruptly, "What sort of man is he?" and received the answer, "A government clerk." "Ah! he can wait, I haven't time now," said the Person of Consequence. Here I must observe that this was a complete lie on the part of the Person of Consequence: he had time; his friend and he had long ago said all they had to say to each other and their conversation had begun to be broken by very long pauses during which they merely slapped each other on the knee, saying, "So that's how things are, Ivan Abramovitch!"—"There it is, Stepan Varlamovitch!" but, for all that, he told the clerk to wait in order to show his friend, who had left the service years before and was living at home in the country, how long clerks had to wait in his anteroom. At last after they had talked, or rather been silent to their heart's content and had smoked a cigar in very comfortable armchairs with sloping backs, he seemed suddenly to recollect, and said to the secretary, who was standing at the door with papers for his signature, "Oh, by the way, there is a clerk waiting, isn't there? Tell him he can come in." When he saw Akaky Akakyevitch's meek appearance and old uniform, he turned to him at once and said, "What do you want?" in a firm and abrupt voice, which he had purposely practiced in his own room in solitude before the looking glass for a week before receiving his present post and the grade of a general. Akaky Akakyevitch, who was overwhelmed with befitting awe beforehand, was somewhat confused and, as far as his tongue would allow him, explained to the best of his powers, with even more frequent "ers" than usual, that he had had a perfectly new overcoat and now he had been robbed of it in the most inhuman way, and that now he had come to beg him by his intervention either to correspond with his honor the head policemaster or anybody else, and find the overcoat. This mode of proceeding struck the general for some reason as taking a great liberty. "What next, sir," he went on as abruptly, "don't you know the way to proceed? To whom are you addressing yourself? Don't you know how things are done? You ought first to have handing in a petition to the office; it would have gone to the head clerk of the room, and to the head clerk of the section, then it would have been handed to the secretary and the secretary would have brought it to me. . . ."

"But, your Excellency," said Akaky Akakyevitch, trying to collect all the small allowance of presence of mind he possessed and feeling at the same time that he was getting into a terrible perspiration, "I ventured, your Excellency, to trouble you because secretaries . . . er . . . are people you can't depend on. . . ."

"What? what? what?" said the Person of Consequence, "where did you get hold of that spirit? Where did you pick up such ideas? What insubordination is spreading among young men against their superiors and betters." The Person of Consequence did not apparently observe that Akaky Akakyevitch was well over fifty, and therefore if he could have been called a young man it would only have been in comparison with a man of seventy. "Do you know to whom you are speaking? Do you understand who I am? Do you understand that, I ask you?" At this point he stamped, and raised his voice to such a powerful note that Akaky Akakyevitch was not the only one to be terrified. Akaky Akakyevitch was positively petrified; he staggered, trembling all over, and could not stand; if the porters had not run up to support him, he would have flopped upon the floor; he was led out almost unconscious. The Person of Consequence, pleased that the effect had surpassed his expectations and enchanted at the idea that his words could even deprive a man of consciousness, stole a sideway glance at his friend to see how he was taking it, and perceived not without satisfaction that his friend was feeling very uncertain and even beginning to be a little terrified himself.

How he got downstairs, how he went out into the street—of all that Akaky Akakyevitch remembered nothing, he had no feeling in his arms or his legs. In all his life he had never been so severely reprimanded by a general, and this was by one of another department, too. He went out into the snowstorm, that was whistling through the streets, with his mouth open, and as he went he stumbled off the pavement; the wind, as its way in Petersburg, blew upon him from all points of the compass and from every side street. In an instant it had blown a quinsy into his throat, and when he got home he was not able to utter a word; with a swollen face and throat he went to bed. So violent is sometimes the effect of a suitable reprimand!

Next day he was in a high fever. Thanks to the gracious assistance of the Petersburg climate, the disease made more rapid progress than could have been expected, and when the doctor came, after feeling his pulse he could find nothing to do but prescribe a fomentation, and that simply that the patient might not be left without the benefit of medical assistance; however, two days later he informed him that his end was at hand, after which he turned to his landlady and said: "And you had better lose no time, my good woman, but order him now a deal coffin—an oak one will be too dear for him." Whether Akaky Akakyevitch heard these fateful words or not, whether they produced a shattering effect upon him, and whether he regretted his pitiful life, no one can tell, for he was all the time in delirium and fever. Apparitions, each stranger than the one before, were continually haunting him: first, he saw Petrovitch and was ordering him to make a greatcoat trimmed with some sort of traps for robbers, who were, he fancied, continually under the bed, and he was calling his landlady every minute to pull out a thief who had even got under the quilt; then he kept asking why his old "dressing jacket" was hanging before him when he had a new overcoat, then he fancied he was standing before the general listening to the appropriate reprimand and saying "I am sorry, your Excellency," then finally he became abusive, uttering the most awful language, so that his old landlady positively crossed herself, having never heard anything of the kind from him before, and the more horrified because these dreadful words followed immediately upon the phrase "your Excellency." Later on, his talk was a mere medley of nonsense, so that it was quite unintelligible; all that could be seen was that his incoherent words and thoughts were concerned with nothing but the overcoat. At last poor Akaky Akakyevitch gave up the ghost. No seal was put upon his room nor upon his things, because, in the first place, he had no heirs and, in the second, the property left was very small, to wit, a bundle of goose-feathers, a quire of white government paper, three pairs of socks, two or three buttons that had come off his trousers, and the "dressing jacket" with which the reader is already familiar. Who came into all this wealth God only knows; even I who tell the tale must own that I have not troubled to inquire. And Petersburg remained without Akaky Akakyevitch, as though, indeed, he had never been in the city. A creature had vanished and departed whose cause no one had championed, who was dear to no one, of interest to no one, who never even attracted the attention of the student of natural history, though the latter does not disdain to fix a common fly upon a pin and look at him under the microscope—a creature who bore patiently the jeers of the office and for no particular reason went to his grave, though even he at the very end of his life was visited by a gleam of brightness in the form of an overcoat that for one instant brought color into his poor life—a creature on whom calamity broke as insufferably as it breaks upon the heads of the mighty ones of this world . . . !

Several days after his death, the porter from the department was sent to his lodgings with instructions that he should go at once to the office, for his chief was asking for him; but the porter was obliged to return without him, explaining that he could not come, and to the inquiry

"Why?" he added, "Well, you see: the fact is he is dead, he was buried three days ago." This was how they learned at the office of the death of Akaky Akakyevitch, and the next day there was sitting in his seat a new clerk who was very much taller and who wrote not in the same upright hand but made his letters more slanting and crooked.

But who could have imagined that this was not all there was to tell about Akaky Akakyevitch, that he was destined for a few days to make a noise in the world after his death, as though to make up for his life having been unnoticed by any one? But so it happened, and our poor story unexpectedly finishes with a fantastic ending. Rumors were suddenly floating about Petersburg that in the neighborhood of the Kalinkin Bridge and for a little distance beyond, a corpse had taken to appearing at night in the form of a clerk looking for a stolen overcoat, and stripping from the shoulders of all passersby, regardless of grade and calling, overcoats of all descriptions—trimmed with cat fur or beaver or wadded, lined with raccoon, fox and bear—made, in fact, of all sorts of skin which men have adapted for the covering of their own. One of the clerks of the department saw the corpse with his own eyes and at once recognized it as Akaky Akakyevitch; but it excited in him such terror, however, that he ran away as fast as his legs could carry him and so could not get a very clear view of him, and only saw him hold up his finger threateningly in the distance.

From all sides complaints were continually coming that backs and shoulders, not of mere titular counsellors, but even of upper court counsellors, had been exposed to taking chills, owing to being stripped of their greatcoats. Orders were given to the police to catch the corpse regardless of trouble or expense, alive or dead, and to punish him in the cruelest way, as an example to others, and, indeed, they very nearly succeeded in doing so. The sentry of one district police station in Kiryushkin Place snatched a corpse by the collar on the spot of the crime in the very act of attempting to snatch a frieze overcoat from a retired musician, who used in his day to play the flute. Having caught him by the collar, he shouted until he had brought two other comrades, whom he charged to hold him while he felt just a minute in his boot to get out a snuffbox in order to revive his nose which had six times in his life been frostbitten, but the snuff was probably so strong that not even a dead man could stand it. The sentry had hardly had time to put his finger over his right nostril and draw up some snuff in the left when the corpse sneezed violently right into the eyes of all three. While they were putting their fists up to wipe them, the corpse completely vanished, so that they were not even sure whether he had actually been in their hands. From that time forward, the sentries conceived such a horror of the dead that they were even afraid to seize the living and confined themselves to shouting from the distance, "Hi, you there, be off!" and the dead clerk began to appear even on the other side of the Kalinkin Bridge, rousing no little terror in all timid people.

We have, however, quite deserted the Person of Consequence, who may in reality almost be said to be the cause of the fantastic ending of this perfectly true story. To begin with, my duty requires me to do justice to the Person of Consequence by recording that soon after poor Akaky Akakyevitch had gone away crushed to powder, he felt something not unlike regret. Sympathy was a feeling not unknown to him; his heart was open to many kindly impulses, although his exalted grade very often prevented them from being shown. As soon as his friend had gone out of his study, he even began brooding over poor Akaky Akakyevitch, and from that time forward, he was almost every day haunted by the image of the poor clerk who had succumbed so completely to the befitting reprimand. The thought of the man so worried him that a week later he actually decided to send a clerk to find out how he was and whether he really could help him in any way. And when they brought him word that Akaky Akakyevitch had died suddenly in delirium and fever, it made a great impression on him, his conscience reproached him and he was depressed all day. Anxious to distract his mind and to forget the unpleasant impression, he went to spend the evening with one of his friends, where he found a genteel company and, what was best of all, almost every one was of the same grade so that he was able to be quite free from restraint. This had a wonderful effect on his spirits, he expanded, became affable and genial—in short, spent a very agreeable evening. At supper he drank a couple of glasses of champagne—a proceeding which we all know has a happy effect in inducing good humor. The champagne made him inclined to do something unusual, and he decided not to go home yet but to visit a lady of his acquaintance, one Karolina Ivanovna—a lady apparently of German extraction, for whom he entertained extremely friendly feelings. It must be noted that the Person of Consequence was a man no longer young, an excellent husband, and the respectable father of a family. He had two sons, one already serving in his office, and a nice-looking daughter of sixteen with a rather turned-up, pretty little nose, who used to come every morning to kiss his hand, saying: "*Bonjour, Papa*." His wife, who was still blooming and decidedly good-looking, indeed, used first to give him her hand to kiss and then would kiss his hand, turning it the other side upwards. But though the Person of Consequence was perfectly satisfied with the kind amenities of his domestic life, he thought it proper to have a lady friend in another quarter of the town. This lady friend was not a bit better looking nor younger than his wife, but these mysterious facts exist in the world and it is not our business to criticize them. And so the Person of Consequence went downstairs, got into his sledge, and said to his coachman, "To Karolina Ivanovna," while luxuriously wrapped in his warm fur coat he remained in that agreeable frame of mind sweeter to a Russian than anything that could be invented, that is, when one thinks of nothing while thoughts come into the mind of themselves, one pleasanter than the other, without the labor of following them or looking for them. Full of satisfaction, he recalled all the amusing moments of the evening he had spent, all the phrases that had set the little circle laughing; many of them he repeating in an undertone and found them as amusing as before, and so, very naturally, laughed very heartily at them again. From time to time, however, he was disturbed by a gust of wind which, blowing suddenly, God knows whence and wherefore, cut him in the face, pelting him with flakes of snow, puffing out his coat collar like a sack, or suddenly flinging it with unnatural force over his head and giving him endless trouble to extricate himself from it. All at once, the Person of Consequence felt that someone had clutched him very tightly by the collar. Turning round he saw a short man in a shabby old uniform, and not without horror recognized him as Akaky Akakyevitch. The clerk's face was white as snow and looked like that of a corpse, but the horror of the Person of Consequence was beyond all bounds when he saw the mouth of the corpse distorted into speech and, breathing upon him the chill of the grave, it uttered the following words: "Ah, so here you are at last! At last I've . . . er . . . caught you by the collar. It's your overcoat I want, you refused to help me and abused me into the bargain! So now give me yours!" The poor Person of Consequence very nearly died. Resolute and determined as he was in his office and before subordinates in general, and though any one looking at his manly air and figure would have said, "Oh, what a man of character!" yet in this plight he felt, like very many persons of athletic appearance, such terror that not without reason he began to be afraid he would have some sort of fit. He actually flung his overcoat off his shoulders as fast as he could and shouted to his coachman in a voice unlike his own, "Drive home and make haste!" The coachman, hearing the tone which he had only heard in critical moments and then accompanied by something even more rousing, hunched his shoulders up to his ears in case of worse following, swung his whip and flew on like an arrow. In a little over six minutes the Person of Consequence was at the entrance of his own house. Pale, panic-stricken, and without his overcoat, he arrived home instead of at Karolina Ivanovna's, dragged himself to his own room and spent the night in great perturbation, so that next morning his daughter said to him at breakfast, "You look quite pale today, Papa," but her papa remained mute and said not a word to anyone of what had happened to him, where he had been, and where he had been going. The incident made a great impression upon him. Indeed, it happened far more rarely that he said to his subordinates, "How dare you? Do you understand who I am?" and he never uttered those words at all until he had first heard all the rights of the case.

What was even more remarkable is that from that time the apparition of the dead clerk ceased entirely. Apparently the general's overcoat had fitted him perfectly; anyway, nothing more was heard of overcoats being snatched from anyone. Many restless and anxious people refused, however, to be pacified, and still maintained that in remote parts of the town the ghost of the dead clerk went on appearing. One sentry in Kolomna, for instance, saw with his own eyes a ghost appear from behind a house; but, being by natural constitution somewhat feeble—so much so that on one occasion an ordinary, well-grown pig, making a sudden dash out of some building, knocked him off his feet to the vast entertainment of the cabmen standing round, from whom he exacted two kopecks each for snuff for such rudeness—he did not dare to stop it, and so followed it in the dark until the ghost suddenly looked round and, stopping, asked him, "What do you want?" displaying a fist such as you never see among the living. The sentry said, "Nothing," and turned back on the spot. This ghost, however, was considerably taller and adorned with immense moustaches, and, directing its steps apparently toward Obuhov Bridge, vanished into the darkness of the night.

Charles Dickens (1812–1870)

Charles Dickens was a great observer and chronicler of the human comedy, though he had strong moral viewpoints and delighted in castigating evil while extolling justice and goodness. His characters, some comic, some heroic, some villainous, are among the most memorable in literature.

Born in Portsmouth, England, the second of eight children, Dickens obtained his early education largely through reading the classics in his father's library. But by the age of twelve, he was forced to find a job blacking bottles when his father suffered reverses and was thrown into debtor's prison. Shortly thereafter, however, his father received an unexpected legacy. Dickens quit work and obtained three more years of schooling before becoming a solicitor's clerk in 1827. From there he graduated into court reporting and then writing sketches for *Monthly Magazine* and *Evening Chronicle*. In 1836, the *Chronicle* invited him to provide comic narratives for a series of engravings, and *The Posthumous Papers of the Pickwick Club* (1837) was the result. A smash hit, it launched him on an almost unparalleled career of fame and fortune, for the next thirty years saw him publish such classics of world literature as *David Copperfield, A Tale of Two Cities, Oliver Twist*, and *Great Expectations*—many written on monthly installments to meet magazine deadlines.

Physically, he was small with brilliant eyes, delicate features, an expressive face, brown hair, and a thin wiry beard. Personally, he was highly energetic, extroverted, generous, and compassionate, though occasionally arrogant and conceited.

His interest in the fantastic and macabre was deep and enduring. As editor of *Households Words* (1849–1858) and *All the Year Round* (1858–1870), he encouraged several persons, including Mrs. Elizabeth Gaskell and Wilkie Collins, to produce some of their best stories of this sort for him. As author, he wrote fifteen fantasies, beginning with "The Story of the Goblins Who Stole a Sexton" (1836) and ending with a charming fairy tale, "The Magic Fishbone" (1868).

But, of course, his most popular excursion into this field is *A Christmas Carol*, conceived and written within a few weeks in 1843. The *Encyclopedia Britannica* describes it as "an extraordinary achievement—the one great Christmas myth of modern literature." Indeed, he performed a condensed version of this story most often of all his works in the dramatic public readings he loved and did so well. It is his final reading copy of this story, arrived at in 1859, that we present here.

When his personal life turned a bit sour in middle age, his reading tours became quite important to him, seemingly providing needed love and adulation. However, his flair for dramatic performances, particularly Sikes' murder of Nancy (from *Oliver Twist*), took a lot out of him and probably had some affect in inducing the apoplectic attack which killed him.

A CHRISTMAS CAROL

Charles Dickens and Christmas—the two are inseparable. "Have you ever read those Christmas tales of Dickens's?" Robert Louis Stevenson asked a friend. "I have cried my eyes out. Had a terrible fight not to sob. Oh, dear God, they are good*—and I feel so good after them—I shall do good and lose no time—I want to go out and comfort someone—I* shall *give money. Oh, what a jolly thing it is for a man to have written books like these and just fill people's hearts with pity."*

Dickens succeeded in filling hearts not only with pity but with a renewal of Christmas itself. Of course, he was obsessed by Christmas. Christmas dinners, Christmas trees, the look on the faces of the children, the fire, the empty seats of other years, the snow, the running home, the crisp and frosty grass, the gray slate-colored twilight, and the stories! So he wrote the greatest of all Christmas stories.

Here is the best of Christmas, A Christmas Carol, *in the very cleverly abbreviated version that Dickens himself used in his ever-popular dramatic readings.*

Stave One: Marley's Ghost

M*arley was dead, to begin with. There is no doubt whatever* about that. The register of his burial was signed by the clergyman, the clerk, the undertaker, and the chief mourner. Scrooge signed it. And Scrooge's name was good upon 'Change for anything he chose to put his hand to.

Old Marley was as dead as a doornail.

Scrooge knew he was dead? Of course he did. How could it be otherwise? Scrooge and he were partners for I don't know how many years. Scrooge was his sole executor, his sole administrator, his sole assign, his sole legatee, his sole friend, his sole mourner.

Scrooge never painted out old Marley's name, however. There it yet stood, years afterwards, above the warehouse door—Scrooge and Marley. The firm was known as Scrooge and Marley. Sometimes people new to the business called Scrooge Scrooge, and sometimes Marley. He answered to both names. It was all the same to him.

Oh! But he was a tightfisted hand at the grindstone, was Scrooge! a squeezing, wrenching, grasping, scraping, clutching, covetous old sinner! External heat and cold had little influence on him. No warmth could warm, no cold could chill him. No wind that blew was bitterer than he, no falling snow was more intent upon its purpose, no pelting rain less open to entreaty. Foul weather didn't know where to have him. The heaviest rain and snow and hail and sleet could boast of the advantage over him in only one respect—they often "came down" handsomely, and Scrooge never did.

Nobody ever stopped him in the street to say, with gladsome looks, "My dear Scrooge, how are you? When will you come to see me?" No beggars implored him to bestow a trifle, no children asked him what it was o'clock, no man or woman ever once in all his life inquired the way to such and such a place, of Scrooge. Even the blind men's dogs appeared to know him, and when they saw him coming on, would tug their owners into doorways and up courts; and then would wag their tails as though they said, "No eyes at all is better than an evil eye, dark master!"

But what did Scrooge care! It was the very thing he liked. To edge his way along the crowded paths of life, warning all human sympathy to keep its distance, was what the knowing ones call "nuts" to Scrooge.

Once upon a time—of all the good days in the year, upon a Christmas Eve—old Scrooge sat busy in his countinghouse. It was cold, bleak, biting, foggy weather; and the city clocks had only just gone three, but it was quite dark already.

The door of Scrooge's countinghouse was open, that he might keep his eye upon his clerk, who, in a dismal little cell beyond, a sort of tank, was copying letters. Scrooge had a very small fire, but the clerk's fire was so very much smaller that it looked like one coal. But he couldn't replenish it, for Scrooge kept the coal box in his own room; and so surely as the clerk came in with the shovel, the master predicted that it would be necessary for them to part. Wherefore the clerk put on his white comforter, and tried to warm himself at the candle; in which effort, not being a man of a strong imagination, he failed.

"A Merry Christmas, uncle! God save you!" cried a cheerful voice. It was the voice of Scrooge's nephew, who came upon him so quickly that this was the first intimation Scrooge had of his approach.

"Bah!" said Scrooge. "Humbug!"

"Christmas a humbug, uncle! You don't mean that, I am sure?"

"I do. Out upon merry Christmas! What's Christmas time to you but a time for paying bills without money; a time for finding yourself a year older, and not an hour richer; a time for balancing your books and having every item in 'em through a round dozen of months presented dead against you? If I had my will, every idiot who goes about with 'Merry Christmas' on his lips should be boiled with his own pudding, and buried with a stake of holly through his heart. He should!"

"Uncle!"

"Nephew, keep Christmas in your own way, and let me keep it in mine."

"Keep it! But you don't keep it."

"Let me leave it alone, then. Much good may it do you! Much good it has ever done you!"

"There are many things from which I might have derived good, by which I have not profited, I dare say, Christmas among the rest. But I am sure I have always thought of Christmas time, when it has come round—apart from the veneration due to its sacred origin, if anything belonging to it *can* be apart from that—as a good time; a kind, forgiving, charitable, pleasant time; the only time I know of, in the long calendar of the year, when men and women seem by one consent to open their shut-up hearts freely, and to think of people below them as if they really were fellow travellers to the grave, and not another race of creatures bound on other journeys. And therefore, uncle, though it has never put a scrap of gold or silver in my pocket, I believe that it *has* done me good, and *will* do me good; and I say, God bless it!"

The clerk in the tank involuntarily applauded.

"Let me hear another sound from *you*," said Scrooge, "and you'll keep your Christmas by losing your situation! You're quite a powerful speaker, sir," he added, turning to his nephew. "I wonder you don't go into Parliament."

"Don't be angry, uncle. Come! Dine with us tomorrow."

Scrooge said that he would see him—yes, indeed he did. He went the whole length of the expression, and said that he would see him in that extremity first.

"But why?" cried Scrooge's nephew. "Why?"

"Why did you get married?"

"Because I fell in love."

"Because you fell in love!" growled Scrooge, as if that were the only one thing in the world more ridiculous than a merry Christmas. "Good afternoon!"

"Nay, uncle, but you never came to see me before that happened. Why give it as a reason for not coming now?"

"Good afternoon."

"I want nothing from you; I ask nothing of you; why cannot we be friends?"

"Good afternoon."

"I am sorry, with all my heart, to find you so resolute. We have never had any quarrel, to which I have been a party. But I have made the trial in homage to Christmas, and I'll keep my Christmas humor to the last. So a Merry Christmas, uncle!"

"Good afternoon!"

"And a happy New Year!"

"Good afternoon!"

His nephew left the room without an angry word, notwithstanding. The clerk, in letting Scrooge's nephew out, had let two other people in. They were portly gentlemen, pleasant to behold, and now stood, with their hats off, in Scrooge's office. They had books and papers in their hands, and bowed to him.

"Scrooge and Marley's, I believe," said one of the gentlemen, referring to his list. "Have I the pleasure of addressing Mr. Scrooge or Mr. Marley?"

"Mr. Marley has been dead these seven years. He died seven years ago, this very night."

"At this festive season of the year, Mr. Scrooge," said the gentleman, taking up a pen, "it is more than usually desirable that we should make some slight provision for the poor and destitute, who suffer greatly at the present time. Many thousands are in want of common necessaries; hundreds of thousands are in want of common comfort, sir."

"Are there no prisons?"

"Plenty of prisons. But under the impression that they scarcely furnish Christian cheer of mind or body to the unoffending multitude, a few of us are endeavouring to raise a fund to buy the poor some meat and drink, and means of warmth. We choose this time, because it is a time, of all others, when Want is keenly felt, and Abundance rejoices. What shall I put you down for?''

''Nothing!''

''You wish to be anonymous?''

''I wish to be left alone. Since you ask me what I wish, gentlemen, that is my answer. I don't make merry myself at Christmas, and I can't afford to make idle people merry. I help to support the prisons and the work-houses—they cost enough—and those who are badly off must go there.''

''Many can't go there; and many would rather die.''

''If they would rather die, they had better do it, and decrease the surplus population.''

At length the hour of shutting up the countinghouse arrived. With an ill will Scrooge, dismounting from his stool,tacitly admitted the fact to the expectant clerk in the tank, who instantly snuffed his candle out, and put on his hat.

''You want all day tomorrow, I suppose?''

''If quite convenient, sir.''

''It's not convenient, and it's not fair. If I was to stop half a crown for it, you'd think yourself mightily ill-used, I'll be bound?''

''Yes, sir.''

''And yet you don't think *me* ill-used, when I pay a day's wages for no work.''

''It's only once a year, sir.''

''A poor excuse for picking a man's pocket every twenty-fifth of December! But I suppose you must have the whole day. Be here all the earlier *next* morning.''

The clerk promised that he would, and Scrooge walked out with a growl. The office was closed in a twinkling, and the clerk, with the long ends of his white comforter dangling below his waist (for he boasted no great-coat), went down a slide, at the end of a lane of boys, twenty times, in honor of its being Christmas Eve, and then ran home as hard as he could pelt to play at blindman's buff.

Scrooge took his melancholy dinner in his usual melancholy tavern; and having read all the newspapers, and beguiled the rest of the evening with his banker's book, went home to bed. He lived in chambers which had once belonged to his deceased partner. They were a gloomy suite of rooms, in a lowering pile of building up a yard. The building was old enough now, and dreary enough, for nobody lived in it but Scrooge, the other rooms being all let out as offices.

Now it is a fact, that there was nothing at all particular about the knocker on the door of this house, except that it was very large; also, that Scrooge had seen it, night and morning, during his whole residence in that place; also, that Scrooge had as little of what is called fancy about him as any man in the city of London. And yet Scrooge, having his key in the lock of the door, saw in the knocker, without its undergoing any intermediate process of change, not a knocker, but Marley's face.

Marley's face, with a dismal light about it, like a bad lobster in a dark cellar. It was not angry or ferocious, but it looked at Scrooge as Marley used to look—ghostly spectacles turned up upon its ghostly forehead.

As Scrooge looked fixedly at this phenomenon, it was a knocker again. He said, "Pooh, pooh!" and closed the door with a bang.

The sound resounded through the house like thunder. Every room above, and every cask in the wine-merchant's cellars below, appeared to have a separate peal of echoes of its own. Scrooge was not a man to be frightened by echoes. He fastened the door, and walked across the hall, and up the stairs. Slowly too, trimming his candle as he went.

Up Scrooge went, not caring a button for its being very dark. Darkness is cheap, and Scrooge liked it. But before he shut his heavy door, he walked through his rooms to see that all was right. He had just enough recollection of the face to desire to do that.

Sitting room, bedroom, lumber room, all as they should be. Nobody under the table, nobody under the sofa; a small fire in the grate; spoon and basin ready; and a little saucepan of gruel (Scrooge had a cold in his head) upon the hob. Nobody under the bed; nobody in the closet; nobody in his dressing gown, which was hanging up in a suspicious attitude against the wall. Lumber room as usual. Old fireguards, old shoes, two fish baskets, washing stand on three legs, and a poker.

Quite satisfied, he closed his door, and locked himself in; double-locked himself in, which was not his custom. Thus secured against surprise, he took off his cravat, put on his dressing gown and slippers and his nightcap, and sat down before the very low fire to take his gruel.

As he threw his head back in the chair, his glance happened to rest upon a bell, a disused bell, that hung in the room, and communicated, for some purpose now forgotten, with a chamber in the highest story of the building. It was with great astonishment, and with a strange, inexplicable dread, that, as he looked, he saw this bell begin to swing. Soon it rang out loudly, and so did every bell in the house.

This was succeeded by a clanking noise, deep down below as if some person were dragging a heavy chain over the casks in the wine-merchant's cellar.

Then he heard the noise much louder, on the floors below; then coming up the stairs; then coming straight towards his door.

It came on through the heavy door, and a spectre passed into the room before his eyes. And upon its coming in, the dying flame leaped up, as though it cried, "I know him! Marley's ghost!"

The same face, the very same. Marley in his pigtail, usual waistcoat, tights, and boots. His body was transparent; so that Scrooge, observing him, and looking through his waistcoat, could see the two buttons on his coat behind.

Scrooge had often heard it said that Marley had no bowels, but he had never believed it until now.

No, nor did he believe it even now. Though he looked the phantom through and through, and saw it standing before him—though he felt the chilling influence of its death-cold eyes, and noticed the very texture of the folded kerchief bound about its head and chin—he was still incredulous.

"How now!" said Scrooge, caustic and cold as ever. "What do you want with me?"

"Much!"—Marley's voice, no doubt about it.

"Who are you?"

"Ask me who I *was*."

"Who *were* you then?"

"In life I was your partner, Jacob Marley."

"Can you—can you sit down?"

"I can."

"Do it, then."

Scrooge asked the question, because he didn't know whether a ghost so transparent might find himself in a condition to take a chair; and felt that, in the event of its being impossible, it might involve the necessity of an embarrassing explanation. But the ghost sat down on the opposite side of the fireplace, as if he were quite used to it.

"You don't believe in me."

"I don't."

"What evidence would you have of my reality beyond that of your senses?"

''I don't know.''

''Why do you doubt your senses?''

''Because a little thing affects them. A slight disorder of the stomach makes them cheats. You may be an undigested bit of beef, a blot of mustard, a crumb of cheese, a fragment of an underdone potato. There's more of gravy than of grave about you, whatever you are!''

Scrooge was not much in the habit of cracking jokes, nor did he feel in his heart by any means waggish then. The truth is, that he tried to be smart, as a means of distracting his own attention, and keeping down his horror.

But how much greater was his horror when, the phantom taking off the bandage round its head, as if it were too warm to wear indoors, its lower jaw dropped down upon its breast!

''Mercy! Dreadful apparition, why do you trouble me? Why do spirits walk the earth, and why do they come to me?''

''It is required of every man that the spirit within him should walk abroad among his fellow men, and travel far and wide; and if that spirit goes not forth in life, it is condemned to do so after death. I cannot tell you all I would. A very little more is permitted to me. I cannot rest, I cannot stay, I cannot linger anywhere. My spirit never walked beyond our counting house—mark me!—in life my spirit never roved beyond the narrow limits of our money-changing hole; and weary journeys lie before me!''

''Seven years dead. And travelling all the time? You travel fast?''

''On the wings of the wind.''

''You might have got over a great quantity of ground in seven years.''

''O blind man, blind man! not to know that ages of incessant labor by immortal creatures for this earth must pass into eternity before the good of which it is susceptible is all developed. Not to know that any Christian spirit working kindly in its little sphere, whatever it may be, will find its mortal life too short for its vast means of usefulness. Not to know that no space of regret can make amends for one life's opportunities misused! Yet I was like this man; I once was like this man!''

''But you were always a good man of business, Jacob,'' faltered Scrooge, who now began to apply this to himself.

''Business!'' cried the Ghost, wringing its hands again. ''Mankind was my business. The common welfare was my business; charity, mercy, forbearance, benevolence, were all my business. The dealings of my trade were but a drop of water in the comprehensive ocean of my business!''

Scrooge was very much dismayed to hear the spectre going on at this rate, and began to quake exceedingly.

''Hear me! My time is nearly gone.''

''I will. But don't be hard upon me! Don't be flowery, Jacob! Pray!''

''I am here tonight to warn you that you have yet a chance and hope of escaping my fate. A chance and hope of my procuring, Ebenezer.''

''You were always a good friend to me. Thank'ee!''

''You will be haunted by Three Spirits.''

''Is that the chance and hope you mentioned, Jacob? I—I think I'd rather not.''

''Without their visits, you cannot hope to shun the path I tread. Expect the first tomorrow night, when the bell tolls One. Expect the second on the next night at the same hour. The third, upon the next night, when the last stroke of Twelve has ceased to vibrate. Look to see me no more; and look that, for your own sake, you remember what has passed between us!''

It walked backward from him; and at every step it took, the window raised itself a little, so that, when the apparition reached it, it was wide open.

Scrooge closed the window, and examined the door by which the Ghost had entered. It was doubled-locked, as he had locked it with his own hands, and the bolts were undisturbed. Scrooge tried to say, ''Humbug!'' but stopped at the first syllable. And being, from the emotion he had undergone, or the fatigues of the day, or his glimpse of the invisible world, or the dull conversation of the Ghost, or the lateness of the hour, much in need of repose, he went straight to bed, without undressing, and fell asleep on the instant.

Stave Two: The First of the Three Spirits

When Scrooge awoke, it was so dark, that, looking out of bed, he could scarcely distinguish the transparent window from the opaque walls of his chamber, until suddenly the church clock tolled a deep, dull, hollow, melancholy ONE.

Light flashed up in the room upon the instant, and the curtains of his bed were drawn aside by a strange figure—like a child; yet not so like a child as like an old man, viewed through some supernatural medium, which gave him the appearance of having receded from the view, and being diminished to a child's proportions. Its hair, which hung about its neck and down its back, was white as if with age; and yet the face had not a wrinkle in it, and the tenderest bloom was on the skin. It held a branch of fresh green holly in its hand; and in singular contradiction of that wintry emblem, had its dress trimmed with summer flowers. But the strangest thing about it was, that from the crown of its head there sprung a bright clear jet of light, by which all this was visible; and which was doubtless the occasion of its using, in its duller moments, a great extinguisher for a cap, which it now held under its arm.

"Are you the Spirit, sir, whose coming was foretold to me?"

"I am!"

"Who and what are you?"

"I am the Ghost of Christmas Past."

"Long Past?"

"No. Your past. The things that you will see with me are shadows of the things that have been; they will have no consciousness of us."

Scrooge then made bold to inquire what business brought him there.

"Your welfare. Rise and walk with me!"

It would have been in vain for Scrooge to plead that the weather and the hour were not adapted to pedestrian purposes; that bed was warm, and the thermometer a long way below freezing; that he was clad but lightly in his slippers, dressing gown, and nightcap; and that he had a cold upon him at that time. The grasp, though gentle as a woman's hand, was not to be resisted. He rose; but finding that the Spirit made toward the window, clasped its robe in supplication.

"I am a mortal, and liable to fall."

"Bear but a touch of my hand *there*," said the Spirit, laying it upon his heart, "and you shall be upheld in more than this!"

As the words were spoken, they passed through the wall, and stood in the busy thoroughfares of a city. It was made plain enough by the dressing of the shops that here, too, it was Christmas time. The Ghost stopped at a certain warehouse door, and asked Scrooge if he knew it.

"Know it! I was apprenticed here!"

They went in. At sight of an old gentleman, in a Welsh wig, sitting behind such a high desk that, if he had been two inches taller, he must have knocked his head against the ceiling, Scrooge cried in great excitement: "Why, it's old Fezziwig! Bless his heart, it's Fezziwig, alive again!"

Old Fezziwig laid down his pen, and looked up at the clock, which pointed at the hour of seven. He rubbed his hands; adjusted his capacious waistcoat; laughed all over himself, from his shoes to his organ of benevolence; and called out in a comfortable, oily, rich, fat, jovial voice: "Yo ho, there! Ebenezer! Dick!"

A living moving picture of Scrooge's former self, a young man, came briskly in, accompanied by his fellow apprentice.

"Dick Wilkins, to be sure!" said Scrooge to the Ghost. "My old fellow 'prentice, bless me, yes. There he is. He was very much attached to me, was Dick. Poor Dick! Dear, dear!"

"Yo ho, my boys!" said Fezziwig. "No more work tonight. Christmas Eve, Dick. Christmas, Ebenezer! Let's have the shutters up, before a man can say Jack Robinson! Clear away, my lads, and let's have lots of room here!"

Clear away! There was nothing they wouldn't have cleared away, or couldn't have cleared away, with old Fezziwig looking on. It was done in a minute. Every movable was packed off, as if it were dismissed from public life for evermore; the floor was swept and watered, the lamps were trimmed, fuel was heaped upon the fire; and the warehouse was as snug and warm and dry and bright a ballroom as you would desire to see on a winter's night.

In came a fiddler with a music book, and went up to the lofty desk, and made an orchestra of it, and tuned like fifty stomachaches. In came Mrs. Fezziwig, one vast substantial smile. In came the three Miss Fezziwigs, beaming and lovable. In came the six young followers whose hearts they broke. In came all the young men and women employed in the business. In came the housemaid, with her cousin the baker. In came the cook, with her brother's particular friend the milkman. In they all came one after another; some shyly, some boldly, some gracefully, some awkwardly, some pushing, some pulling; in they all came, anyhow and everyhow. Away they all went, twenty couples at once; hands half round and back again the other way; down the middle and up again; round and round in various stages of affectionate grouping; old top couple always turning up in the wrong place; new top couple starting off again, as soon as they got there; all top couples at last, and not a bottom one to help them. When this result was brought about, old Fezziwig, clapping his hands to stop the dance, cried out, "Well done"; and the fiddler plunged his hot face into a pot of porter especially provided for that purpose.

There were more dances, and there were forfeits, and more dances, and there was cake, and there was negus, and there was a great piece of

Cold Roast, and there was a great piece of Cold Boiled, and there were mince pies, and plenty of beer. But the great effect of the evening came after the Roast and Boiled, when the fiddler struck up "Sir Roger de Coverley." Then old Fezziwig stood out to dance with Mrs. Fezziwig. Top couple, too; with a good stiff piece of work cut out for them; three or four and twenty pair of partners; people who were not to be trifled with; people who *would* dance, and had no notion of walking.

But if they had been twice as many—four times—old Fezziwig would have been a match for them, and so would Mrs. Fezziwig. As to *her*, she was worthy to be his partner in every sense of the term. A positive light appeared to issue from Fezziwig's calves. They shone in every part of the dance. You couldn't have predicted, at any given time, what would become of 'em next. And when old Fezziwig and Mrs. Fezziwig had gone all through the dance—advance and retire, turn your partner, bow and curtsy, corkscrew, thread the needle, and back again to your place—Fezziwig "cut"—cut so deftly, that he appeared to wink with his legs.

When the clock struck eleven this domestic ball broke up. Mr. and Mrs. Fezziwig took their stations, one on either side of the door, and, shaking hands with every person individually as he or she went out, wished him or her a Merry Christmas. When everybody had retired but the two 'prentices, they did the same to them; and thus the cheerful voices died away, and the lads were left to their beds, which were under a counter in the back shop.

"A small matter," said the Ghost, "to make these silly folks so full of gratitude. He has spent but a few pounds of your mortal money—three or four perhaps. Is that so much that he deserves this praise?"

"It isn't that," said Scrooge, heated by the remark, and speaking unconsciously like his former, not his latter self—"it isn't that, Spirit. He has the power to render us happy or unhappy; to make our service light or burdensome; a pleasure or a toil. Say that his power lies in words and looks; in things so slight and insignificant that it is impossible to add and count 'em up: what then? The happiness he gives is quite as great as if it cost a fortune."

He felt the Spirit's glance, and stopped.

"What is the matter?"

"Nothing particular."

"Something, I think?"

"No, no. I should like to be able to say a word or two to my clerk just now. That's all."

"My time grows short," observed the Spirit. "Quick!"

This was not addressed to Scrooge, or to any one whom he could see, but it produced an immediate effect. For again he saw himself. He was older now; a man in the prime of life.

He was not alone, but sat by the side of a fair young girl in a black dress, in whose eyes there were tears.

"It matters little," she said softly to Scrooge's former self. "To you very little. Another idol has displaced me; and if it can comfort you in time to come, as I would have tried to do, I have no just cause to grieve."

"What idol has displaced you?"

"A golden one. You fear the world too much. I have seen your nobler aspirations fall off one by one, until the master passion, Gain, engrosses you. Have I not?"

"What then? Even if I have grown so much wiser, what then? I am not changed toward you. Have I ever sought release from our engagement?"

"In words, no. Never."

"In what, then?"

"In a changed nature; in an altered spirit; in another atmosphere of life; another Hope as its great end. If you were free today, tomorrow, yesterday, can even I believe that you would choose a dowerless girl; or, choosing her, do I not know that your repentance and regret would surely follow? I do; and I release you. With a full heart, for the love of him you once were."

"Spirit! remove me from this place."

"I told you these were shadows of the things that have been," said the Ghost. "That they are what they are, do not blame me!"

"Remove me!" Scrooge exclaimed. "I cannot bear it! Leave me! Take me back. Haunt me no longer!"

As he struggled with the Spirit he was conscious of being exhausted, and ovedrcome by an irresistible drowsiness; and, further, of being in his own bedroom. He had barely time to reel to bed before he sank into a heavy sleep.

Stave Three: The Second of the Three Spirits

Scrooge awoke in his own bedroom. There was no doubt about that. But it and his own adjoining sitting room, into which he shuffled in his slippers, attracted by a great light there, had undergone a surprising transformation. The walls and ceiling were so hung with living green, that it looked a perfect grove. The leaves of holly, mistletoe, and ivy reflected back the light, as if so many little mirrors had been scattered there; and such a mightly blaze went roaring up the chimney, as that petrifaction of a hearth had never known in Scrooge's time, or Marley's, or for many and many a winter season gone. Heaped upon the floor, to form a kind of throne, were turkeys, geese, game, brawn, great joints of meat, sucking pigs, long wreaths of sausages, mince pies, plum puddings, barrels of oysters, red-hot chestnuts, cherry-cheeked apples, juicy oranges, luscious pears, immense twelfth-cakes, and great bowls of punch. In easy state upon this couch there sat a Giant glorious to see; who bore a glowing torch, in shape not unlike Plenty's horn, and who raised it high to shed its light on Scrooge, as he came peeping round the door.

''Come in—come in! and know me better, man! I am the Ghost of Christmas Present. Look upon me! You have never seen the like of me before.''

''Never.''

''Have never walked forth with the younger members of my family; meaning (for I am very young) my elder brothers born in these later years?'' pursued the Phantom.

''I don't think I have, I am afraid I have not. Have you had many brothers, Spirit?''

''More than eighteen hundred.''

''A tremendous family to provide for! Spirit, conduct me where you will. I went forth last night on compulsion, and I learnt a lesson which is working now. Tonight, if you have aught to teach me, let me profit by it.''

''Touch my robe!''

Scrooge did as he was told, and held it fast.

The room and its contents all vanished instantly, and they stood in the city streets upon a snowy Christmas morning.

Scrooge and the Ghost passed on, invisible, straight to Scrooge's clerk's; and on the threshold of the door the Spirit smiled, and stopped to bless Bob Cratchit's dwelling with the sprinklings of his torch. Think of that! Bob had but fifteen ''bob'' a week himself; he pocketed on Saturdays but fifteen copies of his Christian name; and yet the Ghost of Christmas Present blessed his four-roomed house!

Then up rose Mrs. Cratchit, Cratchit's wife, dressed out but poorly in a twice-turned gown, but brave in ribbons, which are cheap and make a goodly show for sixpence; and she laid the cloth, assisted by Belinda Cratchit, second of her daughters, also brave in ribbons; while Master Peter Cratchit plunged a fork into the saucepan of potatoes, and, getting the corners of his monstrous shirt-collar (Bob's private property, conferred upon his son and heir in honor of the day) into his mouth, rejoiced to find himself so gallantly attired, and yearned to show his linen in the fashionable Parks. And now two smaller Cratchits, boy and girl, came tearing in, screaming that outside the baker's they had smelt the goose, and known it for their own; and, basking in luxurious thoughts of sage and onion, these young Cratchits danced about the table, and exalted Master Peter Cratchit to the skies, while he (not proud, although his collars nearly choked him) blew the fire, until the slow potatoes, bubbling up, knocked loudly at the saucepan lid to be let out and peeled.

"What has ever got your precious father then?" said Mrs. Cratchit. "And your brother Tiny Tim! And Martha warn't as late last Christmas day by half an hour!"

"Here's Martha, mother!" said a girl, appearing as she spoke.

"Here's Martha, mother!" cried the two young Cratchits. "Hurrah! There's *such* a goose, Martha!"

"Why, bless your heart alive, my dear, how late you are!" said Mrs. Cratchit, kissing her a dozen times, and taking off her shawl and bonnet for her.

"We'd a deal of work to finish up last night," replied the girl, "and had to clear away this morning, mother!"

"Well! Never mind so long as you are come," said Mrs. Cratchit. "Sit ye down before the fire, my dear, and have a warm, Lord bless ye!"

"No, no! There's father coming," cried the two young Cratchits, who were everywhere at once. "Hide, Martha, hide!"

So Martha hid herself, and in came little Bob, the father, with at least three feet of comforter, exclusive of the fringe, hanging down before him; and his threadbare clothes darned up and brushed, to look seasonable; and Tiny Tim upon his shoulder. Alas for Tiny Tim, he bore a little crutch, and had his limbs supported by an iron frame!

"Why, where's our Martha?" cried Bob Cratchit, looking round.

"Not coming," said Mrs. Cratchit.

"Not coming!" said Bob, with a sudden declension in his high spirits; for he had been Tim's blood-horse all the way from church, and had come home rampant—"not coming upon Christmas day!"

Martha didn't like to see him disappointed, if it were only in joke; so she came out prematurely from behind the closet door, and ran into his arms, while the two young Cratchits hustled Tiny Tim, and bore him off into the wash house, that he might hear the pudding singing in the copper.

"And how did little Tim behave?" asked Mrs. Cratchit, when she had rallied Bob on his credulity, and Bob had hugged his daughter to his heart's content.

"As good as gold," said Bob, "and better. Somehow he gets thoughtful, sitting by himself so much, and thinks the strangest things you ever heard. He told me, coming home, that he hoped the people saw him in the church, because he was a cripple, and it might be pleasant to them to remember, upon Christmas day, who made lame beggars walk and blind men see."

Bob's voice was tremulous when he told them this, and trembled more when he said that Tiny Tim was growing strong and hearty.

His active little crutch was heard upon the floor, and back came Tiny Tim before another word was spoken, escorted by his brother and sister to his stool beside the fire; and while Bob, turning up his cuffs—as if, poor fellow, they were capable of being made more shabby—compounded some hot mixture in a jug with gin and lemons, and stirred it round and round, and put it on the hob to simmer, Master Peter and the two ubiquitous young Cratchits went to fetch the goose, with which they soon returned in high procession.

Mrs. Cratchit made the gravy (ready beforehand in a little saucepan) hissing hot; Master Peter mashed the potatoes with incredible vigour; Miss Belinda sweetened up the apple-sauce; Martha dusted the hot plates; Bob took Tiny Tim beside him in a tiny corner at the table; the two young Cratchits set chairs for everybody, not forgetting themselves, and mounted guard upon their posts, crammed spoons into their mouths, lest they should shriek for goose before their turn came to be helped. At last the dishes were set on, and grace was said. It was succeeded by a breathless pause, as Mrs. Cratchit, looking slowly all along the carving knife, prepared to plunge it in the breast; but when she did, and when the long-expected gush of stuffing issued forth, one murmur of delight arose all round the board, and even Tiny Tim, excited by the two young Cratchits, beat on the table with the handle of his knife, and feebly cried, Hurrah!

There never was such a goose. Bob said he didn't believe there ever was such a goose cooked. Its tenderness and flavor, size and cheapness, were the themes of universal admiration. Eked out by applesauce and mashed potatoes, it was a sufficient dinner for the whole family; indeed, as Mrs. Cratchit said with great delight (surveying one small atom of a bone upon the dish) they hadn't ate it all at last! Yet every one had had enough, and the youngest Cratchits in particular were steeped in sage and onion to the eyebrows! But now, the plates being changed by Miss Belinda, Mrs. Cratchit left the room alone—too nervous to bear witnesses—to take the pudding up, and bring it in.

Suppose it should not be done enough! Suppose it should break in turning out! Suppose somebody should have got over the wall of the back yard, and stolen it, while they were merry with the goose—a supposition at which the two young Cratchits became livid! All sorts of horrors were supposed.

Hallo! A great deal of steam! The pudding was out of the copper. A smell like a washing day! That was the cloth. A smell like an eating house and a pastry cook's next door to each other, with a laundress's next door to that! That was the pudding! In half a minute Mrs. Cratchit entered—flushed but smiling proudly—with the pudding, like a speckled cannon ball, so hard and firm, blazing in half of half a quartern of ignited brandy, and bedight with Christmas holly stuck in the top.

Oh, a wonderful pudding! Bob Cratchit said, and calmly too, that he regarded it as the greatest success achieved by Mrs. Cratchit since their marriage. Mrs. Cratchit said that now the weight was off her mind, she would confess she had had her doubts about the quantity of flour. Everybody had something to say about it, but nobody said or thought it was at all a small pudding for a large family. Any Cratchit would have blushed to hint at such a thing.

At last the dinner was all done, the cloth was cleared, the hearth swept, and the fire made up. The compound in the jug being tasted, and considered perfect, apples and oranges were put upon the table, and a shovelful of chestnuts on the fire.

Then all the Cratchit family drew round the hearth, in what Bob Cratchit called a circle, and at Bob Cratchit's elbow stood the family display of glass—two tumblers, and a custard-cup without a handle.

These held the hot stuff from the jug, however, as well as golden goblets would have done; and Bob served it out with beaming looks, while the chestnuts on the fire spluttered and crackled noisily. Then Bob proposed:—

"A Merry Christmas to us all, my dears. God bless us!"

Which all the family re-echoed.

"God bless us every one!" said Tiny Tim, the last of all.

He sat very close to his father's side, upon his little stool. Bob held his withered little hand in his, as if he loved the child, and wished to keep him by his side, and dreaded that he might be taken from him.

Scrooge raised his head speedily, on hearing his own name.

"Mr. Scrooge!" said Bob; "I'll give you Mr. Scrooge, the Founder of the Feast!"

"The Founder of the Feast indeed!" cried Mrs. Cratchit, reddening. "I wish I had him here. I'd give him a piece of my mind to feast upon, and I hope he'd have a good appetite for it."

"My dear," said Bob, "the children! Christmas day."

"It should be Christmas day, I am sure," said she, "on which one drinks the health of such an odious, stingy, hard, unfeeling man as Mr. Scrooge. You know he is, Robert! Nobody knows it better than you do, poor fellow!"

"My dear," was Bob's mild answer, "Christmas day."

"I'll drink his health for your sake and the day's," said Mrs. Cratchit, "not for his. Long life to him! A merry Christmas and a happy New Year! He'll be very merry and very happy, I have no doubt!"

The children drank the toast after her. It was the first of their proceedings which had no heartiness in it. Tiny Tim drank it last of all, but he didn't care twopence for it. Scrooge was the Ogre of the family. The mention of his name cast a dark shadow on the party, which was not dispelled for full five minutes.

After it had passed away, they were ten times merrier than before, from the mere relief of Scrooge the Baleful being done with. Bob Cratchit told them how he had a situation in his eye for Master Peter, which would bring him, if obtained, full five and sixpence weekly. The two young Cratchits laughed tremendously at the idea of Peter's being a man of business; and Peter himself looked thoughtfully at the fire from between his collars, as if he were deliberating what particular investments he should favour when he came into the receipt of that bewildering income. Martha, who was a poor apprentice at a milliner's, then told them what kind of work she had to do, and how many hours she worked at a stretch, and how she meant to lie abed tomorrow morning for a good long rest; tomorrow being a holiday she passed at home. Also how she had seen a countess and a lord some days before, and how the lord "was much about as tall as Peter"; at which Peter pulled up his collars so high that you couldn't have seen his head if you had been there. All this time the chestnuts and the jug went round and round; and by and by they had a song, about a lost child travelling in the snow, from Tiny Tim, who had a plaintive little voice, and sang it very well indeed.

There was nothing of high mark in this. They were not a handsome family; they were not well dressed; their shoes were far from being waterproof; their clothes were scanty; and Peter might have known, and very likely did, the inside of a pawnbroker's. But they were happy, grateful, pleased with one another, and contented with the time; and when they faded, and looked happier yet in the bright sprinklings of the Spirit's torch at parting, Scrooge had his eye upon them, and especially on Tiny Tim, until the last.

It was a great surprise to Scrooge, as this scene vanished, to hear a hearty laugh. It was a much greater surprise to Scrooge to recognize it as his own nephew's and to find himself in a bright, dry, gleaming room, with the Spirit standing smiling by his side, and looking at that same nephew.

It is a fair, even-handed, noble adjustment of things, that while there is infection in disease and sorrow, there is nothing in the world so irresistibly contagious as laughter and good humor. When Scrooge's nephew laughed, Scrooge's niece by marriage laughed as heartily as he. And their assembled friends, being not a bit behindhand, laughed out lustily.

"He said that Christmas was a humbug, as I live!" cried Scrooge's nephew. "He believed it too!"

"More shame for him, Fred!" said Scrooge's niece, indignantly. Bless those women! they never do anything by halves. They are always in earnest.

She was very pretty; exceedingly pretty. With a dimpled, surprised-looking, capital face; a ripe little mouth that seemed made to be kissed—as no doubt it was; all kinds of good little dots about her chin, that melted into one another when she laughed; and the sunniest pair of eyes you ever saw in any little creature's head. Altogether she was what you would have called provoking, but satisfactory, too. Oh, perfectly satisfactory.

"He's a comical old fellow," said Scrooge's nephew, "that's the truth; and not so pleasant as he might be. However, his offences carry their own punishment, and I have nothing to say against him. Who suffers by his ill whims? Himself, always. Here he takes it into his head to dislike us, and he won't come and dine with us. What's the consequence? He don't lose much of a dinner."

"Indeed, I think he loses a very good dinner," interrupted Scrooge's niece. Everybody else said the same, and they must be allowed to have been competent judges, because they had just had dinner; and, with the desert upon the table, were clustered round the fire, by lamplight.

"Well, I am very glad to hear it," said Scrooge's nephew, "because I haven't any great faith in these young housekeepers. What do you say, Topper?"

Topper clearly had his eye on one of Scrooge's niece's sisters, for he answered that a bachelor was a wretched outcast, who had no right to express an opinion on the subject. Whereat Scrooge's niece's sister—the plump one with the lace tucker; not the one with the roses—blushed.

After tea they had some music. For they were a musical family, and knew what they were about, when they sung a Glee or a Catch, I can assure you—especially Topper, who could growl away in the bass like a good one, and never swell the large veins in his forehead, or get red in the face over it.

But they didn't devote the whole evening to music. After a while they played at forfeits; for it is good to be children sometimes, and never better than at Christmas, when its mighty Founder was a child himself. There was first a game at blindman's buff though. And I no more believe Topper was really blinded than I believe he had eyes in his boots. Because the way in which he went after that plump sister in the lace tucker was an outrage on the credulity of human nature. Knocking down the fire irons, tumbling over the chairs, bumping up against the piano, smothering himself among the curtains, wherever she went there went he! He always knew where the plump sister was. He wouldn't catch anybody else. If you had fallen up against him, as some of them did, and stood there, he would have made a feint of endeavouring to seize you, which would have been an affront to your understanding, and would instantly have sidled off in the direction of the plump sister.

"Here is a new game," said Scrooge. "One half-hour, Spirit, only one!"

It was a Game called Yes and No, where Scrooge's nephew had to think of something, and the rest must find out what; he only answering to their questions yes or no, as the case was. The fire of questioning to which he was exposed elicited from him that he was thinking of an animal, a live animal, rather a disagreeable animal, a savage animal, an animal that growled and grunted sometimes, and talked sometimes, and lived in London, and walked about the streets, and wasn't made a show of, and wasn't led by anybody, and didn't live in a menagerie, and was never killed in a market, and was not a horse, or an ass, or a cow, or a bull, or a tiger, or a dog, or a pig, or a cat, or a bear. At every new question put to him, this nephew burst into a fresh roar of laughter; and was so inexpressibly tickled, that he was obliged to get up off the sofa and stamp. At last the plump sister cried out:

"I have found it out! I know what it is, Fred! I know what it is!"

"What is it?" cried Fred.

"It's your uncle Scro–o–o–o–oge!"

Which it certainly was. Admiration was the universal sentiment, though some objected that the reply to "Is it a bear?" ought to have been "Yes."

Uncle Scrooge had imperceptibly become so gay and light of heart, that he would have drank to the unconscious company in an inaudible speech. But the whole scene passed off in the breath of the last word spoken by his nephew; and he and the Spirit were again upon their travels.

Much they saw, and far they went, and many homes they visited, but always with a happy end. The Spirit stood beside sickbeds, and they were cheerful; on foreign lands, and they were close at home; by struggling men, and they were patient in their greater hope; by poverty, and it was rich. In almshouse, hospital, and jail, in misery's every refuge, where vain man in his little brief authority had not made fast the door, and barred the Spirit out, he left his blessing, and taught Scrooge his precepts. Suddenly, as they stood together in an open place, the bell struck twelve.

Scrooge looked about him for the Ghost, and saw it no more. As the last stroke ceased to vibrate, he remembered the prediction of old Jacob Marley, and, lifting up his eyes, beheld a solemn Phantom, draped and hooded, coming like a mist along the ground toward him.

Stave Four: The Last of the Spirits

The Phantom slowly, gravely, silently approached. When it came near him, Scrooge bent down upon his knee; for in the air through which this Spirit moved it seemed to scatter gloom and mystery.

It was shrouded in a deep black garment, which concealed its head, its face, its form, and left nothing of it visible save one outstretched hand. He knew no more, for the Spirit neither spoke nor moved.

"I am in the presence of the Ghost of Christmas Yet to Come? Ghost of the Future! I fear you more than any spectre I have seen. But as I know your purpose is to do me good, and as I hope to live to be another man from what I was, I am prepared to bear you company, and do it with a thankful heart. Will you speak to me?"

It gave him no reply. The hand was pointed straight before them.

"Lead on! Lead on! The night is waning fast, and it is precious time to me, I know. Lead on, Spirit!"

They scarcely seemed to enter the city; for the city rather seemed to spring up about them. But there they were in the heart of it, on 'Change, amongst the merchants.

The Spirit stopped beside one little knot of businessmen. Observing that the hand was pointed to them, Scrooge advanced to listen to their talk.

"No," said a great fat man with a monstrous chin. "I don't know much about it either way. I only know he's dead."

"When did he die?" inquired another.

"Last night, I believe."

"Why, what was the matter with him? I thought he'd never die."

"God knows," said the first, with a yawn.

"What has he done with his money?" asked a red-faced gentleman.

"I haven't heard," said the man with the large chin. "Company, perhaps. He hasn't left it to me. That's all I know. Bye, bye."

Scrooge was at first inclined to be surprised that the Spirit should attach importance to conversation apparently so trivial; but feeling assured that it must have some hidden purpose, he set himself to consider what it was likely to be. It could scarcely be supposed to have any bearing on the death of Jacob, his old partner, for that was Past, and this Ghost's province was the Future.

He looked about in that very place for his own image; but another man stood in his accustomed corner, and though the clock pointed to his usual time of day for being there, he saw no likeness of himself amongst the multitudes that poured in through the Porch. It gave him little surprise, however; for he had been revolving in his mind a change of life, and he thought and hoped he saw his newborn resolutions carried out in this.

They left this busy scene, and went into an obscure part of the town, to a low shop where iron, old rags, bottles, bones, and greasy offal were bought. A gray-haired rascal, of great age, sat smoking his pipe. Scrooge and the Phantom came into the presence of this man, just as a woman with a heavy bundle slunk into the shop. But she had scarcely entered, when another woman, similarly laden, came in too; and she was closely followed by a man in faded black. After a short period of blank astonishment, in which the old man with the pipe had joined them, they all three burst into a laugh.

"Let the charwoman alone to be the first!" cried she who had entered first. "Let the laundress alone to be the second; and let the undertaker's man alone to be the third. Look here, old Joe, here's a chance! If we haven't all three met here without meaning it!"

"You couldn't have met in a better place. You were made free of it long ago, you know; and the other two ain't strangers. What have you got to sell? What have you got to sell?"

"Half a minute's patience, Joe, and you shall see."

"What odds then! What odds, Mrs. Dilber?" said the woman. "Every person has a right to take care of themselves. *He* always did! Who's the worse for the loss of a few things like these? Not a dead man, I suppose."

Mrs. Dilber, whose manner was remarkable for general propitiation, said, "No, indeed, ma'am."

"If he wanted to keep 'em after he was dead, a wicked old screw, why wasn't he natural in his lifetime? If he had been, he'd have had somebody to look after him when he was struck with Death, instead of lying gasping out his last there, alone by himself."

"It's the truest word that ever was spoke, it's a judgment on him."

"I wish it was a little heavier judgment, and it should have been, you may depend upon it, if I could have laid my hands on anything else. Open that bundle, old Joe, and let me know the value of it. Speak out plain. I'm not afraid to be the first, nor afraid for them to see it."

Joe went down on his knees for the greater convenience of opening the bundle, and dragged out a large and heavy roll of some dark stuff.

"What do you call this? Bed curtains!"

"Ah! Bed curtains! Don't drop that oil upon the blankets, now."

"*His* blankets?"

"Whose else's do you think? He isn't likely to take cold without 'em, I dare say. Ah! You may look through that shirt till your eyes ache;

but you won't find a hole in it, nor a threadbare place. It's the best he had, and a fine one too. They'd have wasted it by dressing him up in it, if it hadn't been for me."

Scrooge listened to this dialogue in horror.

"Spirit! I see, I see. The case of this unhappy man might be my own. My life tends that way, now. Merciful Heaven, what is this!"

The scene had changed, and now he almost touched a bare, uncurtained bed. A pale light, rising in the outer air, fell straight upon this bed; and on it, unwatched, unwept, uncared for, was the body of this plundered unknown man.

"Spirit, let me see some tenderness connected with a death, or this dark chamber, Spirit, will be forever present to me."

The Ghost conducted him to poor Bob Cratchit's house—the dwelling he had visited before—and found the mother and the children seated round the fire.

Quiet. Very quiet. The noisy little Cratchits were as still as statues in one corner, and sat looking up at Peter, who had a book before him. The mother and her daughters were engaged in needlework. But surely they were very quiet!

" 'And he took a child, and set him in the midst of them.' "

Where had Scrooge heard those words? He had not dreamed them. The boy must have read them out, as he and the Spirit crossed the threshold. Why did he not go on?

The mother laid her work upon the table, and put her hand up to her face. "The color hurts my eyes," she said.

The color? Ah, poor Tiny Tim!

"They're better now again. It makes them weak by candlelight; and I wouldn't show weak eyes to your father when he comes home, for the world. It must be near his time."

"Past it rather," Peter answered, shutting up his book. "But I think he has walked a little slower than he used, these last few evenings, mother."

"I have known him walk with—I have known him walk with Tiny Tim upon his shoulder, very fast indeed.

"And so have I," cried Peter. "Often."

"And so have I," exclaimed another. So had all.

"But he was very light to carry, and his father loved him so, that it was no trouble—no trouble. And there is your father at the door!"

She hurried out to meet him; and little Bob in his comforter—he had need of it, poor fellow—came in. His tea was ready for him on the hob, and they all tried who should help him to it most. Then the two young Cratchits got upon his knees and laid, each child, a little cheek against his face, as if they said, "Don't mind it, father. Don't be grieved!"

Bob was very cheerful with them, and spoke pleasantly to all the family. He looked at the work upont he table, and praised the industry and speed of Mrs. Cratchit and the girls. They would be done long before Sunday, he said.

"Sunday! You went today, then, Robert?"

"Yes, my dear," returned Bob. "I wish you could have gone. It would have done you good to see how green a place it is. But you'll see it often. I promised him that I would walk there on a Sunday. My little, little child! My little child!"

He broke down all at once. He couldn't help it. If he could have helped it, he and his child would have been farther apart, perhaps, than they were.

"Spectre," said Scrooge, "sometimes informs me that our parting moment is at hand. I know it, but I know not how. Tell me what man that was, with the covered face, whom we saw lying dead?"

The Ghost of Christmas Yet to Come conveyed him to a dismal, wretched, ruinous churchyard.

The Spirit stood amongst the graves and pointed down to one.

"Before I draw nearer to that stone to which you point, answer me one question. Are these the shadows of the things that Will be, or are they shadows of the things that May be only?"

Still the Ghost pointed downward to the grave by which it stood.

"Men's courses will foreshadow certain ends, to which, if persevered in, they must lead. But if the courses be departed from, the ends will change. Say it is thus with what you show me!"

The Spirit was immovable as ever.

Scrooge crept towards it, trembling as he went; and, following the finger, read upon the stone of the neglected grave his own name—-EBENEZER SCROOGE.

"Am *I* that man who lay upon the bed? No, Spirit! Oh no, no! Spirit! hear me! I am not the man I was. I will not be the man I must have been but for this intercourse. Why show me this, if I am past all hope? Assure me that I yet may change these shadows you have shown me by an altered life."

For the first time the kind hand faltered.

"I will honor Christmas in my heart, and try to keep it all the year. I will live in the Past, the Present and the Future. The Spirits of all three shall strive within me. I will not shut out the lessons that they teach. Oh, tell me I may sponge away the writing on this stone!"

Holding up his hands in one last prayer to have his fate reversed, he saw an alteration in the Phantom's hood and dress. It shrunk, collapsed, and dwindled down into a bedpost.

Yes, and the bedpost was his own. The bed was his own, the room was his own. Best and happiest of all, the Time before him was his own, to make amends in!

He was checked in his transports by the churches ringing out the lustiest peals he had ever heard.

Running to the window, he opened it, and put out his head. No fog, no mist, no night; clear, bright, stirring, golden day.

"What's today?" cried Scrooge, calling downward to a boy in Sunday clothes, who perhaps had loitered in to look about him.

"*Eh*?"

"What's today, my fine fellow?"

"Today! Why *Christmas day*."

"It's Christmas day! I haven't missed it. Hallo, my fine fellow!"

"Hallo!"

"Do you know the Poulterer's, in the next street but one, at the corner?"

"I should hope I did."

"An intelligent boy! A remarkable boy! Do you know whether they've sold the prize turkey that was hanging up there? Not the little prize turkey—the big one?"

"What, the one as big as me?"

"What a delightful boy! It's a pleasure to talk to him. Yes, my buck!"

"It's hanging there now."

"Is it? Go and buy it."

"Walk-*er*!" exclaimed the boy.

"No, no, I am in earnest. Go and buy it, and tell 'em to bring it here, that I may give them the direction where to take it. Come back with the man, and I'll give you a shilling. Come back with him in less than five minutes, and I'll give you half a crown!"

The boy was off like a shot.

"I'll send it to Bob Cratchit's! He sha'n't know who sends it. It's twice the size of Tiny Tim. Joe Miller never made such a joke as sending it to Bob's will be!"

The hand in which he wrote the address was not a steady one; but write it he did, somehow, and went down stairs to open the street door, ready for the coming of the poulterer's man.

It was a turkey! He never could have stood upon his legs, that bird. He would have snapped 'em short off in a minute, like sticks of sealing wax.

Scrooge dressed himself "all in his best," and at last got out into the streets. The people were by this time pouring forth, as he had seen them with the Ghost of Christmas Present; and, walking with his hands behind him, Scrooge regarded every one with a delighted smile. He looked so irresistibly pleasant, in a word, that three or four good-humored fellows said, "Good morning, sir! A merry Christmas to you!" And Scrooge said often afterwards, that, of all the blithe sounds he had ever heard, those were the blithest in his ears.

In the afternoon, he turned his steps towards his nephew's house.

He passed the door a dozen times, before he had the courage to go up and knock. But he made a dash, and did it.

"Is your master at home, my dear?" said Scrooge to the girl. Nice girl! Very.

"Yes, sir."

"Where is he, my love?"

"He's in the dining room, sir, along with mistress."

"He knows me," said Scrooge, with his hand already on the dining-room lock. "I'll go in here, my dear."

"Fred!"

"Why, bless my soul!" cried Fred, "who's that?"

"It's I. Your uncle Scrooge. I have come to dinner. Will you let me in, Fred?"

Let him in! It is a mercy he didn't shake his arm off. He was at home in five minutes. Nothing could be heartier. His niece looked just the same. So did Topper when *he* came. So did the plump sister when *she* came. So did every one when *they* came. Wonderful party, wonderful games, wonderful unanimity, wonderful happiness!

But he was early at the office next morning. Oh, he was early there. If he could only be there first, and catch Bob Cratchit coming late! That was the thing he had set his heart upon.

And he did it. The clock struck nine. No Bob. A quarter past. No Bob. Bob was full eighteen minutes and a half behind his time. Scrooge sat with his door wide open, that he might see him come into the tank.

Bob's hat was off before he opened the door; his comforter too. He was on his stool in a jiffy; driving away with his pen, as if he were trying to overtake nine o'clock.

''Hallo!'' growled Scrooge, in his accustomed voice, as near as he could feign it. ''What do you mean by coming here at this time of day?''

''I am very sorry, sir. I *am* behind my time.''

''You are? Yes. I think you are. Step this way if you please.''

''It's only once a year, sir. It shall not be repeated. I was making rather merry yesterday, sir.''

''Now, I'll tell you what, my friend. I am not going to stand this sort of thing any longer. And therefore,'' Scrooge continued, leaping from his stool, and giving Bob such a dig in the waistcoat that he staggered back into the tank again—''and therefore I am about to raise your salary!''

Bob trembled, and got a little nearer to the ruler.

''A merry Christmas, Bob!'' said Scrooge, with an earnestness that could not be mistaken, as he clapped him on the back. ''A merrier Christmas, Bob, my good fellow, than I have given you for many a year! I'll raise your salary, and endeavour to assist your struggling family, and we will discuss your affairs this very afternoon, over a Christmas bowl of smoking bishop, Bob! Make up the fires, and buy a second coal scuttle before you dot another *i*, Bob Cratchit!''

Scrooge was better than his word. He did it all, and infinitely more; and to Tiny Tim, who did NOT die, he was a second father. He became as good a friend, as good a master, and as good a man as the good old city knew, or any other good old city, town, or borough in the good old world. Some people laughed to see the alteration in him; but his own heart laughed, and that was quite enough for him.

He had no further intercourse with Spirits, but lived in that respect upon the Total Abstinence Principle ever afterwards; and it was always said of him that he knew how to keep Christmas well, if any man alive possessed the knowledge. May that be truly said of us, and all of us! And so, as Tiny Tim observed, God Bless Us, Every One!

Hans Christian Andersen (1805–1875)

As a literary art form, original fairy tales developed in the nineteenth century, and Hans Christian Andersen was the greatest and most prolific writer of them. Even today he remains one of the world's most widely read authors whose works have been translated into over one hundred languages.

He was born of poor parents in the extremely class conscious country of Denmark. Though receiving little formal education as a child, he was driven by ambition and left home at fourteen to pursue an acting career. As a performer, the Royal Theater of Copenhagen was not impressed with him; however, as a playwright, Andersen's highly imaginative, but barely literate, works seemed to demonstrate potential. So one of the directors, Jonas Collin, took the young man under his wing.

In 1822 Collin secured a government grant to send the gangling seventeen year old off to grammar school. There Andersen was bullied unmercifully by the headmaster, but worked assiduously, eventually gaining admission to Copenhagen University.

In 1829 he produced his first successful literary work, "A Walk from Holmen's Canal to the East Point of the Island of Amager in the Years 1828 and 1829." It was a fantastic travel sketch much in the style of an author Andersen greatly admired, E.T.A. Hoffman.

Then he began traveling around Europe, finishing *Improvisatoren*, his first novel, in 1835. A critical and financial success, it greatly overshadowed the small volume of four fairy tales (*Eventyr, fortalte for born*) he had also published that year. Indeed, Danish critics in general were not very impressed with Andersen's tales for children. For he violated their precepts about literary works by using contemporary idioms and the simple constructions of spoken language.

But children everywhere were captivated by these stories, as were many adults, and by the mid-1840s Andersen had achieved international fame. Royalty and other famous people of the day sought him out, and since he never married and had no family, he spent most of the rest of his life much like a tourist, journeying from place to place and host to host.

Physically, he was the ugly duckling he wrote about: very tall and thin with long arms and legs, huge feet, and a gigantic triangular nose jutting out from his face like a ship's prow. Even his carriage and movements were bizarre and strange. Personally very childlike in nature, he had a talent for attracting people, a good sense of humor, and a kindly, but neurotic, nature. He was deeply scarred by his early experiences and odd physique, suffering from insatiable cravings for affection and praise, a deep sense of inferiority and loneliness, and a host of obsessive fears, including hypochondria.

Not all of the 168 stories he supposedly wrote for children are actual fairy tales (involving supernatural beings and magic), and even those which are tend to focus on human weaknesses rather than on the villainy of ogres or witches. For example, on her quest to find her lost playmate, the plucky feminine protagonist of "The Snow Queen" doesn't fight the Queen herself so much as the idea many get that the world would be better off without emotions.

THE SNOW QUEEN
A TALE IN SEVEN STORIES

FIRST STORY
Deals with a Mirror and Its Fragments

Now we are about to begin and you must attend! And when we get to the end of the story, you will know more than you do now about a very wicked hobgoblin. He was one of the worst kind; in fact he was a real demon.

One day this demon was in a high state of delight because he had invented a mirror with this peculiarity: that every good and pretty thing reflected in it shrank away to almost nothing. On the other hand, every bad and good-for-nothing thing stood out and looked its worst. The most beautiful landscapes reflected in it looked like boiled spinach, and the best people became hideous, or else they were upside down and had no bodies. Their faces were distorted beyond recognition, and if they had even one freckle it appeared to spread all over the nose and mouth. The demon thought this immensely amusing. If a good thought passed through anyone's mind, it turned to a grin in the mirror, and this caused real delight to the demon.

All the pupils in the demon's school—for he kept a school—reported that a miracle had taken place: now for the first time, they said, it was possible to see what the world and mankind were really like. They ran about everywhere with the mirror, till at last there was not a country or a person which had not been seen in this distorting mirror.

They even wanted to fly up to heaven with it to mock the angels. But the higher they flew the more it grinned, so much so that they could hardly hold it. And at last it slipped out of their hands and fell to the earth, shivered into hundreds of millions and billions of bits. Even then it did more harm than ever. Some of these bits were not as big as a grain of sand, and these flew about all over the world, getting into people's eyes. Once in, they stuck there and distorted everything they looked at, or made them see everything that was amiss. Each tiniest grain of glass kept the same power as that possessed by the whole mirror. Some people even got a bit of the glass into their hearts, and that was terrible for the heart became like a lump of ice. Some of the fragments were so big that they were used for window panes, but it was not advisable to look at one's friends through these panes. Other bits were made into spectacles, and it was a bad business when people meaning to be just put on these spectacles.

The bad demon laughed till he split his sides! It tickled him to see the mischief he had done. But some of these fragments were still left floating about the world, and you shall hear what happened to them.

SECOND STORY

About a Little Boy and a Little Girl

In a big town crowded with houses and people, where there is no room for gardens, people have to be content with flowers in pots instead. In one of these towns lived two children who managed to have something bigger than a flowerpot for a garden. They were not brother and sister, but they were just as fond of each other as if they had been. Their parents lived opposite each other in two attic rooms. The roof of one house just touched the roof of the next one, with only a rain-water gutter between them. They each had a little dormer window, and one had only to step over the gutter to get from one house to the other.

Each of the parents had a large window box in which they grew pot herbs and a little rose tree. There was one in each box and they both grew splendidly. Then it occurred to the parents to put the boxes across the gutter, from house to house, and they looked just like two banks of flowers. The pea vines hung down over the edges of the boxes, and the roses threw out long creepers which twined round the windows. It was almost like a green triumphal arch. The boxes were high and the children knew they must not climb up onto them, but they were often allowed to have their little stools out under the rose trees; and there they had delightful games.

Of course in the winter there was an end to these amusements. The windows were often covered with hoar frost. Then they would warm coppers on the stove and stick them on the frozen panes, where they made lovely peepholes as round as possible. Then bright eyes would peep through these holes, one from each window. The little boy's name was Kay and the little girl's, Gerda.

In the summer they could reach each other with one bound, but in the winter they had to go down all the stairs in one house and up all the stairs in the other, and outside there were snowdrifts.

"Look! The white bees are swarming," said the old grandmother.

"Have they a queen bee too?" asked the little boy, for he knew that there was a queen among the real bees.

"Yes, indeed they have," said the grandmother. "She flies where the swarm is thickest. She is the biggest of them all and she never remains on the ground. She always flies up again to the sky. Many a winter's night she flies through the streets and peeps in at the windows, and then the ice freezes on the panes into wonderful patterns like flowers."

"Oh yes, we have seen that," said both children, and then they knew it was true.

"Can the Snow Queen come in here?" asked the little girl.

"Just let her come," said the boy, "and I will put her on the stove, where she will melt."

But the grandmother smoothed his hair and told him more stories.

In the evening when little Kay was at home and half undressed, he crept up onto the chair by the window and peeped out of the little hole. A few snowflakes were falling, and one of these, the biggest, remained on the edge of the window box. It grew bigger and bigger, till it became the figure of a woman dressed in the finest white gauze, which appeared to be made of millions of starry flakes. She was delicately lovely, but all ice—glittering, dazzling ice. Still she was alive. Her eyes shone like two bright stars, but there was no rest or peace in them. She nodded to the window and waved her hand. The little boy was frightened and jumped down off the chair, and then he fancied that a big bird flew past the window.

The next day was bright and frosty, and then came the thaw—and after that the spring. The sun shone, green buds began to appear, the swallows built their nests, and people began to open their windows. The little children began to play in their garden on the roof again. The roses were in splendid bloom that summer. The little girl had learned a hymn, and there was something in it about roses, and that made her think of her own. She sang it to the little boy, and then he sang it with her:

"Where roses deck the flowery vale,
There, Infant Jesus, we thee hail!"

The children took each other by the hands, kissed the roses and rejoiced in God's bright sunshine, and spoke to it as if the Child Jesus were there. What lovely summer days they were, and how delightful it was to sit under the fresh rose trees which seemed never to tire of blooming.

Kay and Gerda were looking at a picture book of birds and animals one day—it had just struck five by the church clock—when Kay said, "Oh! Something struck my heart and I have got something in my eye."

The little girl put her arms round his neck. He blinked his eye, but there was nothing to be seen.

"I believe it is gone," he said, but it was not gone. It was one of those very grains of glass from the mirror, the magic mirror. You remember that horrid mirror in which all good and great things reflected in it became small and mean, while the bad things were magnified and every flaw became very apparent.

Poor Kay! A grain of it had gone straight to his heart and would soon turn it to a lump of ice. He did not feel it any more but it was still there.

"Why do you cry?" he asked. "It makes you look ugly. There's nothing the matter with me. How horrid!" he suddenly cried. "There's a worm in that rose, and that one is quite crooked. After all, they are nasty roses and so are the boxes they are growing in!" He kicked the box and broke off two of the roses.

"What are you doing, Kay?" cried the little girl. When he saw her alarm, he broke off another rose, and then ran in by his own window and left dear little Gerda alone.

When she next got out the picture book he said it was only fit for babies in long clothes. When his grandmother told them stories he always had a *but*—. And if he could manage it, he liked to get behind her chair, put on her spectacles, and imitate her. He did it very well and people laughed at him. He was soon able to imitate everyone in the street. He could make fun of all their peculiarities and failings. "He will turn out a clever fellow,'' said people. But it was all that bit of glass in his heart, that bit of glass in his eye, and it made him tease little Gerda who was so devoted to him. He played quite different games now; he seemed to have grown older. One winter's day when the snow was falling fast, he brought in a big magnifying glass. He held out the tail of his blue coat and let the snowflakes fall upon it.

''Now look through the glass, Gerda!'' he said. Every snowflake was magnified and looked like a lovely flower or a sharply pointed star.

''Do you see how cleverly they are made?'' said Kay. ''Much more interesting than looking at real flowers and there is not a single flaw in them. They are perfect. If only they would not melt!''

Shortly afterwards he appeared in his thick gloves, with his sled on his back. He shouted right into Gerda's ear, ''I have got leave to drive in the big square where the other boys play.'' And away he went.

In the big square the bolder boys used to tie their little sleds to the farm carts and go a long way in this fashion. They had no end of fun over it. Just in the middle of their games, a big sled came along. It was painted white and the occupant wore a white fur coat and cap. The sled drove twice round the square, and Kay quickly tied his sled on behind. Then off they went, faster and faster, into the next street. The driver turned round and nodded to Kay in the most friendly way, just as if they knew each other. Every time Kay wanted to loose his sled, the person nodded again and Kay stayed where he was, and they drove right out through the town gates. Then the snow began to fall so heavily that the little boy could not see a hand before him as they rushed along. He undid the cords and tried to get away from the big sled, but it was no use. His little sled stuck fast. And on they rushed, faster than the wind. He shouted aloud but nobody heard him, and the sled tore on through the snowdrifts. Every now and then it gave a bound, as if they were jumping over hedges and ditches. He was very frightened and he wanted to say his prayers, but he could only remember the multiplication tables.

The snowflakes grew bigger and bigger till at last they looked like big white chickens. All at once they sprang on one side, the big sled stopped, and the person who drove got up, coat and cap smothered in snow. It was a tall and upright lady all shining white, the Snow Queen herself.

''We have come along at a good pace,'' she said, ''but it's cold enough to kill one. Creep inside my bearskin coat.''

She took him into the sled by her, wrapped him in her furs, and he felt as if he were sinking into a snowdrift.

"Are you still cold?" she asked and kissed him on the forehead. Ugh! It was colder than ice. It went to his very heart, which was already more than half ice. He felt as if he were dying, but only for a moment, and then it seemed to have done him good. He no longer felt the cold.

"My sled! Don't forget my sled!" He only now remembered it. It was tied to one of the white chickens which flew along behind them. The Snow Queen kissed Kay again and then he forgot all about little Gerda, grandmother, and all the others at home.

"Now I mustn't kiss you any more," she said, "or I should kiss you to death!"

Kay looked at her and she was so pretty! A more beautiful face could hardly be imagined. She did not seem to be made of ice now, as she was when she waved her hand to him outside the window. In his eyes she was quite perfect, and he was not a bit afraid of her. He told her that he could do mental arithmetic as far as fractions, and that he knew the number of square miles and the number of inhabitants of the country. She always smiled at him, and he then thought that he surely dd not know enough; and he looked up into the wide expanse of heaven, into which they rose higher and higher as she flew with him on a dark cloud, while the storm surged around them, the wind ringing in their ears like well-known old songs.

They flew over woods and lakes, over oceans and islands. The cold wind whistled down below them, the wolves howled, the black crows flew screaming over the sparkling snow. But up above, the moon shone bright and clear—and Kay looked at it all the long, long winter nights. In the day he slept at the Snow Queen's feet.

THIRD STORY

The Garden of the Woman Learned in Magic

But how was little Gerda getting on all this long time since Kay left her? Where could he be? Nobody knew. Nobody could say anything about him. All that the other boys knew was that they had seen him tie his little sled to a splendid big one which drove away down the street and out of the town gates. Nobody knew where he was, and many tears were shed. Little Gerda cried long and bitterly. At last, people said he was dead. He must have fallen into the river which ran close by the town. Oh, what long, dark, winter days those were!

At last the spring came and the sunshine.

"Kay is dead and gone," said little Gerda.

"I don't believe it," said the sunshine.

"He is dead and gone," she said to the swallows.

"We don't believe it," said the swallows, and at last little Gerda did not believe it either.

"I will put on my new red shoes," she said one morning. "Kay never saw them. And then I will go down to the river and ask it about him."

It was very early in the morning. She kissed the old grandmother, who was still asleep, put on the red shoes, and went quite alone out by the gate to the river.

"Is it true that you have taken my little playfellow? I will give you my red shoes if you will bring him back to me again."

She thought the little ripples nodded in such a curious way that she took off her red shoes, her most cherished possessions, and threw both into the river. They fell close by the shore and were carried straight back to her by the little wavelets. It seemed as if the river would not accept her offering, as it had not taken little Kay.

She only thought she had not thrown them far enough, so she climbed into a boat which lay among the rushes. Then she went right out to the farther end of it and threw the shoes into the water again. But the boat was loose and her movements started it off, and it floated away from the shore. She felt it moving and tried to get out, but before she reached the other end the boat was more than a yard from the shore and was floating away quite quickly.

Little Gerda was terribly frightened and began to cry, but nobody heard her except the sparrows. They could not carry her ashore, but they flew alongside twittering as if to cheer her, "We are here! We are here!"

The boat floated rapidly away with the current. Little Gerda sat quite still with only her stockings on. Her little red shoes floated behind but they could not catch up with the boat, which drifted away faster and faster.

The banks on both sides were very pretty with beautiful flowers, fine old trees, and slopes dotted with sheep and cattle, but not a single person.

"Perhaps the river is taking me to little Kay," thought Gerda, and that cheered her. She sat up and looked at the beautiful green banks for hours.

Then they came to a big cherry garden. There was a little house in it with curious blue and red windows. It had a thatched roof, and two wooden soldiers stood outside, who presented arms as she sailed past. Gerda called out to them. She thought they were alive, but of course they did not answer. She was quite close to them, for the current drove the boat close the the bank. Gerda called out again louder than before, and then an old, old woman came out of the house. She was leaning upon a big hooked stick, and she wore a big sun hat which was covered with beautiful painted flowers.

"You poor little child," said the old woman. "However were you driven out on this big strong river into the wide, wide world alone?" Then she walked right into the water and caught hold of the boat with her hooked stick. She drew it ashore and lifted little Gerda out.

Gerda was delighted to be on dry land again, but she was a little bit frightened by the strange old woman.

"Tell me who you are and how you got here," said she.

When Gerda had told her the whole story and asked her if she had seen Kay, the woman said she had not seen him but that she expected him. Gerda must not be sad; she was to come and taste her cherries and see her flowers, which were more beautiful than any picture book. Each one had a story to tell. Then she took Gerda by the hand, they went into the little house, and the old woman locked the door.

The windows were very high up, and they were red, blue, and yellow. They threw a very curious light into the room. On the table were quantities of the most delicious cherries, of which Gerda had leave to eat as many as ever she liked. While she was eating, the old woman combed her hair with a golden comb, so that her hair curled and shone like gold round the pretty little face, which was as sweet as a rose.

"I have long wanted a little girl like you," said the old woman. "You will see how well we shall get on together." While she combed her hair Gerda had forgotten all about Kay, for the old woman was learned in the magic art. But she was not a bad witch. She only cast spells over people for a little amusement, and she wanted to keep Gerda. She therefore went into the garden and waved her hooked stick over all the rosebushes, and however beautifully they were flowering, all sank down into the rich black earth without leaving a trace behind them. The old woman was afraid if Gerda saw the roses she would be reminded of Kay and would want to run away. Then she took Gerda into the flower garden. What a delicious scent there was! Every imaginable flower for every season was in that lovely garden. No picture book could be brighter or more beautiful. Gerda jumped for joy and played till the sun went down behind the tall cherry trees. Then she was put into a lovely bed with rose-colored silken coverings stuffed with violets. She slept and dreamt as lovely dreams as any queen on her wedding day.

The next day she played with the flowers in the garden again—and many days passed in the same way. Gerda knew every flower, but however many there were she always thought there was one missing, but which it was she did not know.

One day she was sitting looking at the old woman's sun hat with its painted flowers, and the very prettiest one of them all was a rose. The old woman had forgotten her hat when she charmed the others away. This is the consequence of being absent-minded.

"What!" said Gerda, "are there no roses here?" And she sprang in among the flower beds and sought, but in vain. Her hot tears fell on the very places where the roses used to be. When the warm drops moistened the earth, the rose trees shot up again just as full of bloom as when they sank. Gerda embraced the roses and kissed them, and then she thought of the lovely roses at home, and this brought the thought of little Kay.

"Oh, how I have been delayed," said the little girl. "I ought to have been looking for Kay. Don't you know where he is?" she asked the roses. "Do you think he is dead and gone?"

"He is not dead," said the roses. "We have been down underground, you know, and all the dead people are there, but Kay is not among them."

"Oh, thank you!" said little Gerda. And then she went to the other flowers and looked into their cups and said, "Do you know where Kay is?"

But each flower stood in the sun and dreamt its own dreams. Little Gerda heard many of these but never anything about Kay.

And what said the tiger lilies?

"Do you hear the drum? Rub-a-dub. It has only two notes: rub-a-dub. Always the same. The wailing of women and the cry of the preacher. The Hindu woman in her long red garment stands on the pile, while the flames surround her and her dead husband. But the woman is only thinking of the living man in the circle round, whose eyes burn with a fiercer fire than that of the flames which consume the body. Do the flames of the heart die in the fire?"

"I understand nothing about that," said little Gerda.

"That is my story," said the tiger lily.

"What does the convolvulus say?"

"An old castle is perched high over a narrow mountain path. It is closely covered with ivy, almost hiding the old red walls and creeping up leaf upon leaf right round the balcony where stands a beautiful maiden. She bends over the balustrade and looks eagerly up the road. No rose on its stem is fresher than she. No apple blossom wafted by the wind moves more lightly. Her silken robes rustle softly as she bends over and says, 'Will he never come?'

"Is it Kay you mean?" asked Gerda.

"I am only talking about my own story—my dream," answered the convolvulus.

What said the little snowdrop?

"Between two trees a rope with a board is hanging. It is a swing. Two pretty little girls in snowy frocks and green ribbons fluttering on their hats are seated on it. Their brother, who is bigger than they are, stands up behind them. He has his arms round the ropes for supports, and holds in one hand a little bowl and in the other a clay pipe. He is blowing soap bubbles. As the swing moves the bubbles fly upwards in all their changing colors. The last one still hangs from the pipe swayed by the wind, and the swing goes on. A little black dog runs up. He is almost as light as the bubbles. He stands up on his hind legs and wants to be taken into the swing, but it does not stop. The little dog falls with an angry bark. They jeer at it. The bubble bursts. A swinging plank, a fluttering foam picture—that is my story!"

"I daresay what you tell me is very pretty, but you speak so sadly and you never mention little Kay."

What said the hyacinth?

"There were three beautiful sisters, all most delicate and quite transparent. One wore a crimson robe, the other a blue, and the third was pure white. These three danced hand in hand by the edge of the lake in the moonlight. They were human beings, not fairies of the wood. The fragrant air attracted them and they vanished into the wood. Here the fragrance was stronger still. Three coffins glide out of the wood toward the lake, and in them lie the maidens. The fireflies flutter lightly around them with their little flickering torches. Do these dancing maidens sleep, or are they dead? The scent of the flower says that they are corpses. The evening bell tolls their knell."

"You make me quite sad," said little Gerda. "Your perfume is so strong it makes me think of those dead maidens. Oh, is little Kay really dead? The roses have been down underground, and they say no."

"Ding, dong," tolled the hyacinth bells. "We are not tolling for little Kay. We know nothing about him. We sing our song, the only one we know."

And Gerda went on to the buttercups, shining among their dark green leaves.

"You are a bright little sun," said Gerda. "Tell me if you know where I shall find my playfellow."

The buttercup shone brightly and returned Gerda's glance. What song could the buttercup sing? It would not be about Kay.

"God's bright sun shone into a little court on the first day of spring. The sunbeams stole down the neighboring white wall, close to which bloomed the first yellow flower of the season. It shone like burnished gold in the sun. An old woman had brought her armchair out into the sun. Her granddaughter, a poor and pretty little maidservant, had come to pay her a short visit, and she kissed her. There was gold, heart's gold, in the kiss. Gold on the lips, gold on the ground, and gold above, in the early morning beams! Now that is my little story," said the buttercup.

"Oh, my poor old grandmother!" sighed Gerda. "She will be longing to see me and grieving about me, as she did about Kay. But I shall soon go home again and take Kay with me. It is useless for me to ask the flowers about him. They know only their own stories and have no information to give me."

Then she tucked up her little dress so that she might run the faster, but the narcissus blossoms struck her on the legs as she jumped over them. So she stopped and said, "Perhaps you can tell me something."

She stooped down close to the flower and listened. What did it say?

"I can see myself. I can see myself," said the narcissus. "Oh, how sweet is my scent. Up there in an attic window stands a little dancing girl half-dressed. First she stands on one leg, then on the other, and looks as if she would tread the whole world under her feet. She is only a delusion.

She pours some water out of a teapot onto a bit of stuff that she is holding. It is her bodice. 'Cleanliness is a good thing,' she says. Her white dress hangs on a peg. It has been washed in the teapot, too, and dried on the roof. She puts it on and wraps a saffron colored scarf round her neck, which makes the dress look whiter. See how high she carries her head, and all upon one stem. I see myself. I see myself."

"I don't care a bit about all that," said Gerda. "It's no use telling me such stuff."

And then she ran to the end of the garden. The door was fastened, but she pressed the rusty latch and it gave way. The door sprang open and little Gerda ran out with bare feet into the wide world. She looked back three times, but nobody came after her. At last she could run no farther and she sat down on a big stone. When she looked around she saw that the summer was over. It was quite late autumn. She would never have known it inside the beautiful garden, where the sun always shone and the flowers of every season were always in bloom.

"Oh, how I have wasted my time," said little Gerda. "It is autumn. I must not rest any longer." And she got up to go on.

Oh, how weary and sore were her little feet, and everything round looked so cold and dreary. The long willow leaves were quite yellow. The damp mist fell off the trees like rain. One leaf dropped after another from the trees, and only the sloe thorn still bore its fruit, but the sloes were sour and set one's teeth on edge. Oh, how gray and sad it looked, out in the wide world!

FOURTH STORY
The Prince and the Princess

Gerda was soon obliged to rest again. A big crow hopped onto the snow, just in front of her. He had been sitting looking at her for a long time and wagging his head. Now he said, "Caw! caw! Good day, good day," as well as he could. He meant to be kind to the little girl, and asked her where she was going alone in the wide world.

Gerda understood the world "alone" and knew how much there was in it, and she told the crow the whole story of her life and adventures and asked if he had seen Kay.

The crow nodded his head gravely and said, "Maybe I have. Maybe I have."

"What, do you really think you have?" cried the little girl, nearly smothering him with her kisses.

"Gently, gently!" said the crow. "I believe it may have been Kay, but he has forgotten you by this time, I expect, for the Princess."

"Does he live with a Princess?" asked Gerda.

"Yes, listen," said the crow. "But it is so difficult to speak your language. If you understand crow's language, I can tell you about it much better."

"No, I have never learned it," said Gerda. "But grandmother did and used to speak it. If only I had learned it!"

"It doesn't matter," said the crow. "I will tell you as well as I can, although I may do it rather badly."

Then he told her what he had heard.

"In this kingdom where we are now," said he, "there lives a Princess who is very clever. She has read all the newspapers in the world and forgotten them again, so clever is she. One day she was sitting on her throne, which is not such an amusing thing to do either, they say. And she began humming a tune, which happened to be:

'Why should I not be married, oh why?'

'Why not, indeed?' said she. And she made up her mind to marry, if she could find a husband who had an answer ready when a question was put to him. She called all the court ladies together, and when they heard what she wanted they were delighted.

" 'I like that now,' they said. 'I was thinking the same thing myself the other day.'

"Every word I say is true," said the crow, "for I have a tame sweetheart who goes about the palace whenever she likes. She told me the story."

Of course his sweetheart was a crow, for "birds of a feather flock together," and one crow always chooses another. "The newspapers all came out immediately with borders of hearts and the Princess's initials. They gave notice that any young man who was handsome enough might go up to the palace to speak to the Princess. The one who spoke as if he were quite at home, and spoke well, would be chosen by the Princess as her husband. Yes, yes, you may believe me. It's as true as I sit here," said the crow. "The people came crowding in. There was such running and crushing, but no one was fortunate enough to be chosen, either on the first day or on the second. They could all of them talk well enough in the street, but when they entered the castle gates and saw the guard in silver uniforms, and when they went up the stairs through rows of lackeys in gold embroidered liveries, their courage forsook them. When they reached the brilliantly lighted reception rooms and stood in front of the throne where the Princess was seated, they could think of nothing to say. They only echoed her last words, and of course that was not what she wanted.

"It was just as if they had all taken some kind of sleeping powder which made them lethargic. They did not recover themselves until they got out into the street again, and then they had plenty to say. There was quite a long line of them, reaching from the town gates up to the palace.

"I went to see them myself," said the crow. "They were hungry and thirsty but they got nothing at the palace, not even as much as a glass of tepid water. Some of the wise ones had taken sandwiches with them, but they did not share them with their neighbors. They thought if the others went in to the Princess looking hungry, there would be more chance for themselves."

"But Kay, little Kay!" asked Gerda, "when did he come? Was he amongst the crowd?"

"Give me time! Give me time! We are just coming to him. It was on the third day that a little person came marching cheerfully along, without either carriage or horse. His eyes sparkled like yours and he had beautiful long hair, but his clothes were very shabby."

"Oh, that was Kay!" said Gerda gleefully. "Then I have found him!" And she clapped her hands.

"He had a little knapsack on his back," said the crow.

"No, it must have been his sled. He had it with him when he went away," said Gerda.

"Maybe so," said the crow. "I did not look very particularly. But I know from my sweetheart that when he entered the palace gates and saw the lifeguards in the silver uniforms, and the lackeys on the stairs in their gold laced liveries, he was not the least bit abashed. He just nodded to them and said, 'It must be very tiresome to stand upon the stairs. I am going inside.' The rooms were blazing with lights. Privy counsellors and excellencies without number were walking about barefoot, carrying golden vessels. It was enough to make you solemn! His boots creaked fearfully too, but he wasn't a bit upset."

"Oh, I am sure that was Kay!" said Gerda. "I know he had a pair of new boots. I heard them creaking in grandmother's room."

"Yes, indeed they did creak!" said the crow. "But nothing daunted, he went straight up to the Princess, who was sitting on a pearl as big as a spinning wheel. Poor, simple boy! All the court ladies and their attendants, and the courtiers and their gentlemen, each attended by a page, were standing round. The nearer the door they stood, the greater was their haughtiness. The footman's boy, who always wore slippers and stood in the doorway, was almost too proud even to be looked at."

"It must be awful!" said little Gerda, "and yet Kay has won the Princess!"

"If I had not been a crow, I should have taken her myself, notwithstanding that I am engaged. They say he spoke as well as I could have done myself when I speak crow language, at least so my sweetheart says. He was a picture of good looks and gallantry, and then he had not come with any idea of wooing the Princess, but simply to hear her wisdom. He admired her just as much as she admired him."

"Indeed it was Kay then," said Gerda. "He was so clever he could do mental arithmetic up to fractions. Oh, won't you take me to the palace?"

"It's easy enough to talk," said the crow, "but how are we to manage it? I will talk to my tame sweetheart about it; she will have some advice to give us, I daresay, but I am bound to tell you that a little girl like you will never be admitted."

"Oh, indeed I shall," said Gerda. "When Kay hears that I am here, he will come out at once to fetch me."

"Wait here for me by the stile," said the crow. Then he wagged his head and flew off.

The evening had darkened in before he came back. "Caw, caw," he said. "She sends you greeting, and here is a little roll for you. She got it out of the kitchen, where there is bread enough, and I daresay you are hungry. It is not possible for you to get into the palace. You have bare feet and the guards in silver and the lackeys in gold would never allow you to pass. But don't cry. We shall get you in somehow. My sweetheart knows a little back staircase which leads up to the bedroom, and she knows where the key is kept."

Then they went quietly into the garden, into the great avenue where the trees were. And when the palace lights went out one after the other, the crow led little Gerda to the back door, which was ajar.

Oh, how Gerda's heart beat with fear and longing! It was just as if she were about to do something wrong, and yet she only wanted to know if this really was little Kay. Oh, it must be he, she thought, picturing to herself his clever eyes and his long hair. She could see his very smile when they used to sit under the rose trees at home. She thought he would be very glad to see her and to hear what a long way she had come to find him, and to hear how sad they had all been at home when he did not come back. Oh, it was joy mingled with fear.

They had now reached the stairs, where a little lamp was burning on a shelf. There stood the tame sweetheart, twisting and turning her head to look at Gerda, who made a curtsey, as grandmother had taught her.

"My betrothed has spokenso charmingly to me about you, my little miss," she said. "Your life, '*Vita,*' as it is called, is most touching! If you will take the lamp, I will go on in front. We shall take the straight road here and we shall meet no one."

"It seems to me that someone is coming up behind us," said Gerda, as she fancied something rushed past her throwing a shadow on the walls: horses with flowing manes and slender legs; huntsmen, ladies and gentlemen, on horseback.

"Oh, those are only the dreams!" said the crow. "They come to take the thoughts of the noble ladies and gentlemen out hunting. That's a good thing, for you will be able to see them all the better in bed. But don't forget, when you are taken into favor, that you show a grateful spirit."

"Now, there's no need to talk about that," said the crow from the woods.

They now came into the first apartment; it was hung with rose-colored satin embroidered with flowers. Here again the dreams overtook them, but they flitted by so quickly that Gerda could not distinguish them. The apartments became one more beautiful than the other. There were enough to bewilder anybody. They now reached the bedroom. The ceiling was like a great palm with crystal leaves, and in the middle of the room were two beds, each like a lily hung from a golden stem. One was white, and in it lay the Princess. The other was red, and there lay he whom Gerda had come to seek—little Kay! She bent aside one of the crimson leaves, and she saw a little brown neck It was Kay! She called his name aloud and held the lamp close to him. Again the dreams rushed through the room on horseback. He awoke, turned his head—and it was not little Kay.

It was only the Prince's neck which was like his, but he was young and handsome. The Princess peeped out of her lily-white bed and asked what was the matter. Then little Gerda cried and told them all her story, and what the crows had done to help her.

"You poor little thing!" said the Prince and Princess. And they praised the crows and said that they were not at all angry with them, but they must not do it again. Then they gave them a reward.

"Would you like your liberty?" said the Princess. "Or would you prefer permanent posts about the court as court crows with perquisites from the kitchen?"

Both crows curtsied and begged for the permanent posts. They thought of their old age and said it would be good to have something for "the old man," as they called it.

The Prince got up and allowed Gerda to sleep in his bed, and he could not have done more. She folded her little hands and thought, "How good the people and the animals are!" Then she shut her eyes and fell fast asleep. All the dreams came flying back again. This time they looked like angels, and they were dragging a little sled with Kay sitting on it, and he nodded. But it was only a dream, so it all vanished when she woke.

Next day she was dressed in silk and velvet from head to foot. They asked her to stay at the palace and have a good time, but she only begged them to give her a little carriage and horse and a little pair of boots, so that she might drive out into the wide world to look for Kay.

They gave her a pair of boots and a muff. She was beautifully dressed, and when she was ready to start, there before the door stood a new chariot of pure gold. The Prince's and Princess's coat of arms was emblazoned on it and shone like a star. Coachman, footman, and outrider, for there was even an outrider, all wore golden crowns. The Prince and Princess themselves helped her into the carriage and wished her joy. The wood crow, who was now married, accompanied her for the first three miles. He sat beside Gerda, for he could not ride with his back to the horses. The other crow stood at the door and flapped her wings. She did not go with them, for she suffered from headache since she had been a kitchen pensioner—the consequence of eating too much. The chariot was stored with sugar biscuits, and there were fruit and ginger nuts under the seat.

"Good-bye! good-bye!" cried the Prince and Princess. Little

Gerda wept and the crow wept too. At the end of the first few miles the crow said good-bye, and this was the hardest parting of all. He flew up into a tree and flapped his big black wings as long as he could see the chariot, which shone like the brightest sunshine.

FIFTH STORY
The Little Robber Girl

They drove on through a dark wood, where the chariot lighted the way and blinded some robbers by its glare. It was more than they could bear.

"It is gold! It is gold!" they cried, and darting forward they seized the horses and killed the postilions, the coachman, and footman. Then they dragged little Gerda out of the carriage.

"She is fat and she is pretty. She has been fattened on nuts," said the old robber woman, who had a long beard, and eyebrows that hung down over her eyes. "She is as good as a fat lamb, and how nice she will taste!" She drew out her sharp knife as she said this. It glittered horribly. "Oh!" screamed the old woman at the same moment, for her little daughter had come up behind her and was biting her ear. She hung on her back, as wild and as savage a little animal as you could wish to find. "You bad, wicked child!" said the mother, but she was prevented from killing Gerda on this occasion.

"She shall play with me," said the little robber girl. "She shall give me her muff and her pretty dress, and she shall sleep in my bed." Then she bit her mother again and made her dance. All the robbers laughed and said, "Look at her dancing with her cub!"

"I want to get into the carriage," said the little robber girl, and she always had her own way because she was so spoilt and stubborn. She and Gerda got into the carriage, and then they drove over stubble and stones farther and farther into the wood. The little robber girl was as big as Gerda, but much stronger. She had broad shoulders and a darker skin. Her eyes were quite black, with almost a melancholy expression. She put her arm around Gerda's waist and said, "They shan't kill you as long as I don't get angry with you. You must surely be a Princess!"

"No," said little Gerda, and then she told her all her adventures and how fond she was of Kay.

The robber girl looked earnestly at her, gave a little nod, and said,

"They shan't kill you even if I am angry with you. I will do it myself." Then she dried Gerda's eyes and stuck her own hands into the pretty muff, which was so soft and warm.

At last the chariot stopped. They were in the courtyard of a robber's castle, the walls of which were cracked from top to bottom. Ravens and crows flew in and out of every hole, and big bulldogs, each of whom looked ready to devour somebody, jumped as high as they could. But they did not bark, for it was not allowed. A big fire was burning in the middle of the stone floor of the smoky old hall. The smoke all went up to the ceiling where it had to find a way out for itself. Soup was boiling in a big caldron over the fire, and hares and rabbits were roasting on the spits.

"You shall sleep with me and all my little pets tonight," said the robber girl.

When they had had something to eat and drink they went along to one corner which was spread with straw and rugs. There were nearly a hundred pigeons roosting overhead on the rafters and beams. They seemed to be asleep, but they fluttered about a little when the children came in.

"They are all mine," said the little robber girl, seizing one of the nearest. She held it by the legs and shook it until it flapped its wings. "Kiss it," she cried, dashing it at Gerda's face. "Those are the wood pigeons," she added, pointing to some laths fixed across a big hole high up on the walls. "They are a regular rabble. They would fly away directly if they were not locked in. And here is my old sweetheart, Be!" Here she dragged forward a reindeer by the horn. He was tied up, and he had a bright copper ring round his neck. "We have to keep him close too, or he would run off. Every single night I tickle his neck with my bright knife. He is so frightened of it!" The little girl produced a long knife out of a hole in the wall and drew it across the reindeer's neck. The poor animal laughed and kicked, and the robber girl laughed and pulled Gerda down into the bed with her.

"Do you have that knife by you while you are asleep?" asked Gerda, looked rather frightened.

"I always sleep with a knife," said the little robber girl. "You never know what will happen. But now tell me again what you told me before about little Kay, and why you went out into the world."

So Gerda told her all about it again, and the wood pigeons cooed up in their cage above them. The other pigeons were alseep. The little robber girl put her arm around Gerda's neck and went to sleep with the knife in her hand, and she was soon snoring. But Gerda would not close her eyes. She did not know whether she was to live or to die. The robbers sat around the fire, eating and drinking, and the old woman was turning somersaults. This sight terrified the poor little girl.

Then the wood pigeons said, "Coo, coo! We have seen little Kay. His sled was drawn by a white chicken, and he was sitting in the Snow Queen's sled. It was floating low over the trees, while we were in our nests. She blew upon us young ones, and they all died except us two. Coo, coo."

"What are you saying up there?" asked Gerda. "Where was the Snow Queen going? Do you know anything about it?"

"She was most likely going to Lapland, because there is always snow and ice there. Ask the reindeer who is tied up below."

"There is ice and snow, and it's a splendid place," said the reindeer. "You can run and jump about where you like on those big glittering plains. The Snow Queen has her summer tent there, but her permanent castle is up at the North Pole, on the island which is called Spitzbergen."

"Oh Kay, little Kay!" sighed Gerda.

"Lie still, or I shall stick the knife into you," said the robber girl.

In the morning Gerda told her all that the wood pigeons had said, and the little robber girl looked quite solemn, but she nodded her head and said, "No matter! No matter! Do you know where Lapland is?" she asked the reindeer.

"Who should know better than I," said the animal, his eyes dancing. "I was born and brought up there, and I used to leap about on the snowfields."

"Listen," said the robber girl. "You see that all our menfolk are away, but mother is still here and she will stay. But later on in the morning she will take a drink out of the big bottle there, and after that she will have a nap. Then I will do something for you." Then she jumped out of bed, ran along to her mother and pulled her beard, and said, "Good morning, my own dear nanny goat!" And her mother filliped her nose till it was red and blue, but it was all affection.

As soon as her mother had had her draught from the bottle and had dropped asleep, the little robber girl went along to the reindeer and said, "I should have the greatest pleasure in the world in keeping you here, to tickle you with my knife, because you are such fun then. However, it does not matter. I will untie your halter and help you outside so that you may run away to Lapland, but you must put your best foot foremost and take this little girl for me to the Snow Queen's palace, where her playfellow is. I suppose you heard what she was telling me, for she spoke loudly enough and you are generally eavesdropping."

The reindeer jumped up into the air for joy. The robber girl lifted little Gerda up, and had the forethought to tie her on, nay, even to give her a little cushion to sit upon. "Here, after all, I will give you your fur boots back, for it will be very cold, but I will keep your muff. It is too pretty to part with. Still you shan't be cold. Here are my mother's big mittens for you. They will reach up to your elbows. Here, stick your hands in! Now your hands look just like my nasty mother's."

Gerda shed tears of joy.

"I don't like you to whimper!" said the little robber girl. "You ought to be looking delighted. And here are two loaves and a ham for you so that you will not starve."

These things were tied onto the back of the reindeer. The little robber girl opened the door and called in all the big dogs, and then she cut the halter with her knife and said to the reindeer, "Now run, but take care of my little girl!"

Gerda stretched out her hands in the big mittens to the robber girl and said good-bye. And then the reindeer darted off over briars and bushes, through the big wood, over swamps and plains, as fast as he could go. The wolves howled and the ravens screamed, while the red lights quivered up in the sky.

"There are my old northern lights," said the reindeer. "See how they flash!" And on he rushed faster than ever, day and night. The loaves were eaten, and the ham too, and then they were in Lapland.

SIXTH STORY

The Lapp Woman and the Finn Woman

They stopped by a little hut, a very poverty-stricken one. The roof sloped right down to the ground, and the door was so low that the people had to creep on hands and knees when they wanted to go in or out. There was nobody at home here but an old Lapp woman who was frying fish over a whale-oil lamp. The reindeer told her all Gerda's story, but he told his own first, for he thought his much the most important. Gerda was so overcome by the cold that she could not speak at all.

"Oh, you poor creatures!" said the Lapp woman. "You've got a long way to go yet. You will have to go hundreds of miles into the Finmark, for the Snow Queen is paying a country visit there, and she burns blue lights every night. I will write a few words on a dried codfish, for I have no paper. I will give it to you to take to the Finn woman up there. She will be better able to direct you than I can."

So when Gerda was warmed and had eaten and drunk something, the Lapp woman wrote a few words on a dried codfish and gave it to her, bidding her take good care of it. Then she tied her onto the reindeer again and off they flew. Flicker, flicker, went the beautiful blue northern lights up in the sky all night long. At last they came to the Finmark, and knocked on the Finn woman's chimney, for she had no door at all.

There was such a heat inside that the Finn woman went about almost naked. She was little and very grubby. She at once loosened Gerda's things and took off the mittens and the boots, or she would have been too hot. Then she put a piece of ice on the reindeer's head, and after that she read what was written on the codfish. She read it three times, and then she knew it by heart, and put the fish into the pot for dinner. There was no reason why it should not be eaten, and she never wasted anything.

Again the reindeer told his own story first and then little Gerda's. The Finn woman blinked with her wise eyes but she said nothing.

"You are so clever," said the reindeer. "I know you can bind all the winds of the world with a bit of sewing cotton. When a skipper unties one knot, he gets a good wind. When he unties two, it blows hard. And if he undoes the third and the fourth, he brings a storm about his head wild enough to blow down the forest trees. Won't you give the little girl a drink, so that she may have the strength of twelve men to overcome the Snow Queen?"

"The strength of twelve men?" said the Finn woman. "Yes, that will be about enough."

She went along to a shelf and took down a big folded skin, which she unrolled. There were curious characters written on it, and thc Finn woman read till the perspiration poured down her forehead.

But the reindeer implored her to give Gerda something, and Gerda looked at her with such beseeching eyes, full of tears, that the Finn woman began blinking again and drew the reindeer into a corner, where she whispered to him, at the same time putting fresh ice on his head.

"Little Kay is certainly with the Snow Queen, and he is delighted with everything there. He thinks it is the best place in the world, but that is because he has got a splinter of glass in his heart and a grain of glass in his eye. They will have to come out first, or he will never be human again, and the Snow Queen will keep him in her power."

"But can't you give little Gerda something to take which will give her power to conquer it all?"

"I can't give her greater power than she already has. Don't you see how great it is? Don't you see how both man and beast have to serve her? How she has got on as well as she has on her bare feet? We must not tell her what power she has. It is in her heart, because she is such a sweet innocent child. If she can't reach the Snow Queen herself, then we can't help her. The Snow Queen's gardens begin just two miles from here. You can carry the little girl as far as that. Put her down by the big bush standing there in the snow covered with red berries. Don't stand gossiping, but hurry back to me!" Then the Finn woman lifted Gerda onto the reindeer's back, and he rushed off as hard as he could.

"Oh, I have not got my boots, and I have not got my mittens!" cried little Gerda.

She soon felt the want of them in that cutting wind, but the reindeer did not dare to stop. He ran on till he came to the bush with the red berries. There he put Gerda down and kissed her on the mouth, while big shining tears trickled down his face. Then he ran back again as fast as ever he could. There stood poor little Gerda without shoes or gloves, in the middle of the freezing icebound Finmark.

She ran forward as quickly as she could. A whole regiment of snowflakes came toward her. They did not fall from the sky, for it was quite clear, with the northern lights shining brightly. No. These snowflakes ran along the ground, and the nearer they came the bigger they grew. Gerda remembered well how big and strange they looked under the magnifying glass. But the size of these was monstrous! They were alive. They were the Snow Queen's advance guard, and they took the most curious shapes. Some looked like big, horrid porcupines; some like bundles of knotted snakes with their heads sticking out. Others again were like fat little bears with bristling hair, but all were dazzling white and living snowflakes.

Then little Gerda said the Lord's Prayer, and the cold was so great that her breath froze as it came out of her mouth, and she could see it like a cloud of smoke in front of her. It grew thicker and thicker till it formed itself into bright little angels who grew bigger and bigger when they touched the ground. They all wore helmets and carried shields and spears in their hands. More and more of them appeared, and when Gerda had finished her prayer she was surrounded by a whole legion. They pierced the snowflakes with their spears and shivered them into a hundred pieces, and little Gerda walked fearlessly and undauntedly through them. The angels touched her hands and her feet, and then she hardly felt how cold it was but walked quickly on towards the Palace of the Snow Queen.

Now we must see what Kay was about. He was not thinking about Gerda at all—least of all that she was just outside the Palace.

SEVENTH STORY

What Happened in the Snow Queen's Palace and Afterwards

The palace walls were made of drifted snow, and the windows and doors of the biting winds. There were over a hundred rooms in it, shaped just as the snow had drifted. The biggest one stretched for many miles. They were all lighted by the strongest northern lights, and were immensely big and empty, and glittering in their iciness. There was never any gaiety in them, not even so much as a ball for the little bears, when the storms might have tuned up as the orchestra, and the polar bears might have walked about on their hind legs and shown off their grand manners. There was never even a little game-playing party for such games as "touch last" or "the biter bit"—no, not even a little gossip over the coffee cups for the white fox misses.

Immense, vast, and cold were the Snow Queen's halls. The northern lights came and went with such regularity that you could count the seconds between their coming and going. In the midst of these never-ending snow halls was a frozen lake. It was broken up on the surface into a thousand bits, but each piece was so exactly like the others that the whole formed a perfect work of art. The Snow Queen sat in the very middle of it when she sat at home. She then said that she was sitting on "The Mirror of Reason," and that it was the best and only one in the world.

Little Kay was blue with cold—nay, almost black—but he did not know it, for the Snow Queen had kissed away the icy shiverings, and his heart was little better than a lump of ice. He went about dragging some sharp flat pieces of ice which he placed in all sorts of patterns, trying to make something out of them, just as when we at home have little tablets of wood, with which we make patterns and call them a "Chinese puzzle."

Kay's patterns were most ingenious, because they were the "Ice Puzzles of Reason." In his eyes they were excellent and of the greatest importance: this was because of the grain of glass still in his eye. He made many patterns forming words, but he never could find the right way to place them for one particular word, a word he was most anxious to make. It was "Eternity." The Snow Queen had said to him that if he could find out this word he should be his own master, and she would give him the whole world and a new pair of skates. But he could not discover it.

"Now I am going to fly away to the warm countries," said the Snow Queen. "I want to go and peep into the black caldrons." She meant the volcanoes Etna and Vesuvius. "I must whiten them a little. It does them good, and the lemons and the grapes too!" And away she flew.

Kay sat quite alone in all those many miles of empty ice halls. He looked at his bits of ice and thought and thought, till something gave way within him. He sat so stiff and immovable that one might have thought he was frozen to death.

Then it was that little Gerda walked into the palace, through the great gates in a biting wind. She said her evening prayer, and the wind dropped as if lulled to sleep, and she walked on into the big empty hall. She saw Kay and knew him at once. She flung her arms round his neck, held him fast, and cried, "Kay, little Kay, have I found you at last?"

But he sat still, rigid and cold.

Then little Gerda shed hot tears. They fell upon his breast and penetrated to his heart. Here they thawed the lump of ice and melted the little bit of the mirror which was in it. He looked at her, and she sang:

"Where roses deck the flowery vale,
There, Infant Jesus, thee we hail!"

Then Kay burst into tears. He cried so much that the grain of glass was washed out of his eye. He knew her and shouted with joy, "Gerda! Dear little Gerda! Where have you been for such a long time? And where have I been?" He looked round and said, "How cold it is here! How empty and vast!"

He kept tight hold of Gerda, who laughed and cried for joy. Their happiness was so heavenly that even the bits of ice danced for joy around them. And when they settled down, there they lay in just the very position the Snow Queen had told Kay he must find out, if he was to become his own master and have the whole world and a new pair of skates.

Gerda kissed his cheeks and they grew rosy. She kissed his eyes and they shone like hers. She kissed his hands and his feet and he became well and strong. The Snow Queen might come home whenever she liked; his order of release was written there in shining letters of ice.

They took hold of each other's hands and wandered out of the big palace. They talked about grandmother and about the roses upon the roof. Wherever they went, the winds lay still and the sun broke through the clouds. When they reached the bush with the red berries, they found the reindeer waiting for them, and he had brought another young reindeer with him whose udders were full. The children drank her warm milk and kissed her on the mouth. Then they carried Kay and Gerda, first to the Finn woman, in whose heated hut they warmed themselves and received directions about the homeward journey. Then they went to the Lapp woman. She had made new clothes for them and prepared her sled. Both the reindeer ran by their side to the boundaries of the country. Here the first green buds appeared, and they said "Good-bye" to the reindeer and the Lapp woman. They heard the first little birds twittering and saw the buds in the forest. Out of it came riding a young girl on a beautiful horse which Gerda knew, for it had drawn the golden chariot. She had a scarlet cap on her head and pistols in her belt. It was the little robber girl, who had tired of staying at home. She was riding northwards to see how she liked it before she tried some other part of the world. She knew them again, and Gerda recognized her with delight.

"You are a nice fellow to go tramping off!" she said to little Kay. "I should like to know if you deserve to have somebody running to the end of the world for your sake."

But Gerda patted her cheek and asked about the Prince and Princess.

"They are traveling in foreign countries," said the robber girl.

"But the crow?" asked Gerda.

"Oh, the crow is dead," she answered. "The tame sweetheart is a widow and goes about with a bit of black wool tied round her leg. She pities herself bitterly, but it's all nonsense! But tell me how you got on yourself, and where you found him."

Gerda and Kay both told her all about it.

"Snip, snap, snur-r! It's all right at last then!" she said. And she took hold of their hands and promised that if she ever passed through their town she would pay them a visit. Then she rode off into the wide world. But Kay and Gerda walked on, hand in hand, and wherever they went they found the most delightful spring and blooming flowers. Soon they recognized the big town where they lived, with its tall towers in which the bells still rang their merry peals. They went straight on to grandmother's door, up the stairs, and into her room.

Everything was just as they had left it. The old clock ticked in the corner, and the hands pointed to the time. As they went through the door into the room, they perceived that they were grown up. The roses clustered around the open window, and there stood their two little chairs. Kay and Gerda sat down upon them, still holding each other by the hand. All the cold empty grandeur of the Snow Queen's palace had passed from their memory like a bad dream. Grandmother sat in God's warm sunshine reading from her Bible.

"Without ye become as little children ye cannot enter into the Kingdom of Heaven."

Kay and Gerda looked into each other's eyes, and then all at once the meaning of the old hymn came to them:

"Where roses deck the flowery vale,
There, Infant Jesus, thee we hail!"

And there they both sat, grown up and yet children, children at heart. And it was summer—warm, beautiful summer.

Edward Everett Hale (1822–1909)

Grandnephew of Nathan Hale, the famous Revolutionary War patriot, Edward Everett Hale was born in Boston, Massachusetts. Beginning school at the age of two, he entered Harvard when thirteen and graduated second in his class. Ordained as a Unitarian minister in 1846, he spent most of his life as a practicing pastor: first at the Church of Unity in Worcester, Massachusetts (1846–1856), then the South Congregational Church in Boston (1846–1901), and finally as chaplain of the United States Senate (1903 until 1909).

Yet religion was only one of his many interests. He used the pulpit and his considerable skills as an orator to campaign for abolition and social reform. Indeed, he was a leader of the "Social Gospel" viewpoint in American theology—arguing for world peace, better living conditions for the working class, and other liberal causes.

Most of his family was literarily inclined, so he began writing early, as a legislative reporter for the *Boston Daily Advertiser* (which his father owned and edited), then as editor and critic, and finally as prolific author of approximately seventy books—ranging from studies of Indian languages to fantasy and science fiction.

His fiction was noted for its verbal cleverness, smoothness, and didactic nature, for he was more concerned with selling ideas than in creating great literature. In fact, one of his fantasy novelettes, about the ethical influence of a dead man's ghost on his friends ("Ten Times One is Ten," 1869), was responsible for the creation of a widespread "Lend a Hand" movement.

Described as "a man of large, angular frame and well-lined features, with a generous heart, a keen and ingenious mind, and a judicious sense of humor,'' he is best remembered today for his classic novella, ''The Man Without a Country'' (1863). It is a story in which Philip Nolan, at his trial, declares his hatred for the United States and is subsequently sentenced to a life of banishment.

But science fiction fans remember Hale as the first to propose building and launching an artificial satellite (''The Brick Moon,'' 1869). His justification, which made a great deal of sense at the time, was that a visible body of this nature would enable ships to determine their longitudinal positions more easily.[1]

Hale's other fantastic works include ''Life in the Brick Moon'' (1870), a sequel to the earlier story; *Sybaris* (1869), an ambitious, but ultimately disappointing, utopian novel; and ''The Queen of California'' (1877), an interesting retelling of a fifteenth century Spanish novella which coined the word ''California.'' Almost forgotten, however, is a powerfully written short story, ''Hands Off,'' published anonymously in 1881. The late Anthony Boucher believed it to be the first alternative world story written, suggesting, as it does, what might happen if an important historical event were changed. In it, one of God's agents gives a dead man a chance to build a better world by tinkering with a duplicate Earth. And the results are perhaps best summed up by Hale's own response to a question he was asked while serving as Senate chaplain:

''Dr. Hale do you pray for the Senate?''

''No,'' he said; ''I look at the senators and pray for the people.''

---

[1]Seventy-six years later, in 1945, another science fiction writer, Arthur C. Clarke, would suggest an even better purpose—relaying TV transmissions via a series of stationary satellites, located in fixed orbits 22,000 miles above the equator.

HANDS OFF

I was in another stage of existence. I was free from the limits of Time, and in new relations to Space.

Such is the poverty of the English language that I am obliged to use past tenses in my descriptions. We might have a verb which should have many forms indifferent to time, but we have not. The Pyramid Indians have.

It happened to me to watch, in this condition, the motions of several thousand solar systems all together. It is fascinating to see all parts of all with equal distinctness—all the more when one has been bothered as much as I have been, in my day, with eyepieces and object-glasses, with refraction, with prismatic colors and achromatic contrivances. The luxury of having practically no distance, of dispensing with these cumbrous telescopes, and at the same time of having nothing too small for observation, and dispensing with microscopes, fussy if not cumbrous, can hardly be described in a language as physical or material as ours.

At the moment I describe, I had intentionally limited my observation to some twenty or thirty thousand solar systems, selecting those which had been nearest to me when I was in my schooling on Earth. Nothing can be prettier than to see the movement, in perfectly harmonic relations, of planets around their centers, of satellites around planets, of suns, with their planets and satellites, around their centers, and of these in turn around theirs. And to persons who have loved Earth as much as I have, and who, while at school there, have studied other worlds and stars, then distant, as carefully as I have, nothing, as I say, can be more charming than to see at once all this play and interplay; to see comets passing from system to system, warming themselves now at one white sun, and then at a parti-colored double; to see the people on them changing customs and costumes as they change their light, and to hear their quaint discussions as they justify the new and ridicule the old.

It cost me a little effort to adjust myself to the old points of view. But I had a Mentor so loving and so patient, whose range—oh! it is infinitely before mine; and he knew how well I loved Earth, and if need had been, he would have spent and been spent till he had adjusted me to the dear old point of vision. No need of large effort, though! There it was, just as he told me. I was in the old plane of the old ecliptic. And again I saw my dear old Orion, and the Dipper, and the Pleiades, and Corona, and all the rest of them, just as if I had never seen other figures made from just the same stars when I had other points of view.

But what I am to tell you of is but one thing.

This guardian of mine and I—not bothered by time—were watching the little systems as the dear little worlds flew around so regularly and so prettily. Well, it was as in old days I have taken a little water on the end of a needle, and have placed it in the field of my compound microscope. I suppose, as I said, that just then there were several thousand solar systems in my ken at once—only the words "then," "there," and "once," have but a modified meaning when one is in these relations. I had only to choose the "epoch" which I would see. And of one world and another I had vision equally distinct—nay, of the blush on a girl's cheek in the planet Neptune, when she sat alone in her bower, I had as distinct vision as of the rush of a comet which cut through a dozen systems, and loitered to flirt with a dozen suns.

In the experience which I describe, I had my choice of epochs as of places. I think scholars, or men of scholarly tastes, will not wonder when I say that in looking at our dear old Earth, after amusing myself for an instant with the history of northern America for ten or twenty thousand of its years, I turned to that queer little land, that neck between Asia and Africa and that mysterious corner of Syria which is north of it. Holy Land, men call it, and no wonder. And I think, also, that nobody will be surprised that I chose to take that instant of time when a great caravan of traders was crossing the isthmus—they were already well on the Egyptian side—who had with them a handsome young fellow whom they had bought just above, a day or two before, and were carrying down south to the slave market at On, in Egypt.

This handsome youngster was Yussuf Ben Yacoub, or, as we say,

Joseph, son of Jacob. He was handsome in the very noblest type of Hebrew beauty. He seemed eighteen or nineteen years old: I am not well enough read to know if he were. The time was early morning. I remember even the freshness of the morning atmosphere, and that exquisite pearliness of the sky. I saw every detail, and my heart was in my mouth as I looked on. It had been a hot night, and the sides of the tents were clewed up. This handsome fellow lay, his wrists tied together by a cord of camel's hair which bound him to the arm of a great Arab, who looked as I remember Keokuk of the Sacs and Foxes. Joseph sat up, on the ground, with his hands so close to the other that the cord did not move with his motion. Then with a queer trick, which I did not follow, and a wrench which must have been agony to him, he twisted and changed the form of the knot in the rope. Then, by a dexterous grip between his front teeth, he loosened the hold of the knot. He bit again, again, and again. Hurrah! It is loose, and the boy is free from that snoring hulk by his side. An instant more, and he is out from the tent; he threads his way daintily down the avenue between the tent ropes: he has come to the wady that stretches dry along the west flank of the encampment. Five hundred yards more will take him to the other side of the Cheril-el-bar (the wall of rock which runs down toward the west from the mountains), and he will be free. At this moment two nasty little dogs from the outlying tent of the caravan—what is known among the Arabs as the tent of the warden of the route—sprang after him, snarling and yelling.

The brave boy turned, and, as if he had David's own blood in his veins, and with it the precision of David's eye, he threw a heavy stone back on the headmost cur so skillfully that it struck his spine, and silenced him forever, as a bullet might have done. The other cur, frightened, stood still and barked worse than ever.

I could not bear it. I had only to crush that yelping cur, and the boy Joseph would be free, and in eight-and-forty hours would be in his father's arms. His brothers would be saved from remorse, and the world—

And the world—?

I stretched out my finger unseen over the dog, when my Guardian, who watched all this as carefully as I did, said: "No. They are all conscious and all free. They are His children just as we are. You and I must not interfere unless we know what we are doing. Come here, and I can show you."

He turned me quite around into the region which the astronomers call the starless region, and there showed me another series—oh! an immense and utterly unaccountable series—of systems, which at the moment seemed just like what we had been watching.

"But they are not the same," said my Guardian, hastily. "You will see they are not the same. Indeed, I do not know myself what these are for," he said, "unless—I think sometimes they are for you and me to learn from. He is so kind. And I never asked. I do not know."

All this time he was looking around among the systems for something, and at last he found it. He pointed it out, and I saw a system just like our dear old system, and a world just like our dear old world. The same ear-shaped South America, the same leg-of-mutton-shaped Africa, the same fiddle-shaped Mediterranean Sea, the same boot for Italy and the same football for Sicily. They were all there. "Now," he said, "here you may try experiments. This is quite a fresh one; no one has touched it. Only these here are not His children—these are only creatures, you know. These are not conscious, though they seem so. You will not hurt them whatever you do; nay, they are not free. Try your dead dog here and see what will happen."

Sure enough there was the gray of the beautiful morning; there was the old hulk of an Arab snoring in his tent; there was the handsome boy in the dry valley, or wady; there was the dead dog—all just as it happened—and there was the other dog snarling and yelping. I just brushed him down, as I have often wiped a green louse off a rosebush; all was silent again, and the boy Joseph turned and ran. The old hulk of an Arab never waked. The master of the caravan did not so much as turn in his bed. The boy passed the corner of the Cheril-el-bar carefully, just looked behind to be sure he was not followed, and then, with the speed of an antelope, ran, and ran, and ran. He need not have run. It was two hours before any one moved in the Midianite camp. Then there was a little alarm. The dead dogs were found, and there was a general ejaculation, which showed that the Midianites of those days were as great fatalists as the Arabs of this. But nobody thought of stopping a minute for one slave more or less. The lazy snorer who had let him go was well lashed for his laziness. And the caravan moved on.

And Joseph? After an hour's running, he came to water, and bathed. Now he dared open his bag and eat a bit of black bread. He kept his eyes all around him, he ran no more, but walked, with that firm, assured step of a frontiersman or skillful hunter. That night he slept between two rocks under a terebinth tree, where even a hawk would not have seen him. The next day he treaded the paths along the hillside, as if he had the eyes of a lynx and the feet of a goat. Toward night he approached a camp, evidently of a sheik of distinction. None of the squalidness here of those trading wanderers, the Midianite children of the desert! Everything here showed Eastern luxury even, and a certain permanency. But one could hear lamentation, and on drawing near one could see whence it came. A long procession of women were beating their arms, striking the most mournful chords, and singing—or, if you please, screaming—in strains of the most heartrending agony. Leah, Bilhah, and Zilpah led the train three times around old Jacob's tent. There, as before, the curtains were drawn aside, and I could see the old man crouched upon the ground, and the splendid cloak or shawl, where even great black stains of blood did not hide the gorgeousness of the parti-colored knitting, hung before him on the tent pole as if he could not bear to have it put away.

Joseph sprang lightly into the tent. "My father, I am here!"

Oh, what a scream of delight! What ejaculations! What praise to God! What questions and what answers! The weird procession of women heard the cry, and Leah, Bilhah, and Zilpah came rushing into the greeting. A moment more, and Judah from his tent, and Reuben from his, headed the line of the false brethren. Joseph turned and clasped Judah's hand. I heard him whisper: "Not a word. The old man knows nothing. Nor need he."

The old man sent out and killed a fatted calf. They ate and drank, and were merry; and for once I felt as if I had not lived in vain.

And this feeling lasted—yes, for some years of their life. True, as I said, they were years which passed in no time. I looked on, and enjoyed them with just that luxury with which you linger over the charming last page of a novel, where everything is spring, and sunshine, and honey, and happiness. And there was the comfortable feeling that this was my work. How clever of me to have mashed that dog! And he was an ugly brute, too! Nobody could have loved him. Yes; though all this passed in no time, still I had one good comfortable thrill of self-satisfaction. But then things began to darken, and one began to wonder.

Jacob was growing very old. I could see that, from the way he kept in the tents while the others went about their affairs. And then, summer after summer, I saw the wheat blight, and a sort of blast come over the olives; there seemed to be a kind of murrain among the cattle, and no end of trouble among the sheep and goats. I could see the anxious looks of the twelve brothers, and their talk was gloomy enough, too. Great herds of camels dying down to one or two mangy, good-for-nothing skeletons; shepherds coming back from the lake country driving three or four wretched sheep, and reporting that these were all that were left from three or four thousand! Things began to grow doubtful, even in the home camp. The women were crying, and the brothers at last held a great council of the head shepherds, and camel drivers, and masters of horse, to know what should be done for forage for the beasts, and even for food at home.

I had succeeded so well with the dog that I was tempted to cry out, in my best Chaldee: "Egypt! Why don't you go down to Egypt? There is plenty of corn there." But first I looked at Egypt, and found things were worse there than they were around Jacob's tents. The inundation had failed there for year after year. They had tried some wretched irrigation, but it was like feeding the hordes of Egypt on peppergrass and radishes to rely on these little watered gardens. "But the granaries," I said, "where are the granaries?" Granaries? There were no granaries. That was but a dull set who were in the Egyptian government then. They had had good crops year in and year out, for a great many years, too. But they had run for luck, as I have known other nations to do. Why, I could see where they had fairly burned the corn of one year to make room for the fresher harvest of the next. There had been no Yussuf Ben Yacoub in the ministry to direct the storing of the harvest in those years of plenty. The man they had at the head was a dreamy dilettante, who was engaged in restoring some old carvings of some two-hundred-and-fifty years before.

And, in short, the fellaheen and the people of higher caste in Egypt were all starving to death. That was, as I began to think, a little uncomfortably, what I had brought about when I put my finger on that ugly, howling yellow dog of the sleepy Midianite sentinel.

Well, it is a long story, and not a pleasant one; though, as I have said, as I and my companion watched it, it all went by in no time—I might even say in less than no time. All the glory and comfort of the encampments of Jacob's sons vanished. All became a mere hand-to-hand fight with famine. Instead of a set of cheerful, rich, prosperous chiefs of the pasture country, with thousands of retainers, and no end of camels, horses, cattle and sheep, here were a few gaunt, half-starved wanderers, living on such game as they could kill on a lucky hunt, or sometimes reduced to locusts, or to the honey from the trees. What grieved me more was to see the good fellows snapped up, one after another, by the beastly garrisons of the Canaanite cities.

Heaven knows where these devils came from, or how they roughed it through the famine. But here they were, in their fortresses, living, as I say, like devils, with the origins of customs so beastly that I will not stain this paper with them. Here they were, and here they got ahead. I remember how disgusted I was when I saw them go down in ships into the Nile country, and clean out, root and branch, the Egyptians who were left after the famine—just as I have seen a swarm of rosebugs settle on a rose garden and clean it out in an hour or two. There was the end of Egypt. Then I watched, with an interest not cheerful now, Dido's colony as she sailed with an immense crew of these Moloch-worshipping Canaanites, and their beastly rites and customs, and planted Carthage. It was interesting to see poor Aeneas dodging about on the Mediterranean, while Dido and her set were faring so well—or well they thought it—on the African shore.

I will own I was rather anxious now. Not but what there was something—and a great gaudy city it was—on the slopes of Mount Moriah and Zion. But it made me sick to see its worship, and I stopped my ears with my fingers rather than hear thc songs. O God! the yells of those poor little children as they burned them to death in Hinnom, a hundred at a time, their own mothers dancing and howling by the fires! I cannot speak of it to this day. I dared not look there long. But it was no better anywhere else. I tried Greece; but I could make nothing of Greece. When I looked for the arrival of Danaus with his Egyptian arts and learning—Toonh, I think they called him in Egypt—why there was no Toonh and no Egyptian arts, because these Canaanite brutes had cleared out Egypt. The Pelasgians were in Greece, and in Greece they stayed. They built great walls—I did not see for what—but they lived in cabins at which a respectable Apache would turn up his nose; and century after century they built the same huts, and lived in them. As for manners, they had none, and their customs were very filthy. When it came time for Cadmus, there was no chance for Cadmus. Perhaps he came, perhaps he did not. All I know is that the Molochite invasion of Egypt had swept all alphabet and letters out of being, and that, if Cadmus came, he was rather more low-lived than the Pelasgians among whom he landed. Really, all Greece was such a mess that I hated to follow along its crass stupidity, and the savage raids which the inhabitants of one valley made upon another. This was what I had done for them when I mashed that little yellow dog so easily.

Aeneas and his set seemed to prosper better at first. I could see his ships, with the green leaves still growing on the top-masts, hurry out from the port of Dido. I saw poor Palinurus tumble over. Yes, indeed, queer enough it was to have the old half-forgotten lines of Dryden—whom I know a great deal better than Virgil, more shame to me—come back as poor Nisus pleaded for his friend, as poor Camilla bled to death, and as Turnus did his best for nothing. Yes, I watched Romulus and the rest of them, just as it was in Harry and Lucy's little inch-square history. I took great comfort in Brutus; I shut my eyes when the noble lady Lucretia stabbed herself; and the quick-moving stereoscope—for I really began to feel that it was one—became more and more fascinating, till we got to the Second Punic War.

Then it seemed to me as if that cursed yellow dog came to the front again. Not that I saw him, of course. Not him! His bones and skin had been gnawed by jackals a thousand years before. But the evil that dogs do lives after them; and when I saw the anxiety on Scipio's face—they did not call him Africanus—when I looked in on little private conferences of manly Roman gentlemen, and heard them count up their waning resources, and match them against the overwhelming force of Carthage, I tell you I felt badly. You see, Carthage was simply an outpost of all that Molochite crew of the East. In the history I am used to, the Levant of that time was divided between Egypt and Greece, and what there was left of Alexander's empire. But in this yellow-dog system, for which I was responsible, it was all one brutal race of Molochism, except that Pelasgian business I told you of in Greece, which was no more to be counted in the balance of power than the Digger Indians are counted in the balance today. This was what made poor Scipio and the rest of them so downhearted. And well it might. I, who saw the whole, as you may say, together, only, as I have explained, it did not mix itself up—I could see Hannibal and his following of all the Mediterranean powers except Italy, come down on the Romans and crush them as easily as I crushed the cur. No, not as easily as that, for they fought like fury. Men fought and women fought, boys and girls fought. They dashed into the harbor of Carthage once with fire ships, and burned the fleet. But it was no good: army after army was beaten; fleet after fleet was sunk by the great Carthaginian triremes. Ah me! I remember one had the cordage of the admiral's ship made from the hair of the Roman matrons. But it was all one. If it had been Manila hemp or wire rope, the ship would not have stood when that brutal Sidonian admiral rammed at her with his hundred oarsmen. That battle was the end of Rome. The brutes burned it first. They tumbled down the very walls of the temples. What they could plough, they ploughed. They dragged the boys and girls into slavery, and that was the end. All the rest were dead on the field of battle, or were sunk in the sea.

And so Molochism reigned century after century. Just that, one century after another century: two centuries in all. What a reign it was! Lust, brutality, terror, cruelty, carnage, famine, agony, horror. If I do not say death, it is because death was a blessing in contrast to such lives. For now that there was nobody to fight who had an idea above the Earth and dead things, these swords that were so sharp had to turn against each other. No Israel to crush, no Egypt, no Iran, no Greece, no Rome. Moloch and Canaan turned on themselves and fought Canaan and Moloch. Do not ask me to tell the story! Where beast meets beast, there is no story to tell worth your hearing or my telling. Brute rage gives you nothing to describe. They poisoned, they starved, they burned; they scourged and flayed and crucified; they invented forms of horror for which our imagination, thank God, has no picture, and our languages no name. And, all this time, lust, and every form of pestilence and disease which depends on lust, raged as fire rages when it has broken bounds. It was seldom and more seldom that children were born; nay, when they were born, they seemed only half alive. And those who grew to manhood and womanhood—only it is desecration to use those names—transmitted such untamed beastliness to those who came after!

One hundred years, as I said. Fewer and fewer of these wretches were left in the world. I could see fields grow up to jungles and to forests. A fire wasted Carthage, and another swept away On, and another finished Sidon, and there was neither heart nor art to rebuild them. Then another hundred years dragged by, with worse horrors, if it were possible, and more. The stream of the world's life began to run in drops, now big drops, with a noisy gurgle; black drops, too, or bloody red. Fewer men, and still fewer women, and all mad with beastly rage. Every man's hand was against his brother, as if this were a world of Cains. All this had come to them because they did not like to retain God in their knowledge.

No, I will not describe it. You do not ask me to. And if you asked, I would say "No." Let me come to the end.

The two centuries had gone. There was but a handful of these furies left. Then the last generation came—and for thirty years more of murder and fight it ground along. At the last, how strange it seemed to me, all that are left, in two unequal parties, each of which had its banner still for fight, and a sort of uniform as if they were armies, but only four on one side and nine on the other, met, as if the world were not wide enough for both, and met in that very Syria where I had helped Joseph, son of Jacob, to fling his arms round his father's neck again.

Nor, indeed, was it very far from that spot. It was close to the wreck and ruin of the Jebusite city which had been one of the strongholds last destroyed of one of these clans. That city was burned, but I saw that the ruins were smoking. Just outside there was an open space. I wonder if it had a weird, deadly look, or whether the horror of the day made me think so? I remember a great rock like a man's skull that peered out from the gray, dry ground. Around that rock these wretches fought, four to nine, hiding behind it, on one side or the other, on that April day, under that black sky.

One is down! Two of the other party are kneeling on him, to take the last breath of life from him. With a yell of rage three or four of his party, dashing their shields on the heads of the two, spring upon them; and I can see one wave his battle-axe above his head, when—

Did the metal attract the spark? A crash! a blaze which dazzled my eyes, and when I opened them the last of these human brutes lay stark dead on the one side and on the other of the grim rock of Calvary!

Not a man or a woman, nor a boy or a girl, not a single soul left in that world!

"Do not be disturbed," said my Mentor. "You yourself have done nothing."

"Nothing!" I groaned. "I have ruined a world in my rashness."

"Nothing," he repeated. "Remember what I told you: these are—what shall I say?—shadows, shadowy forms. They are not His children. They are only forms which act as if they were—that you and I may see and learn, perhaps begin to understand—only it passes knowledge."

As he spoke, I remember that I moaned and struggled with him like a crying child. I was all overwhelmed by the sight of the mischief I had done. I would not be comforted.

"Listen to me," he said again. "You have only done, or wanted to do, what we all try for at first. You wanted to save your poor Joseph. What wonder?"

"Of course I did," sobbed I. "Could I have thought? Should you have thought?"

"No," said he, with that royal smile of his—"no. Once I should not have thought it—I could not have thought it—till I, too, tried my experiments." And he paused.

Perhaps he was thinking what his experiments also were.

Then he began again, and the royal smile had hardly faded away: "Let me show you. Or let me try. You wanted to save your poor Joseph—all sole alone."

"Yes," I said. "Why should I not want to?"

"Because he was not alone; could not be alone. None of them was alone; none of them could be alone. Why, you know yourself that not a raindrop in that shower yonder but balances against a dust-grain on the other side of creation. How could Joseph live or die alone? How could that brute he was chained to live or die alone? None of them is alone. None of us is alone. He is not alone. Even He is in us, and we are in Him. But the way with men—and it is not so long, dear friend, since you were a man—the way with men is to try what you tried. I never yet knew a man—and how many have I known, thank God!—I never yet knew a man but he wanted to single out some one Joseph to help—as if the rest were nothing, or as if our Father had no plans."

"I shall never try that again!" sobbed I, after a long pause.

"Never," said he, "is a long word. You will learn not to say 'never.' But I'll tell you what you will do. When you get a glimpse of the life in common, when you find out what is the drift—shall I say of the game, or shall I say of the law?—in which they all and we all, He in us and we in Him, are living, then, oh, it is such fun to strike in and live for all!"

He paused a minute, and then he went on, hesitating at first, as if he feared to pain me even more, but resolutely afterward, as if this must be said.

"Another thing I notice in most men, though not in all, is this: they do not seem at first to understand that the Idea is the whole. Abraham had left Ur rather than have any part with those smoke-and-dust men—Nature-worshippers I think they call them. How was it that you did not see that Joseph was going down to Egypt with the Idea? He could take what they did not have there. And as you saw, in the other place, without it, why, your world died."

Then he turned around and left that horrid world of phantoms, to go back to our own dear real world. And this time I looked on today. How bright it seemed, and how comforting to me to think that I had never touched the yellow dog, and that he came to his death in his own way!

I saw some things I liked, and some I disliked. It happened that I was looking at Zululand, when poor Prince Lulu's foot slipped at the saddle-flap. I saw the assegai that stabbed him. Had I been a trooper at his side, by his side I would have died too. But no, I was not at his side. And I remembered Joseph, and I said, "From what I call evil, He educes good."

Count Leo Tolstoy (1828–1910)

Author of what many consider the world's greatest novel—*War and Peace* (1865–1869)—Count Leo Tolstoy was born on his family's estate, about a hundred miles south of Moscow. Both parents died while he was young, but he and his brothers enjoyed a happy childhood with their aunts. After spending three years at Kazan University, Tolstoy withdrew and drifted into Moscow's social whirl. There he discovered the dark, or licentious, side of his nature which he struggled against throughout most of his life.

Finally, in 1851, disgusted with himself, Tolstoy left to join his soldier brother Nikolay who was fighting in the Caucasus. His first book, *Childhood*, a lyrical account of his own youth, was published the next year. However, his first major literary successes were the *Sevastopol Sketches* (1855), a series of descriptions about his experiences in the Crimean War.

In 1856 he left the army, and after some travel, started a school for peasant children on his estate at Yasnaya Polyana. Yet he turned away from social causes after marrying (1862) to devote the next fifteen years to family life, writing, and managing his estate. Both *War and Peace* and *Anna Karenina* (1875–1877) were written during this period, but the basic pessimism of the latter reflected Tolstoy's increasing doubts about the type of life he was leading.

Searching for answers, he studied the Bible and eventually worked out his own interpretation of its meaning. Christ had good ideas, but was not the son of God; there was no afterlife; the church should have no authority; and each man must serve God.

As an artist, therefore, he felt it was his duty to help others find the truth. So he devoted a good portion of the rest of his life to churning out reams of didactic essays and short stories. As opposed to his earlier fiction, these later works were simply constructed and devoid of much detail. Still many of them, including our selection for this volume (''How Much Land Does a Man Need?''), are considered ''little masterpieces'' by many critics. And the technique of using fantasy to help make his point (in this case a warning against greed) was one that Tolstoy increasingly utilized in later life (see *Fables and Fairy Tales*, 1962).

Unfortunately, however, many people did not appreciate Tolstoy's messages. In 1901, the Russian Orthodox Church excommunicated him. The government, though taking no direct action, did aid the church in an effort to discourage others from attempting to enact Tolstoy's secular ideas, which included eliminating government, abolishing private property, and practicing passive resistance. Even his wife and family became estranged. They were embarrassed by his working in the fields and wearing peasant garb, annoyed by his followers who flocked around, and outraged by his attempts to give away the copyrights that brought in the money necessary to support them.

Finally, at the age of eighty-two, to search for a peaceful refuge, he ran away from home, dying from pneumonia in an obscure railway station in Ryazan Province.

HOW MUCH LAND DOES A MAN NEED?

An elder sister came to visit her younger sister in the country. The elder was married to a tradesman in town, the younger to a peasant in the village. As the sisters sat over their tea talking, the elder began to boast of the advantages of town life: saying how comfortably they lived there, how well they dressed, what fine clothes her children wore, what good things they ate and drank, and how she went to the theater, promenades, and entertainments.

The younger sister was piqued, and in turn disparaged the life of a tradesman, and stood up for that of a peasant.

"I would not change my way of life for yours," said she. "We may live roughly, but at least we are free from anxiety. You live in better style than we do, but though you often earn more than you need, you're very likely to lose all you have. We know the proverb, 'Loss and gain are brothers twain.' It often happens that people who are wealthy one day are begging their bread the next. Our way is safer. Though a peasant's life is not a fat one, it is long. We shall never grow rich, but we shall always have enough to eat."

The elder sister said sneeringly:

"Enough? Yes, if you like to share with the pigs and the calves! What do you know of elegance or manners! However much your good man may slave, you will die as you are living—on a dung heap—and your children the same."

"Well, what of that?" replied the younger. "Of course our work is rough and coarse. But, on the other hand, it is sure; and we need not bow to anyone. But you, in your towns, are surrounded by temptations; today all may be right, but tomorrow the Evil One may tempt your husband with cards, wine, or women, and all will go to ruin. Don't such things happen often enough?''

Pahóm, the master of the house, was lying on the top of the oven, and he listened to the women's chatter.

''It is perfectly true,'' thought he. ''Busy as we are from childhood tilling mother earth, we peasants have no time to let any nonsense settle in our heads. Our only trouble is that we haven't land enough. If I had plenty of land, I shouldn't fear the Devil himself!''

The women finished their tea, chatted a while about dress, and then cleared away the tea things and lay down to sleep.

But the Devil had been sitting behind the oven, and had heard all that had been said. He was pleased that the peasant's wife had led her husband into boasting, and that he had said that if he had plenty of land he would not fear the Devil himself.

''All right,'' thought the Devil. ''We will have a tussle. I'll give you land enough; and by means of that land I will get you into my power.''

II

Close to the village there lived a lady, a small landowner who had an estate of about three hundred acres or 120 *desyatins*. The *desyatina* is properly 2.7 acres; but in this story round numbers are used. She had always lived on good terms with the peasants until she engaged as her steward an old soldier, who took to burdening the people with fines. However careful Pahóm tried to be, it happened again and again that now a horse of his got among the lady's oats, now a cow strayed into her garden, now his calves found their way into her meadows—and he always had to pay a fine.

Pahóm paid up, but grumbled, and, going home in a temper, was rough with his family. All through that summer Pahóm had much trouble because of this steward; and he was even glad when winter came and the cattle had to be stabled. Though he grudged the fodder when they could no longer graze on the pasture land, at least he was free from anxiety about them.

In the winter the news got about that the lady was going to sell her land and that the keeper of the inn on the high road was bargaining for it. When the peasants heard this they were very much alarmed.

"Well," thought they, "if the innkeeper gets the land, he will worry us with fines worse than the lady's steward. We all depend on that estate."

So the peasants went on behalf of their Commune, and asked the lady not to sell the land to the innkeeper, offering her a better price for it themselves. The lady agreed to let them have it. Then the peasants tried to arrange for the Commune to buy the whole estate, so that it might be held by them all in common. They met twice to discuss it, but could not settle the matter; the Evil One sowed discord among them and they could not agree. So they decided to buy the land individually, each according to his means; and the lady agreed to this plan as she had to the other.

Presently Pahóm heard that a neighbor of his was buying fifty acres, and that the lady had consented to accept one half in cash and to wait a year for the other half. Pahóm felt envious.

"Look at that," thought he, "the land is all being sold, and I'll get none of it." So he spoke to his wife.

"Other people are buying," said he, "and we must also buy twenty acres or so. Life is becoming impossible. That steward is simply crushing us with his fines."

So they put their heads together and considered how they could manage to buy it. They had one hundred rubles laid by. They sold a colt and one half of their bees; hired out one of their sons as a laborer, and took his wages in advance; borrowed the rest from a brother-in-law, and so scraped together half the purchase money.

Having done this, Pahóm chose a farm of forty acres, some of it wooded, and went to the lady to bargain for it. They came to an agreement, and he shook hands with her upon it and paid her a deposit in advance. Then they went to town and signed the deeds; he paying half the price down, and undertaking to pay the remainder within two years.

So now Pahóm had land of his own. He borrowed seed, and sowed it on the land he had bought. The harvest was a good one, and within a year he had managed to pay off his debts both to the lady and to his brother-in-law. So he became a landowner, ploughing and sowing his own land, making hay on his own land, cutting his own trees, and feeding his cattle on his own pasture. When he went out to plow his fields, or to look at his growing corn, or at his grassmeadows, his heart would fill with joy. The grass that grew and the flowers that bloomed there seemed to him unlike any that grew elsewhere. Formerly, when he had passed by that land, it had appeared the same as any other land, but now it seemed quite different.

III

So Pahóm was well-contented, and everything would have been right if the neighboring peasants would only not have trespassed on his corn-fields and meadows. He appealed to them most civilly, but they still went on: now the Communal herdsmen would let the village cows stray into his meadows; then horses from the night pasture would get among his corn. Pahóm turned them out again and again, and forgave their owners, and for a long time he forbore to prosecute anyone. But at last he lost patience and complained to the District Court. He knew it was the peasants' want of land, and no evil intent on their part, that caused the trouble, but he thought:

"I can't go on overlooking it, or they will destroy all I have. They must be taught a lesson."

So he had them up, gave them one lesson, and then another, and two or three of the peasants were fined. After a time Pahóm's neighbors began to bear him a grudge for this, and would now and then let their cattle on to his land on purpose. One peasant even got into Pahóm's wood at night and cut down five young lime trees for their bark. Pahóm, passing through the wood one day, noticed something white. He came nearer and saw the stripped trunks lying on the ground, and close by stood the stumps where the trees had been. Pahóm was furious.

"If he'd only cut one here and there it would have been bad enough," thought Pahóm, "but the rascal has actually cut down a whole clump. If I could only find out who did this, I would pay him out."

He racked his brains as to who it could be. Finally he decided: "It must be Simon—no one else could have done it." So he went to Simon's homestead to have a look around, but he found nothing, and only had an angry scene. However, he now felt more certain than ever that Simon had done it, and he lodged a complaint. Simon was summoned. The case was tried, and re-tried, and at the end of it all Simon was acquitted, there being no evidence against him. Pahóm felt still more aggrieved, and let his anger loose upon the Elder and the Judges.

"You let thieves grease your palms," said he. "If you were honest folk yourselves you would not let a thief go free."

So Pahóm quarrelled with the judges and with his neighbors. Threats to burn his building began to be uttered. So though Pahóm had more land, his place in the Commune was much worse than before.

About this time a rumor got about that many people were moving to new parts.

"There's no need for me to leave my land," thought Pahóm. "But some of the others might leave our village and then there would be more room for us. I would take over their land myself and make my estate a bit bigger. I could then live more at ease. As it is, I'm still too cramped to be comfortable."

One day Pahóm was sitting at home, when a peasant, passing through the village, happened to call in. He was allowed to stay the night, and supper was given him. Pahóm had a talk with this peasant and asked him where he came from. The stranger answered that he came from beyond the Volga, where he had been working. One word led to another, and the man went on to say that many people were settling in those parts. He told how some people from his village had settled there. They had joined the Commune there and had had twenty-five acres per man granted them. The land was so good, he said, that the rye sown on it grew as high as a horse, and so thick that five cuts of a sickle made a sheaf. One peasant, he said, had brought nothing with him but his bare hands, and now he had six horses and two cows of his own.

Pahóm's heart kindled with desire. He thought:

"Why should I suffer in this narrow hole, if one can live so well elsewhere? I will sell my land and my homestead here, and with the money I will start afresh over there and get everything new. In this crowded place one is always having trouble. But I must first go and find out all about it myself."

Toward summer he got ready and started. He went down the Volga on a steamer to Samára, then walked another three hundred miles on foot, and at last reached the place. It was just as the stranger had said. The peasants had plenty of land: every man had twenty-five acres of Communal land given him for his use, and anyone who had money could buy, besides, at a two shillings an acre (three rubles per *desyatina*) as much good freehold land as he wanted.

Having found out all he wished to know, Pahóm returned home as autumn came on, and began selling off his belongings. He sold his land at a profit, sold his homestead and all his cattle, and withdrew from membership of the Commune. He only waited till the spring, and then started with his family for the new settlement.

IV

As soon as Pahóm and his family arrived at their new abode, he applied for admission into the Commune of a large village. He stood treat to the Elders and obtained the necessary documents. Five shares of Communal land were given him for his own and his sons' use: that is to say—125 acres (not all together, but in different fields) besides the use of the Communal pasture. Pahóm put up the buildings he needed and bought cattle. Of the Communal land alone he had three times as much as at his former home, and the land was good corn land. He was ten times better off than he had been. He had plenty of arable land and pasturage, and could keep as many head of cattle as he liked.

At first, in the bustle of building and settling down, Pahóm was pleased with it all, but when he got used to it he began to think that even here he had not enough land. The first year he sowed wheat on his share of the Communal land and had a good crop. He wanted to go on sowing wheat, but had not enough Communal land for the purpose, and what he had already used was not available; for in those parts wheat is sown only on virgin soil or on fallow land. It is sown for one or two years, and then the land lies fallow till it is again overgrown with prairie grass. There were many who wanted such land, and there was not enough for all; so that people quarreled about it. Those who were better off wanted it for growing wheat, and those who were poor wanted it to let to dealers, so that they might raise money to pay their taxes. Pahóm wanted to sow more wheat, so he rented land from a dealer for a year. He sowed much wheat and had a fine crop, but the land was too far from the village—the wheat had to be carted more than ten miles. After a time Pahóm noticed that some peasant dealers were living on separate farms and were growing wealthy; and he thought:

"If I were to buy some freehold land and have a homestead on it, it would be a different thing altogether. Then it would all be nice and compact."

The question of buying freehold land recurred to him again and again.

He went on in the same way for three years, renting land and sowing wheat. The seasons turned out well and the crops were good, so that he began to lay money by. He might have gone on living contentedly, but he grew tired of having to rent other people's land every year, and having to scramble for it. Wherever there was good land to be had, the peasants would rush for it and it was taken up at once, so that unless you were sharp about it you got none. It happened in the third year that he and a dealer together rented a piece of pasture land from some peasants; and they had already ploughed it up, when there was some dispute and the peasants went to law about it, and things fell out so that the labor was all lost.

"If it were my own land," thought Pahóm, "I should be independent, and there would not be all this unpleasantness."

So Pahóm began looking out for land which he could buy; he came across a peasant who had bought thirteen hundred acres, but having got into difficulties was willing to sell again cheap. Pahóm bargained and haggled with him, and at last they settled the price at 1,500 rubles, part in cash and part to be paid later. They had all but clinched the matter when a passing dealer happened to stop at Pahóm's one day to get a feed for his horses. He drank tea with Pahóm, and they had a talk. The dealer said that he was just returning from the land of the Bashkírs, far away, where he had bought thirteen thousand acres of land, all for 1,000 rubles. Pahóm questioned him further, and the tradesman said:

"All one need do is to make friends with the chiefs. I gave away about one hundred rubles worth of dressig gowns and carpets, besides a case of tea, and I gave wine to those who would drink it; and I got the land for less than twopence an acre (five *kopeks* for a *desyatina*)." And he showed Pahóm the title-deeds, saying:

"The land lies near a river, and the whole prairie is virgin soil."

Pahóm plied him with questions, and the tradesman said:

"There is more land there than you could cover if you walked a year, and it all belongs to the Bashkírs. They are as simple as sheep, and land can be got almost for nothing."

"There now," thought Pahóm, "with my one thousand rubles, why should I get only thirteen hundred acres, and saddle myself with a debt besides. If I take it out there, I can get more than ten times as much for the money."

V

Pahóm inquired how to get to the place, and as soon as the tradesman had left him, he prepared to go there himself. He left his wife to look after the homestead, and started on his journey taking his hired man with him. They stopped at a town on their way, and bought a case of tea, some wine, and other presents, as the tradesman had advised. On and on they went until they had gone more than three hundred miles, and on the seventh day they came to a place where the Bashkírs had pitched their tents. It was all just as the tradesman had said. The people lived on the steppes, by a river, in felt-covered tents. They neither tilled the ground nor ate bread. Their cattle and horses grazed in herds on the steppe. The colts were tethered behind the tents, and the mares were driven to them twice a day. The mares were milked, and from the milk kefir was made. It was the women who prepared kefir, and they also made cheese. As far as the men were concerned, drinking kefir and tea, eating mutton, and playing on their pipes was all they cared about. They were all stout and merry, and all the summer long they never thought of doing any work. They were quite ignorant, and knew no Russian, but were good-natured enough.

As soon as they saw Pahóm, they came out of their tents and gathered round their visitor. An interpreter was found, and Pahóm told them he had come about some land. The Bashkírs seemed very glad; they took Pahóm and led him into one of the best tents, where they made him sit on some down cushions placed on a carpet, while they sat round him. They gave him some tea and kefir, and had a sheep killed, and gave him mutton to eat. Pahóm took presents out of his cart and distributed them among the Bashkírs, and divided amongst them the tea. The Bashkírs were delighted. They talked a great deal among themselves, and then told the interpreter to translate.

"They wish to tell you," said the interpreter, "that they like you, and that it is our custom to do all we can to please a guest and to repay him for his gifts. You have given us presents, now tell us which of the things we possess please you best, that we may present them to you."

"What pleases me best here," answered Pahóm, "is your land. Our land is crowded and the soil is exhausted; but you have plenty of land, and it is good land. I never saw the like of it."

The interpreter translated. The Bashkírs talked among themselves for a while. Pahóm could not understand what they were saying, but saw that they were much amused, and that they shouted and laughed. Then they were silent and looked at Pahóm while the interpreter said:

"They wish me to tell you that in return for your presents they will gladly give you as much land as you want. You have only to point it out with your hand and it is yours."

The Bashkírs talked again for a while and began to dispute. Pahóm asked what they were disputing about, and the interpreter told him that some of them thought they ought to ask their Chief about the land and not act in his absence, while others thought there was no need to wait for his return.

VI

While the Bashkírs were disputing, a man in a large fox fur cap appeared on the scene. They all became silent and rose to their feet. The interpreter said, "This is our Chief himself."

Pahóm immediately fetched the best dressing gown and five pounds of tea, and offered these to the Chief. The Chief accepted them, and seated himself in the place of honor. The Bashkírs at once began telling him something. The Chief listened for a while, then made a sign with his head for them to be silent, and addressing himself to Pahóm, said in Russian:

"Well, let it be so. Choose whatever piece of land you like; we have plenty of it."

"How can I take as much as I like?" thought Pahóm. "I must get a deed to make it secure, or else they may say, 'It is yours,' and afterwards may take it away again."

"Thank you for your kind words," he said aloud. "You have much land, and I only want a little. But I should like to be sure which bit is mine. Could it not be measured and made over to me? Life and death are in God's hands. You good people give it to me, but your children might wish to take it away again."

"You are quite right," said the Chief. "We will make it over to you."

"I heard that a dealer had been here," continued Pahóm, "and that you gave him a little land, too, and signed title deeds to that effect. I should like to have it done in the same way."

The Chief understood.

"Yes," replied he, "that can be done quite easily. We have a scribe, and we will go to town with you and have the deed properly sealed."

"And what will be the price?" asked Pahóm.

"Our price is always the same: one thousand rubles a day."

Pahóm did not understand.

"A day? What measure is that? How many acres would that be?"

"We do not know how to reckon it out," said the Chief. "We sell it by the day. As much as you can go round on your feet in a day is yours, and the price is one thousand rubles a day."

Pahóm was surprised.

"But in a day you can get around a large tract of land," he said.

The Chief laughed.

"It will all be yours!" said he. "But there is one condition: If you don't return on the same day to the spot whence you started, your money is lost."

"But how am I to mark the way that I have gone?"

"Why, we shall go to any spot you like, and stay there. You must start from that spot and make your round, taking a spade with you. Whereever you think necessary, make a mark. At every turning, dig a hole and pile up the turf; then afterwards we will go round with a plow from hole to hole. You may make as large a circuit as you please, but before the sun sets you must return to the place you started from. All the land you cover will be yours."

Pahóm was delighted. It was decided to start early next morning. They talked a while, and after drinking some more kefir and eating some more mutton, they had tea again, and then the night came on. They gave Pahom a feather bed to sleep on, and the Bashkirs dispersed for the night, promising to assemble the next morning at daybreak and ride out before sunrise to the appointed spot.

VII

Pahóm lay on the feather bed, but could not sleep. He kept thinking about the land.

"What a large tract I'll mark off!" thought he. "I can easily do thirty-five miles in a day. The days are long now, and within a circuit of thirty-five miles what a lot of land there will be! I'll sell the poorer land, or let it to peasants, but I'll pick out the best and farm it. I will buy two ox teams and hire two more laborers. About a hundred and fifty acres shall be plough land, and I will pasture cattle on the rest.''

Pahóm lay awake all night, and dozed off only just before dawn. Hardly were his eyes closed when he had a dream. He thought he was lying in that same tent and heard somebody chuckling outside. He wondered who it could be, and rose and went out, and he saw the Bashkír Chief sitting in front of the tent holding his sides and rolling about with laughter. Going nearer to the Chief, Pahóm asked: ''What are you laughing at?'' But he saw that it was no longer the Chief, but the dealer who had recently stopped at his house and had told him about the land. Just as Pahóm was going to ask, ''Have you been here long?'' he saw that it was not the dealer, but the peasant who had come up from the Volga, long ago, to Pahóm's old home. Then he saw that it was not the peasant either, but the Devil himself with hoofs and horns, sitting there and chuckling, and before him lay a man barefoot, prostrate on the ground, with only trousers and a shirt on. And Pahóm dreamt that he looked more attentively to see what sort of a man it was that was lying there, and he saw that the man was dead, and that it was himself! He awoke horror struck.

''What things one does dream,'' thought he.

Looking round he saw through the open door that the dawn was breaking.

''It's time to wake them up,'' thought he. ''We ought to be starting.''

He got up, roused his man (who was sleeping in his cart), bade him harness; and went to call the Bashkírs.

''It's time to go to the steppe to measure the land,'' he said.

The Bashkírs rose and assembled, and the Chief came too. Then they began drinking kefir again, and offered Pahóm some tea, but he would not wait.

''If we are to go, let us go. It is high time,'' said he.

VIII

The Bashkírs got ready and they all started: some mounted on horses and some in carts. Pahóm drove in his own small cart with his servant and took a spade with him. When they reached the steppe, the morning red was beginning to kindle. They ascended a hillock (called by the Bashkírs a *shikhan*) and, dismounting from their carts and their horses, gathered in one spot. The Chief came up to Pahóm and stretching out his arm towards the plain:

"See," said he, "all this, as far as your eye can reach, is ours. You may have any part of it you like."

Pahóm's eyes glistened: it was all virgin soil, as flat as the palm of your hand, as black as the seed of a poppy, and in the hollows different kinds of grasses grew breast high.

The Chief took off his fox fur cap, placed it on the ground, and said:

"This will be the mark. Start from here, and return here again. All the land you go round shall be yours."

Pahóm took out his money and put it on the cap. Then he took off his outer coat, remaining in his sleeveless undercoat. He unfastened his girdle and tied it tight below his stomach, put a little bag of bread into the breast of his coat, and tying a flask of water to his girdle, he drew up the tops of his boots, took the spade from his man, and stood ready to start. He considered for some moments which way he had better go—it was tempting everywhere.

"No matter," he concluded, "I'll go towards the rising sun."

He turned his face to the east, stretched himself, and waited for the sun to appear above the rim.

"I must lose no time," he thought, "and it is easier walking while it is still cool."

The sun's rays had hardly flashed above the horizon before Pahóm, carrying the spade over his shoulder, went down into the steppe.

Pahóm started walking neither slowly nor quickly. After having gone a thousand yards he stopped, dug a hole, and placed pieces of turf one on another to make it more visible. Then he went on; and now that he had walked off his stiffness he quickened his pace. After a while he dug another hole.

Pahóm looked back. The hillock could be distinctly seen in the sunlight, with the people on it, and the glittering tyres of the cartwheels. At a rough guess Pahóm concluded that he had walked three miles. It was growing warmer; he took off his undercoat, flung it across his shoulder, and went on again. It had grown quite warm now; he looked at the sun, it was time to think of breakfast.

''The first shift is done, but there are four in a day, and it is too soon yet to turn. But I will just take off my boots,'' said he to himself.

He sat down, took off his boots, stuck them into his girdle, and went on. It was easy walking now.

''I will go on for another three miles,'' thought he, ''and then turn to the left. This spot is so fine that it would be a pity to lose it. The further one goes, the better the land seems.''

He went straight on for a while, and when he looked round, the hillock was scarcely visible and the people on it looked like black ants, and he could just see something glistening there in the sun.

''Ah,'' thought Pahóm, ''I have gone far enough in this direction, it is time to turn. Besides, I am in a regular sweat, and very thirsty.''

He stopped, dug a large hole, and heaped up pieces of turf. Next he untied his flask, had a drink, and then turned sharply to the left. He went on and on; the grass was high, and it was very hot.

Pahóm began to grow tired: he looked at the sun and saw that it was noon.

''Well,'' he thought, ''I must have a rest.''

He sat down, and ate some bread and drank some water; but he did not lie down, thinking that if he did he might fall asleep. After sitting a little while, he went on again. At first he walked easily: the food had strengthened him; but it had become terribly hot and he felt sleepy. Still he went on, thinking: ''An hour to suffer, a lifetime to live.''

He went a long way in this direction also, and was about to turn to the left again, when he perceived a damp hollow: ''It would be a pity to leave that out,'' he thought, ''flax would do well there.'' So he went on past the hollow and dug a hole on the other side of it before he turned the corner. Pahóm looked towards the hillock. The heat made the air hazy: it seemed to be quivering, and through the haze the people on the hillock could scarcely be seen.

''Ah,'' thought Pahóm, ''I have made the sides too long; I must make this one shorter.'' And he went along the third side, stepping faster. He looked at the sun: it was nearly half way to the horizon, and he had not yet done two miles of the third side of the square. He was still ten miles from the goal.

''No,'' he thought, ''though it will make my land lopsided, I must hurry back in a straight line now. I might go too far, and as it is I have a great deal of land.''

So Pahóm hurriedly dug a hole and turned straight towards the hillock.

IX

Pahóm went straight towards the hillock, but he now walked with difficulty. He was done up with the heat, his bare feet were cut and bruised, and his legs began to fail. He longed to rest, but it was impossible if he meant to get back before sunset. The sun waits for no man, and it was sinking lower and lower.

"Oh dear," he thought, "if only I have not blundered trying for too much! What if I am too late?"

He looked towards the hillock and at the sun. He was still far from his goal, and the sun was already near the rim.

Pahóm walked on and on; it was very hard walking, but he went quicker and quicker. He pressed on, but was still far from the place. He began running, threw away his coat, his boots, his flask, and his cap, and kept only the spade which he used as a support.

"What shall I do?" he thought again. "I have grasped too much, and ruined the whole affair. I can't get there before the sun sets."

And this fear made him still more breathless. Pahóm went on running, his soaking shirt and trousers stuck to him, and his mouth was parched. His breast was working like a blacksmith's bellows, his heart was beating like a hammer, and his legs were giving way as if they did not belong to him. Pahóm was seized with terror lest he should die of the strain.

Though afraid of death, he could not stop.

"After having run all that way they will call me a fool if I stop now," thought he. And he ran on and on, and drew near and heard the Bashkírs yelling and shouting to him, and their cries inflamed his heart still more. He gathered his last strength and ran on.

The sun was close to the rim, and cloaked in mist, looked large, and red as blood. Now, yes now, it was about to set! The sun was quite low, but he was also quite near his aim. Pahóm could already see the people on the hillock waving their arms to hurry him up. He could see the fox fur cap on the ground and the money in it, and the Chief sitting on the ground holding his sides. And Pahóm remembered his dream.

"There is plenty of land," thought he, "but will God let me live on it? I have lost my life, I have lost my life! I shall never reach that spot!''

Pahóm looked at the sun, which had reached the earth: one side of it had already disappeared. With all his remaining strength he rushed on, bending his body forward so that his legs could hardly follow fast enough to keep him from falling. Just as he reached the hillock it suddenly grew dark. He looked up—the sun had already set!

He gave a cry: ''All my labor has been in vain,'' thought he, and was about to stop, but he heard the Bashkírs still shouting, and remembered that though to him, from below, the sun seemed to have set, they on the hillock could still see it. He took a long breath and ran up the hillock. It was still light there. He reached the top and saw the cap. Before it sat the Chief laughing and holding his sides. Again Pahóm remembered his dream, and he uttered a cry: his legs gave way beneath him, he fell forward and reached the cap with his hands.

''Ah, that's a fine fellow!'' exclaimed the Chief. ''He has gained much land!''

Pahóm's servant came running up and tried to raise him, but he saw that blood was flowing from his mouth. Pahóm was dead.

The Bashkírs clicked their tongues to show their pity.

His servant picked up the spade and dug a grave long enough for Pahóm to lie in, and buried him in it.

Six feet from his head to his heels was all he needed.

Oscar Wilde (1854–1900)

Born in Dublin, Ireland, the controversial Oscar Wilde was a playwright, poet, fantasist, and wit. He was the second son of a prominent, but morally suspect, eye surgeon and an elephantine, but magnetic, poet. A brilliant scholar, he studied one year at Trinity College, Dublin (1873) and six years at Magdalen College, Oxford (1874–1879). At Oxford, in addition to winning first-class degrees in classical moderations (1876) and *litterae humaniores* (1878), he developed his outrageous (for the times) aesthetic pose so helpful in spreading his fame.

He professed art for art's sake and stocked his centrally located rooms with strange objects of art such as blue china and peacock feathers. He let his hair grow long, carried a single flower, and dressed in silk stockings, knee-breeches, velvet jacket, and flowing bow tie. These tactics guaranteed to, depending upon the viewer, elicit gawks or growls.

After graduation he moved to London (1879), gathering attention by the same approach, then counting on his considerable conversational skills and wit (along with genuine talent) to convert curiosity to friendship and admiration.

While he actually produced very little during the next eight years, he managed to marry a woman of some means and succeeded in his dream of becoming well-known. But in 1887 he assumed the editorship of *Woman's World* and began an eight year run of productivity which saw him produce his fairy tales (see *The Happy Prince, The Selfish Giant, and Other Stories,* 1890), his novel (*The Picture of Dorian Grey,* 1890), his most important essays (*Intentions*, 1891), and his five best plays (of which the first, *Lady Windermere's Fan*, 1892, brought critical recognition and financial success).

Still, these best of times were rapidly becoming the worst of times. Wilde started reassessing his sexual orientation in the mid-1880s, engaging in homosexual alliances and ending up infatuated with young Lord Alfred Douglas, the rather evil son of the Marquis of Queensberry. By the mid-1890s Wilde seemed to lose touch with reality, becoming completely taken in by his own persona. He acted in increasingly outrageous ways, apparently believing society would forgive him any sin. And when the Marquis of Queensberry publicly accused him of sodomy, Wilde was unwisely provoked into suing and then forced into making damaging admissions to the court. Afterwards, he refused to flee the country, thus forcing the government to prosecute him for homosexual offenses. After leaving prison, he emigrated to France. Spiritually and financially broken, he succumbed to cerebral meningitis sometime later.

Today, Wilde's reputation as fantasist exceeds that which he enjoyed during life. The unwarranted condemnation of *The Picture of Dorian Gray* is now recognized as a parochial rejection of theme and contemporary critics, such as Diana Waggoner, believe that at least some of Wilde's fairy tales are among the best ever written.

However, the novelette selected for this volume achieved immediate popularity through its pointed lampooning of nouveau riche Americans. Yet, even now, "The Canterville Ghost" continues to satisfy because of its poignant portrayal of the harried spirit and the plucky young female protagonist.

THE CANTERVILLE GHOST

Chapter 1

*When Mr. Hiram B. Otis, the American Minister, bought Canter-*ville Chase, every one told him he was doing a very foolish thing, as there was no doubt at all that the place was haunted. Indeed, Lord Canterville himself, who was a man of the most punctilious honour, had felt it his duty to mention the fact to Mr. Otis, when they came to discuss terms.

"We have not cared to live in the place ourselves," said Lord Canterville, "since my grand-aunt, the Dowager Duchess of Bolton, was frightened into a fit, from which she never really recovered, by two skeleton hands being placed on her shoulders as she was dressing for dinner, and I feel bound to tell you, Mr. Otis, that the ghost has been seen by several living members of my family, as well as by the rector of the parish, the Rev. Augustus Dampier, who is a fellow of King's College, Cambridge. After the unfortunate accident to the Duchess, none of our younger servants would stay with us, and Lady Canterville often got very little sleep at night, in consequence of the mysterious noises that came from the corridor and the library."

"My Lord," answered the Minister, "I will take the furniture and the ghost at a valuation. I come from a modern country, where we have everything that money can buy; and with all our spry young fellows painting the Old World red, and carrying off your best actresses and primadonnas, I reckon that if there were such a thing as a ghost in Europe, we'd have it at home in a very short time in one of our public museums, or on the road as a show."

"I fear that the ghost exists," said Lord Canterville, smiling, "though it may have resisted the overtures of your enterprising impresarios. It has been well-known for three centuries, since 1584 in fact, and always makes its appearance before the death of any member of our family."

"Well, so does the family doctor for that matter, Lord Canterville. But there is no such thing, sir, as a ghost, and I guess the laws of nature are not going to be suspended for the British aristocracy."

"You are certainly very natural in America," answered Lord Canterville, who did not quite understand Mr. Otis's last observation, "and if you don't mind a ghost in the house, it is all right. Only you must remember I warned you."

A few weeks after this, the purchase was completed, and at the close of the season the Minister and his family went down to Canterville Chase. Mrs. Otis, who as Miss Lucretia R. Tappan, of West 53rd Street, had been a celebrated New York belle, was now a very handsome middle-aged woman, with fine eyes, and a superb profile. Many American ladies on leaving their native land adopt an appearance of chronic ill health, under the impression that it is a form of European refinement, but Mrs. Otis had never fallen into this error. She had a magnificent constitution, and a really wonderful amount of animal spirits. Indeed, in many respects, she was quite English, and was an excellent example of the fact that we have really everything in common with America nowadays, except, of course, language. Her eldest son, christened Washington by his parents in a moment of patriotism, which he never ceased to regret, was a fair-haired, rather good-looking young man, who had qualified himself for American diplomacy by leading the German at the Newport Casino for three successive seasons, and even in London was well-known as an excellent dancer. Gardenias and the peerage were his only weaknesses. Otherwise he was extremely sensible. Miss Virginia E. Otis was a little girl of fifteen, lithe and lovely as a fawn, and with a fine freedom in her large blue eyes. She was a wonderful amazon, and had once raced old Lord Bilton on her pony twice around the park, winning by a length and a half, just in front of Achilles' statue, to the huge delight of the young Duke of Cheshire, who proposed to her on the spot, and was sent back to Eton that very night by his guardians, in floods of tears. After Virginia came the twins, who were usually called "The Stars and Stripes" as they were always getting swished. They were delightful boys, and with the exception of the worthy Minister the only true republicans of the family.

As Canterville Chase is seven miles from Ascot, the nearest railway station, Mr. Otis had telegraphed for a waggonette to meet them, and they started on their drive in high spirits. It was a lovely July evening, and the air was delicate with the scent of the pinewoods. Now and then they heard a wood pigeon brooding over its own sweet voice, or saw, deep in the rustling fern, the burnished breast of the pheasant. Little squirrels peered at them from the beech-trees as they went by, and the rabbits scudded away through the brushwood and over the mossy knolls, with their white tails in the air. As they entered the avenue of Canterville Chase, however, the sky became suddenly overcast with clouds, a curious stillness seemed to hold the atmosphere, a great flight of rooks passed silently over their heads, and, before they reached the house, some big drops of rain had fallen.

Standing on the steps to receive them was an old woman, neatly dressed in black silk, with a white cap and apron. This was Mrs. Umney, the housekeeper, whom Mrs. Otis, at Lady Canterville's earnest request, had consented to keep on in her former position. She made them each a low curtsey as they alighted, and said in a quaint, old-fashioned manner, "I bid you welcome to Canterville Chase." Following her, they passed through the fine Tudor hall into the library, a long, low room, panelled in black oak, at the end of which was a large stained-glass window. Here they found tea laid out for them, and, after taking off their wraps, they sat down and began to look round, while Mrs. Umney waited on them.

Suddenly Mrs. Otis caught sight of a dull red stain on the floor just by the fireplace and, quite unconscious of what it really signified, said to Mrs. Umney, "I am afraid something has been spilt there."

"Yes, madam," replied the old housekeeper in a low voice, "blood has been spilt on that spot."

"How horrid," cried Mrs. Otis. "I don't at all care for bloodstains in a sitting room. It must be removed at once."

The old woman smiled, and answered in the same low, mysterious voice, "It is the blood of Lady Eleanore de Canterville, who was murdered on that very spot by her own husband, Sir Simon de Canterville, in 1575. Sir Simon survived her nine years, and disappeared suddenly under very mysterious circumstances. His body has never been discovered, but his guilty spirit still haunts the Chase. The bloodstain has been much admired by tourists and others, and cannot be removed.''

''That is all nonsense,'' cried Washington Otis; ''Pinkerton's Champion Stain Remover and Paragon Detergent will clean it up in no time,'' and before the terrified housekeeper could interfere he had fallen upon his knees, and was rapidly scouring the floor with a small stick of what looked like a black cosmetic. In a few moments no trace of the bloodstain could be seen.

''I knew Pinkerton would do it,'' he exclaimed triumphantly, as he looked round at his admiring family; but no sooner had he said these words than a terrible flash of lightning lit up the sombre room, a fearful peal of thunder made them all start to their feet, and Mrs. Umney fainted.

''What a monstrous climate!'' said the American Minister calmly, as he lit a long cheroot. ''I guess the old country is so overpopulated that they have not enough decent weather for everybody. I have always been of opinion that emigration is the only thing for England.''

''My dear Hiram,'' cried Mrs. Otis, ''what can we do with a woman who faints?''

''Charge it to her like breakages,'' answered the Minister; ''she won't faint after that''; and in a few moments Mrs. Umney certainly came to. There was no doubt, however, that she was extremely upset, and she sternly warned Mr. Otis to beware of some trouble coming to the house.

''I have seen things with my own eyes, sir,'' she said, ''that would make any Christian's hair stand on end, and many and many a night I have not closed my eyes in sleep for the awful things that are done here.'' Mr. Otis, however, and his wife warmly assured the honest soul that they were not afraid of ghosts, and, after invoking the blessings of Providence on her new master and mistress, and making arrangements for an increase of salary, the old housekeeper tottered off to her own room.

Chapter 2

The storm raged fiercely all that night, but nothing of particular note occurred. The next morning, however, when they came down to breakfast, they found the terrible stain of blood once again on the floor. ''I don't think it can be the fault of the Paragon Detergent,'' said Washington, ''for I have tried it with everything. It must be the ghost.'' He accordingly rubbed out the stain a second time, but the second morning it appeared again. The third morning also it was there, though the library had been locked up at night by Mr. Otis himself, and the key carried upstairs. The whole family were now quite interested; Mr. Otis began to suspect that he had been too dogmatic in his denial of the existence of ghosts; Mrs. Otis expressed her intention of joining the Psychical Society, and Washington prepared a long letter to Messrs. Myers and Podmore on the subject of the Permanence of Sanguineous Stains when connected with crime. That night all doubts about the objective existence of phantasmata were removed for ever.

The day had been warm and sunny; and, in the cool of the evening, the whole family went out for a drive. They did not return home till nine o'clock, when they had a light supper. The conversation in no way turned upon ghosts, so there were not even those primary conditions of receptive expectation which so often precede the presentation of psychical phenomena. The subjects discussed, as I have since learned from Mr. Otis, were merely such as form the ordinary conversation of cultured Americans of the better class, such as the immense superiority of Miss Fanny Davenport over Sarah Bernhardt as an actress; the difficulty of obtaining green corn, buckwheat cakes, and hominy, even in the best English houses; the importance of Boston in the development of the world-soul; the advantages of the baggage check system in railway travelling; and the sweetness of the New York accent as compared to the London drawl. No mention at all was made of the supernatural, nor was Sir Simon de Canterville alluded to in any way. At eleven o'clock the family retired, and by half past all the lights were out. Some time after, Mr. Otis was awakened by a curious noise in the corridor, outside his room. It sounded like the clank of metal, and seemed to be coming nearer every moment. He got up at once, struck a match, and looked at the time. It was exactly one o'clock. He was quite calm, and felt his pulse, which was not at all feverish. The strange noise still continued, and with it he heard distinctly the sound of footsteps. He put on his slippers, took a small oblong phial out of his dressing case, and opened the door. Right in front of him he saw, in the wan moonlight, an old man of terrible aspect. His eyes were as red as burning coals; long grey hair fell over his shoulders in matted coils; his garments, which were of antique cut, were soiled and ragged, and from his wrists and ankles hung heavy manacles and rusty gyves.

"My dear sir," said Mr. Otis, "I really must insist on your oiling those chains, and have brought you for that purpose a small bottle of the Tammany Rising Sun Lubricator. It is said to be completely efficacious upon one application, and there are several testimonials to that effect on the wrapper from some of our most eminent native divines. I shall leave it here for you by the bedroom candles, and will be happy to supply you with more should you require it.'' With these words the United States Minister laid the bottle down on a marble table, and, closing his door, retired to rest.

For a moment the Canterville stood quite motionless in natural indignation; then, dashing the bottle violently upon the polished floor, he fled down the corridor, uttering hollow groans, and emitting a ghastly green light. Just, however, as he reached the top of the great oak staircase, a door was flung open, two little white-robed figures appeared, and a large pillow whizzed past his head! There was evidently no time to be lost, so, hastily adopting the Fourth Dimension of Space as a means of escape, he vanished through the wainscoting, and the house became quite quiet.

On reaching a small secret chamber in the left wing, he leaned up against a moonbeam to recover his breath, and began to try and realise his position. Never, in a brilliant and uninterrupted career of three hundred years, had he been so grossly insulted. He thought of the Dowager Duchess, whom he had frightened into a fit as she stood before the glass in her lace and diamonds; of the four housemaids, who had gone off into hysterics when he merely grinned at them through the curtains of one of the spare bedrooms; of the rector of the parish, whose candle he had blown out as he was coming late one night from the library, and who had been under the care of Sir William Gull ever since, a perfect martyr to nervous disorders; and of old Madame de Tremouillac, who, having wakened up one morning early and seen a skeleton seated in an armchair by the fire reading her diary, had been confined to her bed for six weeks with an attack of brain fever, and, on her recovery, had become reconciled to the Church, and had broken her connection with that notorious sceptic Monsieur de Voltaire. He remembered the terrible night when the wicked Lord Canterville was found choking in his dressing room, with the knave of diamonds halfway down his throat, and confessed, just before he died, that he had cheated Charles James Fox out of £50,000 at Crockford's by means of that very card, and swore that the ghost had made him swallow it. All his great achievements came back to him again, from the butler who had shot himself in the pantry because he had seen a green hand tapping at the window pane, to the beautiful Lady Stutfield, who was always obliged to wear a black velvet band round her throat to hide the mark of five fingers burnt upon her white skin, and who drowned herself at last in the carp pond at the end of the King's Walk. With the enthusiastic egotism of the true artist he went over his most celebrated performances, and smiled bitterly to himself as he recalled to mind his last appearance as 'Red Ruben, or the Strangled Babe,' his debut as 'Gaunt Gibeon, the Blood-sucker of Bexley Moor,' and the furor he had excited one lovely June evening by merely playing ninepins with his own bones upon the lawn-tennis ground. And after all this, some wretched modern Americans were to come and offer him the Rising Sun Lubricator, and throw pillows at his head! It was quite unbearable. Besides, no ghosts in history had ever been treated in this manner. Accordingly, he determined to have vengeance, and remained till daylight in an attitude of deep thought.

Chapter 3

The next morning when the Otis family met at breakfast, they discussed the ghost at some length. The United States Minister was naturally a little annoyed to find that his present had not been accepted. "I have no wish," he said, "to do the ghost any personal injury, and I must say that, considering the length of time he has been in the house, I don't think it is at all polite to throw pillows at him"—a very just remark, at which, I am sorry to say, the twins burst into shouts of laughter. "Upon the other hand," he continued, "if he really declines to use the Rising Sun Lubricator, we shall have to take his chains from him. It would be quite impossible to sleep, with such a noise going on outside the bedrooms."

For the rest of the week, however, they were undisturbed, the only thing that excited any attention being the continual renewal of the bloodstain on the library floor. This certainly was very strange, as the door was always locked at night by Mr. Otis, and the windows kept closely barred. The chameleon-like color, also, of the stain excited a good deal of comment. Some mornings it was a dull (almost Indian) red, then it would be vermilion, then a rich purple, and once when they came down for family prayers, according to the simple rites of the Free American Reformed Episcopalian Church, they found it a bright emerald-green. These kaleidoscopic changes naturally amused the party very much, and bets on the subject were freely made every evening. The only person who did not enter into the joke was little Virginia, who, for some unexplained reason, was always a good deal distressed at the sight of the bloodstain, and very nearly cried the morning it was emerald-green.

The second appearance of the ghost was on Sunday night. Shortly after they had gone to bed they were suddenly alarmed by a fearful crash in the hall. Rushing downstairs, they found that a large suit of old armor had become detached from its stand, and had fallen on the stone floor, while, seated in a high-backed chair, was the Canterville ghost, rubbing his knees with an expression of acute agony on his face. The twins, having brought their peashooters with them, at once discharged two pellets on him, with that accuracy of aim which can only be attained by long and careful practice on a writing master, while the United States Minister covered him with his revolver, and called upon him, in accordance with Californian etiquette, to hold up his hands! The ghost started up with a wild shriek of rage, and swept through them like a mist, extinguishing Washington Otis's candle as he passed, and so leaving them all in total darkness. On reaching the top of the staircase he recovered himself, and determined to give his celebrated peal of demoniac laughter. This he had on more than one occasion found extremely useful. It was said to have turned Lord Raker's wig grey in a single night, and had certainly made three of Lady Canterville's French governesses give warning before their month was up. He accordingly laughed his most horrible laugh, till the old vaulted roof rang and rang again, but hardly had the fearful echo died away when a door opened, and Mrs. Otis came out in a light blue dressing gown. "I am afraid you are far from well," she said, "and have brought you a bottle of Dr. Dobell's tincture. If it is indigestion, you will find it a most excellent remedy." The ghost glared at her in fury, and began at once to make preparations for turning himself into a large black dog, an accomplishment for which he was justly renowned, and to which the family doctor always attributed the permanent idiocy of Lord Canterville's uncle, the Hon. Thomas Horton. The sound of approaching footsteps, however, made him hesitate in his fell purpose, so he contented himself with becoming faintly phosphorescent, and vanished with a deep churchyard groan, just as the twins had come up to him.

On reaching his room he entirely broke down, and became a prey to the most violent agitation. The vulgarity of the twins, and the gross materialism of Mrs. Otis, were naturally extremely annoying, but what really distressed him most was, that he had been unable to wear the suit of mail. He had hoped that even modern Americans would be thrilled by the sight of a Spectre In Armour, if for no more sensible reason, at least out of respect for their national poet Longfellow, over whose graceful and attractive poetry he himself had whiled away many a weary hour when the Cantervilles were up in town. Besides, it was his own suit. He had worn it with success at the Kenilworth tournament, and had been highly complimented on it by no less a person than the Virgin Queen herself. Yet when he had put it on, he had been completely overpowered by the weight of the huge breastplate and steel casque, and had fallen heavily on the stone pavement, barking both his knees severely, and bruising the knuckles of his right hand.

For some days after this he was extremely ill, and hardly stirred out of his room at all, except to keep the bloodstain in proper repair. However, by taking great care of himself, he recovered, and resolved to make a third attempt to frighten the United States Minister and his family. He selected Friday, the 17 of August, for his appearance, and spent most of that day in looking over his wardrobe, ultimately deciding in favor of a large slouched hat with a red feather, a winding sheet frilled at the wrists and neck, and a rusty dagger. Toward evening a violent storm of rain came on, and the wind was so high that all the windows and doors in the old house shook and rattled. In fact, it was just such weather as he loved. His plan of action was this. He was to make his way quietly to Washington Otis's room, gibber at him from the foot of the bed, and stab himself three times in the throat to the sound of slow music. He bore Washington a special grudge, being quite aware that it was he who was in the habit of removing the famous Canterville bloodstain, by means of Pinkerton's Paragon Detergent. Having reduced the reckless and foolhardy youth to a condition of abject terror, he was then to proceed to the room occupied by the United States Minister and his wife, and there to place a clammy hand on Mrs. Otis's forehead, while he hissed into her trembling husband's ear the awful secrets of the charnel house. With regard to little Virginia, he had not quite made up his mind. She had never insulted him in any way, and was pretty and gentle. A few hollow groans from the wardrobe, he thought, would be more than sufficient, or, if that failed to wake her, he might grabble at the counterpane with palsy-twitching fingers. As for the twins, he was quite determined to teach them a lesson. The first thing to be done was, of course, to sit upon their chests, so as to produce the stifling sensation of nightmare. Then, as their beds were quite close to each other, to stand between them in the form of a green icy-cold corpse, till they became paralysed with fear, and finally, to throw off the winding sheet, and crawl round the room, with white bleached bones and one rolling eyeball, in the character of ''Dumb Daniel, or the Suicide's Skeleton,'' a role in which he had on more than one occasion produced a great effect, and which he considered quite equal to his famous part of ''Martin the Maniac, or the Masked Mystery.''

At half-past ten he heard the family going to bed. For some time he was disturbed by wild shrieks of laughter from the twins, who, with the light-hearted gaiety of schoolboys, were evidently amusing themselves before they retired to rest, but at a quarter past eleven all was still, and, as midnight sounded, he sallied forth. The owl beat against the window panes, the raven croaked from the old yew tree, and the wind wandered moaning round the house like a lost soul; but the Otis family slept unconscious of their doom, and high above the rain and storm he could hear the steady snoring of the Minister for the United States. He stepped stealthily out of the wainscoting, with an evil smile on his cruel, wrinkled mouth, and the moon hid her face in a cloud as he stole past the great oriel window, where his own arms and those of his murdered wife were blazoned in azure and gold. On and on he glided, like an evil shadow, the very darkness seeming to loathe him as he passed. Once he thought he heard something call, and stopped; but it was only the baying of a dog from the Red Farm, and he went on, muttering strange sixteenth-century curses, and ever and anon brandishing the rusty dagger in the midnight air. Finally he reached the corner of the passage that led to luckless Washington's room. For a moment he paused there, the wind blowing his long grey locks about his head, and twisting into grotesque and fantastic folds the nameless horror of the dead man's shroud. Then the clock struck the quarter, and he felt the time was come. He chuckled to himself, and turned the corner; but no sooner had he done so, than, with a piteous wail of terror, he fell back, and hid his blanched face in his long, bony hands. Right in front of him was standing a horrible spectre, motionless as a carven image, and monstrous as a madman's dream! Its head was bald and burnished; its face round, and fat, and white; and hideous laughter seemed to have writhed its features into an eternal grin. From the eyes streamed rays of scarlet light, the mouth was a wide well of fire, and a hideous garment, like to his own, swathed with its silent snows the Titan form. On its breast was a placard with strange writing in antique characters, some scroll of shame it seemed, some record of wild sins, some awful calendar of crime, and, with its right hand, it bore aloft a falchion of gleaming steel.

Never having seen a ghost before, he naturally was terribly frightened, and, after a second hasty glance at the awful phantom, he fled back to his room, tripping up in his long winding sheet as he sped down the corridor, and finally dropping the rusty dagger into the Minister's jack-boots, where it was found in the morning by the butler. Once in the privacy of his own apartment, he flung himself down on a small pallet-bed, and hid his face under the clothes. After a time, however, the brave old Canterville spirit asserted itself, and he determined to go and speak to the other ghost as soon as it was daylight. Accordingly, just as the dawn was touching the hills with silver, he returned toward the spot where he had first laid eyes on the grisly phantom, feeling that, after all, two ghosts were better than one, and that, by the aid of his new friend, he might safely grapple with the twins. On reaching the spot, however, a terrible sight met his gaze. Something had evidently happened to the spectre, for the light had entirely faded from its hollow eyes, the gleaming falchion had fallen from its hand, and it was leaning up against the wall in a strained and uncomfortable attitude. He rushed forward and seized it in his arms, when to his horror, the head slipped off and rolled on the floor, the body assumed a recumbent posture, and he found himself clasping a white dimity bed-curtain, with a sweeping brush, a kitchen cleaver, and a hollow turnip lying at his feet! Unable to understand this curious transformation, he clutched the placard with feverish haste, and there, in the grey morning light, he read these fearful words:

YE OTIS GHOSTE.
Ye Onlie True and Originale Spook.
Beware of Ye Imitations.
All others are Counterfeite.

The whole thing flashed across him. He had been tricked, foiled, and outwitted! The old Canterville look came into his eyes; he ground his toothless gums together; and, raising his withered hands high above his head, swore, according to the picturesque phraseology of the antique school, that when Chanticleer had sounded twice his merry horn, deeds of blood would be wrought, and Murder walk abroad with silent feet.

Hardly had he finished this awful oath when, from the red-tiled roof of a distant homestead, a cock crew. He laughed a long, low, bitter laugh, and waited. Hour after hour he waited, but the cock, for some strange reason, did not crow again. Finally, at half-past seven, the arrival of the housemaids made him give up his fearful vigil, and he stalked back to his room, thinking of his vain hope and baffled purpose. There he consulted several books of ancient chivalry, of which he was exceedingly fond, and found that, on every occasion on which his oath had been used, Chanticleer had always crowed a second time. "Perdition seize the naughty fowl," he muttered, "I have seen the day when, with my stout spear, I would have run him through the gorge, and made him crow for me an 'twere in death!" He then retired to a comfortable lead coffin, and stayed there till evening.

Chapter 4

The next day the ghost was very weak and tired. The terrible excitement of the last four weeks was beginning to have its effect. His nerves were completely shattered, and he started at the slightest noise. For five days he kept his room, and at last made up his mind to give up the point of the bloodstain on the library floor. If the Otis family did not want it, they clearly did not deserve it. They were evidently people on a low, material plane of existence, and quite incapable of appreciating the symbolic value of sensuous phenomena. The question of phantasmic apparitions, and the development of astral bodies, was of course quite a different matter, and really not under his control. It was his solemn duty to appear in the corridor once a week, and to gibber from the large oriel window on the first and third Wednesday in every month, and he did not see how he could honorably escape from his obligations. It is quite true that his life had been very evil, but, upon the other hand, he was most conscientious in all things connected with the supernatural. For the next three Saturdays, accordingly, he traversed the corridor as usual between midnight and three o'clock, taking every possible precaution against being either heard or seen. He removed his boots, trod as lightly as possible on the old worm-eaten boards, wore a large black velvet cloak, and was careful to use the Rising Sun Lubricator for oiling his chains. I am bound to acknowledge that it was with a good deal of difficulty that he brought himself to adopt this last mode of protection. However, one night, while the family were at dinner, he slipped into Mr. Otis's bedroom and carried off the bottle. He felt a little humiliated at first, but afterwards was sensible enough to see that there was a great deal to be said for the invention, and, to a certain degree, it served his purpose. Still, in spite of everything, he was not left unmolested. Strings were continually being stretched across the corridor, over which he tripped in the dark, and on one occasion, while dressed for the part of "Black Isaac, or the Huntsman of Hogley Woods," he met with a severe fall, through treading on a butter slide, which the twins had constructed from the entrance of the Tapestry Chamber to the top of the oak staircase. This last insult so enraged him, that he resolved to assert his dignity, and determined to visit the insolent young Etonians the next night in his celebrated character of "Reckless Rupert, or the Headless Earl."

He had not appeared in this disguise for more than seventy years; in fact, not since he had so frightened pretty Lady Barbara Modish by means of it, that she suddenly broke off her engagement with the present Lord Canterville's grandfather, and ran away to Gretna Green with handsome Jack Castleton, declaring that nothing in the world would induce her to marry into a family that allowed such a horrible phantom to walk up and down the terrace at twilight. Poor Jack was afterwards shot in a duel by Lord Canterville on Wandsworth Common, and Lady Barbara died of a broken heart at Tunbridge Wells before the year was out, so, in every way, it had been a great success. It was, however, an extremely difficult "make-up," if I may use such a theatrical expression in connection with one of the greatest mysteries of the supernatural, or, to employ a more scientific term, the higher-natural world and it took him fully three hours to make his preparations. At last everything was ready, and he was very pleased with his appearance. The big leather riding boots that went with the dress were just a little too large for him, and he could only find one of the two horse pistols, but, on the whole, he was quite satisfied, and at a quarter past one he glided out of the wainscoting and crept down the corridor. On reaching the room occupied by the twins, which I should mention was called the Blue Bed Chamber, on account of the color of its hangings, he found the door just ajar. Wishing to make an effective entrance, he flung it wide open, when a heavy jug of water fell right down on him, wetting him to the skin, and just missing his left shoulder by a couple of inches. At the same moment he heard stifled shrieks of laughter proceeding from the four-post bed.

The shock to his nervous system was so great that he fled back to his room as hard as he could go, and the next day he was laid up with a severe cold. The only thing that at all consoled him in the whole affair was the fact that he had not brought his head with him, for, had he done so, the consequences might have been very serious.

He now gave up all hope of ever frightening this rude American family, and contented himself, as a rule, with creeping about the passages in list slippers, with a thick red muffler round his throat for fear of draughts, and a small arquebuse, in case he should be attacked by the twins. The final blow he received occurred on the 19 of September. He had gone downstairs to the great entrance hall, feeling sure that there, at any rate, he would be quite unmolested, and was amusing himself by making satirical remarks on the large Saroni photographs of the United States Minister and his wife, which had now taken the place of the Canterville family pictures. He was simply but neatly clad in a long shroud, spotted with churchyard mould, had tied up his jaw with a strip of yellow linen, and carried a small lantern and a sexton's spade. In fact, he was dressed for the character of "Jonas the Graveless, or the Corpse-Snatcher of Chertsey Barn," one of his most remarkable impersonations, and one which the Cantervilles had every reason to remember, as it was the real origin of their quarrel with their neighbor Lord Rufford. It was about a quarter past two o'clock in the morning, and, as far as he could ascertain, no one was stirring. As he was strolling toward the library, however, to see if there were any traces left of the bloodstain, suddenly there leaped out on him from a dark corner two figures, who waved their arms wildly above their heads, and shrieked out "BOO!" in his ear.

Seized with a panic, which, under the circumstances, was only natural, he rushed for the staircase, but found Washington Otis waiting for him there with a big garden-syringe; and being thus hemmed in by his enemies on every side, and driven almost to bay, he vanished into the great iron stove, which, fortunately for him, was not lit, and had to make his way home through the flues and chimneys, arriving at his own room in a terrible state of dirt, disorder, and despair.

After this he was not seen again on any nocturnal expedition. The twins lay in wait for him on several occasions, and strewed the passages with nutshells every night to the great annoyance of their parents and the servants, but it was of no avail. It was quite eveident that his feelings were so wounded that he would not appear. Mr. Otis consequently resumed his great work on the history of the Democratic Party, on which he had been engaged for some years; Mrs. Otis organized a wonderful clambake, which amazed the whole county; the boys took to lacrosse, euchre, poker, and other American national games; and Virginia rode about the lanes on her pony, accompanied by the young Duke of Cheshire, who had come to spend the last week of his holidays at Canterville Chase. It was generally assumed that the ghost had gone away, and, in fact, Mr. Otis wrote a letter to that effect to Lord Canterville, who, in reply, expressed his great pleasure at the news, and sent his best congratulations to the Minister's worthy wife.

The Otises, however, were deceived, for the ghost was still in the house, and though now almost an invalid, was by no means ready to let matters rest, particularly as he heard that among the guests was the young Duke of Cheshire, whose grand-uncle, Lord Francis Stilton, had once bet a hundred guineas with Colonel Carbury that he would play dice with the Canterville ghost, and was found the next morning lying on the floor of the card room in such a helpless paralytic state, that though he lived on to a great age, he was never able to say anything again but "Double Sixes." The story was well-known at the time, though, of course, out of respect for the feelings of the two noble families, every attempt was made to hush it up; and a full account of all the circumstances connected with it will be found in the third volume of Lord Tattle's *Recollections of the Prince Regent and his Friends*. The ghost, then, was naturally very anxious to show that he had not lost his influence over the Stilton's, with whom, indeed, he was distantly connected, his own first cousin having been married *en secondes noces* to the Sieur de Bulkeley, from whom, as everyone knows, the Dukes of Cheshire are lineally descended. Accordingly, he made arrangements for appearing to Virginia's little lover in his celebrated impersonation of "The Vampire Monk, or the Bloodless Benedictine," a performance so horrible that when old Lady Startup saw it, which she did on one fatal New Year's Eve, in the year 1764, she went off into the most piercing shrieks, which culminated in violent apoplexy, and died in three days, after disinheriting the Cantervilles, who were her nearest relations, and leaving all her money to her London apothecary. At the last moment, however, his terror of the twins prevented his leaving his room, and the little Duke slept in peace under the great feathered canopy in the Royal Bedchamber, and dreamed of Virginia.

Chapter 5

A few days after this, Virginia and her curly haired cavalier went out riding on Brockley meadows, where she tore her habit so badly in getting through a hedge, that, on her return home, she made up her mind to go up by the back staircase so as not to be seen. As she was running past the Tapestry Chamber, the door of which happened to be open, she fancied she saw someone inside, and thinking it was her mother's maid, who sometimes used to bring her work there, looked in to ask her to mend her habit. To her immense surprise, however, it was the Canterville Ghost himself! He was sitting by the window, watching the ruined gold of the yellow trees fly through the air, and the red leaves dancing madly down the long avenue. His head was leaning on his hand, and his whole attitude was one of extreme depression. Indeed, so forlorn, and so much out of repair did he look, that little Virginia, whose first idea had been to run away and lock herself in her room, was filled with pity, and determined to try and comfort him. So light was her footfall, and so deep his melancholy, that he was not aware of her presence till she spoke to him.

"I am so sorry for you," she said, "but my brothers are going back to Eton tomorrow, and then, if you behave yourself, no one will annoy you."

"It is absurd asking me to behave myself," he answered, looking round in astonishment at the pretty little girl who had ventured to address him, "quite absurd. I must rattle my chains, and groan through key-holes, and walk about at night, if that is what you mean. It is my only reason for existing."

"It is no reason at all for existing, and you know you have been very wicked. Mrs. Umney told us, the first day we arrived here, that you had killed your wife."

"Well, I quite admit it," said the Ghost petulantly, "but it was a purely family matter, and concerned no one else."

"It is very wrong to kill any one," said Virginia, who at times had a sweet Puritan gravity, caught from some old New England ancestor.

"Oh, I hate the cheap severity of abstract ethics! My wife was very plain, never had my ruffs properly starched, and knew nothing about cookery. Why, there was a buck I had shot in Hogley Woods, a magnificent pricket, and do you know how she had it sent up to table?

However, it is no matter now, for it is all over, and I don't think it was very nice of her brothers to starve me to death, though I did kill her."

"Starve you to death? Oh, Mr. Ghost, I mean Sir Simon, are you hungry? I have a sandwich in my case. Would you like it?"

"No, thank you, I never eat anything now; but it is very kind of you, all the same, and you are much nicer than the rest of your horrid, rude, vulgar, dishonest family."

"Stop!" cried Virginia, stamping her foot, "it is you who are rude, and horrid, and vulgar; and as for dishonesty, you know you stole the paints out of my box to try and furbish up that ridiculous bloodstain in the library. First you took all my reds, including the vermilion, and I couldn't do any more sunsets, then you took the emerald-green and the chrome-yellow, and finally I had nothing left but indigo and Chinese white, and could only do moonlight scenes, which are always depressing to look at, and not at all easy to paint. I never told on you, though I was very much annoyed, and it was most ridiculous, the whole thing; for who ever heard of emerald-green blood?"

"Well, really," said the Ghost, rather meekly, "what was I to do? It is a very difficult thing to get real blood nowadays, and, as your brother began it all with his Paragon Detergent, I certainly saw no reason why I should not have your paints. As for color, that is always a matter of taste: the Cantervilles have blue blood, for instance, the very bluest in England; but I know you Americans don't care for things of this kind."

"You know nothing about it, and the best thing you can do is to emigrate and improve your mind. My father will be only too happy to give you a free passage, and though there is a heavy duty on spirits of every kind, there will be no difficulty about the Custom House, as the officers are all Democrats. Once in New York, you are sure to be a great success. I know lots of people there who would give a hundred thousand dollars to have a grandfather, and much more than that to have a family Ghost."

"I don't think I should like America."

"I suppose because we have no ruins and no curiosities," said Virginia satirically.

"No ruins! no curiosities!" answered the Ghost; "you have your navy and your manners."

"Good evening; I will go and ask papa to get the twins an extra week's holiday."

"Please don't go, Miss Virginia," he cried; "I am so lonely and so unhappy, and I really don't know what to do. I want to go to sleep and I cannot."

"That's quite absurd. You have merely to go to bed and blow out the candle. It is very difficult sometimes to keep awake, especially at church, but there is no difficulty at all about sleeping. Why, even babies know how to do that, and they are not very clever."

"I have not slept for three hundred years," he said sadly, and Virginia's beautiful blue eyes opened in wonder; "for three hundred years I have not slept, and I am so tired."

Virginia grew quite grave, and her little lips trembled like rose leaves. She came towards him, and kneeling down at his side, looked up into his old withered face.

"Poor, poor Ghost," she murmured; "have you no place where you can sleep?"

"Far away beyond the pine woods," he answered, in a low dreamy voice, "there is a little garden. There the grass grows long and deep, there are the great white stars of the hemlock flower, there the nightingale sings all night long. All night long he sings, and the cold, crystal moon looks down, and the yew tree spreads out its giant arms over the sleepers."

Virginia's eyes grew dim with tears, and she hid her face in her hands.

"You mean the Garden of Death," she whispered.

"Yes, Death. Death must be so beautiful. To lie in the soft brown earth, with the grasses waving above one's head, and listen to silence. To have no yesterday, and no tomorrow. To forget time, to forgive life, to be at peace. You can help me. You can open for me the portals of Death's house, for Love is always with you, and Love is stronger than Death is."

Virginia trembled, a cold shudder ran through her, and for a few moments there was silence. She felt as if she was in a terrible dream.

Then the Ghost spoke again, and his voice sounded like the sighing of the wind.

"Have you ever read the old prophecy on the library window?"

"Oh, often," cried the little girl, looking up; "I know it quite well. It is painted in curious black letters, and it is difficult to read. There are only six lines.

When a golden girl can win
Prayer from out the lips of sin,
When the barren almond bears,
And a little child gives away its tears,
Then shall all the house be still
And peace come to Canterville.

But I don't know what they mean."

"They mean," he said sadly, "That you must weep for me for my sins, because I have no tears, and pray with me for my soul, because I have no faith, and then, if you have always been sweet, and good, and gentle, the Angel of Death will have mercy on me. You will see fearful shapes in darkness, and wicked voices will whisper in your ear, but they will not harm you, for against the purity of a little child the powers of Hell cannot prevail."

Virginia made no answer, and the Ghost wrung his hands in wild despair as he looked down at her bowed golden head. Suddenly she stood up, very pale, and with a strange light in her eyes. "I am not afraid," she said firmly, "and I will ask the Angel to have mercy on you."

He rose from his seat with a faint cry of joy, and taking her hand bent over it with old-fashioned grace and kissed it. His fingers were as cold as ice, and his lips burned like fire, but Virginia did not falter, as he led her across the dusky room. On the faded green tapestry were broidered little huntsmen. They blew their tasselled horns and with their tiny hands waved to her to go back. "Go back! little Virginia," they cried, "go back!" but the Ghost clutched her hand more tightly, and she shut her eyes against them. Horrible animals with lizard tails, and goggle eyes, blinked at her from the carven chimney piece, and murmured "Beware! little Virginia, beware! we may never see you again," but the Ghost glided on more swiftly, and Virginia did not listen. When they reached the end of the room he stopped, and muttered some words she could not understand. She opened her eyes, and saw the wall slowly fading away like a mist, and a great black cavern in front of her. A bitter cold wind swept round them, and she felt something pulling at her dress. "Quick, quick," cried the Ghost, "or it will be too late," and, in a moment, the wainscoting had closed behind them, and the Tapestry Chamber was empty.

Chapter 6

About ten minutes later, the bell rang for tea, and, as Virginia did not come down, Mrs. Otis sent up one of the footmen to tell her. After a little time he returned and said that he could not find Miss Virginia anywhere. As she was in the habit of going out to the garden every evening to get flowers for the dinner table, Mrs. Otis was not at all alarmed at first, but when six o'clock struck, and Virginia did not appear, she became really agitated, and sent the boys out to look for her, while she herself and Mr. Otis searched every room in the house. At half-past six the boys came back and said that they could find no trace of their sister anywhere. They were all now in the greatest state of excitement, and did not know what to do, when Mr. Otis suddenly remembered that, some few days before, he had given a band of gypsies permission to camp in the park. He accordingly at once set off for Blackfell Hollow, where he knew they were, accompanied by his eldest son and two of the farm servants. The little Duke of Cheshire, who was perfectly frantic with anxiety, begged hard to be allowed to go too, but Mr. Otis would not allow him, as he was afraid there might be a scuffle. On arriving at the spot, however, he found that the gypsies had gone, and it was evident that their departure had been rather sudden, as the fire was still burning, and some plates were lying on the grass. Having sent off Washington and the two men to scour the district, he ran home, and despatched telegrams to all the police inspectors in the county, telling them to look out for a little girl who had been kidnapped by tramps or gypsies. He then ordered his horse to be brought around, and, after insisting on his wife and the three boys sitting down to dinner, rode off down the Ascot Road with a groom. He had hardly, however, gone a couple of miles when he heard somebody galloping after him, and, looking round, saw the little Duke coming up on his pony, with his face very flushed and no hat. "I'm awfully sorry, Mr. Otis," gasped out the boy, "but I can't eat any dinner as long as Virginia is lost. Please, don't be angry with me; if you had let us be engaged last year, there would never have been all this trouble. You won't send me back, will you? I can't go! I won't go!"

The Minister could not help smiling at the handsome young scapegrace, and was a good deal touched at his devotion to Virginia, so leaning down from his horse, he patted him kindly on the shoulders, and said, "Well, Cecil, if you won't go back I suppose you must come with me, but I must get you a hat at Ascot."

"Oh, bother my hat! I want Virginia!" cried the little Duke, laughing, and they galloped on to the railway station. There Mr. Otis inquired of the stationmaster if any one answering the description of Virginia had been seen on the platform, but could get no news of her. The stationmaster, however, wired up and down the line, and assured him that a strict watch would be kept for her, and, after having bought a hat for the little Duke from a linen-draper, who was just putting up his shutters, Mr. Otis rode off to Bexley, a village about four miles away, which he was told was a well-known haunt of the gypsies, as there was a large common next to it. Here they roused up the rural policeman, but could get no information from him, and, after riding all over the common, they turned their horses' head homewards, and reached the Chase about eleven o'clock, dead-tired and almost heartbroken. They found Washington and the twins waiting for them at the gate-house with lanterns, as the avenue was very dark. Not the slightest trace of Virginia had been discovered. The gypsies had been caught on Broxley meadows, but she was not with them, and they had explained their sudden departure by saying that they had mistaken the date of Chorton Fair, and had gone off in a hurry for fear they might be late. Indeed, they had been quite distressed at hearing of Virginia's disappearance, as they were very grateful to Mr. Otis for having allowed them to camp in his park, and four of their number had stayed behind to help in the search. The carp pond had been dragged, and the whole Chase thoroughly gone over, but without any result. It was evident that, for that night at any rate, Virginia was lost to them; and it was in a state of the deepest depression that Mr. Otis and the boys walked up to the house, the groom following behind with the two horses and the pony. In the hall they found a group of frightened servants, and lying on a sofa in the library was poor Mrs. Otis, almost out of her mind with terror and anxiety, and having her forehead bathed with eau-de-cologne by the old housekeeper. Mr. Otis at once insisted on her having something to eat, and ordered up supper for the whole party. It was a melancholy meal, as hardly any one spoke, and even the twins were awestruck and subdued, as they were very fond of their sister. When they had finished, Mr. Otis, in spite of the entreaties of the little Duke, ordered them all to bed, saying that nothing more could be done that night, and that he would telegraph in the morning to Scotland Yard for some detectives to be sent down immediately. Just as they were passing out of the dining room, midnight began to boom from the clock tower, and when the last stroke sounded they heard a crash and a sudden shrill cry; a dreadful peal of thunder shook the house, a strain of unearthly music floated through the air, a panel at the top of the staircase flew back with a loud noise, and out on the landing, looking very pale and white, with a little casket in her hand, stepped Virginia. In a moment they had all rushed up to her. Mrs. Otis clasped her passionately in her arms, the Duke smothered her with violent kisses, and the twins executed a wild war dance around the group.

"Good heavens, child, where have you been?" said Mr. Otis, rather angrily, thinking that she had been playing some foolish trick on them. "Cecil and I have been riding all over the country looking for you, and your mother has been frightened to death. You must never play these practical jokes any more."

"Except on the Ghost! except on the Ghost!" shrieked the twins, as they capered about.

"My own darling, thank God you are found; you must never leave my side again," murmured Mrs. Otis, as she kissed the trembling child, and smoothed the tangled gold of her hair. "Papa," said Virginia quietly, "I have been with the Ghost. He is dead, and you must come and see him. He had been very wicked, but he was really sorry for all that he had done, and he gave me this box of beautiful jewels before he died."

The whole family gazed at her in mute amazement, but she was quite grave and serious; and, turning round, she led them through the opening in the wainscoting down a narrow secret corridor, Washington following with a lighted candle, which he had caught up from the table. Finally, they came to a great oak door, studded with rusty nails. When Virginia touched it, it swung back on its heavy hinges, and they found themselves in a little low room, with a vaulted ceiling, and one tiny grated window. Imbedded in the wall was a huge iron ring, and chained to it was a gaunt skeleton, that was stretched out at full length on the stone floor, and seemed to be trying to grasp with its long fleshless fingers an old-fashioned trencher and ewer, that were placed just out of its reach. The jug had evidently been once filled with water, as it was covered inside with green mould. There was nothing on the trencher but a pile of dust. Virginia knelt down beside the skeleton, and, folding her little hands together, began to pray silently, while the rest of the party looked on in wonder at the terrible tragedy whose secret was now disclosed to them.

"Hallo!" suddenly exclaimed one of the twins, who had been

looking out of the window to try and discover in what wing of the house the room was situated. "Hallo! the old withered almond tree has blossomed. I can see the flowers quite plainly in the moonlight."

"God has forgiven him," said Virginia gravely, as she rose to her feet, and a beautiful light seemed to illumine her face.

"What an angel you are!" cried the young Duke, and he put his arm round her neck and kissed her.

Chapter 7

Four days after these curious incidents a funeral started from Canterville Chase at about eleven o'clock at night. The hearse was drawn by eight black horses, each of which carried on its head a great tuft of nodding ostrich plumes, and the leaden coffin was covered by a rich purple pall, on which was embroidered in gold the Canterville coat-of-arms. By the side of the hearse and the coaches walked the servants with lighted torches, and the whole procession was wonderfully impressive. Lord Canterville was the chief mourner, having come up specially from Wales to attend the funeral, and sat in the first carriage along with little Virginia. Then came the United States Minister and his wife, then Washington and the three boys, and in the last carriage was Mrs. Umney. It was generally felt that, as she had been frightened by the ghost for more than fifty years of her life, she had a right to see the last of him. A deep grave had been dug in the corner of the churchyard, just under the old yew tree, and the service was read in the most impressive manner by the Rev. Augustus Dampier. When the ceremony was over, the servants, according to an old custom observed in the Canterville family, extinguished their torches, and, as the coffin was being lowered into the grave, Virginia stepped forward and laid on it a large cross made of white and pink almond blossoms. As she did so, the moon came out from behind a cloud, and flooded with its silent silver the little churchyard, and from a distant copse a nightingale began to sing. She thought of the ghost's description of the Garden of Death, her eyes became dim with tears, and she hardly spoke a word during the drive home.

The next morning, before Lord Canterville went up to town, Mr. Otis had an interview with him on the subject of the jewels the Ghost had given to Virginia. They were perfectly magnificent, especially a certain ruby necklace with old Venetian setting, which was a really a superb specimen of sixteenth-century work, and their value was so great that Mr. Otis felt considerable scruples about allowing his daughter to accept them.

"My Lord," he said, "I know that in this country mortmain is held to apply to trinkets as well as to land, and it is quite clear to me that these jewels are, or should be, heirlooms in your family. I must beg you, accordingly, to take them to London with you, and to regard them simply as a portion of your property which has been restored to you under certain strange conditions. As for my daughter, she is merely a child, and has as yet, I am glad to say, but little interest in such appurtenances of idle luxury. I am also informed by Mrs. Otis, who, I may say, is no mean authority upon Art—having had the privilege of spending several winters in Boston when she was a girl—that these gems are of great monetary worth, and if offered for sale would fetch a tall price. Under these circumstances, Lord Canterville, I feel sure that you will recognize how impossible it would be for me to allow them to remain in the possession of any member of my family; and, indeed, all such vain gauds and toys, however suitable or necessary to the dignity of the British aristocracy, would be completely out of place among those who have been brought up on the severe, and I believe immortal, principles of republican simplicity. Perhaps I should mention that Virginia is very anxious that you should allow her to retain the box as a memento of your unfortunate but misguided ancestor. As it is extremely old, and consequently a good deal out of repair, you may perhaps think fit to comply with her request. For my own part, I confess I am a good deal surprised to find a child of mine expressing sympathy with medievalism in any form, and can only account for it by the fact that Virginia was born in one of your London suburbs shortly after Mrs. Otis had returned from a trip to Athens."

Lord Canterville listened very gravely to the worthy Minister's speech, pulling his grey mustache now and then to hide an involuntary smile, and when Mr. Otis had ended, he shook him cordially by the hand, and said, "My dear sir, your charming little daughter rendered my unlucky ancestor, Sir Simon, a very important service, and I and my family are much indebted to her for her marvellous courage and pluck. The jewels are clearly hers, and, egad, I believe that if I were heartless enough to take them from her, the wicked old fellow would be out of his grave in a fortnight, leading me the devil of a life. As for their being heirlooms, nothing is an heirloom that is not so mentioned in a will or legal document, and the existence of these jewels has been quite unknown. I assure you I have no more claim on them than your butler, and when Miss Virginia grows up I daresay she will be pleased to have pretty things to wear. Besides, you forget, Mr. Otis, that you took the furniture and the ghost at a valuation, and anything that belonged to the ghost passed at once into your possession, as, whatever activity Sir Simon may have shown in the corridor at night, in point of law he was really dead, and you acquired his property by purchase."

Mr. Otis was a good deal distressed at Lord Canterville's refusal, and begged him to reconsider his decision, but the good-natured peer was quite firm, and finally induced the Minister to allow his daughter to retain the present the ghost had given her, and when, in the spring of 1890, the young Duchess of Cheshire was presented at the Queen's first drawing room on the occasion of her marriage, her jewels were the universal theme of admiration. For Virginia received the coronet, which is the reward of all good little American girls, and was married to her boy-lover as soon as he came of age. They were both so charming, and they loved each other so much, that every one was delighted at the match, except the old Marchioness of Dumbleton, who had tried to catch the Duke for one of her seven unmarried daughters, and had given no less than three expensive dinner parties for that purpose, and, strange to say, Mr. Otis himself. Mr. Otis was extremely fond of the young Duke personally, but, theoretically, he objected to titles, and, to use his words, "was not without apprehension lest, amid the enervating influences of a pleasure-loving aristocracy, the true principles of republican simplicity should be forgotten." His objections, however, were completely overruled, and I believe that when he walked up the aisle of St. George's, Hanover Square, with his daughter leaning on his arm, there was not a prouder man in the whole length and breadth of England.

The Duke and Duchess, after the honeymoon was over, went down to Canterville Chase, and on the day after their arrival they walked over in the afternoon to the lonely churchyard by the pine woods. There had been a great deal of difficulty at first about the inscription on Sir Simon's tombstone, but finally it had been decided to engrave on it simply the initials of the old gentleman's name, and the verse from the library window. The Duchess had brought with her some lovely roses, which she strewed upon the grave, and after they had stood by it for some time they strolled into the ruined chancel of the old abbey. There the Duchess sat down on a fallen pillar, while her husband lay at her feet smoking a cigarette and looking up at her beautiful eyes. Suddenly he threw his cigarette away, took hold of her hand, and said to her, "Virginia, a wife should have no secrets from her husband."

"Dear Cecil! I have no secrets from you."

"Yes, you have," he answered, smiling, "you have never told me what happened to you when you were locked up with the ghost."

"I have never told any one, Cecil," said Virginia gravely.

"I know that, but you might tell me."

"Please don't ask me, Cecil. I cannot tell you. Poor Sir Simon! I owe him a great deal. Yes, don't laugh, Cecil, I really do. He made me see what Life is, and what Death signifies, and why Love is stronger than both."

The Duke rose and kissed his wife lovingly.

"You can have your secret as long as I have your heart," he murmured.

"You have always had that, Cecil."

"And you will tell our children someday, won't you?"

Virginia blushed.

Sir Arthur Conan Doyle (1859–1930)

Noted for creating Sherlock Holmes, ''the most famous man who never lived,'' Sir Arthur Conan Doyle was a strange blend of rationalist, idealist, romantic, and mystic who also produced outstanding works of adventure, fantasy, science fiction, and horror. Born in Edinburgh, Scotland, Doyle began writing while studying medicine at the University of Edinburgh in 1879. (It was there, incidently, where he met his models, professors Rutherford and Bell, for George Challenger and Holmes.) He had difficulty building a successful practice after graduating in 1881, so he signed on as ship's doctor for an Arctic whaler and African steamer, while continuing to supplement his income through writing.

However, in 1891, the editors of *The Strand Magazine* profoundly altered Doyle's career. Impressed by his first Sherlock Holmes novel, *A Study in Scarlet* (1882), they commissioned him to write a series featuring the same character. The public went wild over them, and, by escalating his prices for subsequent series, Doyle gained financial security. Thereafter he began devoting his energies to what interested him more: participating in current affairs and writing nonfiction.

These efforts led to mixed results. In public affairs he twice campaigned unsuccessfully for political office—as unionist candidate for Parliament in 1900, and reform candidate in 1906. But twice he was successful in averting miscarriages of justice, obtaining the releases of men accused of murder and horse-maiming. In nonfiction, he wrote two books explaining and justifying the Boer War (*The Great Boer War,* 1900, and *The War in South Africa: Its Cause and Conduct,* 1902) which resulted in his being knighted. But when his son Kingsley died of pneumonia after being severely wounded in World War I, Doyle became an avid spiritualist and wasted much of his remaining life penning embarrassing books about psychic phenomena and the existence of an afterlife.

Physically, he possessed a sturdy build and plain honest face. A lover of sports and the outdoor life, he was also personally courageous and tenacious in temperament. For Holmes's sidekick Watson, Doyle appropriated many of these same characteristics. Intellectually, however, he was brighter than Watson and, in total, probably closer in nature to the medical student protagonist of our selection for this volume, "Lot No. 249."

The shorter fantastic works of Doyle began with the second story he wrote in 1879 ("The American's Tale"), and continued until the year before he died ("The Disintegration Machine" and "When the World Screamed," 1929). However, it is only recently that most of these have been brought together in two important collections: *The Best Science Fiction of Arthur Conan Doyle* (1981) and *The Great Supernatural Stories of Arthur Conan Doyle* (1979).

The story selected for this volume is a suspenseful thriller—with a fascinating portrait of Victorian university life—that just might have served as uncredited inspiration for the first of the mummy movies (*The Mummy*, 1932).

LOT NO. 249

Of the dealings of Edward Bellingham with William Monkhouse Lee, and of the cause of the great terror of Abercrombie Smith, it may be that no absolute and final judgment will ever be delivered. It is true that we have the full and clear narrative of Smith himself, and such corroboration as he could look for from Thomas Styles the servant, from the Reverend Plumptree Peterson, Fellow of Old's, and from such other people as chanced to gain some passing glance at this or that incident in a singular chain of events. Yet, in the main, the story must rest upon Smith alone, and the most will think that it is more likely that one brain, however outwardly sane, has some subtle warp in its texture, some strange flaw in its workings, than that the path of Nature has been overstepped in open day in so famed a center of learning and light as the University of Oxford. Yet when we think how narrow and how devious this path of Nature is, how dimly we can trace it, for all our lamps of science, and how from the darkness which girds it round great and terrible possibilities loom ever shadowly upwards, it is a bold and confident man who will put a limit to the strange by-paths into which the human spirit may wander.

In a certain wing of what we will call Old College in Oxford there is a corner turret of an exceeding great age. The heavy arch which spans the open door has bent downward in the center under the weight of its years, and the grey, lichen-blotched blocks of stone are bound and knitted together with withes and strands of ivy, as though the old mother had set herself to brace them up against wind and weather. From the door a stone stair curves upward spirally, passing two landings, and terminating in a third one, its steps all shapeless and hollowed by the tread of so many generations of the seekers after knowledge. Life has flowed like water down this winding stair, and, waterlike, has left these smooth-worn grooves behind it. From the long-gowned, pedantic scholars of Plantagenet days down to the young bloods of a later age, how full and strong had been that tide of young, English life. And what was left now of all those hopes, those strivings, those fiery energies, save here and there in some old-world churchyard a few scratches upon a stone, and perchance a handful of dust in a mouldering coffin? Yet here were the silent stair and the grey, old wall, with bend and saltire and many another heraldic device still to be read upon its surface, like grotesque shadows thrown back from the days that had passed.

In the month of May, in the year 1884, three young men occupied the sets of rooms which opened onto the separate landings of the old stair. Each set consisted simply of a sitting room and of a bedroom, while the two corresponding rooms upon the ground floor were used, the one as a coal cellar, and the other as the living room of the servant, or scout, Thomas Styles, whose duty it was to wait upon the three men above him. To right and to left was a line of lecture rooms and of offices, so that the dwellers in the old turret enjoyed a certain seclusion, which made the chambers popular among the more studious undergraduates. Such were the three who occupied them now—Abercrombie Smith above, Edward Bellingham beneath him, and William Monkhouse Lee upon the lowest storey.

It was ten o'clock on a bright, spring night, and Abercrombie Smith lay back in his armchair, his feet upon the fender, and his briar-root pipe between his lips. In a similar chair, and equally at his ease, there lounged on the other side of the fireplace his old school friend Jephro Hastie. Both men were in flannels, for they had spent their evening upon the river, but apart from their dress no one could look at their hard-cut, alert faces without seeing that they were open-air men—men whose minds and tastes turned naturally to all that was manly and robust. Hastie, indeed, was stroke of his college boat, and Smith was an even better oar, but a coming examination had already cast its shadow over him and held him to his work, save for the few hours a week which health demanded. A litter of medical books upon the table, with scattered bones, models, and anatomical plates, pointed to the extent as well as the nature of his studies, while a couple of single-sticks and a set of boxing-gloves above the mantelpiece hinted at the means by which, with Hastie's help, he might take his exercise in its most compressed and least-distant form. They knew each other very well—so well that they could sit now in that soothing silence which is the very highest development of companionship.

"Have some whisky," said Abercrombie Smith at last between two cloudbursts. "Scotch in the jug and Irish in the bottle."

"No, thanks. I'm in for the sculls. I don't liquor when I'm training. How about you?"

"I'm reading hard. I think it best to leave it alone."

Hastie nodded, and they relapsed into a contented silence.

"By the way, Smith," asked Hastie, presently, "have you made the acquaintance of either of the fellows on your stair yet?"

"Just a nod when we pass. Nothing more."

"Hum! I should be inclined to let it stand at that. I know something of them both. Not much, but as much as I want. I don't think I should take them to my bosom if I were you. Not that there's much amiss with Monkhouse Lee."

"Meaning the thin one?"

"Precisely. He is a gentlemanly little fellow. I don't think there is any vice in him. But then you can't know him without knowing Bellingham."

"Meaning the fat one?"

"Yes, the fat one. And he's a man whom I, for one, would rather not know."

Abercrombie Smith raised his eyebrows and glanced across at his companion.

"What's up, then?" he asked. "Drink? Cards? Cad? You used not to be censorious."

"Ah! you evidently don't know the man, or you wouldn't ask. There's something damnable about him—something reptilian. My gorge always rises at him. I should put him down as a man with secret vices—an evil liver. He's no fool, though. They say that he is one of the best men in his line that they have ever had in the college."

"Medicine or classics?"

"Eastern languages. He's a demon at them. Chillingworth met him somewhere above the second cataract last long, and he told me that he just prattled to the Arabs as if he had been born and nursed and weaned among them. He talked Coptic to the Copts, and Hebrew to the Jews, and

Arabic to the Bedouins, and they were all ready to kiss the hem of his frock coat. There are some old hermit Johnnies up in those parts who sit on rocks and scowl and spit at the casual stranger. Well, when they saw this chap Bellingham, before he had said five words they just lay down on their bellies and wriggled. Chillingworth said that he never saw anything like it. Bellingham seemed to take it as his right, too, and strutted about among them and talked down to them like a Dutch uncle. Pretty good for an undergrad of Old's, wasn't it?''

''Why do you say you can't know Lee without knowing Bellingham?''

''Because Bellingham is engaged to his sister Eveline. Such a bright little girl, Smith! I know the whole family well. It's disgusting to see that brute with her. A toad and a dove, that's what they always remind me of.''

Abercrombie Smith grinned and knocked his ashes out against the side of the grate.

''You show every card in your hand, old chap,'' said he. ''What a prejudiced, green-eyed, evil-thinking old man he is! You have really nothing against the fellow except that.''

''Well, I've know her ever since she was as long as that cherry-wood pipe, and I don't like to see her taking risks. And it is a risk. He looks beastly. And he has a beastly temper, a venomous temper. You remember his row with Long Norton?''

''No; you always forget that I am a freshman.''

''Ah, it was last winter. Of course. Well, you know the towpath along by the river. There were several fellows going along it, Bellingham in front, when they came on an old market-woman coming the other way. It had been raining—you know what those fields are like when it has rained—and the path ran between the river and a great puddle that was nearly as broad. Well, what does this swine do but keep the path, and push the old girl into the mud, where she and her marketings came to terrible grief. It was a blackguard thing to do, and Long Norton, who is as gentle a fellow as ever stepped, told him what he thought of it. One word led to another, and it ended in Norton laying his stick across the fellow's shoulders. There was the deuce of a fuss about it, and it's a treat to see the way in which Bellingham looks at Norton when they meet now. By Jove, Smith, it's nearly eleven o'clock!''

''No hurry. Light your pipe again.''

"Not I. I'm supposed to be in training. Here I've been sitting gossiping when I ought to have been safely tucked up. I'll borrow your skull, if you can share it. Williams has had mine for a month. I'll take the little bones of your ear, too, if you are sure you won't need them. Thanks very much. Never mind a bag, I can carry them very well under my arm. Good night, my son, and take my tip as to your neighbor."

When Hastie, bearing his anatomical plunder, had clattered off Hadown the winding stair, Abercrombie Smith hurled his pipe into the wastepaper basket, and drawing his chair nearer to the lamp, plunged into a formidable, green-covered volume, adorned with great, colored maps of that strange, internal kingdom of which we are the hapless and helpless monarchs. Though a freshman at Oxford, the student was not so in medicine, for he had worked for four years at Glasgow and at Berlin, and this coming examination would place him finally as a member of his profession. With his firm mouth, broad forehead, and clear-cut, somewhat hard-featured face, he was a man who, if he had no brilliant talent, was yet so dogged, so patient, and so strong that he might in the end overtop a more showy genius. A man who can hold his own among Scotchmen and North Germans is not a man to be easily set back. Smith had left a name at Glasgow and at Berlin, and he was bent now upon doing as much at Oxford, if hard work and devotion could accomplish it.

He had sat reading for about an hour, and the hands of the noisy carriage clock upon the side-table were rapidly closing together upon the twelve, when a sudden sound fell upon the student's ear—a sharp, rather shrill sound, like the hissing intake of a man's breath who gasps under some strong emotion. Smith laid down his book and slanted his ear to listen. There was no one on either side or above him, so that the interruption came certainly from the neighbor beneath—the same neighbor of whom Hastie had given so unsavoury an account. Smith knew him only as a flabby, pale-faced man of silent and studious habits, a man whose lamp threw a golden bar from the old turret even after he had extinguished his own. This community in lateness had formed a certain silent bond between them. It was soothing to Smith when the hours stole on towards dawning to feel that there was another so close who set as small a value upon his sleep as he did. Even now, as his thoughts turned toward him, Smith's feelings were kindly. Hastie was a good fellow, but he was rough, strong-fibered, with no imagination or sympathy. He could not tolerate departures from what he looked upon as the model type of manliness. If a man could not be measured by a public-school standard, then he was beyond the pale with Hastie. Like so many who are themselves robust, he was apt to confuse the constitution with the character, to ascribe to want of principle what was really a want of circulation. Smith, with his stronger mind, knew his friend's habit, and made allowance for it now as his thoughts turned toward the man beneath him.

There was no return of the singular sound, and Smith was about to turn to his work once more, when suddenly there broke out in the silence of the night a hoarse cry, a positive scream—the call of a man who is moved and shaken beyond all control. Smith sprang out of his chair and dropped his book. He was a man of fairly firm fiber, but there was something in this sudden, uncontrollable shriek of horror which chilled his blood and pringled in his skin. Coming in such a place and at such an hour, it brought a thousand fantastic possibilities into his head. Should he rush down, or was it better to wait? He had all the national hatred of making a scene, and he knew so little of his neighbor that he would not lightly intrude upon his affairs. For a moment he stood in doubt and even as he balanced the matter there was a quick rattle of footsteps upon the stairs, and young Monkhouse Lee, half-dressed and as white as ashes, burst into his room.

"Come down!" he gasped. "Bellingham's ill."

Abercrombie Smith followed him closely downstairs into the sitting room which was beneath his own, and intent as he was upon the matter in hand, he could not but take an amazed glance around him as he crossed the threshold. It was such a chamber as he had never seen before—a museum rather than a study. Walls and ceiling were thickly covered with a thousand strange relics from Egypt and the East. Tall, angular figures bearing burdens or weapons stalked in an uncouth frieze round the apartments. Above were bull-headed, stork-headed, cat-headed, owl-headed statues, with viper-crowned, almond-eyed monarchs, and strange, beetlelike deities cut out of the blue Egyptian lapis lazuli. Horus and Isis and Osiris peeped down from every niche and shelf, while across the ceiling a true son of Old Nile, a great, hanging-jawed crocodile, was slung in a double noose.

In the center of this singular chamber was a large, square table, littered with papers, bottles, and the dried leaves of some graceful, palmlike plant. These varied objects had all been heaped together in order to make room for a mummy case, which had been conveyed from the wall, as was evident from the gap there, and laid across the front of the table. The mummy itself, a horrid, black, withered thing, like a charred head on a gnarled bush, was lying half out of the case, with its clawlike hand and bony forearm resting upon the table. Propped up against the sarcophagus was an old, yellow scroll of papyrus, and in front of it, in a wooden armchair, sat the owner of the room, his head thrown back, his widely opened eyes directed in a horrified stare to the crocodile above him, and his blue, thick lips puffing loudly with every expiration.

"My God! he's dying!" cried Monkhouse Lee, distractedly.

He was a slim, handsome young fellow, olive-skinned and dark-eyed, of a Spanish rather than of an English type, with a Celtic intensity of manner which contrasted with the Saxon phlegm of Abercrombie Smith.

"Only a faint, I think," said the medical student. "Just give me a hand with him. You take his feet. Now on to the sofa. Can you kick all those little wooden devils off? What a litter it is! Now he will be all right if we undo his collar and give him some water. What has he been up to at all?"

"I don't know. I heard him cry out. I ran up. I know him pretty well, you know. It is very good of you to come down."

"His heart is going like a pair of castanets," said Smith, laying his hand on the breast of the unconscious man. "He seems to me to be frightened all to pieces. Chuck the water over him! What a face he has got on him!"

It was indeed a strange and most repellent face, for color and outline were equally unnatural. It was white, not with the ordinary pallor of fear, but with an absolutely bloodless white, like the under side of a sole. He was very fat, but gave the impression of having at some time been considerably fatter, for his skin hung loosely in creases and folds, and was shot with a meshwork of wrinkles. Short, stubbly brown hair bristled up from his scalp, with a pair of thick, wrinkled ears protruding at the sides. His light-grey eyes were still open, the pupils dilated and the balls projecting in a fixed and horrid stare. It seemed to Smith as he looked down upon him that he had never seen Nature's danger signals flying so plainly upon a man's countenance, and his thoughts turned more seriously to the warning which Hastie had given him an hour before.

"What the deuce can have frightened him so?" he asked.

"It's the mummy."

"The mummy? How, then?"

"I don't know. It's beastly and morbid. I wish he would drop it. It's the second fright he has given me. It was the same last winter. I found him just like this, with that horrid thing in front of him."

"What does he want with the mummy, then?"

"Oh, he's a crank, you know. It's his hobby. He knows more about these things than any man in England. But I wish he wouldn't! Ah, he's beginning to come to."

A faint tinge of color had begun to steal back into Bellingham's ghastly cheeks, and his eyelids shivered like a sail after a calm. He clasped and unclasped his hands, drew a long, thin breath between his teeth, and suddenly jerking up his head, threw a glance of recognition around him. As his eyes fell upon the mummy, he sprang off the sofa, seized the roll of papyrus, thrust it into a drawer, turned the key, and then staggered back on to the sofa.

"What's up?" he asked. "What do you chaps want?"

"You've been shrieking out and making no end of a fuss," said Monkhouse Lee. "If our neighbor here from above hadn't come down, I'm sure I don't know what I should have done with you."

"Ah, it's Abercrombie Smith," said Bellingham, glancing up at him. "How very good of you to come in! What a fool I am! Oh, my God, what a fool I am!"

He sank his head on to his hands, and burst into peal after peal of hysterical laughter.

"Look here! Drop it!" cried Smith, shaking him roughly by the shoulder.

"Your nerves are all in a jangle You must drop these little midnight games with mummies, or you'll be going off your chump. You're all on wires now."

"I wonder," said Bellingham, "whether you would be as cool as I am if you had seen—"

"What then?"

"Oh, nothing. I meant that I wonder if you could sit up at night with a mummy without trying your nerves. I have no doubt that you are quite right. I dare say that I have been taking it out of myself too much lately. But I am all right now. Please don't go, though. Just wait for a few minutes until I am quite myself."

"The room is very close," remarked Lee, throwing open the window and letting in the cool night air.

"It's balsamic resin," said Bellingham. He lifted up one of the dried palmate leaves from the table and frizzled it over the chimney of the lamp. It broke away into heavy smoke wreaths, and a pungent, biting odor filled the chamber. "It's the sacred plant—the plant of the priests," he remarked. "Do you know anything of Eastern languages, Smith?"

"Nothing at all. Not a word."

The answer seemed to lift a weight from the Egyptologist's mind.

"By the way," he continued, "how long was it from the time that you ran down, until I came to my senses?"

"Not long. Some four or five minutes."

"I thought it could not be very long," said he, drawing a long breath. "But what a strange thing unconsciousness is! There is no measurement to it. I could not tell from my own sensations if it were seconds or weeks. Now that gentleman on the table was packed up in the days of the eleventh dynasty, some forty centuries ago, and yet if he could find his tongue, he would tell us that this lapse of time has been but a closing of the eyes and a reopening of them. He is a singularly fine mummy, Smith."

Smith stepped over to the table and looked down with a professional eye at the black and twisted form in front of him. The features, though horribly discolored, were perfect, and two little nutlike eyes still lurked in the depths of the black, hollow sockets. The blotched skin was drawn tightly from bone to bone, and a tangled wrap of black, coarse hair fell over the ears. Two thin teeth, like those of a rat, overlay the shrivelled lower lip. In its crouching position, with bent joints and craned head, there was a suggestion of energy about the horrid thing which made Smith's gorge rise. The gaunt ribs, with their parchment-like covering, were exposed, and the sunken, leaden-hued abdomen, with the long slit where the embalmer had left his mark; but the lower limbs were wrapped round with coarse, yellow bandages. A number of little clovelike pieces of myrrh and of cassia were sprinkled over the body, and lay scattered on the inside of the case.

"I don't know his name," said Bellingham, passing his hand over the shrivelled head. "You see the outer sarcophagus with the inscriptions is missing. Lot 249 is all the title he has now. You see it printed on his case. That was his number in the auction at which I picked him up."

"He has been a very pretty sort of fellow in his day," remarked Abercrombie Smith.

"He has been a giant. His mummy is six feet seven in length, and that would be a giant over there, for they were never a very robust race. Feel these great, knotted bones, too. He would be a nasty fellow to tackle."

"Perhaps these very hands helped to build the stones into the pyramids," suggested Monkhouse Lee, looking down with disgust in his eyes at the crooked, unclean talons.

"No fear. This fellow has been pickled in natron, and looked after in the most approved style. They did not serve hodmen in that fashion. Salt or bitumen was enough for them. It has been calculated that this sort of thing cost about seven hundred and thirty pounds in our money. Our friend was a noble at the least. What do you make of that small inscription near his feet, Smith?"

"I told you that I know no Eastern tongue."

"Ah, so you did. It is the name of the embalmer, I take it. A very conscientious worker he must have been. I wonder how many modern works will survive four thousand years?"

He kept on speaking lightly and rapidly, but it was evident to Abercrombie Smith that he was still palpitating with fear. His hands shook, his lower lip trembled, and look where he would, his eye always came sliding round to his gruesome companion. Through all his fear, however, there was a suspicion of triumph in his tone and manner. His eyes shone, and his footstep, as he paced the room, was brisk and jaunty. He gave the impression of a man who has gone through an ordeal, the marks of which he still bears upon him, but which has helped him to his end.

"You're not going yet?" he cried, as Smith rose from the sofa.

At the prospect of solitude, his fears seemed to crowd back upon him, and he stretched out a hand to detain him.

"Yes, I must go. I have my work to do. You are all right now. I think that with your nervous system you should take up some less morbid study."

"Oh, I am not nervous as a rule; and I have unwrapped mummies before."

"You fainted last time," observed Monkhouse Lee.

"Ah, yes, so I did. Well, I must have a nerve tonic or a course of electricity. You are not going, Lee?"

"I'll do whatever you wish, Ned."

"Then I'll come down with you and have a shakedown on your sofa. Good night, Smith. I am so sorry to have disturbed you with my foolishness."

They shook hands, and as the medical student stumbled up the spiral and irregular stair he heard a key turn in a door, and the steps of his two new acquaintances as they descended to the lower floor.

In this strange way began the acquaintance between Edward Bellingham and Abercrombie Smith, an acquaintance which the latter, at least, had no desire to push further. Bellingham, however, appeared to have taken a fancy to his rough-spoken neighbor, and made his advances in such a way that he could hardly be repulsed without absolute brutality. Twice he called to thank Smith for his assistance, and many times afterwards he looked in with books, papers, and such other civilities as two bachelor neighbours can offer each other. He was, as Smith soon found, a man of wide reading, with catholic tastes and an extraordinary memory. His manner, too, was so pleasing and suave that one came, after a time, to overlook his repellent appearance. For a jaded and wearied man he was no unpleasant companion, and Smith found himself, after a time, looking forward to his visits, and even returning them.

Clever as he undoubtedly was, however, the medical student seemed to detect a dash of insanity in the man. He broke out at times into a high, inflated style of talk which was in contrast with the simplicity of his life.

"It is a wonderful thing," he cried, "to feel that one can command powers of good and of evil—a ministering angel or a demon of vengeance." And again, of Monkhouse Lee, he said—"Lee is a good fellow, an honest fellow, but he is without strength or ambition. He would not make a fit partner for a man with a great enterprise. He would not make a fit partner for me."

At such hints and innuendoes stolid Smith, puffing solemnly at his pipe, would simply raise his eyebrows and shake his head, with little interjections of medical wisdom as to earlier hours and fresher air.

One habit Bellingham had developed of late which Smith knew to be a frequent herald of a weakening mind. He appeared to be forever talking to himself. At late hours of the night, when there could be no visitor with him, Smith could still hear his voice beneath him in a low, muffled monologue, sunk almost to a whisper, and yet very audible in the silence. This solitary babbling annoyed and distracted the student, so that he spoke more than once to his neighbour about it. Bellingham, however, flushed up at the charge, and denied curtly that he had uttered a sound; indeed, he showed more annoyance over the matter than the occasion seemed to demand.

Had Abercrombie Smith had any doubt as to his own ears he had not to go far to find corroboration. Tom Styles, the little wrinkled man-servant who had attended to the wants of the lodgers in the turret for a longer time than any man's memory could carry him, was sorely put to it over the same matter.

"If you please, sir," said he, as he tidied down the top chamber one morning, "do you think Mr. Bellingham is all right, sir?"

"All right, Styles?"

"Yes, sir. Right in his head, sir."

"Why should he not be, then?"

"Well, I don't know, sir. His habits has changed of late. He's not the same man he used to be, though I make free to say that he was never quite one of my gentlemen, like Mr. Hastie or yourself, sir. He's took to talkin' to himself something awful. I wonder it don't disturb you. I don't know what to make of him, sir."

"I don't know what business it is of yours, Styles."

"Well, I takes an interest, Mr. Smith. It may be forward of me, but I can't help it. I feel sometimes as if I was mother and father to my young gentlemen. It all falls on me when things go wrong and the relations come. But Mr. Bellingham, sir. I want to know what it is that walks about his room sometimes when he's out and when the door's locked on the outside."

"Eh? you're talking nonsense, Styles."

"Maybe so, sir; but I heard it more'n once with my own ears."

"Rubbish, Styles."

"Very good, sir. You'll ring the bell if you want me."

Abercrombie Smith gave little heed to the gossip of the old man-servant, but a small incident occurred a few days later which left an unpleasant effect upon his mind, and brought the words of Styles forcibly to his memory.

Bellingham had come up to see him late one night, and was entertaining him with an interesting account of the rock tombs of Beni Hassan in Upper Egypt, when Smith, whose hearing was remarkable acute, distinctly heard the sound of a door opening on the landing below.

"There's some fellow gone in or out of your room," he remarked.

Bellingham sprang up and stood helpless for a moment, with the expression of a man who is half-incredulous and half-afraid.

"I surely locked it. I am almost positive that I locked it," he stammered. "No one could have opened it."

"Why, I hear someone coming up the steps now," said Smith.

Bellingham rushed out through the door, slammed it loudly behind him, and hurried down the stairs. About halfway down Smith heard him stop, and thought he caught the sound of whispering. A moment later the door beneath him shut, a key creaked in a lock, and Bellingham, with beads of moisture upon his pale face, ascended the stairs once more, and re-entered the room.

"It's all right," he said, throwing himself down in a chair. "It was that fool of a dog. He had pushed the door open. I don't know how I came to forget to lock it."

"I didn't know you kept a dog," said Smith, looking very thoughtfully at the disturbed face of his companion.

"Yes, I haven't had him long. I must get rid of him. He's a great nuisance."

"He must be, if you find it so hard to shut him up. I should have thought that shutting the door would have been enough, without locking it."

"I want to prevent old Styles from letting him out. He's of some value, you know, and it would be awkward to lose him."

"I am a bit of a dog-fancier myself," said Smith, still gazing hard at his companion from the corner of his eyes. "Perhaps you'll let me have a look at it."

"Certainly. But I am afraid it cannot be tonight; I have an appointment. Is that clock right? Then I am a quarter of an hour late already. You'll excuse me, I am sure."

He picked up his cap and hurried from the room. In spite of his appointment, Smith heard him re-enter his own chamber and lock his door upon the inside.

This interview left a disagreeable impression upon the medical student's mind. Bellingham had lied to him, and lied so clumsily that it looked as if he had desperate reasons for concealing the truth. Smith knew that his neighbour had no dog. He knew, also, that the step which he had heard upon the stairs was not the step of an animal. But if it were not, then what could it be? There was old Style's statement about the something which used to pace the room at times when the owner was absent. Could it be a woman? Smith rather inclined to the view. If so, it would mean disgrace and expulsion to Bellingham if it were discovered by the authorities, so that his anxiety and falsehoods might be accounted for. And yet it was inconceivable that an undergraduate could keep a woman in his rooms without being instantly detected. Be the explanation what it might, there was something ugly about it, and Smith determined, as he turned to his books, to discourage all further attempts at intimacy on the part of his soft-spoken and ill-favored neighbor.

But his work was destined to interruption that night. He had hardly caught up the broken threads when a firm, heavy footfall came three steps at a time from below, and Hastie, in blazer and flannels, burst into the room.

"Still at it!" said he, plumping down into his wonted armchair. "What a chap you are to stew! I believe an earthquake might come and knock Oxford into a cocked hat, and you would sit perfectly placid with your books among the ruins. However, I won't bore you long. Three whiffs of baccy, and I am off."

"What's the news, then?" asked Smith, cramming a plug of bird's-eye into his briar with his forefinger.

"Nothing very much. Wilson made seventy for the freshmen against the eleven. They say that they will play him instead of Buddicomb, for Buddicomb is clean off colour. He used to be able to bowl a little, but it's nothing but half-volleys and long hops now."

"Medium right," suggested Smith, with the intense gravity which comes upon a varsity man when he speaks of athletics.

"Inclining to fast, with a work from leg. Comes with the arm about three inches or so. He used to be nasty on a wet wicket. Oh, by the way, have you heard about Long Norton?"

"What's that?"

"He's been attacked."

"Attacked?"

"Yes, just as he was turning out of the High Street, and within a hundred yards of the gate of Old's."

"But who—"

"Ah, that's the rub! If you said 'what,' you would be more

grammatical. Norton swears that it was not human, and, indeed, from the scratches on his throat, I should be inclined to agree with him."

"What, then? Have we come down to spooks?"

Abercrombie Smith puffed his scientific contempt.

"Well, no; I don't think that is quite the idea, either. I am inclined to think that if any showman has lost a great ape lately, and the brute is in these parts, a jury would find a true bill against it. Norton passes that way every night, you know, about the same hour. There's a tree that hangs low over the path—the big elm from Rainy's garden. Norton thinks the thing dropped on him out of the tree. Anyhow, he was nearly strangled by two arms, which, he says, were as strong and as thin as steel bands. He saw nothing; only those beastly arms that tightened and tightened on him. He yelled his head nearly off, and a couple of chaps came running, and the thing went over the wall like a cat. He never got a fair sight of it the whole time. It gave Norton a shake up, I can tell you. I tell him it has been as good as a change at the seaside for him."

"A garrotter, most likely," said Smith.

"Very possibly. Norton says not; but we don't mind what he says. The garrotter had long nails, and was pretty smart at swinging himself over walls. By the way, your beautiful neighbor would be pleased if he heard about it. He had a grudge against Norton, and he's not a man, from what I know of him, to forget his little debts. But hallo, old chap, what have you got in your noddle?"

"Nothing," Smith answered curtly.

He had started in his chair, and the look had flashed over his face which comes upon a man who is struck suddenly by some unpleasant idea.

"You looked as if something I had said had taken you on the raw. By the way, you have made the acquaintance of Master B. since I looked in last, have you not? Young Monkhouse Lee told me something to that effect."

"Yes; I know him slightly. He has been up here once or twice."

"Well, you're big enough and ugly enough to take care of yourself. He's not what I should call exactly a healthy sort of Johnny, though, no doubt, he's very clever, and all that. But you'll soon find out for yourself. Lee is all right; he's a very decent little fellow. Well, so long, old chap! I row Mullins for the Vice-Chancellor's pot on Wednesday week, so mind you come down, in case I don't see you before."

Bovine Smith laid down his pipe and turned stolidly to his books once more. But with all the will in the world, he found it very hard to keep his mind upon his work. It would slip away to brood upon the man beneath him, and upon the little mystery which hung round his chambers. Then his thoughts turned to this singular attack of which Hastie had spoken, and to the grudge which Bellingham was said to owe the object of it. The two ideas would persist in rising together in his mind, as though there were some close and intimate connection between them. And yet the suspicion was so dim and vague that it could not be put down in words.

"Confound the chap!" cried Smith, as he shied his book on pathology across the room. "He has spoiled my night's reading, and that's reason enough, if there were no other, why I should steer clear of him in the future."

For ten days the medical student confined himself so closely to his studies that he neither saw nor heard anything of either of the men beneath him. At the hours when Bellingham had been accustomed to visit him, he took care to sport his oak, and though he more than once heard a knocking at his outer door, he resolutely refused to answer it. One afternoon, however, he was descending the stairs when, just as he was passing it, Bellingham's door flew open, and young Monkhouse Lee came out with his eyes sparkling and a dark flush of anger upon his olive cheeks. Close at his heels followed Bellingham, his fat, unhealthy face all quivering with malignant passion.

"You fool!" he hissed. "You'll be sorry."

"Very likely," cried the other. "Mind what I say. It's off! I won't hear of it!"

"You've promised, anyhow."

"Oh, I'll keep that! I won't speak. But I'd rather little Eva was in her grave. Once for all, it's off. She'll do what I say. We don't want to see you again."

So much Smith could not avoid hearing, but he hurried on, for he had no wish to be involved in their dispute. There had been a serious breach between them, that was clear enough, and Lee was going to cause the engagement with his sister to be broken off. Smith thought of Hastie's comparison of the toad and the dove, and was glad to think that the matter was at an end. Bellingham's face when he was in a passion was not pleasant to look upon. He was not a man to whom an innocent girl could be trusted for life. As he walked, Smith wondered languidly what could have caused the quarrel, and what the promise might be which Bellingham had been so anxious that Monkhouse Lee should keep.

It was the day of the sculling match between Hastie and Mullins, and a stream of men were making their way down to the banks of the Isis. A May sun was shining brightly, and the yellow path was barred with the black shadows of the tall elm trees. On either side the grey colleges lay back from the road, the hoary old mothers of minds looking out from their high, mullioned windows at the tide of young life which swept so merrily past them. Black-clad tutors, prim officials, pale, reading men, brown-faced, straw-hatted young athletes in white sweaters or many-colored blazers, all were hurrying towards the blue, winding river which curves through the Oxford meadows.

Abercrombie Smith, with the intuition of an old oarsman, chose his position at the point where he knew that the struggle, if there were a struggle, would come. Far off he heard the hum which announced the start, the gathering roar of the approach, the thunder of running feet, and the shouts of the men in the boats beneath him. A spray of half-clad, deep-breathing runners shot past him, and craning over their shoulders, he saw Hastie pulling a steady thirty-six, while his opponent, with a jerky forty, was a good boat's length behind him. Smith gave a cheer for his friend, and pulling out his watch, was starting off again for his chambers, when he felt a touch upon his shoulder, and found that young Monkhouse Lee was beside him.

"I saw you there," he said, in a timid, deprecating way. "I wanted to speak to you, if you could spare me a half-hour. This cottage is mine. I share it with Harrington of King's. Come in and have a cup of tea."

"I must be back presently," said Smith. "I am hard on the grind at present. But I'll come in for a few minutes with pleasure. I wouldn't have come out only Hastie is a friend of mine."

"So he is of mine. Hasn't he a beautiful style? Mullins wasn't in it. But come into the cottage. It's a little den of a place, but it is pleasant to work in during the summer months."

It was a small, square, white building, with green doors and shutters, and a rustic trellis-work porch, standing back some fifty yards from the river's bank. Inside, the main room was roughly fitted up as a study—deal table, unpainted shelves with books, and a few cheap oleographs upon the wall. A kettle sang upon a spirit-stove, and there were tea things upon a tray on the table.

"Try that chair and have a cigarette," said Lee. "Let me pour you out a cup of tea. It's so good of you to come in, for I know that your time is a good deal taken up. I wanted to say to you that, if I were you, I should change my rooms at once."

"Eh?"

Smith sat staring with a lighted match in one hand and his unlit cigarette in the other.

"Yes; it must seem very extraordinary, and the worst of it is that I cannot give my reasons, for I am under a solemn promise—a very solemn promise. But I may go so far as to say that I don't think Bellingham is a very safe man to live near. I intend to camp out here as much as I can for a time."

"Not safe! What do you mean?"

"Ah, that's what I musn't say. But do take my advice and move your rooms. We had a grand row today. You must have heard us, for you came down the stairs."

"I saw that you had fallen out."

"He's a horrible chap, Smith. That is the only word for him. I have had doubts about him ever since that night when he fainted—you remember, when you came down. I taxed him today, and he told me things that made my hair rise, and wanted me to stand in with him. I'm not straight-laced, but I am a clergyman's son, you know, and I think there are some things which are quite beyond the pale. I only thank God that I found him out before it was too late, for he was to have married into my family."

"This is all very fine, Lee," said Abercrombie Smith curtly. "But either you are saying a great deal too much or a great deal too little."

"I give you a warning."

"If there is real reason for warning, no promise can bind you. If I see a rascal about to blow a place up with dynamite no pledge will stand in my way of preventing him."

"Ah, but I cannot prevent him, and I can do nothing but warn you."

"Without saying what you warn me against."

"Against Bellingham."

"But that is childish. Why should I fear him, or any man?"

"I can't tell you. I can only entreat you to change your rooms. You are in danger where you are. I don't even say that Bellingham would wish to injure you. But it might happen, for he is a dangerous neighbor just now."

"Perhaps I know more than you think," said Smith, looking keenly at the young man's boyish, earnest face. "Suppose I tell you that someone else shares Bellingham's rooms."

Monkhouse Lee sprang from his chair in uncontrollable excitement.

"You know, then?" he gasped.

"A woman."

Lee dropped back again with a groan.

"My lips are sealed," he said. "I must not speak."

"Well, anyhow," said Smith, rising, "it is not likely that I should allow myself to be frightened out of rooms which suit me very nicely. It would be a little too feeble for me to move out all my goods and chattels because you say that Bellingham might in some unexplained way do me an injury. I think that I'll just take my chance, and stay where I am, and as I see that it's nearly five o'clock, I must ask you to excuse me."

He bade the young student adieu in a few curt words, and made his way homeward through the sweet spring evening, feeling half-ruffled, half-amused, as any other strong, unimaginative man might who has been menaced by a vague and shadowy danger.

There was one little indulgence which Abercrombie Smith always allowed himself, however closely his work might press upon him. Twice a week, on the Tuesday and the Friday, it was his invariable custom to walk over to Farlingford, the residence of Doctor Plumptree Peterson, situated about a mile and a half out of Oxford. Peterson had been a close friend of Smith's elder brother, Francis, and as he was a bachelor, fairly well-to-do, with a good cellar and a better library, his house was a pleasant goal for a man who was in need of a brisk walk. Twice a week, then, the medical student would swing out there along the dark country roads and spend a pleasant hour in Peterson's comfortable study, discussing, over a glass of old port, the gossip of the varsity or the latest developments of medicine or of surgery.

On the day which followed his interview with Monkhouse Lee, Smith shut up his books at a quarter past eight, the hour when he usually started for his friend's house. As he was leaving his room, however, his eyes chanced to fall upon one of the books which Bellingham had lent him, and his conscience pricked him for not having returned it. However repellent the man might be, he should not be treated with discourtesy. Taking the book, he walked downstairs and knocked at his neighbor's door. There was no answer; but on turning the handle he found that it was unlocked. Pleased at the thought of avoiding an interview, he stepped inside, and placed the book with his card upon the table.

The lamp was turned half down, but Smith could see the details of the room plainly enough. It was all much as he had seen it before—the frieze, the animal-headed gods, the hanging crocodile, and the table littered over with papers and dried leaves. The mummy case stood upright against the wall, but the mummy itself was missing. There was no sign of any second occupant of the room, and he felt as he withdrew that he had probably done Bellingham an injustice. Had he a guilty secret to preserve, he would hardly leave his door open so that all the world might enter.

The spiral stair was as black as pitch, and Smith was slowly making his way down its irregular steps, when he was suddenly conscious that something had passed him in the darkness. There was a faint sound, a whiff of air, a light brushing past his elbow, but so slight that he could scarcely be certain of it. He stopped and listened, but the wind was rustling among the ivy outside, and he could hear nothing else.

"Is that you, Styles?" he shouted.

There was no answer, and all was still behind him. It must have been a sudden gust of air, for there were crannies and cracks in the old turret. And yet he could almost have sworn that he heard a footfall by his very side. He had emerged into the quadrangle, still turning the matter over in his head, when a man came running swiftly across the smooth-cropped lawn.

"Is that you Smith?"

"Hullo, Hastie!"

"For God's sake come at once! Young Lee is drowned! Here's Harrington of King's with the news. The doctor is out. You'll do, but come along at once. There may be life in him."

"Have you brandy?"

"No."

"I'll bring some. There's a flask on my table."

Smith bounded up the stairs, taking three at a time, seized the flask, and was rushing down with it, when, as he passed Bellingham's room, his eyes fell upon something which left him gasping and staring upon the landing.

The door, which he had closed behind him, was now open, and right in front of him, with the lamplight shining upon it, was the mummy case. Three minutes ago it had been empty. He could swear to that. Now it framed the lank body of its horrible occupant, who stood, grim and stark, with his black, shrivelled face toward the door. The form was lifeless and inert, but it seemed to Smith as he gazed that there still lingered a lurid spark of vitality, some faint sign of consciousness in the little eyes which lurked in the depths of the hollow sockets. So astounded and shaken was he that he had forgotten his errand, and was still staring at the lean, sunken figure when the voice of his friend below recalled him to himself.

"Come on, Smith!" he shouted. "It's life and death, you know. Hurry up! Now, then," he added, as the medical student reappeared, "let us do a sprint. It is well under a mile, and we should do it in five minutes. A human life is better worth running for than a pot."

Neck and neck they dashed through the darkness, and did not pull up until panting and spent, they had reached the little cottage by the river. Young Lee, limp and dripping like a broken water-plant, was stretched upon the sofa, the green scum of the river upon his black hair, and a fringe of white foam upon his leaden-hued lips. Beside him knelt his fellow student, Harrington, endeavoring to chafe some warmth back into his rigid limbs.

"I think there's life in him," said Smith, with his hand to the lad's side. "Put your watch glass to his lips. Yes, there's dimming on it. You take one arm, Hastie. Now work it as I do, and we'll soon pull him round."

For ten minutes they worked in silence, inflating and depressing the chest of the unconscious man. At the end of that time a shiver ran through his body, his lips trembled, and he opened his eyes. The three students burst out into an irrepressible cheer.

"Wake up, old chap. You've frightened us quite enough."

"Have some brandy. Take a sip from the flask."

"He's all right now," said his companion Harrington. "Heavens, what a fright I got! I was reading here, and he had gone out for a stroll as far as the river, when I heard a scream and a splash. Out I ran, and by the time I could find him and fish him out, all life seemed to have gone. Then

Simpson couldn't get a doctor, for he has a game leg, and I had to run, and I don't know what I'd have done without you fellows. That's right, old chap. Sit up.''

Monkhouse Lee had raised himself on his hands, and looked wildly about him.

''What's up?'' he asked. ''I've been in the water. Ah, yes; I remember.''

A look of fear came into his eyes, and he sank his face into his hands.

''How did you fall in?''

''I didn't fall in.''

''How then?''

''I was thrown in. I was standing by the bank, and something from behind picked me up like a feather and hurled me in. I heard nothing, and I saw nothing. But I know what it was, for all that.''

''And so do I,'' whispered Smith.

Lee looked up with a quick glance of surprise.

''You've learned, then?'' he said. ''You remember the advice I gave you?''

''Yes, and I begin to think that I shall take it.''

''I don't know what the deuce you fellows are talking about,'' said Hastie, ''but I think, if I were you, Harrington, I should get Lee to bed at once. It will be time enough to discuss the why and the wherefore when he is a little stronger. I think, Smith, you and I can leave him alone now. I am walking back to college; if you are coming in that direction, we can have a chat.''

But it was little chat that they had upon their homeward path. Smith's mind was too full of the incidents of the evening, the absence of the mummy from his neighbor's rooms, the step that passed him on the stair, the reappearance—the extraordinary, inexplicable reapparance of the grisly thing—and then this attack upon Lee, corresponding so closely to the previous outrage upon another man against whom Bellingham bore a grudge. All this settled in his thoughts, together with the many little incidents which had previously turned him against his neighbor, and the singular circumstances under which he was first called in to him. What had been a dim suspicion, a vague, fantastic conjecture, had suddenly taken form, and stood out in his mind as a grim fact, a thing not to be denied. And yet, how monstrous it was! how unheard of! how entirely beyond all bounds of human experience. An impartial judge, or even the friend who walked by his side, would simply tell him that his eyes had deceived him, that the mummy had been there all the time, that young Lee had tumbled into the river as any other man tumbles into a river, and the blue pill was the best thing for a disordered liver. He felt that he would have said as much if the positions had been reversed. And yet he could swear that Bellingham was a murderer at heart, and that he wielded a weapon such as no man had ever used in all the grim history of crime.

Hastie had branched off to his rooms with a few crisp and emphatic comments upon his friend's unsociability, and Abercrombie Smith acrossed the quadrangle to his corner turret with a strong feeling of repulsion for his chambers and their associations. He would take Lee's advice, and move his quarters as soon as possible, for how could a man study when his ear was ever straining for every murmur or footstep in the room below? He observed, as he crossed over the lawn, that the light was still shining in Bellingham's window, and as he passed up the staircase the door opened, and the man himself looked out at him. With his fat, evil face he was like some bloated spider fresh from the weaving of his poisonous web.

"Good evening," said he. "Won't you come in?"

"No," cried Smith fiercely.

"No? You are as busy as ever? I wanted to ask you about Lee. I was sorry to hear that there was a rumor that something was amiss with him."

His features were grave, but there was the gleam of a hidden laugh in his eyes as he spoke. Smith saw it, and he could have knocked him down for it.

"You'll be sorrier still to hear that Monkhouse Lee is doing very well, and is out of all danger," he answered. "Your hellish tricks have not come off this time. Oh, you needen't try to brazen it out. I know all about it."

Bellingham took a step back from the angry student, and half-closed the door as if to protect himself.

"You are mad," he said. "What do you mean? Do you assert that I had anything to do with Lee's accident?"

"Yes," thundered Smith. "You and that bag of bones behind you; you worked it between you. I tell you what it is, Master B., they have given up burning folk like you, but we still keep a hangman, and, by George! if any man in this college meets his death while you are here, I'll have you up, and if you don't swing for it, it won't be my fault. You'll find that your filthy Egyptian tricks won't answer in England."

"You're a raving lunatic," said Bellingham.

"All right. You just remember what I say, for you'll find that I'll be better than my word."

The door slammed, and Smith went fuming up to his chamber, where he locked the door upon the inside, and spent half the night in smoking his old briar and brooding over the strange events of the evening.

Next morning Abercrombie Smith heard nothing of his neighbor, but Harrington called upon him in the afternoon to say that Lee was almost himself again. All day Smith stuck fast to his work, but in the evening he determined to pay the visit to his friend Doctor Peterson upon which he had started the night before. A good walk and a friendly chat would be welcome to his jangled nerves.

Bellingham's door was shut as he passed, but glancing back when he was some distance from the turret, he saw his neighbor's head at the window outlined against the lamplight, his face pressed apparently against the glass as he gazed out into the darkness. It was a blessing to be away from all contact with him, if but for a few hours, and Smith stepped out briskly, and breathed the soft spring air into his lungs. The half-moon lay in the west between two Gothic pinnacles, and threw upon the silvered street a dark tracery from the stonework above. There was a brisk breeze, and light, fleecy clouds drifted swiftly across the sky. Old's was on the very border of the town, and in five minutes Smith found himself beyond the houses and between the hedges of a May-scented, Oxfordshire lane.

It was a lonely and little-frequented road which led to his friend's house. Early as it was, Smith did not meet a single soul upon his way. He walked briskly along until he came to the avenue gate, which opened into the long, gravel drive leading up to Farlingford. In front of him he could see the cosy, red light of the windows glimmering through the foliage. He stood with his hand upon the iron latch of the swinging gate, and he glanced back at the road along which he had come. Something was coming swiftly down it.

It moved in the shadow of the hedge, silently and furtively, a dark, crouching figure, dimly visible against the black background. Even as he gazed back at it, it had lessened its distance by twenty paces, and was fast closing upon him. Out of the darkness he had a glimpse of a scraggy neck, and of two eyes that will ever haunt him in his dreams. He turned, and with a cry of terror he ran for his life up the avenue. There were the red lights, the signals of safety, almost within a stone's throw of him. He was a famous runner, but never had he run as he ran that night.

The heavy gate had swung into place behind him but he heard it dash open again before his pursuer. As he rushed madly and wildly through the night, he could hear a swift, dry patter behind him, and could see, as he threw back a glance, that this horror was bounding like a tiger at his heels, with blazing eyes and one stringy arm out-thrown. Thank God, the door was ajar. He could see the thin bar of light which shot from the lamp in the hall. Nearer yet sounded the clatter from behind. He heard a hoarse gurgling at his very shoulder. With a shriek he flung himself against the door, slammed and bolted it behind him, and sank half-fainting onto the hall chair.

"My goodness, Smith, what's the matter?" asked Peterson, appearing at the door of his study.

"Give me some brandy."

Peterson disappeared, and came rushing out again with a glass and a decanter.

"You need it," he said, as his visitor drank off what he poured out for him. "Why, man, you are as white as a cheese."

Smith laid down his glass, rose up, and took a deep breath.

"I am my own man again now," said he. "I was never so unmanned before. But, with your leave, Peterson, I will sleep here tonight, for I don't think I could face that road again except by daylight. It's weak, I know, but I can't help it."

Peterson looked at his visitor with a very questioning eye.

"Of course you shall sleep here if you wish. I'll tell Mrs. Burney to make up the spare bed. Where are you off to now?"

"Come up with me to the window that overlooks the door. I want you to see what I have seen."

They went up to the window of the upper hall whence they could look down upon the approach to the house. The drive and the fields on either side lay quiet and still, bathed in the peaceful moonlight.

"Well, really, Smith," remarked Peterson, "it is well that I know you to be an abstemious man. What in the world can have frightened you?"

"I'll tell you presently. But where can it have gone? Ah, now, look, look! See the curve of the road just beyond your gate."

"Yes, I see; you needn't pinch my arm off. I saw someone pass. I should say a man, rather thin, apparently, and tall, very tall. But what of him? And what of yourself? You are still shaking like an aspen leaf."

"I have been within handgrip of the devil, that's all. But come down to your study, and I shall tell you the whole story."

He did so. Under the cheery lamplight with a glass of wine on the table beside him, and the portly form and florid face of his friend in front, he narrated, in their order, all the events, great and small, which had formed so singular a chain, from the night on which he had found Bellingham fainting in front of the mummy case until this horrid experience of an hour ago.

"There now," he said as he concluded, "that's the whole, black business. It is monstrous and incredible, but it is true."

Doctor Plumptree Peterson sat for some time in silence with a very puzzled expression upon his face.

"I never heard of such a thing in my life, never!" he said at last. "You have told me the facts. Now tell me your inferences."

"You can draw your own."

"But I should like to hear yours. You have thought over the matter, and I have not."

"Well, it must be a little vague in detail, but the main points seem to me to be clear enough. This fellow Bellingham, in his Eastern studies, has got hold of some infernal secret by which a mummy—or possibly only this particular mummy—can be temporarily brought to life. He was trying this disgusting business on the night when he fainted. No doubt the sight of the creature moving had shaken his nerve, even though he had expected it. You remember that almost the first words he said were to call out upon himself as a fool. Well, he got more hardened afterwards, and carried the matter through without fainting. The vitality which he could put into it was evidently only a passing thing, for I have seen it continually in its case as dead as this table. He has some elaborate process, I fancy, by which he brings the thing to pass. Having done it, he naturally bethought him that he might use the creature as an agent. It has intelligence and it has strength. For some purpose he took Lee into his confidence; but Lee, like a decent Christian, would have nothing to do with such a business. Then they had a row, and Lee vowed that he would tell his sister of Bellingham's true character. Bellingham's game was to prevent him, and he nearly managed it, by setting this creature of his on his track. He had already tried its powers upon another man—Norton—toward whom he had a grudge. It is the merest chance that he has not two murders upon his soul. Then, when I taxed him with the matter, he had the strongest reasons for wishing to get me out of the way before I could convey my knowledge to anyone else. He got his chance when I went out, for he knew my habits and where I was bound for. I have had a narrow shave, Peterson, and it is mere luck you didn't find me on your doorstep in the morning. I'm not a nervous man as a rule, and I never thought to have the fear of death put upon me as it was tonight."

"My dear boy, you take the matter too seriously," said his companion. "Your nerves are out of order with your work, and you make too much of it. How could such a thing as this stride about the streets of Oxford, even at night, without being seen?"

"It has been seen. There is quite a scare in the town about an escaped ape, as they imagine the creature to be. It is the talk of the place."

"Well, it's a striking chain of events. And yet, my dear fellow, you must allow that each incident in itself is capable of a more natural explanation."

"What! even my adventure of tonight?"

"Certainly. You come out with your nerves all unstrung, and your head full of this theory of yours. Some gaunt, half-famished tramp steals after you, and seeing you run, is emboldened to pursue you. Your fears and imagination do the rest."

"It won't do, Peterson; it won't do."

"And again, in the instance of your finding the mummy case empty, and then a few moments later with an occupant, you know that it was lamplight, that the lamp was half-turned down, and that you had no special reason to look hard at the case. It is quite possible that you may have overlooked the creature in the first instance."

"No, no; it is out of the question."

"And then Lee may have fallen into the river, and Norton been garrotted. It is certainly a formidable indictment that you have against Bellingham; but if you were to place it before a police magistrate, he would simply laugh in your face."

"I know he would. That is why I mean to take the matter into my own hands."

"Eh?"

"Yes; I feel that a public duty rests upon me, and, besides, I must do it for my own safety, unless I choose to allow myself to be hunted by this beast out of the college, and that would be a little too feeble. I have quite made up my mind what I shall do. And first of all, may I use your paper and pens for an hour?"

"Most certainly. You will find all that you want upon that side-table."

Abercrombie Smith sat down before a sheet of foolscap, and for an hour, and then for a second hour his pen travelled swiftly over it. Page after page was finished and tossed aside while his friend leaned back in his armchair, looking across at him with patient curiosity. At last, with an exclamation of satisfaction, Smith sprang to his feet, gathered his papers up into order, and laid the last one upon Peterson's desk.

"Kindly sign this as a witness," he said.

"A witness? Of what?"

"Of my signature, and of the date. The date is the most important. Why, Peterson, my life might hang upon it."

"My dear Smith, you are talking wildly. Let me beg you to go to bed."

"On the contrary, I never spoke so deliberately in my life. And I will promise to go to bed the moment you have signed it."

"But what is it?"

"It is a statement of all that I have been telling you tonight. I wish you to witness it."

"Certainly," said Peterson, signing his name under that of his companion. "There you are! But what is the idea?"

"You will kindly retain it, and produce it in case I am arrested."

"Arrested? For what?"

"For murder. It is quite on the cards. I wish to be ready for every event. There is only one course open to me, and I am determined to take it."

"For Heaven's sake, don't do anything rash!"

"Believe me, it would be far more rash to adopt any other course. I hope that we won't need to bother you, but it will ease my mind to know that you have this statement of my motives. And now I am ready to take your advice and to go to roost, for I want to be at my best in the morning."

Abercrombie Smith was not an entirely pleasant man to have as an enemy. Slow and easy-tempered, he was formidable when driven to action. He brought to every purpose in life the same deliberate resoluteness which had distinguished him as a scientific student. He had laid his studies aside for a day, but he intended that the day should not be wasted. Not a word did he say to his host as to his plans, but by nine o'clock he was well on his way to Oxford.

In the High Street he stopped at Clifford's, the gunmaker's, and bought a heavy revolver, with a box of central-fire cartridges. Six of them he slipped into the chambers, and half-cocking the weapon, placed it in the pocket of his coat. He then made his way to Hastie's rooms, where the big oarsman was lounging over his breakfast, with the *Sporting Times* propped up against the coffeepot.

"Hullo! What's up?" he asked. "Have some coffee?"

"No, thank you. I want you to come with me, Hastie, and do what I ask you."

"Certainly, my boy."

"And bring a heavy stick with you."

"Hullo!" Hastie stared. "Here's a hunting crop that would fell an ox."

"One other thing. You have a box of amputating knives. Give me the longest of them."

"There you are. You seem to be fairly on the war trail. Anything else?"

"No; that will do." Smith placed the knife inside his coat, and led the way to the quadrangle. "We are neither of us chickens, Hastie," said he. "I think I can do this job alone, but I take you as a precaution. I am going to have a little talk with Bellingham. If I have only him to deal with, I won't, of course, need you. If I shout, however, up you come, and lam out with your whip as hard as you can lick. Do you understand?"

"All right. I'll come if I hear you bellow."

"Stay here, then. I may be a little time, but don't budge until I come down."

"I'm a fixture."

Smith ascended the stairs, opened Bellingham's door and stepped in. Bellingham was seated behind his table, writing. Beside him, among his litter of strange possesions, towered the mummy case, with its sale number 249 still stuck upon its front, and its hideous occupant stiff and stark within it. Smith looked very deliberately round him, closed the door, and then, stepping across to the fireplace, struck a match and set the fire alight. Bellingham sat staring, with amazement and rage upon his bloated face.

"Well, really now, you make yourself at home," he gasped.

Smith sat himself deliberately down, placing his watch upon the table, drew out his pistol, cocked it, and laid it in his lap. Then he took the long amputating knife from his bosom, and threw it down in front of Bellingham.

"Now, then," said he, "just get to work and cut up that mummy."

"Oh, is that it?" said Bellingham with a sneer.

"Yes, that is it. They tell me that the law can't touch you. But I have a law that will set matters straight. If in five minutes you have not set to work, I swear by the God who made me that I will put a bullet through your brain!"

"You would murder me?"

Bellingham had half-risen, and his face was the color of putty.

"Yes."

"And for what?"

"To stop your mischief. One minute has gone."

"But what have I done?"

"I know and you know."

"This is mere bullying."

"Two minutes are gone."

"But you must give reasons. You are a madman—a dangerous madman. Why should I destroy my own property? It is a valuable mummy."

"You must cut it up, and you must burn it."

"I will do no such thing."

"Four minutes are gone."

Smith took up the pistol and he looked towards Bellingham with an inexorable face. As the second hand stole round, he raised his hand, and the finger twitched upon the trigger.

"There! there! I'll do it!" screamed Bellingham.

In frantic haste he caught up the knife and hacked at the figure of the mummy, ever glancing round to see the eye and the weapon of his terrible visitor bent upon him. The creature crackled and snapped under every stab of the keen blade. A thick, yellow dust rose up from it. Spices and dried essences rained down upon the floor. Suddenly, with a rending crack, its backbone snapped asunder, and it fell, a brown heap of sprawling limbs, upon the floor.

"Now into the fire!" said Smith.

The flames leaped and roared as the dried and tinder-like debris was piled upon it. The little room was like the stokehole of a steamer and the sweat ran down the faces of the two men; but still the one stooped and worked, while the other sat watching him with a set face. A thick, fat smoke oozed out from the fire, and a heavy smell of burned resin and singed hair filled the air. In a quarter of an hour a few charred and brittle sticks were all that was left of Lot No. 249.

"Perhaps that will satisfy you," snarled Bellingham, with hate and fear in his little grey eyes as he glanced back at his tormentor.

"No; I must make a clean sweep of all your materials. We must have no more devil's tricks. In with all these leaves! They may have something to do with it."

"And what now?" asked Bellingham, when the leaves also had been added to the blaze.

"Now the roll of papyrus which you had on the table that night. It is in that drawer, I think."

"No, no," shouted Bellingham. "Don't burn that. Why, man, you don't know what you do. It is unique, it contains wisdom which is nowhere else to be found."

"Out with it!"

"But look here, Smith, you can't really mean it. I'll share the knowledge with you. I'll teach you all that is in it. Or, stay, let me only copy it before you burn it!"

Smith stepped forward and turned the key in the drawer. Taking out the yellow, curled roll of paper, he threw it into the fire, and pressed it down with his heel. Bellingham screamed, and grabbed at it; but Smith pushed him back and stood over it until it was reduced to a formless, grey ash.

"Now, Master B.," said he, "I think I have pretty well drawn your teeth. You'll hear from me again, if you return to your old tricks. And now good morning, for I must go back to my studies."

And such is the narrative of Abercrombie Smith as to the singular events which occurred in Old College, Oxford, in the spring of '84. As Bellingham left the university immediately afterwards, and was last heard of in the Soudan, there is no one who can contradict his statement. But the wisdom of men is small, and the ways of Nature are strange, and who shall put a bound to the dark things which may be found by those who seek for them?

Robert Louis Stevenson (1850–1894)

One of the world's most widely read authors, Stevenson was born in Edinburgh, Scotland, the only son of a prosperous civil engineer. Stevenson was greatly loved, and, with the possible exception of an overabundance of Calvinism, he appears to have had a happy childhood. But from an early age on experienced health problems which eventually developed into tuberculosis.

He always wanted to write. However, his father wanted him to become an engineer, so in 1867 he was packed off to the University of Edinburgh, where he was, at best, an indifferent student. Finally, in 1871 he confronted his father. They reached an unenthusiastic compromise and Stevenson began reading law at an Edinburgh firm.

In 1873 he made the acquaintance of Sidney Colvin, a fellow of Trinity College, who offered the young man encouragement and an introduction to some important literary gate-keepers. Two years later Stevenson passed his bar exam, but never practiced because of the increasing acceptance of his various submissions. In 1876 Stevenson published his first book (*An Inland Voyage*) and met the woman (Fanny Osbourne) who would be his wife. She was ten years older than he, married, and the mother of two surviving children. But he fell madly in love with her almost immediately, even following her back to California (1879) when she returned to secure her divorce.

In 1880 they married, made peace with Stevenson's parents, and began a series of travels to search for a climate conducive to preserving his frail health.

About five foot ten, cadaverously thin, with intense wide-set eyes, and a full voice, Stevenson was extremely happy with his marriage. To support his family, he threw himself into his work, producing, within seven years, such great books and collections as *New Arabian Nights* (1882), *Treasure Island* (1883), *The Strange Case of Dr. Jekyll and Mr. Hyde* (1886), *Kidnapped* (1886), and *The Merry Men and Other Tales and Fables* (1887). These brought fame and fortune.

Still his health remained poor. So, when he returned to California in 1888, he decided to cruise around the South Seas. The climate proved beneficial, and, after stops at several islands including Tahiti and Hawaii, the Stevensons settled in Samoa. Here Stevenson's power grew, and when he died of a cerebral hemorrhage, he was working on a novel (*Weir of Hemriston*) critics claim to have been his masterpiece.

A concerted stylist, Stevenson developed the ability to pack atmosphere, accurate dialect, and rapid pacing into cleverly constructed adventure tales. His fantastic adventures include *The Strange Case of Dr. Jekyll and Mr. Hyde* (a classic novel of multiple personalities "based on the double life of Edinburgh's notorious Deacon Brodie"), "The Body-Snatcher" (a story of supernatural horror), "Thrawn Janet" (a Scottish ghost story), and our selection for this volume, "The Bottle Imp" (a retelling of Baron Fouqué's similarly titled deal-with-the-devil story in a South Seas setting).

THE BOTTLE IMP

There was a man of the island of Hawaii, whom I shall call Keawe; for the truth is, he still lives, and his name must be kept secret; but the place of his birth was not far from Honaunau, where the bones of Keawe the Great lie hidden in a cave. This man was poor, brave, and active; he could read and write like a schoolmaster; he was a first-rate mariner besides, sailed for some time in the island steamers, and steered a whaleboat on the Kamakua coast. At length it came in Keawe's mind to have a sight of the great world and foreign cities, and he shipped on a vessel bound to San Francisco.

This is a fine town, with a fine harbor, and rich people uncountable; and, in particular, there is one hill which is covered with palaces. Upon this hill Keawe was one day taking a walk, with his pocket full of money, viewing the great houses upon either hand with pleasure. "What fine houses there are!" he was thinking, "and how happy must these people be who dwell in them, and take no care for the morrow!" The thought was in his mind when he came abreast of a house that was smaller than some others, but all finished and beautified like a toy; the steps of that house shone like silver, and the borders of the garden bloomed like garlands, and the windows were bright like diamonds; and Keawe stopped and wondered at the excellence of all he saw. So stopping, he was aware of a man that looked forth upon him through a window, so clear that Keawe could see him as you see a fish in a pool upon the reef. The man was elderly, with a bald head and a black beard; and his face was heavy with sorrow, and he bitterly sighed. And the truth of it is, that as Keawe looked in upon the man, and the man looked out upon Keawe, each envied the other.

All of a sudden the man smiled and nodded, and beckoned Keawe to enter, and met him at the door of the house.

"This is a fine house of mine," said the man, and bitterly sighed. "Would you not care to view the chambers?"

So he led Keawe all over it, from the cellar to the roof, and there was nothing there that was not perfect of its kind, and Keawe was astonished.

"Truly," said Keawe, "this is a beatufiul house; if I lived in the like of it, I should be laughing all day long. How comes it, then, that you should be sighing?"

"There is no reason," said the man, "why you should not have a house in all points similar to this, and finer, if you wish. You have some money, I suppose?"

"I have fifty dollars," said Keawe; "but a house like this will cost more than fifty dollars."

The man made a computation. "I am sorry you have no more," said he, "for it may raise you trouble in the future; but it shall be yours at fifty dollars."

"The house?" asked Keawe.

"No, not the house," replied the man; "but the bottle. For I must tell you, although I appear to you so rich and fortunate, all my fortune, and this house itself and its garden, came out of a bottle not much bigger than a pint. This is it."

And he opened a lockfast place, and took out a round-bellied bottle with a long neck; the glass of it was white like milk, with changing rainbow colors in the grain. Withinside something obscurely moved, like a shadow and a fire.

"This is the bottle," said the man; and, when Keawe laughed, "You do not believe me?" he added. "Try, then, for yourself. See if you can break it."

So Keawe took the bottle up and dashed it on the floor till he was weary; but it jumped on the floor like a child's ball, and was not injured.

"This is a strange thing," said Keawe. "For by the touch of it, as well as by the look, the bottle should be of glass."

"Of glass it is," replied the man, sighing more heavily than ever; "but the glass of it was tempered in the flames of hell. An imp lives in it, and that is the shadow we behold there moving; or, so I suppose. If any man buy this bottle the imp is at his command; all that he desires—love, fame, money, houses like this house, ay, or a city like this city—all are his at the word uttered. Napoleon had this bottle, and by it he grew to be the king of the world; but he sold it at the last and fell. Captain Cook had this bottle, and by it he found his way to so many islands; but he too sold it, and was slain upon Hawaii. For, once it is sold, the power goes and the protection; and unless a man remain content with what he has, ill will befall him."

"And yet you talk of selling it yourself?" Keawe said.

"I have all I wish, and I am growing elderly," replied the man. "There is one thing the imp cannot do—he cannot prolong life; and it would not be fair to conceal from you there is a drawback to the bottle; for if a man die before he sells it, he must burn in hell forever."

"To be sure, that is a drawback and no mistake," cried Keawe. "I would not meddle with the thing. I can do without a house, thank God; but there is one thing I could not be doing with one particle, and that is to be damned."

"Dear me, you must not run away with things," returned the man. "All you have to do is to use the power of the imp in moderation, and then sell it to someone else, as I do to you, and finish your life in comfort."

"Well, I observe two things," said Keawe. "All the time you keep sighing like a maid in love—that is one; and for the other, you sell this bottle very cheap."

"I have told you already why I sigh," said the man. "It is because I fear my health is breaking up; and, as you said yourself, to die and go to the devil is a pity for any one. As for why I sell so cheap, I must explain to you there is a peculiarity about the bottle. Long ago, when the devil brought it first upon earth, it was extremely expensive, and was sold first of all to Prester John for many millions of dollars; but it cannot be sold at all, unless sold at a loss. If you sell it for as much as you paid for it, back it comes to you again like a homing pigeon. It follows that the price has kept falling in these centuries, and the bottle is now remarkably cheap. I bought it myself from one of my great neighbors on this hill, and the price I paid was only ninety dollars. I could sell it for as high as eighty-nine dollars and ninety-nine cents, but not a penny dearer, or back the thing must come to me. Now, about this there are two bothers. First, when you offer a bottle so singular for eighty-odd dollars, people suppose you to be jesting. And second—but there is not hurry about that—and I need not go into it. Only remember it must be coined money that you sell it for.''

''How am I to know that this is all true?'' asked Keawe.

''Some of it you can try at once,'' replied the man. ''Give me your fifty dollars, take the bottle, and wish your fifty dollars back into your pocket. If that does not happen, I pledge you my honor I will cry off the bargain and restore your money.''

''You are not deceiving me?'' said Keawe.

The man bound himself with a great oath.

''Well, I will risk that much,'' said Keawe, ''for that can do no harm,'' and he paid over his money to the man, and the man handed him the bottle.

''Imp of the bottle,'' said Keawe, ''I want my fifty dollars back.'' And sure enough, he had scarce said the word before his pocket was as heavy as ever.

''To be sure this is a wonderful bottle,'' said Keawe.

''And now good morning to you, my fine fellow, and the devil go with you for me,'' said the man.

''Hold on,'' said Keawe, ''I don't want any more of this fun. Here, take your bottle back.''

''You have bought it for less than I paid for it,'' replied the man, rubbing his hands. ''It is yours now; and, for my part, I am only concerned to see the back of you.'' And with that he rang for his Chinese servant, and had Keawe shown out of the house.

Now, when Keawe was in the street, with the bottle under his arm, he began to think. ''If all is true about this bottle, I may have made a losing bargain,'' thinks he. ''But perhaps the man was only fooling me.'' The first thing he did was to count his money; the sum was exact—forty-nine dollars American money, and one Chili piece. ''That looks like the truth,'' said Keawe. ''Now I will try another part.''

The streets in that part of the city were as clean as a ship's decks, and though it was noon, there were no passengers. Keawe set the bottle in the gutter and walked away. Twice he looked back, and there was the milky, round-bellied bottle where he left it. A third time he looked back and turned a corner; but he had scarce done so, when something knocked upon his elbow, and behold! it was the long neck sticking up; and as for the round belly, it was jammed into the pocket of his pilot coat.

''And that looks like the truth,'' said Keawe.

The next thing he did was to buy a corkscrew in a shop, and go apart in a secret place in the fields. And there he tried to draw the cork, but as often as he put the screw in, out it came again, and the cork was as whole as ever.

"There is some new sort of cork," said Keawe, and all at once he began to shake and sweat, for he was afraid of that bottle.

On his way back to the port side he saw a shop where a man sold shells and clubs from the wild islands, old heathen deities, old coined money, pictures from China and Japan, and all manner of things that sailors bring in their sea chests. And here he had an idea. So he went in and offered the bottle for a hundred dollars. The man of the shop laughed at him at first, and offered him five; but, indeed, it was a curious bottle, such glass was never blown in any human glassworks, so prettily the colors shone under the milky way, and so strangely the shadow hovered in the midst; so, after he had disputed a while after the manner of his kind, the shopman gave Keawe sixty silver dollars for the thing and set it on a shelf in the midst of his window.

"Now," said Keawe, "I have sold that for sixty which I bought for fifty—or, to say truth, a little less, because one of my dollars was from Chili. Now I shall know the truth upon another point."

So he went back on board his ship, and when he opened his chest, there was the bottle, which had come more quickly than himself. Now Keawe had a mate on board whose name was Lopaka.

"What ails you," said Lopaka, "that you stare in your chest?"

They were alone in the ship's forecastle, and Keawe bound him to secrecy, and told all.

"This is a very strange affair," said Lopaka; "and I fear you will be in trouble about this bottle. But there is one point very clear—that you are sure of the trouble, and you had better have the profit in the bargain. Make up your mind what you want with it; give the order, and it is done as you desire, I will buy the bottle myself; for I have an idea of my own to get a schooner, and go trading through the islands."

"That is not my idea," said Keawe; "but to have a beautiful house and garden on the Kona Coast, where I was born, the sun shining in at the door, flowers in the garden, glass in the windows, pictures on the walls, and toys and fine carpets on the tables, for all the world like the house I was in this day—only a story higher, and with balconies all about like the King's palace; and to live there without care and make merry with my friends and relatives."

"Well," said Lopaka, "let us carry it back with us to Hawaii; and if all comes true as you suppose, I will buy the bottle, as I said, and ask a schooner."

Upon that they were agreed, and it was not long before the ship returned to Honolulu, carrying Keawe and Lopaka, and the bottle. They were scarce come ashore when they met a friend upon the beach, who began at once to condole with Keawe.

"I do not know what I am to be condoled about," said Keawe.

"Is it possible you have not heard," said the friend, "your uncle—that good old man—is dead, and your cousin—that beautiful boy—was drowned at sea?"

Keawe was filled with sorrow, and, beginning to weep and to lament, he forgot about the bottle. But Lopaka was thinking to himself, and presently, when Keawe's grief was a little abated, "I have been thinking," said Lopaka, "had not your uncle lands in Hawaii, in the district of Kaü?"

"No," said Keawe, "not in Kaü: they are on the mountain side—a little be-south Kookena."

"These lands will now be yours?" asked Lopaka.

"And so they will," says Keawe, and began again to lament for his relatives.

"No," said Lopaka, "do not lament at present. I have a thought in my mind. How if this should be the doing of the bottle? For here is the place ready for your house."

"If this be so," cried Keawe, "it is a very ill way to serve me by killing my relatives. But it may be, indeed; for it was in just such a station that I saw the house with my mind's eye."

"The house, however, is not yet built," said Lopaka.

"No, nor like to be!" said Keawe; "for though my uncle has some coffee and ava and bananas, it will not be more than will keep me in comfort; and the rest of that land is the black lava."

"Let us go to the lawyer," said Lopaka; "I have still this idea in my mind."

Now, when they came to the lawyer's, it appeared Keawe's uncle had grown monstrous rich in the last days, and there was a fund of money.

"And here is the money for the house!" cried Lopaka.

"If you are thinking of a new house," said the lawyer, "here is the card of a new architect of whom they tell me great things."

"Better and better!" cried Lopaka. "Here is all made plain for us. Let us continue to obey orders."

So they went to the architect, and he had drawings of houses on his table.

"You want something out of the way," said the architect. "How do you like this?" and he handed a drawing to Keawe.

Now, when Keawe set eyes on the drawing, he cried out aloud, for it was the picture of his thought exactly drawn.

"I am in for this house," thought he. "Little as I like the way it comes to me, I am in for it now, and I may as well take the good along with the evil."

So he told the architect all that he wished, and how he would have that house furnished, and about the pictures on the wall and the knick-knacks on the tables; and he asked the man plainly for how much he would undertake the whole affair.

The architect put many questions, and took his pen and made a computation; and when he had done he named the very sum that Keawe had inherited.

Lopaka and Keawe looked at one another and nodded.

"It is quite clear," thought Keawe, "that I am to have this house, whether or no. It comes from the devil, and I fear I will get little good by that; and of one thing I am sure, I will make no more wishes as long as I have this bottle. But with the house I am saddled, and I may as well take the good along with the evil."

So he made his terms with the architect, and they signed a paper; and Keawe and Lopaka took ship again and sailed to Australia; for it was concluded between them they should not interfere at all, but leave the architect and the bottle imp to build and to adorn the house at their own pleasure.

The voyage was a good voyage, only all the time Keawe was holding in his breath, for he had sworn he would utter no more wishes, and take no more favors, from the devil. The time was up when they got back. The architect told them that the house was ready, and Keawe and Lopaka took a passage in the *Hall*, and went down Kona way to view the house, and see if all had been done fitly according to the thought that was in Keawe's mind.

Now, the house stood on the mountain side, visible to ships. Above, the forest ran up into the clouds of rain; below, the black lava fell in cliffs, where the kings of old lay buried. A garden bloomed about the house with every hue of flowers; and there was an orchard of papaya on the one hand and an orchard of breadfruit on the other, and right in front, toward the sea, a ship's mast had been rigged up and bore a flag. As for the house, it was three stories high, with great chambers and broad balconies on each. The windows were of glass, so excellent that it was as clear as water and as bright as day. All manner of furniture adorned the chambers. Pictures hung upon the wall in golden frames—pictures of ships, and men fighting, and of the most beautiful women, and of singular places; nowhere in the world are there pictures of so bright a color as those Keawe found hanging in his house. As for the knick-knacks, they were extraordinarily fine: chiming clocks and musical boxes, little men with nodding heads, books filled with pictures, weapons of price from all quarters of the world, and the most elegant puzzles to entertain the leisure of a solitary man. And as no one would care to live in such chambers, only to walk through and view them, the balconies were made so broad that a whole town might have lived upon them in delight; and Keawe knew not which to prefer, whether the back porch, where you get the land breeze and looked upon the orchards and the flowers, or the front balcony, where you could drink the wind of the sea, and look down the steep wall of the mountain and see the *Hall* going by once a week or so between Hookea and the hills of Pele, or the schooners plying up the coast for wood and ava and bananas.

When they had viewed all, Keawe and Lopaka sat on the porch.

"Well," asked Lopaka, "is it all as you designed?"

"Words cannot utter it," said Keawe. "It is better than I dreamed, and I am sick with satisfaction."

"There is but one thing to consider," said Lopaka, "all this may be quite natural, and the bottle imp have nothing whatever to say to it. If I were to buy the bottle, and got no schooner after all, I should have put my hand in the fire for nothing. I gave you my word, I know; but yet I think you would not grudge me one more proof."

"I have sworn I would take no more favours," said Keawe. "I have gone already deep enough."

"This is no favor I am thinking of," replied Lopaka. "It is only to see the imp himself. There is nothing to be gained by that, and so nothing to be ashamed of, and yet, if I once saw him, I should be sure of the whole matter. So indulge me so far, and let me see the imp; and, after that, here is the money in my hand; and I will buy it."

"There is only one thing I am afraid of," said Keawe. "The imp may be very ugly to view, and if you once set eyes upon him you might be very undesirous of the bottle."

"I am a man of my word," said Lopaka. "And here is the money betwixt us."

"Very well," replied Keawe, "I have a curiosity myself. So come, let us have one look at you, Mr. Imp."

Now as soon as that was said, the imp looked out of the bottle, and in again, swift as a lizard; and there sat Keawe and Lapaka turned to stone. The night had quite come, before either found a thought to say or voice to say it with; and then Lopaka pushed the money over and took the bottle.

"I am a man of my word," said he, "and had need to be so, or I would not touch this bottle with my foot. Well, I shall get my schooner and a dollar or two for my pocket; and then I will be rid of this devil as fast as I can. For, to tell you the plain truth, the look of him has cast me down."

"Lopaka," said Keawe, "do not you think any worse of me than you can help; I know it is night, and the roads bad, and the pass by the tombs an ill place to go by so late, but I declare since I have seen that little face, I cannot eat or sleep or pray till it is gone from me. I will give you a lantern, and a basket to put the bottle in, and any picture or fine thing in all my house that takes your fancy; and be gone at once, and go sleep at Hookena with Nahinu."

"Keawe," said Lopaka, "many a man would take this ill; above all, when I am doing you a turn so friendly, as to keep my word and buy the bottle; and for that matter, the night and the dark, and the way by the tombs, must be all tenfold more dangerous to a man with such a sin upon his conscience and such a bottle under his arm. But for my part, I am so extremely terrified myself, I have not the heart to blame you. Here I go, then; and I pray God you may be happy in your house, and I fortunate with my schooner, and both get to heaven in the end in spite of the devil and the bottle."

So Lopaka went down the mountain; and Keawe stood in his front balcony, and listened to the clink of the horses' shoes, and watched the lantern go shining down the path, and along the cliff of caves where the old dead are buried; and all the time he trembled and clasped his hands, and prayed for his friend, and gave glory to God that he himself was escaped out of that trouble.

But the next day came very brightly, and that new house of his was so delightful to behold that he forgot his terrors. One day followed another, and Keawe dwelt there in perpetual joy. He had his place on the back porch; it was there he ate and lived, and read the stories in the Honolulu newspapers; but when anyone came by they would go in and view the chambers and the pictures. And the fame of the house went far and wide; it was called *Ka-Hale Nui*—the Great House—in all Kona; and sometimes the Bright House, for Keawe kept a Chinaman, who was all day dusting and furbishing; and the glass, and the gilt, and the fine stuffs, and the pictures, shone as bright as the morning. As for Keawe himself, he could not walk in the chambers without singing, his heart was so enlarged; and when ships sailed by upon the sea, he would fly his colors on the mast.

So time went by, until one day Keawe went upon a visit as far as Kailua to certain of his friends. There he was well feasted; and left as soon as he could the next morning, and rode hard, for he was impatient to behold his beautiful house; and besides, the night then coming on was the night in which the dead of old days go abroad in the sides of Kona; and having already meddled with the devil, he was the more chary of meeting with the dead. A little beyond Honaunau, looking far ahead, he was aware of a woman bathing in the edges of the sea; and she seemed a well-grown girl, but he thought no more of it. Then he saw her white shift flutter as she put it on, and then her red holoku; and by the time he came abreast of her she was done with her toilet, and had come up from the sea, and stood by the trackside in her red holoku, and she was all freshened with the bath, and her eyes shone and were kind. Now Keawe no sooner beheld her than he drew rein.

"I thought I knew every one in this country," said he. "How comes it that I do not know you?"

"I am Kokua, daughter of Kiano," said the girl, "and I have just returned from Oahu. Who are you?"

"I will tell you who I am in a little," said Keawe, dismounting from his horse, "but not now. For I have a thought in my mind, and if you knew who I was, you might have heard of me, and would not give me a true answer. But tell me, first of all, one thing: are you married?"

At this Kokua laughed out aloud. "It is you who ask questions," she said. "Are you married yourself?"

"Indeed, Kokua, I am not," replied Keawe, "and never thought to be until this hour. But here is the plain truth. I have met you here at the roadside, and I saw your eyes, which are like the stars, and my heart went to you as swift as a bird. And so now, if you want none of me, say so, and I will go on to my own place; but if you think me no worse than any other young man, say so, too, and I will turn aside to your father's for the night, and tomorrow I will talk with the good man."

Kokua said never a word, but she looked at the sea and laughed.

"Kokua," said Keawe, "if you say nothing, I will take that for the good answer; so let us be stepping to your father's door."

She went on ahead of him, still without speech; only sometimes she glanced back and glanced away again, and she kept the strings of her hat in her mouth.

Now, when they had come to the door, Kiano came out on his veranda, and cried out and welcomed Keawe by name. At that the girl looked over, for the fame of the great house had come to her ears; and, to be sure, it was a great temptation. All that evening they were very merry together; and the girl was as bold as brass under the eyes of her parents, and made a mark of Keawe, for she had a quick wit. The next day he had a word with Kiano, and found the girl alone.

"Kokua," said he, "you made a mark of me all the evening; and it is still time to bid me go. I would not tell you who I was, because I have so fine a house, and I feared you would think too much of that house, and too little of the man that loves you. Now you know all, and if you wish to have seen the last of me, say so at once."

"No," said Kokua, but this time she did not laugh, nor did Keawe ask for more.

This was the wooing of Keawe; things had gone quickly; but so an arrow goes, and the ball of a rifle swifter still, and yet both may strike the target. Things had gone fast, but they had gone far also, and the thought of Keawe rang in the maiden's head; she heard his voice in the breach of the surf upon the lava, and for this young man that she had seen but twice she would have left father and mother and her native islands. As for Keawe himself, his horse flew up the path of the mountain under the cliff of tombs, and the sound of the hoofs, and the sound of Keawe singing to himself for pleasure, echoed in the caverns of the dead. He came to the Bright House, and still he was singing. He sat and ate in the broad balcony, and the Chinaman wondered at his master, to hear how he sang between the mouthfuls. The sun went down into the sea, and the night came; and Keawe walked the balconies by lamplight, high on the mountains, and the voice of his singing startled men on ships.

"Here am I now upon my high place," he said to himself. "Life may be no better; this is the mountain top; and all shelves about me toward the worse. For the first time I will light up the chambers, and bathe in my fine bath with the hot water and the cold, and sleep above in the bed of my bridal chamber."

So the Chinaman had word, and he must rise from sleep and light the furnaces; and as he walked below, beside the boilers, he heard his master singing and rejoicing above him in the lighted chambers. When the water began to be hot the Chinaman cried to his master: and Keawe went into the bathroom; and the Chinaman heard him sing as he filled the marble basin; and heard him sing, and the singing broken, as he undressed; until of a sudden, the song ceased. The Chinaman listened, and listened; he called up the house to Keawe to ask if all were well, and Keawe answered him "Yes," and bade him go to bed; but there was no more singing in the Bright House; and all night long the Chinaman heard his master's feet go round and round the balconies without repose.

Now, the truth of it was this: as Keawe undressed for his bath, he spied upon his flesh a patch like a patch of lichen on a rock, and it was then that he stopped singing. For he knew the likeness of that patch, and knew that he was fallen in the Chinese Evil.*

Now, it is a sad thing for any man to fall into this sickness. And it would be a sad thing for anyone to leave a house so beautiful and so commodious, and depart from all his friends to the north coast of Molokai, between the mighty cliff and the sea-breakers. But what was that to the case of the man Keawe, he had met his love but yesterday and won her but that morning, and now saw all his hopes break, in a moment, like a piece of glass?

A while he sat upon the edge of the bath, then sprang, with a cry, and ran outside; and to and fro, to and fro, along the balcony, like one despairing.

"Very willingly could I leave Hawaii, the home of my fathers," Keawe was thinking. "Very lightly could I leave my house, the high-placed, the many-windowed, here upon the mountains. Very bravely could I go to Molokai, to Kalaupapa by the cliffs, to live with the smitten

*Leprosy.

and to sleep there, far from my fathers. But what wrong have I done, what sin lies upon my soul, that I should have encountered Kokua coming cool from the sea-water in the evening? Kokua, the soul ensnarer! Kokua, the light of my life! Her may I never wed, her may I look upon no longer, her may I no more handle with my loving hand; and it is for this, it is for you, O Kokua! that I pour my lamentations!''

Now you are to observe what sort of a man Keawe was, for he might have dwelt there in the Bright House for years, and no one been the wiser of his sickness; but he reckoned nothing of that, if he must lose Kokua. And again he might have wed Kokua even as he was; and so many would have done, because they have the souls of pigs; but Keawe loved the maid manfully, and he would do her no hurt and bring her in no danger.

A little beyond the midst of the night, there came in his mind the recollection of that bottle. He went round to the back porch, and called to memory the day when the devil had looked forth; and at the thought ice ran in his veins.

''A dreadful thing is in the bottle,'' thought Keawe, ''and dreadful is the imp, and it is a dreadful thing to risk the flames of hell. But what other hope have I to cure my sickness or to wed Kokua? What!'' he thought, ''would I beard the devil once, only to get me a house, and not face him again to win Kokua?''

Thereupon he called to mind it was the next day the *Hall* went by on her return to Honolulu. ''There must I go first,'' he thought, ''and see Lopaka. For the best hope that I have now is to find that same bottle I was so pleased to be rid of.''

Never a wink could he sleep; the food stuck in his throat; but he sent a letter to Kiano, and about the time when the steamer would be coming, rode down beside the cliff of the tombs. It rained; his horse went heavily; he looked up at the black mouths of the caves, and he envied the dead that slept there and were done with trouble; and called to mind how he had galloped by the day before, and was astonished. So he came down to Hookena, and there was all the country gathered for the steamer as usual. In the shed before the store they sat and jested and passed the news; but there was no matter of speech in Keawe's bosom, and he sat in their midst and looked without on the rain falling on the houses, and the surf beating among the rocks, and the sighs arose in his throat.

''Keawe of the Bright House is out of spirits,'' said one to another. Indeed, and so he was, and little wonder.

Then the *Hall* came, and the whaleboat carried him on board. The afterpart of the ship was full of Haoles*—who had been to visit the volcano, as their custom is; and the midst was crowded with Kanakas, and the forepart with wild bulls from Hilo and horses from Kaü; but Keawe sat apart from all in his sorrow, and watched for the house of Kiano. There it sat low upon the shore in the black rocks, and shaded by the cocoa palms, and there by the door was a red holoku, no greater than a fly, and going to and fro with a fly's busyness. 'Ah, queen of my heart,'' he cried, ''I'll venture my dear soul to win you!''

Soon after darkness fell and the cabins were lit up, and the Haoles sat and played at the cards and drank whisky as their custom is; but Keawe walked the deck all night; and all the next day, as they steamed under the lee of Maui or of Molokai, he was still pacing to and fro like a wild animal in a menagerie.

Toward evening they passed Diamond Head, and came to the pier of Honolulu. Keawe stepped out among the crowd and began to ask for Lopaka. It seemed he had become the owner of a schooner—none better in the islands—and was gone upon an adventure as far as Pola-Pola or Kahiki; so there was no help to be looked for from Lopaka. Keawe called to mind a friend of his, a lawyer in the town (I must not tell his name), and inquired of him. They said he was grown suddenly rich, and had a fine new house upon Waikiki shore; and this put a thought in Keawe's head, and he called a hack and drove to the lawyer's house.

The house was all brand new, and the trees in the garden no greater than walking sticks, and the lawyer, when he came, had the air of a man well pleased.

''What can I do to serve you?'' said the lawyer.

''You are a friend of Lopaka's,'' replied Keawe, ''and Lopaka purchased from me a certain piece of goods that I thought you might enable me to trace.''

The lawyer's face became very dark. ''I do not profess to misunderstand you, Mr. Keawe,'' said he, ''though this is an ugly business to be stirring in. You may be sure I know nothing, but yet I have a guess, and if you would apply in a certain quarter I think you might have news.''

And he named the name of a man, which, again, I had better not repeat. So it was for days, and Keawe went from one to another, finding

*Whites.

everywhere new clothes and carriages, and fine new houses, and men everywhere in great contentment, although, to be sure, when he hinted at his business their faces would cloud over.

"No doubt I am upon the track," thought Keawe. "These new clothes and carriages are all the gifts of the little imp, and these glad faces are the faces of men who have taken their profit and got rid of the accursed thing in safety. When I see pale cheeks and hear sighing, I shall know that I am near the bottle."

So it befell at last he was recommended to a Haole in Beritania Street. When he came to the door, about the hour of the evening meal, thee were the usual marks of the new house, and the young garden, and the electric light shining in the windows; but when the owner came, a shock of hope and fear ran through Keawe; for here was a young man, white as a corpse, and black about the eyes, the hair shedding from his head, and such a look in his countenance as a man may have when he is waiting for the gallows.

"Here it is, to be sure," thought Keawe, and so with this man he noways veiled his errand. "I am come to buy the bottle," said he.

At the word, the young Haole of Beritania Street reeled against the wall.

"The bottle!" he gasped. "To buy the bottle!" Then he seemed to choke, and seizing Keawe by the arm, carried him into a room and poured out wine in two glasses.

"Here is my respects," said Keawe, who had been much about with Haoles in his time. "Yes," he added, "I am come to buy the bottle. What is the price by now?"

At that word the young man let his glass slip through his fingers, and looked upon Keawe like a ghost.

"The price," says he; "the price! You do not know the price?"

"It is for that I am asking you," returned Keawe. "But why are you so much concerned? Is there anything wrong about the price?"

"It has dropped a great deal in value since your time, Mr. Keawe," said the young man, stammering.

"Well, well, I shall have the less to pay for it," said Keawe. "How much did it cost you?"

The young man was as white as a sheet.

"Two cents," said he.

"What!" cried Keawe, "two cents? Why, then, you can only sell it for one. And he who buys it—'' The words died upon Keawe's tongue; he who bought it could never sell it again, the bottle and the bottle imp must abide with him until he died, and when he died must carry him to the red end of hell.

The young man of Beritania Street fell upon his knees. ''For God's sake, buy it!'' he cried. ''You can have all my fortune in the bargain. I was mad when I bought it at that price. I had embezzled money at my store; I was lost else; I must have gone to jail.''

''Poor creature,'' said Keawe, ''you would risk your soul upon so desperate an adventure, and to avoid the proper punishment of your own disgrace; and you think I could hesitate with love in front of me. Give me the bottle, and the change which I make sure you have all ready. Here is a five-cent piece.''

It was as Keawe supposed; the young man had the change ready in a drawer; the bottle changed hands, and Keawe's fingers were no sooner clasped upon the stalk than he had breathed his wish to be a clean man. And sure enough, when he got home to his room, and stripped himself before a glass, his flesh was whole like an infant's. And here was the strange thing: he had no sooner seen this miracle than his mind was changed within him, and he cared naught for the Chinese Evil, and little enough for Kokua; and had but the one thought, that here he was bound to the bottle imp for time and for eternity, and had no better hope but to be a cinder for ever in the flames of hell. Away ahead of him he saw them blaze with his mind's eye, and his soul shrank, and darkness fell upon the light.

When Keawe came to himself a little, he was aware it was the night when the band played at the hotel. Thither he went, because he feared to be alone; and there, among happy faces, walked to and fro, and heard the tunes go up and down, and saw Berger beat the measure, and all the while he heard the flames crackle and saw the red fire burning in the bottomless pit. Of a sudden the band played *Hiki-ao-ao*; that was a song that he had sung with Kokua, and at the strain courage returned to him.

''It is done now,'' he thought, ''and once more let me take the good along with the evil.''

So it befell that he returned to Hawaii by the first steamer, and as soon as it could be managed he was wedded to Kokua, and carried her up the mountain side to the Bright House.

Now it was so with these two, that when they were together

Keawe's heart was stilled; but as soon as he was alone he fell into a brooding horror, and heard the flames crackle, and saw the red fire burn in the bottomless pit. The girl, indeed, had come to him wholly; her heart leaped in her side at sight of him, her hand clung to his; and she was so fashioned, from the hair upon her head to the nails upon her toes, that none could see her without joy. She was pleasant in her nature. She had the good word always. Full of song she was, and went to and fro in the Bright House, the brightest thing in its three stories, carolling like the birds. And Keawe beheld and heard her with delight, and then must shrink upon one side, and weep and groan to think upon the price that he had paid for her; and then he must dry his eyes, and wash his face, and go and sit with her on the broad balconies, joining in her songs, and, with a sick spirit, answering her smiles.

There came a day when her feet began to be heavy and her songs more rare; and now it was not Keawe only that would weep apart, but each would sunder from the other and sit in opposite balconies with the whole width of the Bright House betwixt. Keawe was so sunk in his despair, he scarce observed the change, and was only glad he had more hours to sit alone and brood upon his destiny, and was not so frequently condemned to pull a smiling face on a sick heart. But one day, coming softly through the house, he heard the sound of a child sobbing, and there was Kokua rolling her face upon the balcony floor, and weeping like the lost.

"You do well to weep in this house, Kokua," he said. "And yet I would give the head off my body that you (at least) might have been happy."

"Happy!" she cried. "Keawe, when you lived alone in your Bright House you were the word of the island for a happy man; laughter and song were in your mouth, and your face was as bright as the sunrise. Then you wedded poor Kokua; and the good God knows what is amiss in her—but from that day you have not smiled. Oh!" she cried, "what ails me? I thought I was pretty, and I knew I loved him. What ails me, that I throw this cloud upon my husband?"

"Poor Kokua," said Keawe. He sat down by her side, and sought to take her hand; but that she plucked away. "Poor Kokua," he said again. "My poor child—my pretty. And I had thought all this while to spare you! Well, you shall know all. Then, at least, you will pity poor Keawe; then you will understand how much he loved you in the past—

that he dared hell for your possession—and how much he loves you still (the poor condemned one), that he can yet call up a smile when he beholds you."

With that he told her all, even from the beginning.

"You have done this for me?" she cried. "Ah, well, then what do I care!" and she clasped and wept upon him.

"Ah, child!" said Keawe, "and yet, when I consider of the fire of hell, I care a good deal!"

"Never tell me," said she, "no man can be lost because he loved Kokua, and no other fault. I tell you, Keawe, I shall save you with these hands, or perish in your company. What! you loved me and gave your soul, and you think I will not die to save you in return?"

"Ah, my dear, you might die a hundred times: and what difference would that make?" he cried, "except to leave me lonely till the time comes for my damnation?"

"You know nothing," said she. "I was educated in a school in Honolulu; I am no common girl. And I tell you I shall save my lover. What is this you say about a cent? But all the world is not American. In England they have a piece they call a farthing, which is about half a cent. Ah! sorrow!" she cried, "that makes it scarcely better, for the buyer must be lost, and we shall find none so brave as my Keawe! But, then, there is France; they have a small coin there which they call a centime, and these go five to the cent, or thereabout. We could not do better. Come, Keawe, let us go to the French islands; let us go to Tahiti as fast as ships can bear us. There we have four centimes, three centimes, two centimes, one centime; four possible sales to come and go on; and two of us to push the bargain. Come, my Keawe! kiss me, and banish care. Kokua will defend you."

"Gift of God!" he cried. "I cannot think that God will punish me for desiring aught so good. Be it as you will then, take me where you please: I put my life and my salvation in your hands."

Early the next day Kokua went about her preparations. She took Keawe's chest that he went with sailoring; and first she put the bottle in a corner, and then packed it with the richest of their clothes and the bravest of the knick-knacks in the house. "For," said she, "we must seem to be rich folks, or who would believe in the bottle?" All the time of her preparation she was as gay as a bird; only when she looked upon Keawe the tears would spring in her eye, and she must run and kiss him. As for Keawe, a weight was off his soul; now that he had his secret shared, and some hope in front of him, he seemed like a new man, his feet went lightly on the earth, and his breath was good to him again. Yet was terror still at his elbow; and ever and again, as the wind blows out a taper, hope died in him, and he saw the flames toss and the red fire burn in hell.

It was given out in the country they were gone pleasuring in the States, which was thought a strange thing, and yet not so strange as the truth, if any could have guessed it. So they went to Honolulu in the *Hall*, and thence in the *Umatilla* to San Francisco with a crowd of Haoles, and at San Francisco took their passage by the mail brigantine, the *Tropic Bird*, for Papeete, the chief place of the French in the south islands. Thither they came, after a pleasant voyage, on a fair day of the Trade Wind, and saw the reef with the surf breaking and Motuiti with its palms, and the schooner riding withinside and the white houses of the town low down along the shore among green trees, and overhead the mountains and the clouds of Tahiti, the wise island.

It was judged the most wise to hire a house, which they did accordingly, opposite the British Consul's, to make a great parade of money, and themselves conspicuous with carriages and horses. This it was very easy to do, so long as they had the bottle in their possession; for Kokua was more bold than Keawe, and, whenever she had a mind, called on the imp for twenty or a hundred dollars. At this rate they soon grew to be remarked in the town; and the strangers from Hawaii, their riding and their driving, the fine holokus, and the rich lace of Kokua, became the matter of much talk.

They got on well after the first with the Tahiti language, which is indeed like to the Hawaiian, with a change of certain letters; and as soon as they had any freedom of speech, began to push the bottle. You are to consider it was not an easy subject to introduce; it was not easy to persuade people you are in earnest, when you offer to sell them for four centimes the spring of health and riches inexhaustible. It was necessary besides to explain the dangers of the bottle; and either people disbelieved the whole thing and laughed, or they thought the more of the darker part, became overcast with gravity, and drew away from Keawe and Kokua, as from persons who had dealings with the devil. So far from gaining ground, these two began to find they were avoided in the town; the children ran away from them screaming, a thing intolerable to Kokua; Catholics crossed themselves as they went by; and all persons began with one accord to disengage themselves from their advances.

Depression fell upon their spirits. They would sit at night in their new house, after a day's weariness, and not exchange one word, or the silence would be broken by Kokua bursting suddenly into sobs. Sometimes they would pray together; sometimes they would have the bottle out upon the floor, and sit all evening watching how the shadow hovered in the midst. At such times they would be afraid to go to rest. It was long ere slumber came to them, and, if either dozed off, it would be to wake and find the other silently weeping in the dark, or, perhaps, to wake alone, the other having fled from the house and the neighborhood of that bottle, to pace under the bananas in the little garden, or to wander on the beach by moonlight.

One night it was so when Kokua awoke. Keawe was gone. She felt in the bed and his place was cold. Then fear fell upon her, and she sat up in bed. A little moonshine filtered through the shutters. The room was bright, and she could spy the bottle on the floor. Outside it blew high, the great trees of the avenue cried aloud, and the fallen leaves rattled in the veranda. In the midst of this Kokua was aware of another sound; whether of a beast or of a man she could scarce tell, but it was as sad as death, and cut her to the soul. Softly she arose, set the door ajar, and looked forth into the moonlit yard. There, under the bananas, lay Keawe, his mouth in the dust, and as he lay he moaned.

It was Kokua's first thought to run forward and console him; her second potently withheld her. Keawe had borne himself before his wife like a brave man; it became her little in the hour of weakness to intrude upon his shame. With the thought she drew back into the house.

"Heaven," she thought, "how careless have I been—how weak! It is he, not I, that stands in this eternal peril; it was he, not I, that took the curse upon his soul. It is for my sake, and for the love of a creature of so little worth and such poor help, that he now beholds so close to him the flames of hell—ay, and smells the smoke of it, lying without there in the wind and moonlight. Am I so dull of spirit that never till now I have surmised my duty, or have I seen it before and turned aside? But now, at least, I take up my soul in both the hands of my affection; now I say farewell to the white steps of heaven and the waiting faces of my friends. A love for a love, and let mine be equalled with Keawe's! A soul for a soul, and be it mine to perish!"

She was a deft woman with her hands, and was soon apparelled. She took in her hand the change—the precious centimes they kept ever at their side; for this coin is little used, and they had made provision at a government office. When she was forth in the avenue clouds came on the wind, and the moon was blackened. The town slept, and she knew not whither to turn till she heard one coughing in the shadow of the trees.

"Old man," said Kokua, "what do you here abroad in the cold night?"

The old man could scarce express himself for coughing, but she made out that he was old and poor, and a stranger in the island.

"Will you do me a service?" said Kokua. "As one stranger to another, and as an old man to a young woman, will you help a daughter of Hawaii?"

"Ah," said the old man. "So you are the witch from the Eight Islands, and even my old soul you seek to entangle. But I have heard of you, and defy your wickedness."

"Sit down here," said Kokua, "and let me tell you a tale." And she told him the story of Keawe from the beginning to the end.

"And now," said she, "I am his wife, whom he bought with his soul's welfare. And what should I do? If I went to him myself and offered to buy it, he will refuse. But if you go, he will sell it eagerly; I will await you here; you will buy it for four centimes, and I will buy it again for three. And the Lord strengthen a poor girl!"

"If you meant falsely," said the old man, "I think God would strike you dead."

"He would!" cried Kokua. "Be sure He would. I could not be so treacherous; God would not suffer it."

"Give me the four centimes and await me here," said the old man.

Now, when Kokua stood alone in the street, her spirit died. The wind roared in the trees, and it seemed to her the rushing of the flames of hell; the shadows towered in the light of the street lamp, and they seemed to her the snatching hands of evil ones. If she had had the strength, she must have run away, and if she had had the breath, she must have screamed aloud; but, in truth, she could do neither, and stood and trembled in the avenue, like an affrighted child.

Then she saw the old man returning, and he had the bottle in his hand.

"I have done your bidding," said he. "I left your husband weeping like a child; tonight he will sleep easy." And he held the bottle forth.

"Before you give it to me," Kokua panted, "take the good with the evil—ask to be delivered from your cough."

"I am an old man," replied the other, "and too near the gate of the grave to take a favor from the devil. But what is this? Why do you not take the bottle? Do you hesitate?"

"Not hesitate!" cried Kokua. "I am only weak. Give me a moment. It is my hand resists, my flesh shrinks back from the accursed thing. One moment only!"

The old man looked upon Kokua kindly. "Poor child!" said he, "you fear: your soul misgives you. Well, let me keep it. I am old, and can never more be happy in this world, and as for the next—"

"Give it me!" gasped Kokua. "There is your money. Do you think I am so base as that? Give me the bottle."

"God bless you, child," said the old man.

Kokua concealed the bottle under her holoku, said farewell to the old man, and walked off along the avenue, she cared not whither. For all roads were now the same to her, and led equally to hell. Sometimes she walked, and sometimes ran; sometimes lay by the wayside in the dust and wept. All that she had heard of hell came back to her; she saw the flames blaze, and she smelled the smoke, and her flesh withered on the coals.

Near day she came to her mind again, and returned to the house. It was even as the old man said—Keawe slumbered like a child. Kokua stood and gazed upon his face.

"Now my husband," said she, "it is your turn to sleep. When you wake it will be your turn to sing and laugh. But for poor Kokua, alas! that meant no evil—for poor Kokua no more sleep, no more singing, no more delight, whether in earth or heaven."

With that she lay down in the bed by his side, and her misery was so extreme that she fell in a deep slumber instantly.

Late in the morning her husband woke her and gave her the good news. It seemed he was silly with delight, for he paid no heed to her distress, ill though she dissembled it. The words stuck in her mouth, it mattered not; Keawe did the speaking. She ate not a bite, but who was to observe it? For Keawe cleared the dish. Kokua saw and heard him, like some strange thing in a dream; there were times when she forgot or doubted, and put her hands to her brow; to know herself doomed and hear her husband babble seemed so monstrous.

All the while Keawe was eating and talking, and planning the time of their return, and thanking her for saving him and fondling her, and calling her the true helper after all. He laughed at the old man that was fool enough to buy that bottle.

"A worthy man he seemed," Keawe said. "But no one can judge by appearances. For why did the old reprobate require the bottle?"

"My husband," said Kokua humbly, "his purpose may have been good."

Keawe laughed like an angry man.

"Fiddle-de-dee!" cried Keawe. "An old rogue, I tell you; and an old ass to boot. For the bottle was hard enough to sell at four centimes; and at three it will be quite impossible. The margin is not broad enough, the thing begins to smell of scorching—brr!" said he, and shuddered. "It is true I bought it myself at a cent, when I knew not there were smaller coins. I was a fool for my pains; there will never be found another, and whoever has that bottle now will carry it to the pit."

"O my husband!" said Kokua. "Is it not a terrible thing to save oneself by the eternal ruin of another? It seems to me I could not laugh. I would be humbled. I would be filled with melancholy. I would pray for the poor holder."

Then Keawe, because he felt the truth of what she said, grew the more angry. "Heighty-teighty!" cried he. "You may be filled with melancholy if you please. It is not the mind of a good wife. If you thought at all of me, you would sit shamed."

Thereupon he went out, and Kokua was alone.

What chance had she to sell that bottle at two centimes? None, she perceived. And if she had any, here was her husband hurrying her away to a country where there was nothing lower than a cent. And here—on the morrow of her sacrifice—was her husband leaving her and blaming her.

She would not even try to profit by what time she had, but sat in the house, and now had the bottle out and viewed it with unutterable fear, and now, with loathing, hid it out of sight.

By-and-by Keawe came back, and would have her take a drive.

"My husband, I am ill," she said. "I am out of heart. Excuse me, I can take no pleasure."

Then was Keawe more wroth than ever. With her, because he thought she was brooding over the case of the old man; and with himself, because he thought she was right and was ashamed to be so happy.

"This is your truth," cried he, "and this your affection! Your husband is just saved from eternal ruin, which he encountered for the love of you—and you can take no pleasure! Kokua, you have a disloyal heart."

He went forth again furious, and wandered in the town all day. He met friends, and drank with them; they hired a carriage and drove into the country, and there drank again. All the time Keawe was ill at ease, because he was taking this pastime while his wife was sad, and because he knew in his heart that she was more right than he; and the knowledge made him drink the deeper.

Now there was an old brutal Haole drinking with him, one that had been a boatswain of a whaler—a runaway, a digger in gold mines, a convict in prisons. He had a low mind and a foul mouth; he loved to drink and to see others drunken; and he pressed the glass upon Keawe. Soon there was no more money in the company.

"Here, you!" says the boatswain, "you are rich, you have been always saying. You have a bottle or some foolishness."

"Yes," says Keawe, "I am rich; I will go back and get some money from my wife, who keeps it."

"That's a bad idea, mate," said the boatswain. "Never you trust a petticoat with dollars. They're all as false as water; you keep an eye on her."

Now this word struck in Keawe's mind; for he was muddled with what he had been drinking.

"I should not wonder but she was false, indeed," thought he. "Why else should she be so cast down at my release? But I will show her I am not the man to be fooled. I will catch her in the act."

Accordingly, when they were back in town, Keawe bade the boatswain wait for him at the corner by the old calaboose, and went forward up the avenue alone to the door of his house. The night had come again; there was a light within, but never a sound; and Keawe crept about the corner, opened the back door softly, and looked in.

There was Kokua on the floor, the lamp at her side; before her was a milk-white bottle, with a round belly and a long neck; and as she viewed it, Kokua wrung her hands.

A long time Keawe stood and looked in the doorway. At first he was struck stupid; and then fear fell upon him that the bargain had been made amiss, and the bottle had come back to him as it came at San Francisco; and at that his knees were loosened, and the fumes of the wine departed from his head like mists off a river in the morning. And then he had another thought; and it was a strange one, that made his cheeks to burn.

"I must make sure of this," thought he.

So he closed the door, and went softly around the corner again, and then came noisily in, as though he were but now returned. And, lo! by the time he opened the front door no bottle was to be seen; and Kokua sat in a chair and started up like one awakened out of sleep.

"I have been drinking all day and making merry," said Keawe. "I have been with good companions, and now I only came back for money, and return to drink and carouse with them again."

Both his face and voice were as stern as judgment, but Kokua was too troubled to observe.

"You do well to use your own, my husband," said she, and her words trembled.

"Oh, I do well in all things," said Keawe, and he went straight to the chest and took out money. But he looked besides in the corner where they kept the bottle, and there was no bottle there.

At that the chest heaved upon the floor like a sea-billow, and the house spun about him like a wreath of smoke, for he saw she was lost now, and there was no escape. "It is what I feared," he thought. "It is she who has bought it."

And then he came to himself a little and rose up; but the sweat streamed on his face as thick as the rain and as cold as the well-water.

"Kokua," said he, "I said to you today what ill became me. Now I return to house with my jolly companions," and at that he laughed a little quietly. "I will take more pleasure in the cup if you forgive me."

She clasped his knees in a moment, she kissed his knees with flowing tears.

"Oh," she cried, "I ask but a kind word!"

"Let us never one think hardly of the other," said Keawe, and was gone out of the house.

Now, the money that Keawe had taken was only some of that store of centime pieces they had laid in at their arrival. It was very sure he had no mind to be drinking. His wife had given her soul for him, now he must give his for hers; no other thought was in the world with him.

At the corner, by the old calaboose, there was the boatswain waiting.

"My wife has the bottle," said Keawe, "and, unless you help me to recover it, there can be no more money and no more liquor tonight."

"You do not mean to say you are serious about that bottle?" cried the boatswain.

"There is the lamp," said Keawe. "Do I look as if I was jesting?"

"That is so," said the boatswain. "You look as serious as a ghost."

"Well, then," said Keawe, "here are two centimes; you just go to my wife in the house, and offer her these for the bottle, which (if I am not much mistaken) she will give you instantly. Bring it to me here, and I will buy it back from you for one; for that is the law with this bottle, that it still must be sold for a less sum. But whatever you do, never breathe a word to her that you have come from me."

"Mate, I wonder are you making a fool of me?" asked the boatswain.

"It will do you no harm if I am," returned Keawe.

"That is so, mate," said the boatswain.

"And if you doubt me," added Keawe, "you can try. As soon as you are clear of the house, wish to have your pocket full of money, or a bottle of the best rum, or what you please, and you will see the virtue of the thing."

"Very well, Kanaka," says the boatswain. "I will try; but if you are having your fun out of me, I will take my fun out of you with a belaying-pin."

So the whalerman went off up the avenue; and Keawe stood and waited. It was near the same spot where Kokua had waited the night before; but Keawe was more resolved, and never faltered in his purpose; only his soul was bitter with despair.

It seemed a long time he had to wait before he heard a voice singing in the darkness of the avenue. He knew the voice to be the boatswain's; but it was strange how drunken it appeared upon a sudden.

Next the man himself came stumbling into the light of the lamp. He had the devil's bottle buttoned in his coat; another bottle was in his hand; and even as he came in view he raised it to his mouth and drank.

"You have it," said Keawe. "I see that."

"Hands off!" cried the boatswain, jumping back. "Take a step near me, and I'll smash your mouth. You thought you could make a catspaw of me, did you?"

"What do you mean?" cried Keawe.

"Mean?" cried the boatswain. "This is a pretty good bottle, this is;

that's what I mean. How I got it for two centimes I can't make out; but I am sure you shan't have it for one."

"You mean you won't sell?" gasped Keawe.

"No, sir," cried the boatswain. "But I'll give you a drink of the rum, if you like."

"I tell you," said Keawe, "the man who has that bottle goes to hell."

"I reckon I'm going anyway," returned the sailor; "and this bottle's the best thing to go with I've struck yet. No, sir!" he cried again, "this is my bottle now, and you can go and fish for another."

"Can this be true?" Keawe cried. "For your own sake, I beseech you, sell it me!"

"I don't value any of your talk," replied the boatswain. "You thought I was a flat, now you see I'm not; and there's an end. If you won't have a swallow of the rum, I'll have one myself. Here's your health, and good night to you!"

So off he went down the avenue toward town, and there goes the bottle out of the story.

But Keawe ran to Kokua light as the wind; and great was their joy that night; and great, since then, has been the peace of all their days in the Bright House.

Frank Stockton (1834–1902)

Today Frank Stockton is remembered primarily for his classic short story "The Lady or the Tiger?" (1882). However, he was so popular during his lifetime that a twenty-three volume edition of his complete works was published between 1899 and 1904. He was America's first major writer of high fantasy—i.e., set in imaginary lands. Much of what he did write was science fiction or fantasy, and virtually all of his shorter works of fantasy remain fresh and readable.

Born and raised in Philadelphia, he enjoyed a happy childhood in which he started reading and writing fairy tales. His family wanted him to pursue a medical career after high school, but, instead, he spent fourteen years (1852–1866) working as a wood engraver. By 1859 he had begun selling stories to magazines such as the *Southern Literary Messenger*, the *Riverside Magazine for Young People*, and *Hearth and Home*. This gradually absorbed more of his time and when his first book of children's fairy tales (*Ting-A-Ling*) appeared in 1870, he resolved to work on his literary career full-time. When *St. Nicholas Magazine* for children started in 1873, Stockton became assistant editor, staying there for eight years before deciding, probably because of the popular reception to *Rudder Grange* (1879), to do nothing but write.

For a number of years thereafter he lived in the quiet rural settings of Nutley and Convent Station, New Jersey, where he often dictated first drafts from the depths of a comfortable hammock. Still, he enjoyed traveling, and the smashing success of such works as "The Lady or the Tiger?" and *The Casting Away of Mrs. Lecks and Mrs. Aleshine* (1886) allowed him to do so extensively.

Finally, in the later part of the 1890s, Stockton bought a house near

Harper's Ferry, West Virginia, where he lived for a few years until his death in Washington, D.C.

A slender, swarthy man who walked with a limp, Stockton was known as a witty, whimsical, and ironic raconteur, and a gentle companion whose stories delivered their infrequent messages in charming and entertaining fashion. A meticulous craftsman, he sometimes labored an hour to revise just one word. But his greatest strength lay in short stories, because they allowed him to generate humor that did not have to be sustained.

The Science Fiction of Frank R. Stockton (1976) collects most of his shorter works in this genre. Unaccountably, however, his twenty or so short fantasies have yet to receive similar treatment. Perhaps *Volume XVII: Stories III* (1900) from Scribner's twenty-three-volume set of *The Novels and Stories of Frank R. Stockton* comes closest. It contains ten fantastic stories, including five of his best: "The Griffin and the Minor Canon," "The Bee-Man of Orn," "Old Pipes and the Dryad," "The Philosophy of Relative Existences," and "The Christmas Shadrach." Of these, we have chosen the last and least known, a droll story of hot passions and a cooling stone.

THE CHRISTMAS SHADRACH

Whenever I make a Christmas present I like it to mean something —not necessarily my sentiments toward the person to whom I give it, but sometimes an expression of what I should like that person to do or to be. In the early part of a certain winter, not very long ago, I found myself in a position of perplexity and anxious concern regarding a Christmas present which I wished to make.

The state of the case was this: There was a young lady, the daughter of a neighbor and old friend of my father, who had been gradually assuming relations toward me which were not only unsatisfactory to me, but were becoming more and more so. Her name was Mildred Bronce. She was between twenty and twenty-five years of age, and as fine a woman in every way as one would be likely to meet in a lifetime. She was handsome, of a tender and generous disposition, a fine intelligence, and a thoroughly well-stocked mind. We had known each other for a long time, and when fourteen or fifteen Mildred had been my favorite companion. She was a little younger than I, and I liked her better than any boy I knew. Our friendship had continued through the years, but of late there had been a change in it. Mildred had become very fond of me, and her fondness seemed to have in it certain elements which annoyed me.

As a girl to make love to, no one could be better than Mildred Bronce. But I had never made love to her—at least not earnestly—and I did not wish that any permanent condition of loving should be established between us. Mildred did not seem to share this opinion, for every day it became plainer to me that she looked upon me as a lover, and that she was perfectly willing to return my affection.

But I had other ideas upon the subject. Into the rural town in which my family passed the greater part of the year there had recently come a young lady, Miss Janet Clinton, to whom my soul went out of my own option. In some respects, perhaps, she was not the equal of Mildred, but she was very pretty. She was small; she had a lovely mouth; she was apparently of a clinging nature, and her dark eyes looked into mine with a tingling effect that no other eyes had ever produced. I was in love with her because I wished to be, and the consciousness of this fact caused me a proud satisfaction. This affair was not the result of circumstances, but of my own free will.

I wished to retain Mildred's friendship, I wished to make her happy; and with this latter intent in view I wished very much that she should not disappoint herself in her anticipations of the future.

Each year it had been my habit to make Mildred a Christmas present, and I was now looking for something to give her which would please her and suit my purpose.

When a man wishes to select a present for a lady which, while it assures her of his kind feeling toward her, shall at the same time indicate that not only has he no matrimonial inclinations in her direction, but that it would be entirely unwise for her to have any such inclinations in his direction; that no matter with what degree of fondness her heart is disposed to turn toward him, his heart does not turn toward her, and that, in spite of all sentiments induced by long association and the natural fitness of things, she need never expect to be to him anything more than a sister, he has, indeed, a difficult task before him. But such was the task I set for myself.

Day after day I wandered through the shops. I looked at odd pieces of jewelry and bric-à-brac, and at many a quaint relic or bit of art work which seemed to have a meaning, but nothing had the meaning I wanted. As to books, I found none which satisfied me—not one which was adapted to produce the exact impression that I desired.

One afternoon I was in a little basement shop kept by a fellow in a long overcoat, who, so far as I was able to judge, bought curiosities, but never sold any. For some minutes I had been looking at a beautifully decorated saucer of rare workmanship for which there was no cup to match, and for which the proprietor informed me no cup could be found or manufactured. There were some points in the significance of an article of this sort, given as a present to a lady, which fitted my purpose, but it would signify too much. I did not wish to suggest to Mildred that she need never expect to find a cup. It would be better, in fact, if I gave her anything of this kind, to send her a cup and saucer entirely unsuited to each other, and which could not, under any conditions, be used together.

I put down the saucer, and continued my search among the dusty shelves and cases.

"How would you like a paper-weight?" the shopkeeper asked. "Here is something a little odd," handing me a piece of dark-colored mineral nearly as big as my fist, flat on the underside, and of a pleasing irregularity above. Around the bottom was a band of arabesque work in some dingy metal, probably German silver. I smiled as I took it.

"This is not good enough for a Christmas present," I said. "I want something odd, but it must have some value."

"Well," said the man, "that has no real value, but there is a peculiarity about it which interested me when I heard of it, and so I bought it. This mineral is a piece of what the ironworkers call shadrach. It is a portion of the iron or iron ore which passes through the smelting furnaces without being affected by the great heat, and so they have given it the name of one of the Hebrew youths who was cast into the fiery furnace by Nebuchadnezzar, and who came out unhurt. Some people think there is a sort of magical quality about this shadrach, and that it can give out to human beings something of its power to keep their minds cool when they are in danger of being overheated. The old gentleman who had this made was subject to fits of anger, and he thought this piece of shadrach helped to keep him from giving way to them. Occasionally he used to leave it in the house of a hot-tempered neighbor, believing that the testy individual would be cooled down for a time, without knowing how the change had been brought about. I bought a lot of things of the old gentleman's widow, and this among them. I thought I might try it some time, but I never have done so."

I held the shadrach in my hand, ideas concerning it rapidly flitting through my mind. Why would not this be a capital thing to give to Mildred? If it should, indeed, possess the quality ascribed to it, if it should be able to cool her liking for me, what better present could I give her? I did not hesitate long.

"I will buy this," I said. "But the ornamentation must be of a better sort. It is now too cheap and tawdry-looking."

"I can attend to that for you," said the shopkeeper. "I can have it set in a band of gold or silver filigree-work like this, if you choose."

I agreed to this proposition, but ordered the band to be made of silver, the cool tone of that metal being more appropriate to the characteristics of the gift than the warmer hues of gold.

When I gave my Christmas present to Mildred, she was pleased with it. Its oddity struck her fancy.

"I don't believe anybody ever had such a paperweight as that," she said, as she thanked me. "What is it made of?"

I told her, and explained what shadrach was, but I did not speak of its presumed influence over human beings, which, after all, might be nothing but the wildest fancy. I did not feel altogether at my ease as I added that it was merely a trifle, a thing of no value except as a reminder of the season.

"The fact that it is a present from you gives it value," she said, as she smilingly raised her eyes to mine.

I left her house—we were all living in the city then—with a troubled conscience. What a deception I was practising upon this noble girl, who, if she did not already love me, was plainly on the point of doing so! She had received my present as if it indicated a warmth of feeling on my part, when, in fact, it was the result of a desire for a cooler feeling on her part.

But I called my reason to my aid, and I showed myself that what I had given Mildred—if it should prove to possess any virtue at all—was, indeed, a most valuable boon. It was something which would prevent the waste of her affections, the wreck of her hopes. No kindness could be truer, no regard for her happiness more sincere, than the motives which prompted me to give her the shadrach.

I did not soon again see Mildred, but as often as possible I visited Janet. She always received me with a charming cordiality, and if this should develop into warmer sentiments I was not the man to wish to cool them. In many ways Janet seemed much better suited to me than Mildred. One of the greatest charms of this beautiful girl was a tender trustfulness, as if I were a being on whom she could lean and to whom she could look up. I liked this. It was very different from Mildred's manner. With the latter I had always been well-satisfied if I felt myself standing on the same plane.

The weeks and months passed on, and again we were all in the country, and here I saw Mildred often. Our homes were not far apart, and our families were very intimate. With my opportunities for frequent observation I could not doubt that a change had come over her. She was always friendly when we met, and seemed as glad to see me as she was to see any other member of my family, but she was not the Mildred I used to know. It was plain that my existence did not make the same impression on her that it once made. She did not seem to consider it important whether I came or went, whether I was in the room or not, whether I joined a party or stayed away. All this had been very different. I knew well that Mildred had been used to consider my presence as a matter of much importance, and I now felt sure that my Christmas shadrach was doing its work. Mildred was cooling toward me. Her affection, or, to put it more modestly, her tendency to affection, was gently congealing into friendship. This was highly gratifying to my moral nature, for every day I was doing my best to warm the soul of Janet. Whether or not I succeeded in this I could not be sure. Janet was as tender and trustful and charming as ever, but no more so than she had been months before.

Sometimes I thought she was waiting for an indication of an increased warmth of feeling on my part before she allowed the temperature of her own sentiments to rise. But, for one reason and another, I delayed the solution of this problem. Janet was very fond of company, and although we saw a great deal of each other, we were not often alone. If we two had more frequently walked, driven, or rowed together, as Mildred and I used to do, I think Miss Clinton would soon have had every opportunity of making up her mind about the fervor of my passion.

The summer weeks passed on, and there was no change in the things which now principally concerned me, except that Mildred seemed to be growing more and more indifferent to me. From having seemed to care no more for me than for her other friends, she now seemed to care less for me than for most people. I do not mean that she showed a dislike, but she treated me with a sort of indifference which I did not fancy at all. This sort of thing had gone too far, and there was no knowing how much further it would go. It was plain enough that the shadrach was overdoing the business.

I was now in a state of much mental disquietude. Greatly as I desired to win the love of Janet, it grieved me to think of losing the generous friendship of Mildred—that friendship to which I had been accustomed for the greater part of my life, and on which, as I now discovered, I had grown to depend.

In this state of mind I went to see Mildred. I found her in the library, writing. She received me pleasantly, and was sorry her father was not at home, and begged that I would excuse her finishing the note on which she was engaged, because she wished to get it into the post office before the mail closed. I sat down on the other side of the table, and she finished her note, after which she went out to give it to a servant.

Glancing about me, I saw the shadrach. It was partly under a litter of papers, instead of lying on them. I took it up, and was looking at it when Mildred returned. She sat down and asked me if I had heard of the changes that were to be made in the timetable of the railroad. We talked a little on the subject, and then I spoke of the shadrach, saying carelessly that it might be interesting to analyze the bit of metal. There was a little knob which might be filed off without injuring it in the least.

"You may take it," she said, "and make what experiments you please. I do not use it much. It is unnecessarily heavy for a paperweight."

From her tone I might have supposed she had forgotten that I had given it to her. I told her that I would be very glad to borrow the paperweight for a time, and, putting it into my pocket, I went away, leaving her arranging her disordered papers on the table, and giving quite as much regard to this occupation as she had given to my little visit.

I could not feel sure that the absence of the shadrach would cause any diminution in the coolness of her feelings toward me, but there was reason to believe that it would prevent them from growing cooler. If she should keep that shadrach she might in time grow to hate me. I was very glad that I had taken it from her.

My mind easier on this subject, my heart turned more freely toward Janet, and going to her house the next day, I was delighted to find her alone. She was as lovely as ever, and as cordial, but she was flushed and evidently annoyed.

"I am in a bad humor today," she said, "and I am glad you came to talk to me and quiet me. Dr. Gilbert promised to take me to drive this afternoon, and we were going over to the hills where they find the wild rhododendron. I am told that it is still in blossom up there, and I want some flowers ever so much—I am going to paint them. Besides, I am crazy to drive with his new horses. And now he sends me a note to say that he is engaged."

This communication shocked me, and I began to talk to her about Dr. Gilbert. I soon found that several times she had been driving with this handsome young physician, but never, she said, behind his new horses, nor to the rhododendron hills.

Dr. Herbert Gilbert was a fine young fellow beginning practice in town, and one of my favorite associates. I had never thought of him in connection with Janet, but I could now see that he might make a most dangerous rival. When a young and talented doctor, enthusiastic in his studies, and earnestly desirous of establishing a practice, and who, if his time were not fully occupied, would naturally wish that the neighbors would think that such were the case, deliberately devotes some hours on I know not how many days to driving a young lady into the surrounding country, it may be supposed that he is really in love with her. Moreover, judging from Janet's present mood, this doctor's attentions were not without encouragement.

I went home, I considered the state of affairs, I ran my fingers through my hair, I gazed steadfastly upon the floor. Suddenly I rose. I had had an inspiration. I would give the shadrach to Dr. Gilbert!

I went immediately to the doctor's office, and found him there. He, too, was not in a very good humor.

"I have had two old ladies here nearly all the afternoon, and they have bored me to death," he said. "I could not get rid of them, because I found they had made an appointment with each other to visit me today and talk over a hospital plan which I proposed some time ago, and which is really very important to me, but I wish they had chosen some other time to come here. What is that thing?"

"That is a bit of shadrach," I said, "made into a paperweight." And then I proceeded to explain what shadrach is, and what peculiar properties it must possess to resist the power of heat, which melts other metal apparently of the same class. I added that I thought it might be interesting to analyze a bit of it and discover what fireproof constituents it possessed.

"I should like to do that," said the doctor, attentively turning over the shadrach in his hand. "Can I take off a piece of it?"

"I will give it to you," said I, "and you can make what use of it you please. If you do analyze it, I shall be very glad indeed to hear the results of your investigations."

The doctor demurred a little at taking the paperweight with such a pretty silver ring around it, but I assured him that the cost of the whole affair was trifling, and I should be gratified if he would take it. He accepted the gift, and was thanking me, when a patient arrived, and I departed.

I really had no right to give away this paperweight, which, in fact, belonged to Mildred, but there are times when a man must keep his eyes on the chief good, and not think too much about other things. Besides, it was evident that Mildred did not care in the least for the bit of metal, and she had virtually given it to me.

There was another point which I took into consideration. It might be that the shadrach might simply cool Dr. Gilbert's feelings toward me, and that would be neither pleasant nor advantageous. If I could have managed matters so that Janet could have given it to him, it would have been all right. But now all that I could do was to wait and see what would happen. If only the thing would cool the doctor in a general way, that would help. He might then give more thought to his practice and his hospital ladies, and let other people take Janet driving.

About a week after this I met the doctor. He seemed in a hurry, but I stopped him. I had a curiosity to know if he had analyzed the shadrach, and asked him about it.

"No," said he, "I haven't done it. I haven't had time. I knocked off a piece of it, and I will attend to it when I get a chance. Good day."

Of course, if the man was busy, he could not be expected to give his mind to a trifling matter of that sort, but I thought he need not have been so curt about it. I stood gazing after him as he walked rapidly down the street. Before I resumed my walk I saw him enter the Clinton house. Things were not going on well. The shadrach had not cooled Dr. Gilbert's feelings toward Janet.

But because the doctor was still warm in his attentions to the girl I loved, I would not in the least relax my attentions to her. I visited her as often as I could find an excuse to do so. There was generally some one else there, but Janet's disposition was of such gracious expansiveness that each one felt obliged to be satisfied with what he got, much as he may have wished for something different.

But one morning Janet surprised me. I met her at Mildred's house, where I had gone to borrow a book of reference. Although I had urged her not to put herself to so much trouble, Mildred was standing on a little ladder looking for the book, because, she said, she knew exactly what I wanted, and she was sure she could find the proper volume better than I could. Janet had been sitting in a window seat, reading, but when I came in she put down her book and devoted herself to conversation with me. I was a little sorry for this, because Mildred was very kindly engaged in doing me a service, and I really wanted to talk to her about the book she was looking for. Mildred showed so much of her old manner this morning that I would have been very sorry to have her think that I did not appreciate her returning interest in me. Therefore, while under other circumstances I would have been delighted to talk to Janet, I did not wish to give her so much of my attention then. But Janet Clinton was a girl who insisted on people attending to her when she wished them to do so, and having stepped through an open door into the garden, she presently called me to her. Of course I had to go.

I will not keep you a minute from your fellow student,'' she said, ''but I want to ask a favor of you.'' And into her dark, uplifted eyes there came a look of tender trustfulness clearer than any I had yet seen there. ''Don't *you* want to drive me to the rhododendron hills?'' she said. ''I suppose the flowers are all gone by this time, but I have never been there, and I should like ever so much to go.''

I could not help remarking that I thought Dr. Gilbert was going to take her there.

''Dr. Gilbert, indeed!'' she said, with a little laugh. ''He promised once, and didn't come, and the next day he planned for it it rained. I don't think doctors make very good escorts, anyway, for you can't tell who is going to be sick just as you are about to start on a trip. Besides, there is no knowing how much botany I should have to hear, and when I go on a pleasure drive I don't care very much about studying things. But of course I don't want to trouble you.''

''Trouble!'' I exclaimed. ''It will give me the greatest delight to take you for that drive or any other, and at whatever time you please.''

''You are always so good and kind,'' she said, with her dark eyes again upraised. ''And now let us go in and see if Mildred has found the book.''

I spoke the truth when I said that Janet's proposition delighted me. To take a long drive with that charming girl, and at the same time to feel that she had chosen me as her companion, was a greater joy than I had yet had reason to expect. But it would have been a more satisfying joy if she had asked me in her own house and not in Mildred's, if she had not allowed the love which I hoped was growing up between her and me to interfere with the revival of the old friendship between Mildred and me.

But when we returned to the library Mildred was sitting at a table with a book before her, opened at the passage I wanted.

''I have just found it,'' she said, with a smile. ''Draw up a chair, and we will look over these maps together. I want you to show me how he travelled when he left his ship."

"Well, if you two are going to the pole," said Janet, with her prettiest smile, "I will go back to my novel."

She did not seem in the least to object to my geographical researches with Mildred, and if the latter had even noticed my willingness to desert her at the call of Janet, she did not show it. Apparently she was as much a good comrade as she had ever been. This state of things was gratifying in the highest degree. If I could be loved by Janet and still keep Mildred as my friend, what greater earthly joys could I ask?

The drive with Janet was postponed by wet weather. Day after day it rained, or the skies were heavy, and we both agreed that it must be in the bright sunshine that we would make this excursion. When we should make it, and should be alone together on the rhododendron hill, I intended to open my soul to Janet.

It may seem strange to others, and at the time it also seemed strange to me, but there was another reason besides the rainy weather which prevented my declaration of love to Janet. This was a certain nervous anxiety in regard to my friendship for Mildred. I did not in the least waver in my intention to use the best endeavors to make the one my wife, but at the same time I was oppressed by a certain alarm that in carrying out this project I might act in such a way as to wound the feelings of the other.

This disposition to consider the feelings of Mildred became so strong that I began to think that my own sentiments were in need of control. It was not right that while making love to one woman I should give so much consideration to my relations with another. The idea struck me that in a measure I had shared the fate of those who had thrown the Hebrew youths into the fiery furnace. My heart had not been consumed by the flames, but in throwing the shadrach into what I supposed were Mildred's affections it was quite possible that I had been singed by them. At any rate, my conscience told me that under the circumstances my sentiments toward Mildred were too warm. In honestly making love to Janet I ought to forget them entirely.

It might have been a good thing, I told myself, if I had not given away the shadrach, but kept it as a gift from Mildred. Very soon after I reached this conclusion it became evident to me that Mildred was again cooling in my direction as rapidly as the mercury falls after sunset on a

September day. This discovery did not make my mercury fall. In fact, it brought it for a time nearly to the boiling point. I could not imagine what had happened. I almost neglected Janet, so anxious was I to know what had made this change in Mildred.

Weeks passed on, and I discovered nothing, except that Mildred had now become more than indifferent to me. She allowed me to see that my companionship did not give her pleasure.

Janet had her drive to the rhododendron hills, but she took it with Dr. Gilbert and not with me. When I heard of this it pained me, though I could not help admitting that I deserved the punishment. But my surprise was almost as great as my pain, for Janet had recently given me reason to believe that she had a very small opinion of the young doctor. In fact, she had criticised him so severely that I had been obliged to speak in his defence. I now found myself in a most doleful quandary, and there was only one thing of which I could be certain: I needed cooling toward Mildred if I still allowed myself to hope to marry Janet.

One afternoon I was talking to Mr. Bronce in his library, when, glancing toward the table used by his daughter for writing purposes, I was astounded to see, lying on a little pile of letters, the Christmas shadrach. As soon as I could get an opportunity I took it in my hand and eagerly examined it. I had not been mistaken. It was the paperweight I had give Mildred. There was the silver band around it, and there was the place where a little piece had been knocked off by the doctor. Mildred was not at home, but I determined that I would wait and see her. I would dine with the Bronces, I would spend the evening, I would stay all night—I would not leave the house until I had had this mystery explained. She returned in about half an hour, and greeted me in the somewhat stiff manner she had adopted of late. But when she noticed my perturbed expression and saw that I held the shadrach in my hand, she took a seat by the table, where for some time I had been waiting for her, alone.

"I suppose you want to ask me about that paperweight," she remarked.

"Indeed I do," I replied. "How in the world did you happen to get it again?"

"Again?" she repeated satirically. "You may well say that. I will explain it to you. Some little time ago I called on Janet Clinton, and on her writing desk I saw that paperweight. I remembered it perfectly. It was the one you gave me last Christmas, and afterward borrowed of me, saying that you wanted to analyze it, or something of the sort. I had never used it very much, and of course was willing that you should take it and make experiments with it if you wanted to, but I must say that the sight of it on Janet Clinton's desk both shocked and angered me. I asked her where she got it, and she told me a gentleman had given it to her. I did not need to waste any words inquiring who this gentleman was, but I determined that she should not rest under a mistake in regard to its proper ownership, and told her plainly that the person who had given it to her had previously given it to me—that it was mine, and he had no right to give it to any one else. 'Oh, if that is the case,' she exclaimed, 'take it, I beg of you. I don't care for it, and, what is more, I don't care any more for the man who gave it to me than I do for the thing itself.' So I took it and brought it home with me. Now you know how I happened to have it again."

For a moment I made no answer. Then I asked how long it had been since she had received the shadrach from Janet Clinton.

"Oh, I don't remember exactly," she said. "It was several weeks ago."

Now I knew everything. All the mysteries of the past were revealed to me. The young doctor, fervid in his desire to please the woman he loved, had given Janet this novel paperweight. From that moment she had begun to regard his attentions with apathy, and finally—her nature was one which was apt to go to extremes—to dislike him. Mildred repossessed herself of the shadrach, which she took, not as a gift from Janet, but as her rightful property, presented to her by me. And this horrid little object, probably with renewed power, had cooled, almost frozen indeed, the sentiments of that dear girl toward me. Then, too, had the spell been taken from Janet's inclinations, and she had gone to the rhododendron hills with Dr. Gilbert.

One thing was certain: I must have that shadrach.

"Mildred," I exclaimed, "will you not give me this paperweight? —give it to me for my own?"

"What do you want to do with it?" she asked sarcastically. "Analyze it again?"

"Mildred," said I, "I did not give it to Janet. I gave it to Dr. Gilbert, and he must have given it to her. I know I had no right to give it away at all, but I did not believe that you would care. But now I beg that you will let me have it—let me have it for my own. I assure you solemnly I will never give it away. It has caused trouble enough already.''

''I don't exactly understand what you mean by trouble,'' she said, ''but take it if you want it. You are perfectly welcome.'' And picking up her gloves and hat from the table, she left me.

As I walked home my hatred of the wretched piece of metal in my hand increased with every step. I looked at it with disgust when I went to bed that night, and when my glance lighted upon it the next morning I involuntarily shrank from it as if it had been an evil thing. Over and over again that day I asked myself why I should keep in my possession something which would make my regard for Mildred grow less and less, which would eventually make me care for her not at all? The very thought of not caring for Mildred sent a pang through my heart.

My feelings all prompted me to rid myself of what I looked upon as a calamitous talisman, but my reason interfered. If I still wished to marry Janet it was my duty to welcome indifference to Mildred.

In this mood I went out to stroll, to think, to decide, and that I might be ready to act on my decision I put the shadrach into my pocket. Without exactly intending it, I walked toward the Bronce place, and soon found myself on the edge of a pretty pond which lay at the foot of the garden. Here, in the shade of a tree, there stood a bench, and on this lay a book, an ivory paper cutter in its leaves as marker.

I knew that Mildred had left that book on the bench. It was her habit to come to this place to read. As she had not taken the volume with her, it was probable that she intended soon to return. But then the sad thought came to me that if she saw me there she would not return. I picked up the book. I read the pages she had been reading. As I read I felt that I could think the very thoughts that she thought as she read. I was seized with a yearning to be with her, to read with her, to think with her. Never had my soul gone out to Mildred as at that moment, and yet, heavily dangling in my pocket, I carried—I could not bear to think of it. Seized by a sudden impulse, I put down the book. I drew out the shadrach, and, tearing off the silver band, I tossed the vile bit of metal into the pond.

''There!'' I cried. ''Go out of my possession, out of my sight! You shall work no charm on me. Let nature take its course, and let things happen as they may.'' Then, relieved from the weight on my heart and the weight in my pocket, I went home.

Nature did take its course, and in less than a fortnight from that day the engagement of Janet and Dr. Gilbert was announced. I had done nothing to prevent this, and the news did not disturb my peace of mind. But my relations with Mildred very much disturbed it. I had hoped that, released from the baleful influence of the shadrach, her friendly feelings toward me would return, and my passion for her had now grown so strong that I waited and watched, as a wrecked mariner waits and watches for the sight of a sail, for a sign that she had so far softened toward me that I might dare to speak to her of my love. But no such sign appeared.

I now seldom visited the Bronce house. No one of that family, once my best friends, seemed to care to see me. Evidently Mildred's feelings toward me had extended themselves to the rest of the household. This was not surprising, for her family had long been accustomed to think as Mildred thought.

One day I met Mr. Bronce at the post office, and, some other gentlemen coming up, we began to talk of a proposed plan to introduce a system of waterworks into the village, an improvement much desired by many of us.

"So far as I am concerned," said Mr. Bronce, "I am not now in need of anything of the sort. Since I set up my steam-pump I have supplied my house from the pond at the end of my garden with all the water we can possibly want for every purpose."

"Do you mean," asked one of the gentlemen, "that you get your drinking water in that way?"

"Certainly," replied Mr. Bronce. "The basin of the pond is kept as clean and in as good order as any reservoir can be, and the water comes from an excellent, rapid-flowing spring. I want nothing better."

A chill ran through me as I listened. The shadrach was in that pond. Every drop of water which Mildred drank, which touched her, was influenced by that demoniacal paperweight, which, without knowing what I was doing, I had thus bestowed upon the whole Bronce family.

When I went home I made diligent search for a stone which might be about the size and weight of the shadrach, and having repaired to a retired spot, I practiced tossing it as I had tossed the bit of metal into the pond. In each instance I measured the distance which I had thrown the stone, and was at last enabled to make a very fair estimate of the distance to which I had thrown the shadrach when I had buried it under the waters of the pond.

That night there was a half-moon, and between eleven and twelve o'clock, when everybody in our village might be supposed to be in bed and asleep, I made my way over the fields to the back of the Bronce place, taking with me a long fish-cord, with a knot in it showing the average distance to which I had thrown the practice stone. When I reached the pond I stood as nearly as possible in the place by the bench from which I had hurled the shadrach, and to this spot I pegged one end of the cord. I was attired in an old tennis suit, and, having removed my shoes and stockings, I entered the water, holding the roll of cord in my hand. This I slowly unwound as I advanced toward the middle of the pond, and when I reached the knot I stopped, with the water above my waist.

I had found the bottom of the pond very smooth, and free from weeds and mud, and I now began feeling about with my bare feet, as I moved from side to side, describing a small arc; but I discovered nothing more than an occasional pebble no larger than a walnut.

Letting out some more of the cord, I advanced a little farther into the center of the pond, and slowly described another arc. The water was now nearly up to my armpits, but it was not cold, though it if had been I do not think I should have minded it in the ardor of my search. Suddenly I put my foot on something hard and as big as my fist, but in an instant it moved away from under my foot; it must have been a turtle. This occurrence made me shiver a little, but I did not swerve from my purpose, and, loosing the string a little more, I went farther into the pond. The water was now nearly up to my chin, and there was something weird, mystical, and awe-inspiring in standing thus in the depths of this silent water, my eyes so near its gently rippling surface, fantastically lighted by the setting moon, and tenanted by nobody knew what cold and slippery creatures. But from side to side I slowly moved, reaching out with my feet in every direction, hoping to touch the thing for which I sought.

Suddenly I set my right foot upon something hard and irregular. Nervously I felt it with my toes. I patted it with my bare sole. It was as big as the shadrach. It felt like the shadrach. In a few moments I was almost convinced that the direful paperweight was beneath my foot.

Closing my eyes and holding my breath, I stooped down into the water and groped on the bottom with my hands. In some way I had moved while stooping, and at first I could find nothing. A sensation of dread came over me as I felt myself in the midst of the dark, solemn water—around me, above me, everywhere—almost suffocated, and apparently deserted even by the shadrach. But just as I felt that I could hold my breath no longer, my fingers touched the thing that had been under my foot, and, clutching it, I rose and thrust my head out of the water. I could do nothing until I had taken two or three long breaths; then, holding up the object in my hand to the light of the expiring moon, I saw that it was like the shadrach—so like, indeed, that I felt that it must be it.

Turning, I made my way out of the water as rapidly as possible, and dropping on my knees on the ground, I tremblingly lighted the lantern which I had left on the bench, and turned its light on the thing I had found. There must be no mistake. If this was not the shadrach I would go in again. But there was no necessity for reentering the pond. It *was* the shadrach.

With the extinguished lantern in one hand and the lump of mineral evil in the other, I hurried home. My wet clothes were sticky and chilly in the night air. Several times, in my haste, I stumbled over clods and briers, and my shoes, which I had not taken time to tie, flopped up and down as I ran. But I cared for none of these discomforts. The shadrach was in my power.

Crossing a wide field, I heard, not far away, the tramping of hoofs, as of a horseman approaching at full speed. I stopped and looked in the direction of the sound. My eyes had now become so accustomed to the dim light that I could distinguish objects somewhat plainly, and I quickly perceived that the animal that was galloping toward me was a bull. I well knew what bull it was. This was Squire Starling's pasture field, and that was his great Alderney bull, Ramping Sir John of Ramapo II.

I was well acquainted with that bull, renowned throughout the neighborhood for his savage temper and his noble pedigree—son of Ramping Sir John of Ramapo I, whose sire was the Great Rodolphin, son of Prince Maximus of Granby, one of whose daughters averaged eighteen pounds of butter a week, and who, himself, had killed two men.

The bull, who had not perceived me when I crossed the field before, for I had then made my way with as little noise as possible, was now bent on punishing my intrusion upon his domains, and bellowed as he came on. I was in a position of great danger. With my flopping shoes it was impossible to escape by flight. I must stand and defend myself. I turned and faced the furious creature, who was not twenty feet distant, and then, with all my strength, I hurled the shadrach, which I held in my right hand, directly at his shaggy forehead. My ability to project a missile was considerable, for I had held, with credit, the position of pitcher in a baseball nine, and as the shadrach struck the bull's head with a great thud, he stopped as if he had suddenly run against a wall.

I do not know that actual and violent contact with the physical organism of a recipient accelerates the influence of a shadrach upon the mental organism of said recipient, but I do know that the contact of my projectile with that bull's skull instantly cooled the animal's fury. For a few moments he stood and looked at me, and then his interest in me as a man and trespasser appeared to fade away, and moving slowly from me, Ramping Sir John of Ramapo II began to crop the grass.

I did not stop to look for the shadrach. I considered it safely disposed of. So long as Squire Starling used that field for a pasture, connoisseurs in mineral fragments would not be apt to wander through it, and when it should be ploughed, the shadrach, to ordinary eyes no more than a common stone, would be buried beneath the sod. I awoke the next morning refreshed and happy, and none the worse for my wet walk.

"Now," I said to myself, "nature shall truly have her own way. If the uncanny comes into my life and that of those I love, it shall not be brought in by me."

About a week after this I dined with the Bronce family. They were very cordial, and it seemed to me the most natural thing in the world to be sitting at their table. After dinner Mildred and I walked together in the garden. It was a charming evening, and we sat down on the bench by the edge of the pond. I spoke to her of some passages in the book I had once seen there.

"Oh, have you read that?" she asked with interest.

"I have seen only two pages of it," I said, "and those I read in the volume you left on this bench, with a papercutter in it for a marker. I long to read more and talk with you of what I have read.

"Why, then, didn't you wait? You might have known that I would come back."

I did not tell her that I knew that because I was there she would not have come. But before I left the bench I discovered that hereafter, wherever I might be, she was willing to come and to stay.

Early in the next spring Mildred and I were married, and on our wedding trip we passed through a mining district in the mountains. Here we visited one of the great ironworks, and were both much interested in witnessing the wonderful power of man, air, and fire over the stubborn king of metals.

"What is this substance?" asked Mildred of one of the officials who was conducting us through the works.

"That," said the man, "is what we call shad——"

"My dear," I cried, "we must hurry away this instant or we shall lose the train. Come, quick; there is not a moment for delay." And with a word of thanks to the guide, I seized her hand and led her, almost running, into the open air.

Mildred was amazed.

"Never before," she exclaimed, "have I seen you in such a hurry! I thought the train we decided to take did not leave for at least an hour."

"I have changed my mind," I said, "and think it will be a great deal better for us to take the one which leaves in ten minutes."

Sir H. Rider Haggard (1856–1925)

Born in Bradenham, England, Sir H. Rider Haggard was a master of the adventure story, a man credited with developing the models of the "Great White Hunter" and the "Lost Race," two of the most alluring literary creations of the nineteenth century. Today millions of moviegoers are familiar with his work through the filmed versions of *King Solomon's Mines* and *She*, though the movies rather badly tamper with the spirit and content of the novels.

Haggard, himself, led a most interesting life. At the age of nineteen, he traveled to South Africa as secretary to the governor of Natal. Later he was made Master of the High Court at Pretoria, became an ostrich farmer, and returned to England to enter the law. By 1884, he had written three unsuccessful novels, but his brother's dare to try for something as good as *Treasure Island* inspired him to produce *King Solomon's Mines* (1885) in six weeks of frenzied activity. Both it and *She*, which he wrote just as quickly two years later, were immense hits. So, assured of financial success, he abandoned law and retired to indulge his three major interests: writing, politics, and farming.

Unfortunately, while he wrote more than thirty subsequent novels, none lived up to the promise of his most famous two. A contributing reason to this decline might have been his psychic experience of dreaming about talking to his family dog on the night it died—an event which induced subsequent revulsion toward hunting and killing.

His attempts at a political career fared only slightly better. A strong imperialist, he ran unsuccessfully for Parliament on the Unionist ticket. He was elected chairman of the bench of magistrates at Ditchingham, Norfolk, but he did his most effective work as an appointee on a number of Royal Commissions.

In farming, he had his greatest success. His writings on agriculture and the deplorable conditions of the rural worker led to his knighting in 1912. Indeed, he was even described as looking like a farmer—tall, angular, and huge of frame.

His works have continued to be popular and it has been suggested that this might be because they feature an escape from our highly technological world into primitivism as well as pandering to our desires for eternal youth, immortality, and reincarnation. However, he was also a master storyteller, with a marvelous imagination and sense of pace, who never bored his readers. And, while he could have taken a bit more care with many of his works, his African and Egyptian novels, in particular, gain great verisimilitude from a strong sense of setting and custom.

Haggard did not consider himself a short story writer and produced relatively few, but most are quite well done, as a reading of *The Best Short Stories of Rider Haggard* (1981) will indicate. Certainly, one of the best is "Black Heart and White Heart" (1896), a tale of Zulu prophecy, empire, and love. It is a work of which Peter Haining has said: "I doubt if a better story has ever been written about these remarkable people."

BLACK HEART AND WHITE HEART

I
A Zulu Idyll

At the date of our introduction to him, Philip Hadden was a transport-rider and a trader in "the Zulu." Still on the right side of forty, in appearance he was singularly handsome: tall, dark, upright, with keen eyes, short-pointed beard, curling hair and clear-cut features. His life had been varied, and there were passages in it which he did not narrate even to his most intimate friends. He was of gentle birth, however, and it was said that he had received a public school and university education in England. At any rate he could quote the classics with aptitude on occasion, an accomplishment which, coupled with his refined voice and a bearing not altogether common in the wild places of the world, had earned for him among his rough companions the soubriquet of "The Prince."

However these things may have been, it is certain that he had emigrated to Natal under a cloud, and equally certain that his relatives at home were content to take no further interest in his fortunes. During the fifteen or sixteen years which he had spent in or about the colony, Hadden followed many trades, and did no good at any of them. A clever man, of agreeable and prepossessing manner, he always found it easy to form friendships and to secure a fresh start in life. But, by degrees, the friends were seized with a vague distrust of him; and, after a period of more or less application, he himself would close the opening that he had made by a sudden disappearance from the locality, leaving behind him a doubtful reputation and some bad debts.

Before the beginning of this story of one of the most remarkable episodes in his life, Philip Hadden was engaged for several years in transport-riding—that is, in carrying goods on ox wagons from Durban or Maritzburg to various points in the interior. A difficulty such as had more than once confronted him in the course of his career, led to his temporary abandonment of this means of earning a livelihood. On arriving at the little frontier town of Utrecht in the Transvaal, in charge of two wagonloads of mixed goods consigned to a storekeeper there, it was discovered that out of six cases of brandy five were missing from his wagon. Hadden explained the matter by throwing the blame upon his Kaffir "boys," but the storekeeper, a rough-tongued man, openly called him a thief and refused to pay the freight on any of the load. From words the men clame to blows, knives were drawn, and before anybody could interfere the storekeeper received a nasty wound in his side. That night, without waiting till the matter could be inquired into by the landdrost or magistrate, Hadden slipped away, and trekked back into Natal as quickly as his oxen would travel. Feeling that even here he was not safe, he left one of his wagons at Newcastle, loaded up the other with Kaffir goods—such as blankets, calico, and hardware—and crossed into Zululand, where in those days no sherrif's officer would be likely to follow him.

Being well acquainted with the language and customs of the natives, he did good trade with them, and soon found himself possessed of some cash and a small herd of cattle, which he received in exchange for his wares. Meanwhile news reached him that the man whom he had injured still vowed vengeance against him, and was in communication with the authorities in Natal. These reasons making his return to civilization undesirable for the moment, and further business being impossible until he could receive a fresh supply of trade stuff, Hadden like a wise man turned his thoughts to pleasure. Sending his cattle and wagon over the border to be left in charge of a native headman with whom he was friendly, he went on foot to Ulundi to obtain permission from the king, Cetywayo, to hunt game in his country. Somewhat to his surprise the Indunas, or headmen received him courteously—for Hadden's visit took place within a few months of the outbreak of the Zulu war in 1878, when Cetywayo was already showing unfriendliness to the English traders and others, though why the king did so they knew not.

On the occasion of his first and last interview with Cetywayo,

Hadden got a hint of the reason. It happened thus. On the second morning after his arrival at the royal kraal, a messenger came to inform him that "the Elephant whose tread shook the earth" had signified that it was his pleasure to see him. Accordingly he was led through the thousands of huts and across the Great Place to the little enclosure where Cetywayo, a royal-looking Zulu seated on a stool, and wearing a *kaross* of leopard skins, was holding an *indaba*, or conference, surrounded by his counsellors. The Induna who had conducted him to the august presence went down upon his hands and knees, and, uttering the royal salute of *Bayéte*, crawled forward to announce that the white man was waiting.

"Let him wait," said the king angrily; and, turning, he continued the discussion with his counsellors.

Now, as has been said, Hadden thoroughly understood Zulu; and when from time to time the king raised his voice, some of the words he spoke reached his ear.

"What!" Cetywayo said, to a wizened and aged man who seemed to be pleading with him earnestly; "am I a dog that these white hyenas should hunt me thus? Is not the land mine, and was it not my father's before me? Are not the people mine to save or to slay? I tell you that I will stamp out these little white men; my *impis* shall eat them up. I have said!"

Again the withered aged man interposed, evidently in the character of a peacemaker. Hadden could not hear his talk, but he rose and pointed toward the sea, while from his expressive gestures and sorrowful mien, he seemed to be prophesying disaster should a certain course of action be followed.

For a while the king listened to him, then he sprang from his seat, his eyes literally ablaze with rage.

"Hearken," he cried to the counsellor; "I have guessed it for long, and now I am sure of it. You are a traitor. You are Sompseu's[1] dog, and the dog of the Natal Government, and I will not keep another man's dog to bite me in my own house. Take him away!"

A slight involuntary murmur rose from the ring of *indunas*, but the old man never flinched, not even when the soldiers, who presently would murder him, came and seized him roughly. For a few seconds, perhaps

[1]Sir Theophilus Shepstone's.

five, he covered his face with the corner of the *kaross* he wore, then he looked up and spoke to the king in a clear voice.

"O King," he said, "I am a very old man; as a youth I served under Chaka the Lion, and I heard his dying prophecy of the coming of the white man. Then the white men came, and I fought for Dingaan at the battle of the Blood River. They slew Dingaan, and for many years I was the counsellor of Panda, your father. I stood by you, O King, at the battle of the Tugela, when its gray waters were turned to red with the blood of Umbulazi your brother, and of the tens of thousands of his people. Afterwards I became your counsellor, O King, and I was with you when Sompseu set the crown upon your head and you made promises to Sompseu—promises that you have not kept. Now you are weary of me, and it is well; for I am very old, and doubtless my talk is foolish, as it chances to the old. Yet I think that the prophecy of Chaka, your great-uncle, wil come true, and that the white men will prevail against you and that through them you shall find your death. I would that I might have stood in one more battle and fought for you, O King, since fight you will, but the end which you choose is for me the best end. Sleep in peace, O King, and farewell. *Bayéte*!"[1]

For a space there was silence, a silence of expectation while men waited to hear the tyrant reverse his judgment. But it did not please him to be merciful, or the needs of policy outweighed his pity.

"Take him away," he repeated. Then, with a slow smile on his face and one word, "Good-night," upon his lips, supported by the arm of a soldier, the old warrior and statesman shuffled forth to the place of death.

Hadden watched and listened in amazement not unmixed with fear. "If he treats his own servants like this, what will happen to me?" he reflected. "We English must have fallen out of favor since I left Natal. I wonder whether he means to make war on us or what? If so, this isn't my place."

Just then the king, who had been gazing moodily at the ground, chanced to look up. "Bring the stranger here," he said.

Hadden heard him, and coming forward offered Cetywayo his hand in as cool and nonchalant a manner as he could command.

Somewhat to his surprise it was accepted. "At least, White Man," said the king, glancing at his visitor's tall spare form and cleanly cut

[1]The royal salute of the Zulus.

face, "you are no *umfagozan* (low fellow); you are of the blood of chiefs."

"Yes, King," answered Hadden, with a little sigh, "I am of the blood of chiefs."

"What do you want in my country, White Man?"

"Very little, King. I have been trading here, as I daresay you have heard, and have sold all my goods. Now I ask your leave to hunt buffalo, and other big game, for a while before I return to Natal."

"I cannot grant it," answered Cetywayo, "you are a spy sent by Sompseu, or by the Queen's Induna in Natal. Get you gone."

"Indeed," said Hadden, with a shrug of his shoulders; "then I hope that Sompseu, or the Queen's Induna, or both of them, will pay me when I return to my own country. Meanwhile I will obey you because I must, but I should first like to make you a present."

"What present?" asked the king. "I want no presents. We are rich here, White Man."

"So be it, King. It was nothing worthy of your taking, only a rifle."

"A rifle, White Man? Where is it?"

"Without. I would have brought it, but your servants told me that it is death to come armed before the 'Elephant who shakes the Earth.' "

Cetywayo frowned, for the note of sarcasm did not escape his quick ear.

"Let this white man's offering be brought; I will consider the thing."

Instantly the Induna who had accompanied Hadden darted to the gateway, running with his body bent so low that it seemed as though at every step he must fall upon his face. Presently he returned with the weapon in his hand and presented it to the king, holding it so that the muzzle was pointed straight at the royal breast.

"I crave leave to say, O Elephant," remarked Hadden in a drawling voice, "that it might be well to command your servant to lift the mouth of that gun from your heart."

"Why?" asked the king.

"Only because it is loaded, and at full cock, O Elephant, who probably desires to continue to shake the earth."

At these words the "Elephant" uttered a sharp exclamation, and rolled from his stool in a most unkingly manner, whilst the terrified Induna, springing backwards, contrived to touch the trigger of the rifle and discharge a bullet through the exact spot that a second before had been occupied by his monarch's head.

"Let him be taken away," shouted the incensed king from the ground, but long before the words had passed his lips the Induna, with a cry that the gun was bewitched, had cast it down and fled at full speed through the gate.

"He has already taken himself away," suggested Hadden, while the audience tittered. "No, King, do not touch it rashly; it is a repeating rifle. Look—" and lifting the Winchester, he fired the four remaining shots in quick succession into the air, striking the top of a tree at which he aimed with every one of them.

"*Wow*, it is wonderful!" said the company in astonishment.

"Has the thing finished?" asked the king.

"For the present it has," answered Hadden. "Look at it."

Cetywayo took the repeater in his hand, and examined it with caution, swinging the muzzle horizontally in an exact line with the stomachs of some of his most eminent Indunas, who shrank to this side and that as the barrel was brought to bear upon them.

"See what cowards they are, White Man," said the king with indignation, "they fear lest there should be another bullet in this gun."

"Yes," answered Hadden, "they are cowards indeed. I believe that if they were seated on stools they would tumble off them as it chanced to your Majesty to do just now."

"Do you understand the making of guns, White Man?" asked the king hastily, while the Indunas one and all turned their heads, and contemplated the fence behind them.

"No, King, I cannot make guns, but I can mend them."

"If I paid you well, White Man, would you stop here at my kraal, and mend guns for me?" asked Cetywayo anxiously.

"It might depend on the pay," answered Hadden; "but for a while I am tired of work, and wish to rest. If the king gives me the permission to hunt for which I asked, and men to go with me, then when I return perhaps we can bargain on the matter. If not, I will bid the king farewell, and journey to Natal."

"In order to make report of what he has seen and learned here," muttered Cetywayo.

At this moment the talk was interrupted, for the soldiers who had led away the old Induna returned at speed, and prostrated themselves before the king.

"Is he dead?" he asked.

"He has travelled the king's bridge," they answered grimly; "he died singing a song of praise of the king."

"Good," said Cetywayo, "that stone shall hurt my feet no more. Go, tell the tale of its casting away to Sompseu and to the Queen's Induna in Natal," he added with bitter emphasis.

"*Baba!* Hear our Father speak. Listen to the rumbling of the Elephant," said the Indunas taking the point, while one bolder than the rest added: "Soon we will tell them another tale, the white Talking Ones, a red tale, a tale of spears, and the regiments shall sing it in their ears."

At the words an enthusiasm caught hold of the listeners, as the sudden flame catches hold of dry grass. They sprang up, for the most of them were seated on their haunches, and stamping their feet upon the ground in unison, repeated:

Indaba ibomwu—indaba ye mikonto
Lizo dunyiswa nge impi ndhlebeni yaho.
(A red tale! A red tale! A tale of spears,
And the *impis* shall sing it in their ears.)

One of them, indeed, a great fierce-faced yellow, drew near to Hadden and shaking his fist before his eyes—fortunately being in the royal presence he had no assegai—shouted the sentences at him.

The king saw that the fire he had lit was burning too fiercely.

"Silence," he thundered in the deep voice for which he was remarkable, and instantly each man became as if he were turned to stone, only the echoes still answered back. "And the *impis* shall sing it in their ears—in their ears."

"I am growing certain that this is no place for me," thought Hadden; "if that scoundrel had been armed he might have temporarily forgotten himself. Hullo! who's this?"

Just then there appeared through the gate of the fence a splendid specimen of the Zulu race. The man, who was about thirty-five years of age, was arrayed in a full war dress of a captain of the Umcityu regiment. From the circlet of otter skin on his brow rose his crest of plumes, round his middle, arms and knees hung the long fringes of black oxtails, and in one hand he bore a little dancing shield, also black in color. The other was empty, since he might not appear before the king bearing arms. In countenance the man was handsome, and though just now they betrayed some anxiety, his eyes were genial and honest, and his mouth sensitive. In height he must have measured six foot two inches, yet he did not strike the observer as being tall, perhaps because of his width of chest and the solidity of his limbs, that were in curious contrast to the delicate and almost womanish hands and feet which so often mark the Zulu of noble blood. In short the man was what he seemed to be, a savage gentleman of birth, dignity and courage.

In company with him was another man plainly dressed in a moocha and a blanket, whose grizzled hair showed him to be over fifty years of age. His face also was pleasant and even refined, but the eyes were timorous, and the mouth lacked character.

''Who are these?'' asked the king.

The two men fell on their knees before him, and bowed till their foreheads touched the ground—the while giving him his *sibonga* or titles of praise.

''Speak,'' he said impatiently.

''O King,'' said the young warrior, seating himself Zulu fashion. ''I am Nahoon, the son of Zomba, a captain of the Umcityu, and this is my uncle, Umgona, the brother of one of my mothers, my father's youngest wife.''

Cetywayo frowned. ''What do you here away from your regiment, Nahoon?''

''May it please the king. I have leave of absence from the head captains, and I come to ask a boon of the king's bounty.''

''Be swift, then, Nahoon.''

''It is this, O King,'' said the captain with some embarrassment: ''A while ago the king was pleased to make a *keshla* of me because of certain service that I did out yonder . . .'' and he touched the black ring which he wore in the hair of his head. ''Being now a ringed man and a captain, I crave the right of a man at the hands of the king—the right to marry.''

''Right? Speak more humbly, son of Zomba; my soldiers and my cattle have no rights.''

Nahoon bit his lip, for he had made a serious mistake.

''Pardon, O King. the matter stands thus: My uncle Umgona here has a fair daughter named Nanea, whom I desire to wife, and who desires me to husband. Awaiting the king's leave I am betrothed to her and in earnest of it I have paid to Umgona a *lobola* of fifteen head of cattle, cows and calves together. But Umgona has a powerful neighbor, an old chief named Maputa, the warden of the Crocodile Drift, who doubtless is known to the king, and this chief also seeks Nanea in marriage and harries Umgona, threatening him with many evils if he will not give the girl to him. But Umgona's heart is white toward me, and toward Maputa it is black, therefore together we come to crave this boon of the king."

"It is so; he speaks the truth," said Umgona.

"Cease," answered Cetywayo angrily. "Is this a time that my soldiers should seek wives in marriage, wives to turn their hearts to water? Know that but yesterday for this crime I commanded that twenty girls who had dared without my leave to marry men of the Undi regiment, should be strangled and their bodies laid upon the crossroads and with them the bodies of their fathers, that all might know their sin and be warned thereby. Ay, Umgona, it is well for you and for your daughter that you sought my word before she was given in marriage to this man. Now this is my award: I refuse your prayer, Nahoon, and since you, Umgona, are troubled with one whom you would not take as son-in-law, the old chief Maputa, I will free you from his importunity. The girl, says Nahoon, is fair—good, I myself will be gracious to her, and she shall be numbered among the wives of the royal house. Within thirty days from now, in the week of the next new moon, let her be delivered into the *Sigodhla*, the royal house of the women, and with her those cattle, the cows and the calves together, that Nahoon has given you, of which I fine him because he has dared to think of marriage without the leave of the king."

II
The Bee Prophesies

" 'A Daniel come to judgment' indeed," reflected Hadden, who had been watching this savage comedy with interest; "our lovesick friend has got more than he bargained for. Well, that comes of appealing to Caesar," and he turned to look at the two suppliants.

The old man, Umgona, merely started, then began to pour out sentences of conventional thanks and praise to the king for his goodness and condescension. Cetywayo listened to his talk in silence, and when he had done answered by reminding him tersely that if Nanea did not appear at the date named, both she and he, her father, would in due course certainly decorate a crossroad in their own neighborhood.

The captain, Nahoon, afforded a more curious study. As the fatal words crossed the king's lips, his face took on an expression of absolute astonishment, which was presently replaced by one of fury—the just fury of a man who suddenly has suffered an unutterable wrong. His whole frame quivered, the veins stood out in knots on his neck and forehead, and his fingers closed convulsively as though they were grasping the handle of a spear. Presently the rage passed away—for as well might a man be wroth with fate as with a Zulu despot—to be succeeded by a look of the most hopeless misery. The proud dark eyes grew dull, the copper-colored face sank in and turned ashen, the mouth drooped, and down one corner of it there trickled a little line of blood springing from the lip bitten through in the effort to keep silence. Lifting his hand in salute to the king, the great man rose and staggered rather than walked toward the gate.

As he reached it, the voice of Cetywayo commanded him to stop. "Stay," he said, "I have a service for you, Nahoon, that shall drive out of your head these thoughts of wives and marriage. You see this white man here; he is my guest, and would hunt buffalo and big game in the bush country. I put him in your charge; take men with you, and see that he comes to no hurt. See also that you bring him before me within a month, or your life shall answer for it. Let him be here at my royal kraal in the first week of the new moon—when Nanea comes—and then I will tell you whether or no I agree with you that she is fair. Go now, my child, and you, White Man, go also; those who are to accompany you shall be with you at the dawn. Farewell, but remember we meet again at the new moon, when we will settle what pay you shall receive as keeper of my guns. Do not fail me, White Man, or I shall send after you, and my messengers are sometimes rough."

"This means that I am a prisoner," thought Hadden, "but it will go hard if I cannot manage to give them the slip somehow. I don't intend to stay in this country if war is declared, to be pounded into *mouti* (medicine), or have my eyes put out, or any little joke of that sort."

Ten days had passed, and one evening Hadden and his escort were encamped in a wild stretch of mountainous country lying between the Blood and Unvunyana rivers, not more than eight miles from that

"Place of the Little Hand" which within a few weeks was to become famous throughout the world by its native name of Isandhlwana. For three days they had been tracking the spoor of a small herd of buffalo that still inhabited the district, but as yet they had not come up with them. The Zulu hunters had suggested that they should follow the Unvunyana down toward the sea where game was more plentiful, but this neither Hadden, nor the captain, Nahoon, had been anxious to do, for reasons which each of them kept secret to himself. Hadden's object was to work gradually down to the Buffalo River across which he hoped to effect a retreat into Natal. That of Nahoon was to linger in the neighborhood of the kraal of Umgona, which was situated not very far from their present camping place, in the vague hope that he might find an opportunity of speaking with or at least of seeing Nanea, the girl to whom he was affianced, who within a few weeks must be taken from him, and given over to the king.

A more eerie-looking spot than that where they were encamped Hadden had never seen. Behind them lay a tract of land—half-swamp and half-bush—in which the buffalo were supposed to be hiding. Beyond, in lonely grandeur, rose the mountain of Isandhlwana, while in front was an amphitheater of the most gloomy forest, ringed round in the distance by sheer-sided hills. Into this forest there ran a river which drained the swamp, placidly enough upon the level. But it was not always level, for within three hundred yards of them it dashed suddenly over a precipice, of no great height but very steep, falling into a boiling rock-bound pool that the light of the sun never seemed to reach.

"What is the name of that forest, Nahoon?" asked Hadden.

"It is named *Emagudu*, 'The Home of the Dead,' " the Zulu replied absently, for he was looking toward the kraal of Nanea, which was situated an hour's walk away over the ridge to the right.

"The Home of the Dead! Why?"

"Because the dead live there, those whom we name the *Esemkofu*, the Speechless Ones, and with them other Spirits, the *Amahlosi*, from whom the breath of life has passed away, and who yet live on."

"Indeed," said Hadden, "and have you ever seen these ghosts?"

"Am I mad that I should go to look for them, White Man? Only the dead enter that forest, and it is on the borders of it that our people make offerings to the dead."

Followed by Nahoon, Hadden walked to the edge of the cliff and looked over it. To the left lay the deep and dreadful-looking pool, while close to the bank of it, placed upon a narrow strip of turf between the cliff and the commencement of the forest, was a hut.

"Who lives there?" asked Hadden.

"The great *Isanusi*—she who is named *Inyanga* or Doctoress; she who is named *Inyosi* (the Bee), because she gathers wisdom from the dead who grow in the forest."

"Do you think that she could gather enough widsom to tell me whether I am going to kill any buffalo, Nahoon?"

"Mayhap, White Man, but," he added with a little smile, "those who visit the Bee's hive may hear nothing, or they may hear more than they wish for. The words of that Bee have a sting."

"Good; I will see if she can sting me."

"So be it," said Nahoon; and turning, he led the way along the cliff till he reached a native path which zig-zagged down its face.

By this path they climbed till they came to the sward at the foot of the descent, and walked up it to the hut which was surrounded by a low fence of reeds, enclosing a small courtyard paved with ant-heap earth beaten hard and polished. In this courtyard sat the Bee, her stool being placed almost at the mouth of the round opening that served as a doorway to the hut. At first all that Hadden could see of her, crouched as she was in the shadow, was a huddled shape wrapped round with a greasy and tattered catskin *kaross*, above the dge of which appeared two eyes, fierce and quick as those of a leopard. At her feet smouldered a little fire, and ranged around it in a semicircle were a number of human skulls, placed in pairs as though they were talking together, whilst other bones, to all appearance also human, were festooned about the hut and the fence of the courtyard.

"I see that the old lady is set up with the usual properties," thought Hadden, but he said nothing.

Nor did the witch doctoress say anything; she only fixed her beady eyes upon his face. Hadden returned the compliment, staring at her with all his might, till suddenly he became aware that he was vanquished in this curious duel. His brain grew confused, and to his fancy it seemed that the woman before him had shifted shape into the likeness of a colossal and horrid spider sitting at the mouth of her trap, and that these bones were the relics of her victims.

"Why do you not speak, White Man?" she said at last in a slow clear voice. "Well, there is no need, since I can read your thoughts.

You are thinking that I who am called the Bee should be better named the Spider. Have no fear; I did not kill these men. What would it profit me when the dead are so many? I suck the souls of men, not their bodies, White Man. It is their living hearts I love to look on, for therein I read much and thereby I grow wise. Now what would you of the Bee, White Man, the Bee that labors in this Garden of Death, and—what brings *you* here, son of Zomba? Why are you not with the Umcityu now that they doctor themselves for the great war—the last war—the war of the white and the black—or if you have no stomach for fighting why are you not at the side of Nanea the tall, Nanea the fair?''

Nahoon made no answer, but Hadden said:

''A small thing, mother. I would know if I shall prosper in my hunting.''

''In your hunting, White Man; what hunting? The hunting of game, of money, or of women? Well, one of them, for a-hunting you must ever be; that is your nature, to hunt and be hunted. Tell me now, how goes the wound of that trader who tasted of your steel yonder in the town of the Maboon (Boers)? No need to answer, White Man, but what fee, Chief, for the poor witch doctoress whose skill you seek,'' she added in a whining voice. ''Surely you would not that an old woman should work without a fee?''

''I have none to offer you, mother, so I will be going,'' said Hadden, who began to feel himself satisfied with this display of the Bee's powers of observation and thought-reading.

''Nay,'' she answered with an unpleasant laugh, ''would you ask a question, and not wait for the answer? I will take no fee from you at present, White Man; you shall pay me later on when we meet again,'' and once more she laughed. ''Let me look in your face, let me look in your face,'' she continued, rising and standing before him.

Then of a sudden Hadden felt something cold at the back of his neck, and the next instant the Bee had sprung from him, holding between her thumb and finger a curl of dark hair which she had cut from his head. The action was so instantaneous that he had neither time to avoid nor to resent it, but stood still staring at her stupidly.

''That is all I need,'' she cried, ''for like my heart my magic is white. Stay—son of Zomba, give me also of your hair, for those who visit the Bee must listen to her humming.''

Nahoon obeyed, cutting a little lock from his head with the sharp edge of his assegai, though it was very evident that he did this not because he wished to do so, but because he feared to refuse.

Then the Bee slipped back her *kaross*, and stood bending over the fire before them, into which she threw herbs taken from a pouch that was bound about her middle. She was still a finely shaped woman, and she wore none of the abominations which Hadden had been accustomed to see upon the persons of witch doctoresses. About her neck, however, was a curious ornament, a small live snake, red and grey in hue, which her visitors recognized as one of the most deadly to be found in that part of the country. It is not unusual for Bantu witch doctors thus to decorate themselves with snakes, though whether or not their fangs have first been extracted no one seems to know.

Presently the herbs began to smoulder, and the smoke of them rose up in a thin straight stream, that, striking upon the face of the Bee, clung about her head enveloping it as though with a strange blue veil. Then of a sudden she stretched out her hands, and let fall the two locks of hair upon the burning herbs, where they writhed themselves to ashes like things alive. Next she opened her mouth, and began to draw the fumes of the hair and herbs into her lungs in great gulps; while the snake, feeling the influence of the medicine, hissed, and uncoiling itself from about her neck, crept upwards and took refuge among the black *saccaboola* feathers of her headdress.

Soon the vapors began to do their work; she swayed to and fro muttering, then sank back against the hut, upon the straw of which her head rested. Now the Bee's face was turned upwards toward the light, and it was ghastly to behold, for it had become blue in color, and the open eyes were sunken like the eyes of one dead, whilst above her forehead the red snake wavered and hissed, reminding Hadden of the Uraeus crest on the brow of statues of Egyptian kings. For ten seconds or more she remained thus, then she spoke in a hollow and unnatural voice:

"O Black Heart and body that is white and beautiful, I look into your heart, and it is black as blood, and it shall be black with blood. Beautiful white body with a black heart, you shall find your game and hunt it, and it shall lead you into the House of the Homeless, into the Home of the Dead, and it shall be shaped as a bull, it shall be shaped as a tiger, it shall be shaped as a woman whom kings and waters cannot harm. Beautiful white body and black heart, you shall be paid your wages, money for money, and blow for blow. Think of my word when the spotted cat purrs above your breast; think of it when the battle roars about you; think of it when you grasp your great reward, and for the last time stand face to face with the ghost of the dead in the Home of the Dead.

"O White Heart and black body, I look into your heart and it is white as milk, and the milk of innocence shall save it. Fool, why do you strike that blow? Let him be who is loved of the tiger, and whose love is as the love of a tiger, Ah! what face is that in the battle? Follow it, follow it, O swift of foot; but follow warily, for the tongue that has lies will never plead for mercy, and the hand that can betray is strong in war. White Heart, what is death? In death life lives, and among the dead you shall find the life you lost, for there awaits you she whom kings and waters cannot harm."

As the Bee spoke, by degrees her voice sank lower and lower till it was almost inaudible. Then it ceased altogether, and she seemed to pass from trance to sleep. Hadden, who had been listening to her with an amused and cynical smile, now laughed aloud.

"Why do you laugh, White Man?" asked Nahoon angrily.

"I laugh at my own folly in wasting time listening to the nonsense of that lying fraud."

"It is no nonsense, White Man."

"Indeed? Then will you tell me what it means?"

"I cannot tell you what it means yet, but her words have to do with a woman and a leopard, and with your fate and my fate."

Hadden shrugged his shoulders, not thinking the matter worth further argument, and at that moment the Bee woke up shivering, drew the red snake from her headdress and coiling it about her throat wrapped herself again in the greasy *kaross*.

"Are you satisfied with my wisdom, *Inkoos*?" she asked of Hadden.

"I am satisfied that you are one of the cleverest cheats in Zululand, mother," he answered coolly. "Now, what is there to pay?"

The Bee took no offense at this rude speech, though for a second or two the look in her eyes grew strangely like that which they had seen in those of the snake when the fumes of the fire made it angry.

"If the white lord says I am a cheat, it must be so," she answered, "for he of all men should be able to discern a cheat. I have said that I ask no fee—yet, give me a little tobacco from your pouch."

Hadden opened the bag of antelope hide and drawing some tobacco from it, gave it to her. In taking it she clasped his hand and examined the gold ring that was upon the third finger, a ring fashioned like a snake with two little rubies set in the head to represent the eyes.

"I wear a snake about my neck, and you wear one upon your hand, *Inkoos*. I should like to have this ring to wear upon my hand, so that the snake about my neck may be less lonely there."

"Then I am afraid you will have to wait till I am dead," said Hadden.

"Yes, yes," she answered in a pleased voice, "it is a good word. I will wait till you are dead and then I will take the ring, and none can say that I have stolen it, for Nahoon there will bear me witness that you gave me permission to do so."

For the first time Hadden started, since there was something about the Bee's tone that jarred upon him. Had she addressed him in her professional manner, he would have thought nothing of it; but in her cupidity she had become natural, and it was evident that she spoke from conviction, believing her own words.

She saw him start, and instantly changed her note.

"Let the white lord forgive the jest of a poor old witch doctoress," she said in a whining voice. "I have so much to do with Death that his name leaps to my lips," and she glanced first at the circle of skulls about her, then toward the waterfall that fed the gloomy pool upon whose banks her hut was placed.

"Look," she said simply.

Following the line of her outstretched hand Hadden's eyes fell upon two withered mimosa trees which grew over the falls almost at right angles to its rocky edge. These trees were joined together by a rude platform made of logs of wood lashed down with *riems* of hide. Upon this platform stood three figures: notwithstanding the distance and the spray of the fall, he could see that they were those of two men and a girl, for their shapes stood out distinctly against the fiery red of the sunset sky. One instant there were three, the next there were two—for the girl had gone, and something dark rushing down the face of the fall, struck the surface of the pool with a heavy thud, while a faint and piteous cry broke upon his ear.

"What is the meaning of that?" he asked, horrified and amazed.

"Nothing," answered the Bee with a laugh. "Do you not know, then, that this is the place where faithless women, or girls who have loved without the leave of the king, are brought to meet their death, and with them their accomplices. Oh! they die here thus each day, and I watch them die and keep the count of the number of them,'' and drawing a tally-stick from the thatch of the hut, she took a knife and added a notch to the many that appeared upon it, looking at Nahoon the while with a half-questioning, half-warning gaze.

''Yes, yes, it is a place of death,'' she muttered. ''Up yonder the quick die day by day and down there''—and she pointed along the course of the river beyond the pool to where the forest began some two hundred yards from her hut—''the ghosts of them have their home. Listen!''

As she spoke, a sound reached their ears that seemed to swell from the dim skirts of the forests, a peculiar and unholy sound which it is impossible to define more accurately than by saying that it seemed beastlike, and almost inarticulate.

''Listen,'' repeated the Bee, ''they are merry yonder.''

''Who?'' asked Hadden; ''the baboons?''

''No, *Inkoos*, the *Amatongo*—the ghosts that welcome her who has just become of their number.''

''Ghosts,'' said Hadden roughly, for he was angry at his own tremors, ''I should like to see those ghosts. Do you think that I have never heard a troop of monkeys in the bush before, mother? Come, Nahoon, let us be going while there is light to climb the cliff. Farewell.''

''Farewell *Inkoos*, and doubt not that your wish will be fulfilled. Go in peace *Inkoos*—to sleep in peace.''

III
The End of the Hunt

The prayer of the Bee notwithstanding, Philip Hadden slept ill that night. He felt in the best of health, and his conscience was not troubling him more than usual, but rest he could not. Whenever he closed his eyes, his mind conjured up a picture of the grim witch doctoress, so strangely named the Bee and the sound of her evil-omened words as he had heard them that afternoon. He was neither a superstitious nor a timid man, and any supernatural beliefs that might linger in his mind were, to say the least of it, dormant. But do what he might, he could not shake off a certain eerie sensation of fear, lest there should be some grains of truth in the prophesyings of this hag. What if it were a fact that he was near his death, and that the heart which beat so strongly in his breast must soon be still for ever—no, he would not think of it. This gloomy place, and the dreadful sight which he saw that day, had upset his nerves. The domestic customs of these Zulus were not pleasant, and for his part he was determined to be clear of them so soon as he was able to escape the country.

In fact, if he could in any way manage it, it was his intention to make a dash for the border on the following night. To do this with a good prospect of success, however, it was necessary that he should kill a buffalo, or some other head of game. Then, as he knew well, the hunters with him would feast upon meat until they could scarcely stir, and that would be his opportunity. Nahoon, however, might not succumb to this temptation; therefore he must trust to luck to be rid of him. If it came to the worst, he could put a bullet through him, which he considered he would be justified in doing, seeing that in reality the man was his jailor. Should this necessity arise, he felt indeed that he could face it without undue compunction, for in truth he disliked Nahoon; at times he even hated him. Their natures were antagonistic, and he knew that the great Zulu distrusted and looked down upon him, and to be looked down upon by a savage "nigger" was more than his pride could stomach.

At the first break of dawn Hadden rose and roused his escort, who were still stretched in sleep around the dying fire, each man wrapped in his kaross or blanket. Nahoon stood up and shook himself, looking gigantic in the shadows of the morning.

"What is your will, *Umlungu* (white man), that you are up before the sun?"

"My will, *Muntumpofu* (yellow man), is to hunt buffalo," answered Hadden coolly. It irritated him that this savage should give him no title of any sort.

"Your pardon," said the Zulu reading his thoughts, "but I cannot call you *Inkoos* because you are not my chief, or any man's; still if the title 'white man' offends you, we will give you a name."

"As you wish," answered Hadden briefly.

Accordingly they gave him a name, *Inhlizin-mgama*, by which he was known among them thereafter, but Hadden was not best pleased when he found that the meaning of those soft-sounding syllables was "Black Heart." That was how the *inyanga* had addressed him—only she used different words.

An hour later, and they were in the swampy bush country that lay behind the encampment searching for their game. Within a very little while Nahoon held up his hand, then pointed to the ground. Hadden looked; there, pressed deep in the marshy soil, and to all appearance not ten minutes old, was the spoor of a small herd of buffalo.

"I knew that we should find game today," whispered Nahoon, "because the Bee said so."

"Curse the Bee," answered Hadden below his breath. "Come on."

For a quarter of an hour or more they followed the spoor through thick reeds, till suddenly Nahoon whistled very softly and touched Hadden's arm. He looked up, and there, about two hundred yards away, feeding on some higher ground among a patch of mimosa trees, were the buffaloes—six of them—an old bull with a splendid head, three cows, a heifer and a calf about four months old. Neither the wind nor the nature of the veldt were favorable for them to stalk the game from their present position, so they made a detour of half a mile and very carefully crept toward them up the wind, slipping from trunk to trunk of the mimosas and when these failed them, crawling on their stomachs under cover of the tall *tambuti* grass. At last they were within forty yards, and a further advance seemed impracticable; for although he could not smell them, it was evident from his movements that the old bull heard some unusual sound and was growing suspicious. Nearest to Hadden, who alone of the party had a rifle, stood the heifer broadside on—a beautiful shot. Remembering that she would make the best beef, he lifted his Martini, and aiming at her immediately behind the shoulder, gently squeezed the trigger. The rifle exploded and the heifer fell dead, shot through the heart. Strangely enough the other buffaloes did not at once run away. On the contrary, they seemed puzzled to account for the sudden noise; and, not being to wind anything, lifted their heads and stared round them.

The pause gave Hadden space to get in a fresh cartridge and to aim again, this time at the old bull. The bullet struck him somewhere in the neck or shoulder, for he came to his knees, but in another second was up and having caught sight of the cloud of smoke he charged straight at it. Because of this smoke, or for some other reason, Hadden did not see him coming, and in consequence would most certainly have been trampled or gored, had not Nahoon sprung forward, at the imminent risk of his own life, and dragged him down behind an ant-heap. A moment more and the great beast had thundered by, taking no further notice of them.

"Forward," said Hadden, and leaving most of the men to cut up the heifer and carry the best of her meat to camp, they started on the blood spoor.

For some hours they followed the bull, till at last they lost the trail on a patch of stony ground thickly covered with bush, and exhausted by the heat, sat down to rest and to eat some *biltong* or sun-dried flesh which they had with them. They finished their meal, and were preparing to return to the camp, when one of the four Zulus who were with them went to drink at a little stream that ran at a distance of not more than ten paces away. Half a minute later they heard a hideous grunting noise and a splashing of water, and saw the Zulu fly into the air. All the while they were eating, the wounded buffalo had been lying in wait for them under a thick bush on the banks of the streamlet, knowing—cunning brute that he was—that sooner or later his turn would come. With a shout of consternation they rushed forward to see the bull vanish over the rise before Hadden could get a chance of firing at him, and to find their companion dying, for the great horn had pierced his lung.

"It is not a buffalo, it is a devil," the poor fellow gasped, and expired.

"Devil or not, I mean to kill it," exclaimed Hadden. So leaving the others to carry the body of their comrade to camp, he started on accompanied by Nahoon only. Now the ground was more open and the chase easier, for they sighted their quarry frequently, though they could not come near enough to fire. Presently they travelled down a steep cliff.

"Do you know where we are?" asked Nahoon, pointing to a belt of forest opposite. "That is *Emagudu*, the Home of the Dead—and look, the bull heads thither."

Hadden glanced round him. It was true; yonder to the left were the falls, the Pool of Doom, and the hut of the Bee.

"Very well," he answered; "then we must head for it too."

Nahoon halted. "Surely you would not enter there," he exclaimed.

"Surely I will," replied Hadden, "but there is no need for you to do so if you are afraid."

"I am afraid—of ghosts," said the Zulu, "but I will come."

So they crossed the strip of turf, and entered the haunted wood. It was a gloomy place indeed; great wide-topped trees grew thick there shutting out the sight of the sky; moreover, the air in it which no breeze stirred, was heavy with the exhalation of rotting foliage. There seemed to be no life here and no sound—only now and again a loathsome spotted snake would uncoil itself and glide away, and now and again a heavy rotten bough fell with a crash.

Hadden was too intent upon the buffalo, however, to be much impressed by his surroundings. He only remarked that the light would be bad for shooting, and went on.

They must have penetrated a mile or more into the forest when the sudden increase of blood upon the spoor told them that the bull's wound was proving fatal to him.

"Run now," said Hadden cheerfully.

"Nay, *hamba gachle*—go softly—" answered Nahoon, "the devil is dying, but he will try to play us another trick before he dies." And he went on peering ahead of him, cautiously.

"It is all right here, anyway," said Hadden, pointing to the spoor that ran straight forward printed deep in the marshy ground.

Nahoon did not answer, but stared steadily at the trunks of two trees a few paces in front of them and to their right. "Look," he whispered.

Hadden did so, and at length made out the outline of something brown that was crouched behind the trees.

"He is dead," he exclaimed.

"No," answered Nahoon, "he has come back on his own path and is waiting for us. He knows that we are following his spoor. Now if you stand here, I think that you can shoot him through the back between the tree trunks."

Hadden knelt down, and aiming very carefully at a point just below the bull's spine, he fired. There was an awful bellow, and the next instant the brute was up and at them. Nahoon flung his broad spear, which sank deep into its chest, then they fled this way and that. The buffalo stood still for a moment, its fore legs straddled wide and its head down, looking first after the one and then the other, till of a sudden it uttered a low moaning sound and rolled over dead, smashing Nahoon's assegai to fragments as it fell.

"There! he's finished," said Hadden, "and I believe it was your assegai that killed him. Hullo! what's that noise?"

Nahoon listened. In several quarters of the forest, but from how far away it was impossible to tell, there rose a curious sound, as of people calling to each other in fear but in no articulate language. Nahoon shivered.

"It is the *Esemkofu*," he said, "the ghosts who have no tongue, and who can only wail like infants. Let us be going; this place is bad for mortals.''

''And worse for buffaloes,'' said Hadden, giving the dead bull a kick, ''but I suppose that we must leave him here for your friends, the *Esemkofu*, as we have got meat enough, and can't carry his head.''

So they started back towards the open country. As they threaded their way slowly through the tree trunks, a new idea came into Hadden's mind. Once out of this forest, he was within an hour's run of the Zulu border, and once over the Zulu border, he would feel a happier man than he did at that moment. As has been said, he had intended to attempt to escape in the darkness, but the plan was risky. All the Zulus might not overeat themselves and go to sleep, especially after the death of their comrade; Nahoon, who watched him day and night, certainly would not. This was his opportunity—there remained the question of Nahoon.

Well, if it came to the worst, Nahoon must die; it would be easy—he had a loaded rifle, and now that his assegai was gone, Nahoon had only a kerry. He did not wish to kill the man, though it was clear to him, seeing that his own safety was at stake, that he would be amply justified in so doing. Why should he not put it to him—and then be guided by circumstances?

Nahoon was walking across a little open space about ten paces ahead of him where Hadden could see him very well, whilst he himself was under the shadow of a large tree with low horizontal branches running out from the trunk.

''Nahoon,'' he said.

The Zulu turned round, and took a step toward him.

''No, do not move, I pray. Stand where you are, or I shall be obliged to shoot you. Listen now: do not be afraid for I shall not fire without warning. I am your prisoner, and you are charged to take me back to the king to be his servant. But I believe that a war is going to break out between your people and mine; and this being so, you will understand that I do not wish to go to the Cetywayo's kraal, because I should either come to a violent death there, or my own brothers will believe that I am a traitor and treat me accordingly. The Zulu border is not much more than an hour's journey away—let us say an hour and a half's: I mean to be across it before the moon is up. Now, Nahoon, will you lose me in the forest and give me this hour and a half's start—or will you stop here with that ghost people of whom you talk? Do you understand? No, please do not move.''

"I understand you," answered the Zulu, in a perfectly composed voice, "and I think that was a good name which we gave you this morning, though, Black Heart, there is some justice in your words and more wisdom. Your opportunity is good, and one which a man named as you are should not let fall."

"I am glad to find that you take this view of the matter, Nahoon. And now will you be so kind as to lose me, and to promise not to look for me till the moon is up?"

"What do you mean, Black Heart?"

"What I say. Come, I have no time to spare."

"You are a strange man," said the Zulu reflectively. "You heard the king's order to me: would you have me disobey the order of the king?"

"Certainly, I would. You have no reason to love Cetywayo, and it does not matter to you whether or not I return to his kraal to mend guns there. If you think that he will be angry because I am missing, you had better cross the border also; we can go together."

"And leave my father and all my brethren to his vengeance? Black Heart, you do not understand. How can you, being so named? I am a soldier, and the king's word is the king's word. I hoped to have died fighting, but I am the bird in your noose. Come, shoot, or you will not reach the border before moonrise," and he opened his arms and smiled.

"If it must be, so let it be. Farewell, Nahoon, at least you are a brave man, but every one of us must cherish his own life," answered Hadden calmly.

Then with much deliberation he raised his rifle and covered the Zulu's breast.

Already—whilst his victim stood there still smiling, although a twitching of his lips betrayed the natural terrors that no bravery can banish—already his finger was contracting on the trigger, when of a sudden, as instantly indeed as though he had been struck by lightning, Hadden went down backwards, and behold! there stood upon him a great spotted beast that waved its long tail to and fro and glared down into his eyes.

It was a leopard—a tiger as they call it in Africa—which, crouched upon a bough of the tree above, had been unable to resist the temptation of satisfying its savage appetite on the man below. For a second or two there was silence, broken only by the purring, or rather the snoring sound made by the leopard. In those seconds, strangely enough, there sprang up before Hadden's mental vision a picture of the *inyanga* called *Inyosi* or the Bee, her deathlike head resting against the thatch of the hut, and her deathlike lips muttering "think of my word when the great cat purrs above your face."

Then the brute put out its strength. The claws of one paw it drove deep into the muscles of his left thigh, while with another it scratched at his breast, tearing the clothes from it and furrowing the flesh beneath. The sight of the white skin seemed to madden it, and in its fierce desire for blood it drooped its square muzzle and buried its fangs in its victim's shoulder. Next moment there was a sound of rushing feet and of a club falling heavily. Up reared the leopard with an angry snarl, up till it stood as high as the attacking Zulu. At him it came, striking out savagely and tearing the black man as it had torn the white. Again the kerry fell full on its jaws, and down it went backwards. Before it could rise again, or rather as it was in the act of rising, the heavy knob-stick struck it once more, and with fearful force, this time as it chanced, full on the nape of the neck, paralysing the brute. It writhed and bit and twisted, throwing up the earth and leaves, while blow after blow was rained upon it, till at length with a convulsive struggle and a stifled roar it lay still—the brains oozing from its shattered skull.

Hadden sat up, the blood running from his wounds.

"You have saved my life, Nahoon," he said faintly, "and I thank you."

"Do not thank me, Black Heart," answered the Zulu, "it was the king's word that I should keep you safely. Still this tiger has been hardly dealt with, for certainly *he* has saved *my* life," and lifting the Martini he unloaded the rifle.

At this juncture Hadden swooned away.

Twenty-four hours had gone by when, after what seemed to him to be but a little time of troubled and dreamful sleep, through which he could hear voices without understanding what they said, and feel himself borne he knew not whither, Hadden awoke to find himself lying upon a *kaross* in a large and beautifully clean Kaffir hut with a bundle of furs for a pillow. There was a bowl of milk at his side and tortured as he was by thirst, he tried to stretch out his arm to lift it to his lips, only to find to his astonishment that his hand fell back to his side like that of a dead man. Looking round the hut impatiently, he found that there was nobody in it to assist him, so he did the only thing which remained for him to do—he lay still. He did not fall asleep, but his eyes closed, and a kind of gentle torpor crept over him, half obscuring his recovered senses. Presently he heard a soft voice speaking; it seemed far away, but he could clearly distinguish the words.

"Black Heart still sleeps," the voice said, "but there is color in his face; I think that he will wake soon, and find his thoughts again."

"Have no fear, Nanea, he will surely wake, his hurts are not dangerous," answered another voice, that of Nahoon. "He fell heavily with the weight of the tiger on top of him, and that is why his senses have been shaken for so long. He went near to death, but certainly he will not die."

"It would have been a pity if he had died," answered the soft voice, "he is so beautiful; never have I seen a white man who was so beautiful."

"I did not think him beautiful when he stood with his rifle pointed at my heart," answered Nahoon sulkily.

"Well, there is this to be said," she replied, "he wished to escape from Cetywayo, and that is not to be wondered at," and she sighed. "Moreover he asked you to come with him, and it might have been well if you had done so, that is, if you would have taken me with you!"

"How could I have done it, girl?" he asked angrily. "Would you have me set at nothing the order of the king?"

"The king!" she replied raising her voice. "What do you owe to the king? You have served him faithfully, and your reward is that within a few days he will take me from you—me, who should have been your wife, and I must—I must . . ." And she began to weep softly, adding between her sobs, "If you loved me truly, you would think more of me and of yourself, and less of the Black One and his orders. Oh! let us fly, Nahoon, let us fly to Natal before this spear pierces me."

"Weep not, Nanea," he said; "why do you tear my heart in two between my duty and my love? You know that I am a soldier, and that I must walk the path whereon the king has set my feet. Soon I think I shall be dead, for I seek death, and then it will matter nothing."

"Nothing to you, Nahoon, who are at peace, but to me? Yet, you are right, and I know it, therefore forgive me, who am no warrior, but a woman who must also obey the will of the king." And she cast her arms about his neck, sobbing her fill upon his breast.

IV
Nanea

Presently, muttering something that the listener could not catch, Nahoon left Nanea, and crept out of the hut by its beehole entrance. Then Hadden opened his eyes and looked around him. The sun was sinking and a ray of its red light streaming through the little opening filled the place with a soft and crimson glow. In the center of the hut—supporting it—stood a thorn-wood roof-tree colored black by the smoke of the fire; and against this, the rich light falling full upon her, leaned the girl Nanea—a very picture of despair.

As is occasionaly the case among Zulu women, she was beautiful—so beautiful that the sight of her went straight to the white man's heart, for a moment causing the breath to catch in his throat. Her dress was very simple. On her shoulders, hanging open in front, lay a mantle of soft white stuff edged with blue beads, about her middle was a buckskin moocha, also embroidered with blue beads, while around her forehead and left knee were strips of gray fur, and on her right wrist a shining bangle of copper. Her naked bronzed-hued figure was tall and perfect in its proportions; while her face had little in common with that of the ordinary native girl, showing as it did strong traces of the ancestral Arabian or Semitic blood. It was oval in shape, with delicate aquiline features, arched eyebrows, a full mouth, that drooped a little at the corners, tiny ears, behind which the wavy coal-black hair hung down to the shoulder, and the very loveliest pair of dark and liquid eyes that it is possible to imagine.

For a minute or more Nanea stood thus, her sweet face bathed in the sunbeam, while Hadden feasted his eyes upon its beauty. Then sighing heavily, she turned, and seeing that he was awake, started, drew her mantel over her breast and came, or rather glided, toward him.

"The chief is awake," she said in her soft Zulu accents. "Does he need aught?"

"Yes, Lady," he answered; "I need to drink, but alas! I am too weak."

She knelt down beside him, and supporting him with her left arm, with her right held the gourd to his lips.

How it came about Hadden never knew, but before that draught was finished a change passed over him. Whether it was a savage girl's touch, or her strange and fawnlike loveliness, or the tender pity in her eyes, matters not—the issue was the same. She struck some cord in his turbulent uncurbed nature, and of a sudden it was filled full with passion for her—a passion which if, not elevated, at least was real. He did not for a moment mistake the significance of the flood of feeling that surged through his veins. Hadden never shirked facts.

"By Heaven!" he said to himself. "I have fallen in love with a black beauty at first sight—more in love than I have ever been before. It's awkward, but there will be compensations. So much the worse for Nahoon, or for Cetywayo, or for both of them. After all, I can always get rid of her if she becomes a nuisance."

Then, in a fit of renewed weakness, brought about by the turmoil of his blood, he lay back upon the pillow of furs, watching Nanea's face while with a native salve of pounded leaves she busied herself dressing the wounds that the leopard had made.

It almost seemed as though something of what was passing in his mind communicated itself to that of the girl. At least, her hand shook a little at her task, and getting done with it as quickly as she could, she rose from her knees with a courteous "It is finished, *Inkoos*," and once more took up her position by the roof-tree.

"I thank you, Lady," he said; "your hand is kind."

"You must not call me lady, *Inkoos*," she answered, "I am no chieftainess, but only the daughter of a headman, Umgona."

"And named Nanea," he said. "Nay, do not be surprised. I have heard of you. Well, Nanea, perhaps you will soon become a chieftainess—up at the king's kraal yonder."

"Alas! and alas!" she said, covering her face with her hands.

"Do not grieve, Nanea, a hedge is never so tall and thick but that it can be climbed or crept through."

She let fall her hands and looked at him eagerly, but he did not pursue the subject.

"Tell me, how did I come here, Nanea?"

"Nahoon and his companions carried you, *Inkoos*."

"Indeed, I begin to be thankful to the leopard that struck me down. Well, Nahoon is a brave man, and he has done me a great service. I trust that I may be able to repay it—to you, Nanea."

This was the first meeting of Nanea and Hadden; but, although she did not seek them, the necessities of his sickness and of the situation brought about many another. Never for a moment did the white man waver in his determination to get into his keeping the native girl who had captivated him, and to attain his end he brought to bear all his powers and charm to detach her from Nahoon, and win her affections for himself. He was no rough wooer, however, but proceeded warily, weaving her about with a web of flattery and attention that must, he thought, produce the desired effect upon her mind. Without a doubt, indeed, it would have done so—for she was but a woman, and an untutored one—had it not been for a simple fact which dominated her whole nature. She loved Nahoon, and there was no room in her heart for any other man, white or black. To Hadden she was courteous and kindly but no more, nor did she appear to notice any of the subtle advances by which he attempted to win a foothold in her heart. For a while this puzzled him, but he remembered that the Zulu women do not usually permit themselves to show feeling toward an undeclared suitor. Therefore it became necessary that he should speak out.

His mind once made up, he had not to wait long for an opportunity. He was now quite recovered from his hurts, and accustomed to walk in the neighborhood of the kraal. About two hundred yards from Umgona's huts rose a spring, and thither it was Nanea's habit to resort in the evening to bring back drinking water for the use of her father's household. The path between this spring and the kraal ran through a patch of bush, where on a certain afternoon toward sundown Hadden took his seat under a tree, having first seen Nanea go down to the little stream as was her custom. A quarter of an hour later she reappeared carrying a large gourd upon her head. She wore no garment now except her moocha, for she had but one mantle and was afraid lest the water should splash it. He watched her advancing along the path, her hands resting on her hips, her splendid naked figure outlined against the westering sun, and wondered what excuse he could make to talk with her. As it chanced fortune favored him, for when she was near him a snake glided across the path in front of the girl's feet, causing her to spring backwards in alarm and overset the gourd of water. He came forward, and picked it up.

"Wait here," he said laughing; "I will bring it to you full."

"Nay, *Inkoos*," she remonstrated, "that is a woman's work."

"Among my people," he said, "the men love to work for the women," and he started for the spring, leaving her wondering.

Before he reached her again, he regretted his gallantry, for it was necessary to carry the handless gourd upon his shoulder, and the contents of it spilling over the edge soaked him. Of this, however, he said nothing to Nanea.

"There is your water, Nanea, shall I carry it for you to the kraal?"

"Nay, *Inkoos*, I thank you, but give it to me, you are weary with its weight."

"Stay awhile, and I will accompany you. Ah! Nanea, I am still weak, and had it not been for you I think that I should be dead."

"It was Nahoon who saved you—not I, *Inkoos*."

"Nahoon saved my body, but you, Nanea, you alone can save my heart."

"You talk darkly, *Inkoos*."

"Then I must make my meaning clear, Nanea, I love you."

She opened her brown eyes wide.

"You, a white lord, love me, a Zulu girl? How can that be?"

"I do not know, Nanea, but it is so, and were you not blind you would have seen it. I love you, and I wish to take you to wife."

"Nay, *Inkoos*, it is impossible. I am already betrothed."

"Ay," he answered, "betrothed to the king."

"No, betrothed to Nahoon."

"But it is the king who will take you within a week; is it not so? And would you not rather that I should take you than the king?"

"It seems to be so, *Inkoos*, and I would rather go with you than with the king, but most of all I desire to marry Nahoon. It may be that I shall not be able to marry him, but if that is so, at least I will never become one of the king's women."

"How will you prevent it, Nanea?"

"There are waters in which a maid may drown, and trees upon which she can hang," she answered with a quick setting of the mouth.

"That would be a pity, Nanea, you are too fair to die."

"Fair or foul, yet I die, *Inkoos*."

"No, no, come with me—I will find a way—and be my wife," and he put his arm about her waist, and strove to draw her to him.

Without any violence of movement, and with the most perfect dignity, the girl disengaged herself from his embrace.

"You have honored me, and I thank you, *Inkoos*," she said quietly, "but you do not understand. I am the wife of Nahoon—I belong to Nahoon; therefore, I cannot look on any other man while Nahoon lives. It is not our custom, *Inkoos*, for we are not as the white women, but ignorant and simple, and when we vow ourselves to a man, we abide by that vow till death.''

''Indeed,'' said Hadden; ''and so now you go to tell Nahoon that I have offered to make you my wife.''

''No, *Inkoos*, why should I tell Nahoon your secrets? I have said 'nay' to you, not 'yea', therefore he has no right to know,'' and she stooped to lift the gourd of water.

Hadden considered the situation rapidly, for his repulse only made him the more determined to succeed. Of a sudden under the emergency he conceived a scheme, or rather its rough outline. It was not a nice scheme, and some men might have shrunk from it, but as he had no intention of suffering himself to be defeated by a Zulu girl, he decided—with regret, it is true—that having failed to attain his ends by means which he considered fair, he must resort to others of more doubtful character.

''Nanea,'' he said, ''you are a good and honest woman, and I respect you. As I have told you, I love you also, but if you refuse to listen to me there is nothing more to be said, and after all, perhaps it would be better that you should marry one of your own people. But, Nanea, you will never marry him, for the king will take you; and, if he does not give you to some other man, either you will become one of his 'sisters,' or to be free of him, as you say, you will die. Now hear me, for it is because I love you and wish your welfare that I speak thus. Why do you not escape into Natal, taking Nahoon with you, for there as you know you may live in peace out of reach of the arm of Cetywayo?''

''That is my desire, *Inkoos*, but Nahoon will not consent. He says that there is to be war between us and you white men, and he will not break the command of the king and desert from his army.''

''Then he cannot love you much, Nanea, and at least you have to think of yourself. Whisper into the ear of your father and fly together, for be sure that Nahoon will soon follow you. Ay! and I myself will fly with you, for I too believe that there must be war, and then a white man in this country will be as a lamb among the eagles.''

''If Nahoon will come, I will go, *Inkoos*, but I cannot fly without Nahoon; it is better I should stay here and kill myself.''

''Surely then being so fair and loving him so well, you can teach him to forget his folly and to escape with you. In four days' time we must start for the king's kraal, and if you win over Nahoon, it will be easy for us to turn our faces southwards and cross the river that lies between the land of the Amazulu and Natal. For the sake of all of us, but most of all for your own sake, try to do this, Nanea, whom I have loved and whom I now would save. See him and plead with him as you know how, but as yet do not tell him that I dream of flight, for then I should be watched."

"In truth, I will, *Inkoos*," she answered earnestly, "and oh! I thank you for your goodness. Fear not that I will betray you—first would I die. Farewell."

"Farewell, Nanea," and taking her hand he raised it to his lips.

Late that night, just as Hadden was beginning to prepare himself for sleep, he heard a gentle tapping at the board which closed the entrance to his hut.

"Enter," he said, unfastening the door, and presently by the light of the little lantern that he had with him, he saw Nanea creep into the hut, followed by the great form of Nahoon.

"*Inkoos*," she said in a whisper when the door was closed again, "I have pleaded with Nahoon, and he has consented to fly; moreover, my father will come also."

"Is it so, Nahoon?" asked Hadden.

"It is so," answered the Zulu, looking down shamefacedly; "to save this girl from the king, and because the love of her eats out my heart, I have bartered away my honor. But I tell you, Nanea, and you, White Man, as I told Umgona just now, that I think no good will come of this flight, and if we are caught or betrayed, we shall be killed every one of us."

"Caught we can scarcely be," broke in Nanea anxiously, "for who could betray us, except the *Inkoos* here—"

"Which he is not likely to do," said Hadden quietly, "seeing that he desires to escape with you, and that his life is also at stake."

"That is so, Black Heart," said Nahoon, "otherwise I tell you that I should not have trusted you."

Hadden took no notice of this outspoken saying, but until very late that night they sat there together making their plans.

On the following morning Hadden was awakened by sounds of violent altercation. Going out of his hut he found that the disputants were Umgona and a fat and evil-looking Kaffir chief who had arrived at the kraal on a pony. This chief, he soon discovered, was named Maputa, being none other than the man who had sought Nanea in marriage and brought about Nahoon's and Umgona's unfortunate appeal to the king. At present he was engaged in abusing Umgona furiously, charging him with having stolen certain of his oxen and bewitched his cows so that they would not give milk. The alleged theft it was comparatively easy to disprove, but the wizardry remained a matter of argument.

"You are a dog, and a son of a dog," shouted Maputa, shaking his fat fist in the face of the trembling but indignant Umgona. "You promised me your daughter in marriage, then having vowed her to that *umfagozan*—that low lout of a soldier, Nahoon, the son of Zomba—you went, the two of you, and poisoned the king's ear against me, bringing me into trouble with the king, and now you have bewitched my cattle. Well, wait, I will be even with you, Wizard; wait till you wake up in the cold morning to find your fence red with fire, and the slayers standing outside your gates to eat up you and yours with spears—"

At this juncture Nahoon, who till now had been listening in silence, intervened with effect.

"Good," he said, "we will wait, but not in your company Chief Maputa. *Hamba*! (go)" and seizing the fat old ruffian by the scruff of his neck, he flung him backwards with such violence that he rolled over and over down the little slope.

Hadden laughed, and passed on toward the stream where he proposed to bathe. Just as he reached it, he caught sight of Maputa riding along the footpath, his head ring covered with mud, his lips purple and his black face livid with rage.

"There goes an angry man," he said to himself. "Now, how would it be . . ." and he looked upwards like one seeking an inspiration. It seemed to come; perhaps the devil finding it open whispered in his ear, at any rate—in a few seconds his plan was formed, and he was walking through the bush to meet Maputa.

"Go in peace, Chief," he said; "they seem to have treated you roughly up yonder. Having no power to interfere, I came away for I could not bear the sight. It is indeed shameful that an old and venerable man of rank should be struck into the dirt, and beaten by a soldier drunk with beer."

"Shameful, White Man!" gasped Maputa; "your words are true indeed. But wait a while. I, Maputa, will roll that stone over, I will throw that bull upon its back. When next the harvest ripens, this I promise, that neither Nahoon nor Umgona, nor any of his kraal shall be left to gather it."

"And how will you manage that, Maputa?"

"I do not know, but I will find a way. Oh! I tell you, a way shall be found."

Hadden patted the pony's neck meditatively, then leaning forward, he looked the chief in the eyes and said:

"What will you give me, Maputa, if I show you that way, a sure and certain one, whereby you may be avenged to the death upon Nahoon, whose violence I also have seen, and upon Umgona, whose witchcraft brought sore sickness upon me?"

"What reward do you seek, White Man?" asked Maputa eagerly.

"A little thing, Chief, a thing of no account, only the girl Nanea, to whom as it chances I have taken a fancy."

"I wanted her for myself, White Man, but he who sits at Ulundi has laid his hand upon her."

"That is nothing, Chief; I can arrange with him who 'sits at Ulundi.' It is with you who are great here that I wish to come to terms. Listen: if you grant my desire, not only will I fulfill yours upon your foes, but when the girl is delivered into my hands I will give you this rifle and a hundred rounds of cartridges."

Maputa looked at the sporting Martini, and his eyes glistened.

"It is good," he said; "it is very good. Often have I wished for such a gun that will enable me to shoot game, and to talk with my enemies from far away. Promise it to me, White Man, and you shall take the girl if I can give her to you."

"You swear it, Maputa?"

"I swear it by the head of Chaka, and the spirits of my fathers."

"Good. At dawn on the fourth day from now it is the purpose of Umgona, his daughter Nanea, and Nahoon, to cross the river into Natal by the drift that is called Crocodile Drift, taking their cattle with them and flying from the king. I also shall be of their company, for they know that I have learned their secret, and would murder me if I tried to leave them. Now you who are chief of the border and guardian of that drift, must hide at night with some men among the rocks in the shallows of the drift and await our coming. First Nanea will cross driving the cows and calves, for so it is arranged, and I shall help her; then will follow Umgona and Nahoon with the oxen and heifers. On these two you must fall, killing them and capturing the cattle, and afterwards I will give you the rifle."

"What if the king ask for the girl, White Man?"

"Then you shall answer that in the uncertain light you did not recognize her and so she slipped away from you; moreover, that at first you feared to seize the girl lest her cries should alarm the men and they should escape you."

"Good, but how can I be sure that you will give me the gun once you are across the river?"

"Thus: before I enter the ford I will lay the rifle and cartridges upon a stone by the bank, telling Nanea that I shall return to fetch them when I have driven over the cattle."

"It is well, White Man; I will not fail you."

So the plot was made, and after some further conversation upon points of detail, the two conspirators shook hands and parted.

"That ought to come off all right," reflected Hadden to himself as he plunged and floated in the waters of the stream, "but somehow I don't quite trust our friend Maputa. It would have been better if I could have relied upon myself to get rid of Nahoon and his respected uncle—a couple of shots would do it in the water. But then that would be murder and murder is unpleasant; whereas the other thing is only the delivery to justice of two base deserters, a laudable action in a military country. Also personal interference upon my part might turn the girl against me; while after Umgona and Nahoon have been wiped out by Maputa, she *must* accept my escort. Of course there is a risk, but in every walk of life the most cautious have to take risks at times."

As it chanced, Philip Hadden was correct in his suspicions of his coadjutor, Maputa. Even before that worthy chief reached his own kraal, he had come to the conclusion that the white man's plan, though attractive in some ways, was too dangerous, since it was certain that if the girl Nanea escaped, the king would be indignant. Moreover, the men he took with him to do the killing in the drift would suspect something and talk. On the other hand he would earn much credit with his majesty by revealing the plot, saying that he had learned it from the lips of the white hunter, whom Umgona and Nahoon had forced to participate in it, and of whose coveted rifle he must trust to chance to possess himself.

An hour later two discreet messengers were bounding across the plains, bearing words from the Chief Maputa, the Warden of the Border, to the "great Black Elephant" at Ulundi.

V
The Doom Pool

Fortune showed itself strangely favorable to the plans of Nahoon and Nanea. One of the Zulu captain's perplexities was as to how he should lull the suspicions and evade the vigilance of his own companions, who together with himself had been detailed by the king to assist Hadden in his hunting and to guard against his escape. As it chanced, however, on the day after the incident of the visit of Maputa, a messenger arrived from no less a person than the great military Induna, Tvingwayo ka Marolo, who afterwards commanded the Zulu army at Isandhlwana, ordering these men to return to their regiment the Umcityu Corps, which was to be placed upon full war footing. Accordingly Nahoon sent them, saying that he himself would follow with Black Heart in the course of a few days, as at present the white man was not sufficiently recovered from his hurts to allow of his travelling fast and far. So the soldiers went, doubting nothing.

Then Umgona gave it out that in obedience to the command of the king he was about to start for Ulundi, taking with him his daughter Nanea to be delivered over into the *Sigodhla*, and also those fifteen head of cattle that had been *lobola'd* by Nahoon in consideration of his forthcoming marriage, whereof he had been fined by Cetywayo. Under pretense that they required a change of veldt, the rest of his cattle he sent away in charge of a Basuto herd who knew nothing of their plans, telling him to keep them by the Crocodile Drift, as there the grass was good and sweet.

All preparations being completed, on the third day the party started, heading straight for Ulundi. After they had travelled some miles, however, they left the road and turning sharp to the right, passed unobserved of any through a great stretch of uninhabited bush. Their path now lay not far from the Pool of Doom, which, indeed, was close to Umgona's kraal, and the forest that was called Home of the Dead, but out of sight of these. It was their plan to travel by night, reaching the broken country near the Crocodile Drift on the following morning. Here they proposed to lie hid that day and through the night; then, having first collected the cattle which had preceded them, to cross the river at the break of dawn and escape into Natal. At least this was the plan of his companions; but, as we know, Hadden had another program, wherein after one last appearance two of the party would play no part.

During that long afternoon's journey Umgona, who knew every inch of the country, walked ahead driving the fifteen cattle and carrying in his hand, a long travelling stick of black and white *umzimbeet* wood, for in truth the old man was in a hurry to reach his journey's end. Next came Nahoon, armed with a broad assegai, but naked except for his moocha and necklet of baboon's teeth, and with him Nanea in her white bead-bordered mantle. Hadden, who brought up the rear, noticed that the girl seemed to be under the spell of an imminent apprehension, for from time to time she clasped her lover's arm, and looking up into his face, addressed him with vehemence, almost with passion.

Curiously enough, the sight touched Hadden, and once or twice he was shaken by so sharp a pang of remorse at the thought of his share in this tragedy, that he cast about in his mind seeking a means to unravel the web of death which he himself had woven. But ever that evil voice was whispering at his ear. It reminded him that he, the white *Inkoos*, had been refused by this dusky beauty, and that if he found a way to save him, within some few hours she would be the wife of the savage gentleman at her side, the man who had named him Black Heart and who despised him, the man whom he had meant to murder and who immediately repaid his treachery by rescuing him from the jaws of the leopard at the risk of his own life. Moreover, it was a law of Hadden's existence never to deny himself anything that he desired if it lay within his power to take it—a law which had led him always deeper into sin. In other respects, indeed, it had not carried him far, for in the past he had desired much, and he had won little; but this particular flower was to his hand, and he would pluck it. If Nahoon stood between him and the flower, so much the worse for Nahoon, and if it should wither in his grasp, so much the worse for the flower; it could always be thrown away. Thus it came about that, not for the first time in his life, Philip Hadden discarded the somewhat spasmodic prickings of conscience and listened to that evil whispering at his ear.

About half-past five o'clock in the afternoon the four refugees passed the stream that a mile or so down fell over the little precipice into the Doom Pool; and, entering a patch of thorn trees on the further side, walked straight into the midst of two-and-twenty soldiers, who were beguiling the tedium of expectancy by the taking of snuff and the smoking of *dakka* or native hemp. With these soldiers, seated on his pony, for he was too fat to walk, waited the Chief Maputa.

Observing that their expected guests had arrived, the men knocked out the *dakka* pipe, replaced the snuff boxes in the slits made in the lobes of their ears, and secured the four of them.

"What is the meaning of this, O King's soldiers," asked Umgona in a quavering voice. "We journey to the kraal of U'Cetywayo; why do you molest us?"

"Indeed. Wherefore then are your faces set toward the south? Does the Black One live in the south? Well, you will journey to another kraal presently," answered the jovial-looking captain of the party with a callous laugh.

"I do not understand," stammered Umgona.

"Then I will explain while you rest," said the captain. "The Chief Maputa yonder sent word to the Black One at Ulundi that he had learned of your intended flight to Natal from the lips of this white man, who had warned him of it. The Black One was angry, and despatched us to catch you and make an end of you. That is all. Come on now, quietly, and let us finish the matter. As the Doom Pool is near, your deaths will be easy."

Nahoon heard the words, and sprang straight at the throat of Hadden; but he did not reach it, for the soldiers pulled him down. Nanea heard them also, and turning, looked the traitor in the eyes; she said nothing, she only looked, but he could never forget that look. The white man for his part was filled with a fiery indignation against Maputa.

"You wicked villain," he gasped, whereat the chief smiled in a sickly fashion, and turned away.

Then they were marched along the banks of the stream till they reached the waterfall that fell into the Pool of Doom.

Hadden was a brave man after his fashion, but his heart quailed as he gazed into that abyss.

"Are you going to throw me in there?" he asked of the Zulu captain in a thick voice.

"You, White Man?" replied the soldier unconcernedly. "No, our orders are to take you to the king, but what he will do with you I do not know. There is to be war between your people and ours, so perhaps he means to pound you into medicine for the use of the witch doctors, or to peg you over an ant-heap as a warning to other white men."

Hadden received this information in silence, but its effect upon his brain was bracing, for instantly he began to search out some means of escape.

By now the party had halted near the two thorn trees that hung over the waters of the pool.

"Who dives first?" asked the captain of the Chief Maputa.

"The old wizard," he replied, nodding at Umgona; "then his daughter after him, and last of all this fellow," and he struck Nahoon in the face with his open hand.

"Come on, Wizard," said the captain, grasping Umgona by the arm, "and let us see how you can swim."

At the words of doom Umgona seemed to recover his self-command, after the fashion of his race.

"No need to lead me, soldier," he said, shaking himself loose, "who am old and ready to die." Then he kissed his daughter at his side, wrung Nahoon by the hand, and turning from Hadden with a gesture of contempt walked out upon the platform that joined the two thorn trunks. Here he stood for a moment looking at the setting sun, then suddenly, and without a sound, he hurled himself into the abyss below and vanished.

"That was a brave one," said the captain with admiration. "Can you spring too, girl, or must we throw you?"

"I can walk my father's path," Nanea answered faintly, "but first I crave leave to say one word. It is true that we were escaping from the king, and therefore by the law we must die; but it was Black Heart here who made the plot, and he who has betrayed us. Would you know why he has betrayed us? Because he sought my favor, and I refused him, and this is the vengeance that he takes—a white man's vengeance."

"*Wow!*" broke in the Chief Maputa, "this pretty one speaks truth, for the white man would have made a bargain with me under which Umgona, the wizard, and Nahoon, the soldier, were to be killed at the Crocodile Drift, and he himself suffered to escape with the girl. I spoke him softly and said 'yes,' and then like a loyal man I reported to the king."

"You hear," sighed Nanea. "Nahoon, fare you well, though presently perhaps we shall be together again. It was I who tempted you from your duty. For my sake you forgot your honor, and I am repaid. Farewell, my husband, it is better to die with you than to enter the house of the king's women," and Nanea stepped onto the platform.

Here, holding to a bough of one of the thorn trees, she turned and addressed Hadden saying:

"Black Heart, you seem to have won the day, but me at least you lose and—the sun is not yet set. After sunset comes the night, Black Heart, and in that night I pray that you may wander eternally, and be given to drink of my blood and the blood of Umgona my father, and the blood of Nahoon my husband, who saved your life, and whom you have murdered. Perchance, Black Heart, we may yet meet yonder—in the House of the Dead."

Then uttering a low cry Nanea clasped her hands and sprang upwards and outwards from the platform. The watchers bent their heads forward to look. They saw her rush headlong down the face of the fall to strike the water fifty feet below. A few seconds, and for the last time, they caught sight of her white garment glimmering on the surface of the gloomy pool. Then the shadows and mist-wreaths hid it, and she was gone.

"Now, husband," cried the cheerful voice of the captain, "yonder is your marriage bed, so be swift to follow a bride who is so ready to lead the way. *Wow!* but you are good people to kill, never have I had to do with any who gave less trouble. You—" and he stopped, for mental agony had done its work, and suddenly Nahoon went mad before his eyes.

With a roar like that of a lion the great man cast off those who held him and seizing one of them round thc waist and thigh, he put out all his terrible strength. Lifting him as though he had been an infant, he hurled him over the edge of the cliff to find his death on the rocks of the Pool of Doom. Then crying:

"Black Heart! your turn, Black Heart the traitor!" he rushed at Hadden, his eyes rolling and foam flying from his lips, as he passed striking the Chief Maputa from his horse with a backward blow of his hand. Ill would it have gone with the white man if Nahoon had caught him. But he could not come at him, for the soldiers sprang upon him and notwithstanding his fearful struggles they pulled him to the ground, as at certain festivals the Zulu regiments with their naked hands pull down a bull in the presence of the king.

"Cast him over before he can work more mischief," said a voice. But the captain cried out, "Nay, nay, he is sacred; the fire from Heaven has fallen on his brain, and we may not harm him, else evil would overtake us all. Bind him hand and foot, and bear him hence tenderly to where he can be cared for. Surely, I thought that these evildoers were giving us too little trouble, and thus it has proved."

So they set themselves to make fast Nahoon's hands and wrists, using as much gentleness as they might, for among the Zulus a lunatic is accounted holy. It was no easy task, and it took time.

Hadden glanced around him, and saw his opportunity. On the ground close beside him lay his rifle, where one of the soldiers had placed it, and about a dozen yards away Maputa's pony was grazing. With a swift movement, he seized the Martini and five seconds later he was on the back of the pony, heading for the Crocodile Drift at a gallop. So quickly indeed did he execute this masterly retreat, that occupied as they all were in binding Nahoon, for half a minute or more none of the soldiers noticed what had happened. Then Maputa chanced to see, and waddled after him to the top of the rise, screaming:

"The white thief, he has stolen my horse, and the gun too, the gun that he promised to give me."

Hadden, who by this time was a hundred yards away, heard him clearly, and a rage filled his heart. This man had made an open murderer of him; more, he had been the means of robbing him of the girl for whose sake he had dipped his hands in these iniquities. He glanced over his shoulder; Maputa was still running, and alone. Yes, there was time; at any rate he would risk it.

Pulling up the pony with a jerk, he leapt from its back, slipping his arms through the rein with an almost simultaneous movement. As it chanced, and as he had hoped would be the case, the animal was a trained shooting horse, and stood still. Hadden planted his feet firmly on the ground and drawing a deep breath, he cocked the rifle and covered the advancing chief. Now Maputa saw his purpose and with a yell of terror turned to fly. Hadden waited a second to get the sight fair on to his broad back, then just as the soldier appeared above the rise he pressed the trigger. He was a noted shot, and in this instance his skill did not fail him; for, before he heard the bullet tell, Maputa flung his arms wide and plunged to the ground dead.

Three seconds more, and with a savage curse, Hadden had re-mounted the pony and was riding for his life toward the river, which a while later he crossed in safety.

VI
The Ghost of the Dead

When Nanea leapt from the dizzy platform that overhung the Pool of Doom, a strange fortune befell her. Close in to the precipice were many jagged rocks, and on these the waters of the fall fell and thundered, bounding from them in spouts of spray into the troubled depths of the foss beyond. It was on these stones that the life was dashed out of the bodies of the wretched victims who were hurled from above. But Nanea, it will be remembered, had not waited to be treated thus, and as it chanced the strong spring with which she had leapt to death carried her clear of the rocks. By a very little she missed the edge of them and striking the deep water head first like some practiced diver, she sank down and down till she thought that she would never rise again. Yet she did rise, at the end of the pool in the mouth of the rapid, along which she sped swiftly, carried down by the rush of the water. Fortunately there were no rocks here; and, since she was a skilful swimmer, she escaped the danger of being thrown against the banks.

For a long distance she was borne thus till at length she saw that she was in a forest, for trees cut off the light from the water, and their drooping branches swept its surface. One of these Nanea caught with her hand, and by thc help of it she dragged herself from the River of Death whence none had escaped before. Now she stood upon the bank gasping but quite unharmed; thcre was not a scratch on her body; even her white garment was still fast about her neck.

But though she had suffered no hurt in her terrible voyage, so exhausted was Nanea that she could scarcely stand. Here the gloom was that of night, and shivering with cold she looked around helplessly to find some refuge. Close to the water's edge grew an enormous yellow-wood tree, and to this she staggered—thinking to climb it, and seek shelter in its boughs where, as she hoped, she would be safe from wild beasts. Again fortune befriended her, for at a distance of a few feet from the ground there was a great hole in the tree which, she discovered, was hollow. Into this hole she crept, taking her chance of its being the home of snakes or other evil creatures, to find that the interior was wide and warm. It was dry also, for at the bottom of the cavity lay a foot or more of rotten tinder and moss brought there by rats or birds. Upon this tinder she lay down, and covering herself with the moss and leaves soon sank into sleep or stupor.

How long Nanea slept she did not know, but at length she was awakened by a sound as of guttural human voices talking in a language that she could not understand. Rising to her knees she peered out of the hole in the tree. It was night, but the stars shone brilliantly, and their light fell upon an open circle of ground close by the edge of the river. In this circle there burned a great fire, and at a little distance from the fire were gathered eight or ten horrible-looking beings, who appeared to be rejoicing over something that lay upon the ground. They were small in stature, men and women together, but no children, and all of them were nearly naked. Their hair was long and thin, growing down almost to the eyes, their jaws and teeth protruded and the girth of their black bodies was out of all proportion to their height. In their hands they held sticks with sharp stones lashed on to them, or rude hatchetlike knives of the same material.

Now Nanea's heart shrank within her, and she nearly fainted with fear, for she knew that she was in the haunted forest, and without a doubt these were the *Esemkofu*, the evil ghosts that dwelt therein. Yes, that was what they were, and yet she could not take her eyes off them—the sight of them held her with a horrible fascination. But if they were ghosts, why did they sing and dance like men? Why did they wave those sharp stones aloft, and quarrel and strike each other? And why did they make a fire as men do when they wish to cook food? More, what was it that they rejoiced over, that long dark thing which lay so quiet upon the ground? It did not look like a head of game, and it could scarcely be a crocodile, yet clearly it was food of some sort, for they were sharpening the stone knives in order to cut it up.

While she wondered thus, one of the dreadful-looking little creatures advanced to the fire, and taking from it a burning bough, held it over the thing that lay upon the ground, to give light to a companion who was about to do something to it with the stone knife. Next instant Nanea drew back her head from the hole, a stifled shriek upon her lips. She saw what it was now—it was the body of a man. Yes, and these were not ghosts; they were cannibals of whom when she was little, her mother had told her tales to keep her from wandering away from home.

But who was the man they were about to eat? It could not be one of themselves, for his stature was much greater. Oh! now she knew; it must be Nahoon, who had been killed up yonder, and whose dead body the waters had brought down to the haunted forest as they had brought her alive. Yes, it must be Nahoon, and she would be forced to see her husband devoured before her eyes. The thought of it overwhelmed her. That he should die by order of the king was natural, but that he should be buried thus? Yet what could she do to prevent it? Well, if it cost her her life, it should be prevented. At the worst they could only kill and eat her also, and now that Nahoon and her father were gone, being untroubled by any religious or spiritual hopes and fears, she was not greatly concerned to keep her own breath in her.

Slipping through the hole in the tree, Nanea walked quietly toward the cannibals—not knowing in the least what she should do when she reached them. As she arrived in line with the fire this lack of program came home to her mind forcibly, and she paused to reflect. Just then one of the cannibals looked up to see a tall and stately figure wrapped in a white garment which, as the flame-light flickered on it, seemed now to advance from the dense background of shadow, and now to recede into it. The poor savage wretch was holding a stone knife in his teeth when he beheld her, but it did not remain there long, for opening his great jaws he uttered the most terrified and piercing yell that Nanea had ever heard. Then the others saw her also, and presently the forest was ringing with shrieks of fear. For a few seconds the outcasts stood and gazed, then they were gone this way and that, bursting their path through the undergrowth like startled jackals. The *Esemkofu* of Zulu tradition had been routed in their own haunted home by what they took to be a spirit.

Poor *Esemkofu*! they were but miserable and starving bushmen who, driven into that place of ill omen many years ago, had adopted this means, the only one open to them, to keep the life in their wretched bodies. Here at least they were unmolested, and as there was little other food to be found amid that wilderness of trees, they took what the river brought them. When executions were few in the Pool of Doom, times were hard for them indeed—for then they were driven to eat each other. That is why there were no children.

As their inarticulate outcry died away in the distance, Nanea ran forward to look at the body that lay on the ground, and staggered back with a sigh of relief. It was not Nahoon, but she recognized the face for that of one of the party of executioners. How did he come here? Had Nahoon killed him? Had Nahoon escaped? She could not tell, and at the best it was improbable, but still the sight of this dead soldier lit her heart with a faint ray of hope, for how did he come to be dead if Nahoon had no hand in his death? She could not bear to leave him lying so near her hiding-place, however; therefore, with no small toil, she rolled the corpse back into the water, which caried it swiftly away. Then she returned to the tree, having first replenished the fire, and awaited the light.

At last it came—so much of it as ever penetrated this darksome den—and Nanea, becoming aware that she was hungry, descended from the tree to search for food. All day long she searched, finding nothing, till toward sunset she remembered that on the outskirts of the forest there was a flat rock where it was the custom of those who had been in any way afflicted, or who considered themselves or their belongings to be bewitched, to place propitiatory offerings of food wherewith the *Esemkofu* and *Amalhosi* were supposed to satisfy their spiritual cravings. Urged by the pinch of starvation, to this spot Nanea journeyed rapidly, and found to her joy that some neighboring kraal had evidently been in recent trouble, for the Rock of Offering was laden with cobs of corn, gourds of milk, porridge and even meat. Helping herself to as much as she could carry, she returned to her lair, where she drank of the milk and cooked meat and mealies at the fire. Then she crept back into the tree, and slept.

For nearly two months Nanea lived thus in the forest, since she could not venture out of it—fearing lest she should be seized, and for a second time taste of the judgment of the king. In the forest at least she was safe, for none dared enter there, nor did the *Esemkofu* give her further trouble. Once or twice she saw them, but on each occasion they fled shrieking from her presence—seeking some distant retreat, where they hid themselves or perished. Nor did food fail her, for finding that it was taken, the pious givers brought it in plenty to the Rock of Offering.

But, oh! the life was dreadful, and the gloom and loneliness coupled with her sorrows at times drove her almost to insanity. Still she lived on, though often she desired to die, for if her father was dead, the corpse she had found was not the corpse of Nahoon, and in her heart there still shone that spark of hope. Yet what she hoped for she could not tell.

When Philip Hadden reached civilized regions, he found that war was about to be declared between the Queen and Cetywayo, King of the Amazulu; also that in the prevailing excitement his little adventure with the Utrecht storekeeper had been overlooked or forgotten. He was the owner of two good buck waggons with spans of salted oxen, and at that time vehicles were much in request to carry military stores for the columns which were to advance into Zululand; indeed the transport authorities were glad to pay £90 a month for the hire of each wagon and to guarantee the owners against all loss of cattle. Although he was not desirous of returning to Zululand, this bait proved too much for Hadden, who accordingly leased out his waggons to the Commissariat, together with his own services as conductor and interpreter.

He was attached to No. 3 column of the invading force, which it may be remembered was under the immediate command of Lord Chelmsford, and on the 20 January, 1879, he marched with it by the road that runs from Rorke's Drift to the Indeni forest, and encamped that night beneath the shadow of the steep and desolate mountain known as Isandhlwana.

That day also a great army of King Cetywayo's, numbering twenty thousand men and more, moved down from the Upindo Hill and camped upon the stony plain that lies a mile and a half to the east of Isandhlwana. No fires were lit, and it lay there in utter silence, for the warriors were "sleeping on their spears."

With that *impi* was the Umcityu regiment, three thousand five hundred strong. At the first break of dawn the Induna in command of the Umcityu looked up from beneath the shelter of the black shield with which he had covered his body, and through the thick mist he saw a great man standing before him, clothed only in a moocha, a gaunt wild-eyed man who held a rough club in his hand. When he was spoken to, the man made no answer; he only leaned upon his club looking from left to right along the dense array of innumerable shields.

"Who is this *Silwana* (wild creature)?" asked the Induna of his captains wondering.

The captains stared at the wanderer, and one of them replied, "This is Nahoon-ka-Zomba, it is the son of Zomba who not long ago held rank in this regiment of the Umcityu. His betrothed, Nanea, daughter of Umgona, was killed together with her father by order of the Black One, and Nahoon went mad with grief at the sight of it, for the fire of Heaven entered his brain, and mad he has wandered ever since."

"What would you here, Nahoon-ka-Zomba?" asked the Induna.

Then Nahoon spoke slowly. "My regiment goes down to war

against the white men, give me a shield and a spear, O Captain of the king, that I may fight with my regiment, for I seek a face in the battle.''

So they gave him a shield and a spear, for they dared not turn away one whose brain was alight with the fire of Heaven.

When the sun was high that day, bullets began to fall among the ranks of the Umcityu. Then the black-shielded, black-plumed Umcityu arose, company by company, and after them arose the whole vast Zulu army, breast and horns together, and swept down in silence upon the doomed British camp, a moving sheen of spears. The bullets pattered on the shields, the shells tore long lines through their array, but they never halted nor wavered. Forward on either side shot out the horns of armed men, clasping the camp in an embrace of steel. Then as these began to close, out burst the war cry of the Zulus, and with the roar of a torrent and the rush of a storm, with a sound like the humming of a billion bees, wave after wave the deep breast of the *impi* rolled down upon the white men. With it went the black-shielded Umcityu and with them went Nahoon, the son of Zomba. A bullet struck him in the side, glancing from his ribs, he did not heed; a white man fell from his horse before him, he did not stab, for he sought but one face in the battle.

He sought—and at last he found. There, among the wagons where the spears were busiest, there standing by his horse and firing rapidly was Black Heart, he who had given Nanea his betrothed to death. Three soldiers stood between them, one of them Nahoon stabbed, and two he brushed aside; then he rushed straight at Hadden.

But the white man saw him come, and even through the mask of his madness he knew Nahoon again, and terror took hold of him. Throwing away the empty rifle, for his ammunition was spent, he leaped upon his horse and drove his spurs into its flanks. Away it went among the carnage, springing over the dead and bursting through the lines of shields, and after it came Nahoon, running long and low with head stretched forward and trailing spear, running as a hound runs when the buck is at view.

Hadden's first plan was to head for Rorke's Drift, but a glance to the left showed him that the masses of the Undi barred that way, so he fled straight on, leaving his path to fortune. In five minutes he was over a ridge, and there was nothing of the battle to be seen, in ten all sounds of it had died away, for few guns were fired in the dread race to Fugitive's

Drift, and the assegai makes no noise. In some strange fashion, even at this moment, the contrast between the dreadful scene of blood and turmoil that he had left, and the peaceful face of Nature over which he was passing, came home to his brain vividly. Here birds sang and cattle grazed; here the sun shone undimmed by the smoke of cannon, only high up in the blue and silent air long streams of vultures could be seen winging their way to the Plain of Isandhlwana.

The ground was very rough, and Hadden's horse begn to tire. He looked over his shoulder—there some two hundred yards behind came the Zulu, grim as Death, unswerving as Fate. He examined the pistol in his belt; there was but one undischarged cartridge left, all the rest had been fired and the pouch was empty. Well, one bullet should be enough for one savage: the question was should he stop and use it now? No, he might miss or fail to kill the man; he was on horseback and his foe on foot, surely he could tire him out.

A while passed, and they dashed through a little stream. It seemed familiar to Hadden. Yes, that was the pool where he used to bathe when he was the guest of Umgona, the father of Nanea; and there on the knoll to his right were the huts, or rather the remains of them, for they had been burnt with fire. What chance had brought him to this place, he wondered; then again he looked behind him at Nahoon, who seemed to read his thoughts, for he shook his spear and pointed to the ruined kraal.

On he went at speed for here the land was level, and to his joy he lost sight of his pursuer. But presently there came a mile of rocky ground, and when it was past, glancing back he saw that Nahoon was once more in his old place. His horse's strength was almost spent, but Hadden spurred it forward blindly, whither he knew not. Now he was travelling along a strip of turf and ahead of him he heard the music of a river, while to his left rose a high bank. Presently the turf belt bent inwards and there, not twenty yards away from him, was a Kaffir hut standing on the brink of a river. He looked at it, yes, it was the hut of that accursed *inyanga*, the Bee, and standing by the fence of it was none other than the Bee herself. At the sight of her the exhausted horse swerved violently, stumbled and came to the ground, where it lay panting. Hadden was thrown from the saddle but sprang to his feet unhurt.

"Ah! Black Heart, is it you? What news of the battle, Black Heart?" cried the Bee in a mocking voice.

"Help me, mother, I am pursued," he gasped.

"What of it, Black Heart, it is but by one tired man. Stand then and face him, for now Black Heart and White Heart are together again. You will not? Then away to the forest and seek shelter among the dead who await you there. Tell me, tell me, was it the face of Nanea that I saw beneath the waters a while ago? Good! bear my greetings to her when you two meet in the House of the Dead."

Hadden looked at the stream; it was in flood. He could not swim it, so followed by the evil laugh of the prophetess, he sped toward the forest. After him came Nahoon, his tongue hanging from his jaws like the tongue of a wolf.

Now he was in the shadow of the forest, but still he sped on following the course of the river, till at length his breath failed, and he halted on the further side of a little glade, beyond which a great tree grew. Nahoon was more than a spear's throw behind him: therefore he had time to draw his pistol and make ready.

"Halt, Nahoon," he cried, as once before he had cried; "I would speak with you."

The Zulu heard his voice, and obeyed.

"Listen," said Hadden. "We have run a long race and fought a long fight, you and I, and we are still alive both of us. Very soon, if you come on, one of us must be dead, and it will be you, Nahoon, for I am armed and as you know I can shoot straight. What do you say?"

Nahoon made no answer, but stood still at the edge of the glade, his wild and glowering eyes fixed on the white man's face and his breath coming in short gasps.

"Will you let me go, if *I* let *you* go?" Hadden asked once more. "I know why you hate me, but the past cannot be undone, nor can the dead be brought to earth again."

Still Nahoon made no answer, and his silence seemed more fateful and more crushing than any speech; no spoken accusation would have been so terrible in Hadden's ear. He made no answer, but lifting his assegai he stalked grimly toward his foe.

When he was within five paces Hadden covered him and fired. Nahoon sprang aside, but the bullet struck him somewhere, for his right arm dropped, and the stabbing spear that he held was jerked from it harmlessly over the white man's head. But still making no sound, the Zulu came on and gripped him by the throat with his left hand. For a space they struggled terribly, swaying to and fro, but Hadden was unhurt and fought with the fury of despair, while Nahoon had been twice wounded, and there remained to him but one sound arm wherewith to strike. Presently forced to earth by the white man's iron strength, the soldier was down, nor could he rise again.

"Now we will make an end," muttered Hadden savagely, and he turned to seek the assegai, then staggered slowly back with starting eyes and reeling gait. For there before him, still clad in her white robe, a spear in her hand, stood the spirit of Nanea!

"Think of it," he said to himself, dimly remembering the words of the *inyanga*, "when you stand face to face with the ghost of the dead in the Home of the Dead."

There was a cry and a flash of steel; the broad spear leapt toward him to bury itself in his breast. He swayed, he fell, and presently Black Heart clasped that great reward which the word of the Bee had promised Him.

"Nahoon! Nahoon!" murmured a soft voice, "awake, it is no ghost, but I—Nanea—I, your living wife, to whom my *Ehlose*[1] has given it me to save you."

Nahoon heard and opened his eyes to look and his madness left him.

"Welcome, wife," he said faintly, "now I will live since Death has brought you back to me in the House of the Dead."

Today Nahoon is one of the Indunas of the English Government in Zululand, and there are children about his kraal. It was from the lips of none other than Nanea his wife that the teller of this tale heard its substance.

The Bee also lives and practices as much magic as she dares under the white man's rule. On her black hand shines a golden ring shaped like a snake with ruby eyes, and of this trinket the Bee is very proud.

---

[1]Guardian Spirit.

H. G. Wells (1866–1946)

Born in Bromley, England, Herbert George Wells was a novelist, social critic, historian, and one of the most important influences on twentieth-century science fiction. His parents were lower middle-class, and in a society that was intensely stratified (if not class conscious), Wells had to struggle ferociously to rise above his origins. He alternated various apprenticeships with classes at Midhurst Grammar School, finally winning a scholarship to the Normal School of Science. There he studied under the great biologist T. H. Huxley, who had a profound influence on Wells's world view. However, Wells left school early (though he graduated from London University in 1888) to embark on a teaching career. But, when he almost died from a tubercular hemorrhage, he chucked job and wife, running away with one of his students to "make one last attempt at authorship before early death."

Almost immediately he achieved success with science fiction works such as *The Time Machine* (1895), *The Star* (1897), *The Invisible Man* (1897), and *The War of the Worlds* (1898). After joining the Fabian Society in 1903, he began writing realistic novels such as *Ann Veronica* (1900) and *Tono-Bungay* (1908). Finally, in the third phase of his career he turned to thesis novels, serving merely to illustrate his sociopolitical theories as well as popular works of nonfiction such as *The Outline of History* (1920; revised 1931), *The Science of Life* (1929–1930), and *The Work, Wealth and Happiness of Mankind* (1932).

Physically, he was a small man with a large head and chest, darting eyes, and a shrill voice. Though bright, imaginative, and energetic, he seemed continually driven by desires to succeed, to save the world, and to satisfy strong sexual needs.

In addition to writing, politics was one of his lifelong passions, and in the early 1920s he unsuccessfully ran for Parliament twice as a Labor Party candidate. But, as the world drifted into World War II, he became disillusioned, pessimistic, and eccentric, By his death in 1946, he had reached absolute despair and the thesis of his last book, *Mind at the End of its Tether*,was "man's scientific advances were totally outdistancing his intellectual and social development."

Although remembered today primarily for his early science fiction, he also wrote approximately twenty fantasy stories, including two novels. *The Wonderful Visit* (1895) follows the misfortunes of an angel who falls to earth in a small English town. *The Sea Lady* (1902) explores the changes a middle-class Englishman experiences as a result of his love for a mermaid. However, it is his shorter fantasties which display the most range and readability. There is horror ("Pollock and the Porrah Man" and "The Red Room"), religious fantasy ("The Story of the Last Trump" and "The Apple"), and an early example of heroic fantasy ("The Valley of the Spiders").

For this volume we have chosen what most consider his greatest contribution to the genre: "The Man Who Could Work Miracles," a story of a man who discovers the weak points of wishing.

THE MAN WHO COULD WORK MIRACLES

A PANTOUM IN PROSE

It is doubtful whether the gift was innate. For my own part, I think it came to him suddenly. Indeed, until he was thirty he was a sceptic, and did not believe in miraculous powers. And here, since it is the most convenient place, I must mention that he was a little man, and had eyes of a hot brown, very erect red hair, a moustache with ends that he twisted up, and freckles. His name was George McWhirter Fotheringay—not the sort of name by any means to lead to any expectation of miracles—and he was clerk at Gomshott's. He was greatly addicted to assertive argument. It was while he was asserting the impossibility of miracles that he had his first intimation of his extraordinary powers. This particular argument was being held in the bar of the Long Dragon, and Toddy Beamish was conducting the opposition by a monotonous but effective "So *you* say," that drove Mr. Fotheringay to the very limit of his patience.

There were present, besides these two, a very dusty cyclist, landlord Cox, and Miss Maybridge, the perfectly respectable and rather portly barmaid of the Dragon. Miss Maybridge was standing with her back to Mr. Fotheringay, washing glasses; the others were watching him, more or less amused by the present ineffectiveness of the assertive method. Goaded by the Torres Vedras tactics of Mr. Beamish, Mr. Fotheringay determined to make an unusual rhetorical effort. "Looky here, Mr. Beamish," said Mr. Fotheringay. "Let us clearly understand what a miracle is. It's something contrariwise to the course of nature done by power of Will, something what couldn't happen without being specially willed."

"So *you* say," said Mr. Beamish, repulsing him.

Mr. Fotheringay appealed to the cyclist, who had hitherto been a silent auditor, and received his assent—given with a hesitating cough and a glance at Mr. Beamish. The landlord would express no opinion, and Mr. Fotheringay, returning to Mr. Beamish, received the unexpected concession of a qualified assent to his definition of a miracle.

"For instance," said Mr. Fotheringay, greatly encouraged. "Here would be a miracle. That lamp, in the natural course of nature, couldn't burn like that upsy-down, could it, Beamish?"

"*You* say it couldn't," said Beamish.

"And you?" said Fotheringay. "You don't mean to say—eh?"

"No," said Beamish reluctantly. "No, it couldn't."

"Very well," said Mr. Fotheringay. "Then here comes someone, as it might be me, along here, and stands as it might be here, and says to that lamp, as I might do, collecting all my will—'Turn upsy-down without breaking, and go on burning steady,' and—Hullo!"

It was enough to make anyone say "Hullo!" The impossible, the incredible, was visible to them all. The lamp hung inverted in the air, burning quietly with its flame pointing down. It was as solid, as indisputable as ever a lamp was, the prosaic common lamp of the Long Dragon bar.

Mr. Fotheringay stood with an extended forefinger and the knitted brows of one anticipating a catastrophic smash. The cyclist, who was sitting next to the lamp, ducked and jumped across the bar. Everybody jumped, more or less. Miss Maybridge turned and screamed. For nearly three seconds the lamp remained still. A faint cry of mental distress came from Mr. Fotheringay. "I can't keep it up," he said, "any longer." He staggered back, and the inverted lamp suddenly flared, fell against the corner of the bar, bounced aside, smashed upon the floor, and went out.

It was lucky it had a metal receiver, or the whole place would have been in a blaze. Mr. Cox was the first to speak, and his remark, shorn of needless excrescences, was to the effect that Fotheringay was a fool. Fotheringay was beyond disputing even so fundamental a proposition as that! He was astonished beyond measure at the thing that had occurred. The subsequent conversation threw absolutely no light on the matter so far as Fotheringay was concerned; the general opinion not only followed Mr. Cox very closely but very vehemently. Everyone accused Fotheringay of a silly trick, and presented him to himself as a foolish destroyer of comfort and security. His mind was in a tornado of perplexity, he was himself inclined to agree with them, and he made a remarkably ineffectual opposition to the proposal of his departure.

He went home flushed and heated, coat-collar crumpled, eyes smarting, and ears red. He watched each of the ten street lamps nervously as he passed it. It was only when he found himself alone in his little bedroom in Church Row that he was able to grapple seriously with his memories of the occurrence, and ask, "What on earth happened?"

He had removed his coat and boots, and was sitting on the bed with his hands in his pockets repeating the text of his defence for the seventeenth time, "*I* didn't want the confounded thing to upset," when it occurred to him that at the precise moment he had said the commanding words he had inadvertently willed the thing he said, and that when he had seen the lamp in the air he had felt that it depended on him to maintain it there without being clear how this was to be done. He had not a particularly complex mind, or he might have stuck for a time at that "inadvertently willed," embracing, as it does, the abstrusest problems of voluntary action; but as it was, the idea came to him with a quite acceptable haziness. And from that, following, as I must admit no clear logical path, he came to the test of experiment.

He pointed resolutely to his candle and collected his mind, though he felt he did a foolish thing. "Be raised up," he said. But in a second that feeling vanished. The candle was raised, hung in the air one giddy moment, and as Mr. Fotheringay gasped, fell with a smash on his toilet table, leaving him in darkness save for the expiring glow of its wick.

For a time Mr. Fotheringay sat in the darkness, perfectly still. "It did happen, after all," he said. "And 'ow I'm to explain it I *don't* know." He sighed heavily, and began feeling in his pockets for a match. He could find none, and he rose and groped about the toilet table. "I wish I had a match," he said. He resorted to his coat, and there were none there, and then it dawned upon him that miracles were possible even with matches. He extended a hand and scowled at it in the dark. "Let there be a match in that hand," he said. He felt some light object fall across his palm, and his fingers closed upon a match.

After several ineffectual attempts to light this, he discovered it was a safety-match. He threw it down, and then it occurred to him that he might have willed it lit. He did, and perceived it burning in the midst of his toilet-table mat. He caught it up hastily, and it went out. His perception of possibilities enlarged, and he felt for and replaced the candle in its candlestick. "Here! *you* be lit," said Mr. Fotheringay, and forthwith the candle was flaring, and he saw a little black hole in the toilet cover, with a wisp of smoke rising from it. For a time he stared from this to the little flame and back, and then looked up and met his own gaze in the looking glass. By this help he communed with himself in silence for a time.

"How about miracles now?" said Mr. Fotheringay at last, addressing his reflection.

The subsequent meditations of Mr. Fotheringay were of a severe but confused description. So far as he could see, it was a case of pure willing with him. The nature of his first experiences disinclined him for any further experiments except of the most cautious type. But he lifted a sheet of paper, and turned a glass of water pink and then green, and he created a snail, which he miraculously annihilated, and got himself a miraculous new toothbrush. Somewhen in the small hours he had reached the fact that his willpower must be of a particularly rare and pungent quality, a fact of which he had certainly had inklings before, but no certain assurance. The scare and perplexity of his first discovery were now qualified by pride in this evidence of singularity and by vague intimations of advantage. He became aware that the church clock was striking one, and as it did not occur to him that his daily duties at Gomshott's might be miraculously dispensed with, he resumed undressing, in order to get to bed without further delay. As he struggled to get his shirt over his head he was struck with a brilliant idea. "Let me be in bed," he said, and found himself so. "Undressed," he stipulated; and, finding the sheets cold, added hastily, "and in my nightshirt—no, in a nice soft woollen nightshirt. Ah!" he said with immense enjoyment. "And now let be comfortably asleep. . . ."

He awoke at his usual hour and was pensive all through breakfast time, wondering whether his overnight experience might not be a particularly vivid dream. At length his mind turned again to cautious experiments. For instance, he had three eggs for breakfast; two his landlady had supplied, good, but shoppy, and one was a delicious fresh goose egg, laid, cooked, and served by his extraordinary will. He hurried off to Gomshott's in a state of profound but carefully concealed excitement, and only remembered the shell of the third egg when his landlady spoke of it that night. All day he could do no work because of this astonishingly new self-knowledge, but this caused him no inconvenience, because he made up for it miraculously in his last ten minutes.

As the day wore on his state of mind passed from wonder to elation, albeit the circumstances of his dismissal from the Long Dragon were still disagreeable to recall, and a garbled account of the matter that had reached his colleagues led to some badinage. It was evident he must be careful how he lifted frangible articles, but in other ways his gift promised more and more as he turned it over in his mind. He intended among other things to increase his personal property by unostentatious acts of creation. He called into existence a pair of very splendid diamond studs, and hastily annihilated them again as young Gomshott came across the countinghouse to his desk. He was afraid young Gomshott might wonder how he had come by them. He saw quite clearly the gift required caution and watchfulness in its exercise, but so far as he could judge the difficulties attending its mastery would be no greater than those he had already faced in the study of cycling. It was that analogy, perhaps, quite as much as the feeling that he would be unwelcome in the Long Dragon, that drove him out after supper into the lane beyond the gasworks, to rehearse a few miracles in private.

There was possibly a certain want of originality in his attempts, for apart from his willpower Mr. Fotheringay was not a very exceptional man. The miracle of Moses' rod came to his mind, but the night was dark and unfavorable to the proper control of large miraculous snakes. Then he recollected the story of "Tannhäuser" that he had read on the back of the Philharmonic program. That seemed to him singularly attractive and harmless. He stuck his walking stick—a very nice Poona-Penang lawyer—into the turf that edged the footpath, and commanded the dry wood to blossom. The air was immediately full of the scent of roses, and by means of a match he saw for himself that his beautiful miracle was indeed accomplished. His satisfaction was ended by advancing footsteps. Afraid of a premature discovery of his powers, he addressed the blossoming stick hastily: "Go back." What he meant was "Change back"; but of course he was confused. The stick receded at a considerable velocity, and incontinently came a cry of anger and a bad word from the approaching person. "Who are you throwing brambles at, you fool?" cried a voice. "That got me on the shin."

"I'm sorry, old chap," said Mr. Fotheringay, and then, realizing the awkward nature of the explanation, caught nervously at his moustache. He saw Winch, one of the three Immering constables, advancing.

"What d'yer mean by it?" asked the constable. "Hullo! It's you, is it? The gent that broke the lamp at the Long Dragon!"

"I don't mean anything by it," said Mr. Fotheringay. "Nothing at all."

"What d'yer do it for then?"

"Oh, bother!" said Mr. Fotheringay.

"Bother, indeed? D'yer know that stick hurt? What d'yer do it for, eh?"

For the moment Mr. Fotheringay could not think what he had done it for. His silence seemed to irritate Mr. Winch. "You've been assaulting the police, young man, this time. That's what *you* done."

"Look here, Mr. Winch," said Mr. Fotheringay, annoyed and confused, "I'm very sorry. The fact is—"

"Well?"

He could think of no way but the truth. "I was working a miracle." He tried to speak in an offhand way, but try as he would he couldn't.

"Working a—! 'Ere, don't you talk rot. Working a miracle, indeed! Miracle! Well, that's downright funny! Why, you's the chap that don't believe in miracles. . . . Fact is, this is another of your silly conjuring tricks—that's what this is. Now, I tell you—"

But Mr. Fotheringay never heard what Mr. Winch was going to tell him. He realized he had given himself away, flung his valuable secret to all the winds of heaven. A violent gust of irritation swept him to action. He turned on the constable swiftly and fiercely. "Here," he said, "I've had enough of this, I have! I'll show you a silly conjuring trick, I will! Go to Hades! Go, now!"

He was alone!

Mr. Fotheringay performed no more miracles that night nor did he trouble to see what had become of his flowering stick. He returned to the town, scared and very quiet, and went to his bedroom. "Lord!" he said, "it's a powerful gift—an extremely powerful gift. I didn't hardly mean as much as that. Not really. . . . I wonder what Hades is like!"

He sat on the bed taking off his boots. Struck by a happy thought he transferred the constable to San Francisco, and without any more interference with normal causation went soberly to bed. In the night he dreamt of the anger of Winch.

The next day Mr. Fotheringay heard two interesting items of news.

Someone had planted a most beautiful climbing rose against the elder Mr. Gomshott's private house in the Lullaborough Road, and the river as far as Rawling's Mill was to be dragged for Constable Winch.

Mr. Fotheringay was abstracted and thoughtful all that day, and performed no miracles except certain provisions for Winch, and the miracle of completing his day's work with punctual perfection in spite of all the bee-swarm of thoughts that hummed through his mind. And the extraordinary abstraction and meekness of his manner was remarked by several people, and made a matter for jesting. For the most part he was thinking of Winch.

On Sunday evening he went to chapel, and oddly enough, Mr. Maydig, who took a certain interest in occult matters, preached about "things that are not lawful." Mr. Fotheringay was not a regular chapel goer, but the system of assertive scepticism, to which I have already alluded, was now very much shaken. The tenor of the sermon threw an entirely new light on these novel gifts, and he suddenly decided to consult Mr. Maydig immediately after the service. So soon as that was determined, he found himself wondering why he had not done so before.

Mr. Maydig, a lean, excitable man with quite remarkably long wrists and neck, was gratified at a request for a private conversation from a young man whose carelessness in religious matters was a subject for general remark in the town. After a few necessary delays, he conducted him to the study of the Manse, which was contiguous to the chapel, seated him comfortably, and standing in front of a cheerful fire—his legs threw a Rhodian arch of shadow on the oppostie wall—requested Mr. Fotheringay to state his business.

At first Mr. Fotheringay was a little abashed, and found some difficulty in opening the matter. "You will scarcely believe me, Mr. Maydig, I am afraid"— and so forth for some time. He tried a question at last, and asked Mr. Maydig his opinion of miracles.

Mr. Maydig was still saying "Well" in an extremely judicial tone, when Mr. Fotheringay interrupted again: "You don't believe, I suppose, that some common sort of person—like myself, for instance—as it might be sitting here now, might have some sort of twist inside him that made him able to do things by his will."

"It's possible," said Mr. Maydig. "Something of the sort, perhaps is possible."

"If I might make free with something here, I think I might show you by a sort of experiment," said Mr. Fotheringay. "Now, take that tobacco jar on the table, for instance. What I want to know is whether what I am going to do with it is a miracle or not. Just half a minute, Mr. Maydig, please."

He knitted his brows, pointed to the tobacco jar and said: "Be a bowl of vi'lets."

The tobacco jar did as it was ordered.

Mr. Maydig started violently at the change, and stood looking from the thaumaturgist to the bowl of flowers. He said nothing. Presently he ventured to lean over the table and smell the violets; they were fresh-picked and very fine ones. Then he stared at Mr. Fotheringay again.

"How did you do that?" he asked.

Mr. Fotheringay pulled his moustache. "Just told it—and there you are. Is that a miracle, or is it black art, or what is it? And what you think's the matter with me? That's what I want to ask."

"It's a most extraordinary occurrence."

"And this day last week I knew no more that I could do things like that than you did. It came quite sudden. It's something odd about my will, I suppose, and that's as far as I can see."

"Is *that*—the only thing? Could you do other things besides that?"

"Lord, yes!" said Mr. Fotheringay. "Just anything." He thought, and suddenly recalled a conjuring entertainment he had seen. "Here!" He pointed. "Change into a bowl of fish—no, not that—change into a glass bowl full of water with goldfish swimming in it. That's better! You see that, Mr. Maydig?"

"It's astonishing. It's incredible. You are either a most extraordinary. . . . But no—"

"I could change it into anything," said Mr. Fotheringay. "Just anything. Here! be a pigeon, will you?"

In another moment a blue pigeon was fluttering round the room and making Mr. Maydig duck every time it came near him. "Stop there, will you," said Mr. Fotheringay; and the pigeon hung motionless in the air. "I could change it back to a bowl of flowers," he said, and after replacing the pigeon on the table worked that miracle. "I expect you will want your pipe in a bit," he said, and restored the tobacco jar.

Mr. Maydig had followed all these later changes in a sort of ejaculatory silence. He stared at Mr. Fotheringay and, in a very gingerly manner, picked up the tobacco jar, examined it, replaced it on the table. *"Well!"* was the only expression of his feelings.

"Now, after that it's easier to explain what I came about," said Mr. Fotheringay; and proceeded to a lengthy and involved narrative of his strange experiences, beginning with the affair of the lamp in the Long Dragon and complicated by persistent allusions to Winch. As he went on, the transient pride Mr. Maydig's consternation had caused passed away; he became the very ordinary Mr. Fotheringay of everyday intercourse again. Mr. Maydig listened intently, the tobacco jar in his hand, and his bearing changed also with the course of the narrative. Presently, while Mr. Fotheringay was dealing with the miracle of the third egg, the minister interrupted with a fluttering extended hand—

"It is possible," he said. "It is credible. It is amazing, of course, but it reconciles a number of difficulties. The power to work miracles is a gift—a peculiar quality like genius or second sight—hitherto it has come very rarely and to exceptional people. But in this case . . . I have always wondered at the miracles of Mahomet, and at Yogi's miracles, and the miracles of Madame Blavatsky. But, of course! Yes, it is simply a gift! It carries out so beautifully the arguments of that great thinker"—Mr. Maydig's voice sank—"his Grace the Duke of Argyll. Here we plumb some profounder law—deeper than the ordinary laws of nature. Yes—yes. Go on. Go on!"

Mr. Fotheringay proceeded to tell of his misadventure with Winch, and Mr. Maydig, no longer overawed or scared, began to jerk his limbs about and interject astonishment, "It's this what troubled me most," proceeded Mr. Fotheringay; "it's this I'm most mijitly in want of advice for; of course he's at San Francisco—wherever San Francisco may be—but of course it's awkward for both of us, as you'll see Mr. Maydig. I don't see how he can understand what has happened, and I dare say he's scared and exasperated something tremendous, and trying to get at me. I dare say he keeps on starting off to come here. I send him back, by a miracle, every few hours, when I think of it. And of course, that's a thing he won't be able to understand, and it's bound to annoy him; and, of course, if he takes a ticket every time it will cost him a lot of money. I done the best I could for him, but of course it's difficult for him to put himself in my place. I thought afterwards that his clothes might have got scorched, you know—if Hades is all it's supposed to be—before I shifted him. In that case I suppose they'd have locked him up in San Francisco. Of course I willed him a new suit of clothes on him directly I thought of it. But, you see, I'm already in a deuce of a tangle—"

Mr. Maydig looked serious. "I see you are in a tangle. Yes, it's a difficult position. How you are to end it . . ." He became diffuse and inconclusive.

"However, we'll leave Winch for a little and discuss the larger question. I don't think this is a case of the black art or anything of the sort. I don't think there is any taint of criminality about it at all, Mr. Fotheringay—none whatever, unless you are suppressing material facts. No, it's miracles—pure miracles—miracles, if I may say so, of the very highest class."

He began to pace the hearthrug and gesticulate, while Mr. Fotheringay sat with his arm on the table and his head on his arm, looking worried. "I don't see how I'm to manage about Winch," he said.

"A gift of working miracles—apparently a very powerful gift," said Mr. Maydig, "will find a way about Winch—never fear. My dear sir, you are a most important man—a man of the most astonishing possibilities. As evidence, for example! And in other ways, the things you may do. . . ."

"Yes, *I've* thought of a thing or two," said Mr. Fotheringay. "But—some of the things came a bit twisty. You saw that fish at first? Wrong sort of bowl and wrong sort of fish. And I thought I'd ask someone."

"A proper course," said Mr. Maydig, "a very proper course—altogether the proper course." He stopped and looked at Mr. Fotheringay. "It's practically an unlimited gift. Let us test your powers, for instance. If they really *are* . . . If they really are all they seem to be."

And so, incredible as it may seem, in the study of the little house behind the Congregational Chapel, on the evening of Sunday, November 10, 1896, Mr. Fotheringay, egged on and inspired by Mr. Maydig, began to work miracles. The reader's attention is specially and definitely called to the date. He will object, probably has already objected, that certain points in this story are improbable, that if any things of the sort already described had indeed occurred, they would have been in all the papers a year ago. The details immediately following he will find particularly hard to accept, because among other things they involve the conclusion that he or she, the reader in question, must have been killed in a violent and unprecedented manner more than a year ago. Now a miracle is nothing if not improbable, and as a matter of fact the reader *was* killed in a violent and unprecedented manner a year ago. In the subsequent course of this story that will become perfectly clear and credible, as every right-minded and reasonable reader will admit. But this is not the place for the end of the story, being but little beyond the hither side of the middle. And at first the miracles worked by Mr. Fotheringay were timid little miracles—little things with the cups and parlor fitments, as feeble as the miracles of Theosophists, and feeble as they were, they were received with awe by his collaborator. He would have preferred to settle the Winch business out of hand, but Mr. Maydig would not let him. But after they had worked a dozen of these domestic trivialities, their sense of power grew, their imagination began to show signs of stimulation, and their ambition enlarged. Their first larger enterprise was due to hunger and the negligence of Mrs. Minchin, Mr. Maydig's housekeeper. The meal to which the minister conducted Mr. Fotheringay was certainly ill-laid and uninviting as refreshment for two industrious miracle workers; but they were seated, and Mr. Maydig was descanting in sorrow rather than in anger upon his housekeeper's shortcomings, before it occurred to Mr. Fotheringay that an opportunity lay before him. "Don't you think, Mr. Maydig," he said, "if it isn't a liberty, I—"

"My dear Mr. Fotheringay! Of course! No—I didn't think."

Mr. Fotheringay waved his hand. "What shall we have?" he said, in a large, inclusive spirit, and, at Mr. Maydig's order, revised the supper very thoroughly. "As for me," he said, eyeing Mr. Maydig's selection, "I am always particularly fond of a tankard of stout and a nice Welsh rarebit, and I'll order that. I ain't much given to Burgundy," and forthwith stout and Welsh rarebit promptly appeared at his command. They sat long at their supper, talking like equals, as Mr. Fotheringay presently perceived with a glow of surprise and gratification, of all the miracles they would presently do. "And by the bye, Mr. Maydig," said Mr. Fotheringay, "I might perhaps be able to help you—in a domestic way."

"Don't quite follow," said Mr. Maydig, pouring out a glass of miraculous old Burgundy.

Mr. Fotheringay helped himself to a second Welsh rarebit out of vacancy, and took a mouthful. "I was thinking," he said, "I might be able (*chum, chum*) to work (*chum, chum*) a miracle with Mrs. Minchin (*chum, chum*)—make her a better woman."

Mr. Maydig put down the glass and looked doubtful. "She's—She strongly objects to interference, you know, Mr. Fotheringay. And—as a matter of fact—it's well past eleven and she's probably in bed and asleep. Do you think, on the whole—"

Mr. Fotheringay considered these objections. "I don't see that it shouldn't be done in her sleep."

For a time Mr. Maydig opposed the idea, and then he yielded. Mr. Fotheringay issued his orders, and a little less at their ease, perhaps, the two gentlemen proceeded with their repast. Mr. Maydig was enlarging on the changes he might expect in his housekeeper next day, with an optimism that seemed even to Mr. Fotheringay's supper senses a little forced and hectic, when a series of confused noises from upstairs began. Their eyes exchanged interrogations, and Mr. Maydig left the room hastily. Mr. Fotheringay heard him calling up to his housekeeper and then his footsteps going softly up to her.

In a minute or so the minister returned, his step light, his face radiant. "Wonderful!" he said, "and touching! Most touching!"

He began pacing the hearthrug. "A repentance—a most touching repentance—through the crack of the door. Poor woman! A most wonderful change! She had got up. She must have got up at once. She had got up out of her sleep to smash a private bottle of brandy in her box. And to confess it, too! . . . But this gives us—it opens—a most amazing vista of possibilities. If we can work this miraculous change in *her* . . ."

"The thing's unlimited seemingly," said Mr. Fotheringay. "And about Mr. Winch—"

"Altogether unlimited." And from the hearthrug Mr. Maydig, waving the Winch difficulty aside, unfolded a series of wonder proposals—proposals he invented as he went along.

Now what these proposals were does not concern the essentials of this story. Suffice it that they were designed in a spirit of infinite benevolence, the sort of benevolence that used to be called postprandial. Suffice it, too, that the problem of Winch remained unsolved. Nor is it necessary to describe how far that series got to its fulfillment. There were astonishing changes. The small hours found Mr. Maydig and Mr. Fotheringay careering across the chilly market-square under the still moon, in a sort of ecstasy of thaumaturgy, Mr. Maydig all flap and gesture, Mr. Fotheringay short and bristling, and no longer abashed at his greatness. They had reformed every drunkard in the Parliamentary division, changed all the beer and alcohol to water (Mr. Maydig had overruled Mr. Fotheringay on this point), they had, further, greatly improved the railway communication of the place, drained Flinder's swamp, improved the soil of One Tree Hill, and cured the Vicar's wart. And they were going to see what could be done with the injured pier at South Bridge. "The place," gasped Mr. Maydig, "won't be the same place tomorrow. How surprised and thankful everyone will be!" And just at that moment the church clock struck three.

"I say," said Mr. Fotheringay, "that's three o'clock! I must be getting back. I've got to be at business by eight. And besides, Mrs. Wimms—"

"We're only beginning," said Mr. Maydig, full of the sweetness of unlimited power. "We're only beginning. Think of all the good we're doing. When people wake—"

"But—" said Mr. Fotheringay.

Mr. Maydig gripped his arm suddenly. His eyes were bright and wild. "My dear chap," he said, "there's no hurry. Look"—he pointed to the moon at the zenith—"Joshua!"

"Joshua?" said Mr. Fotheringay.

"Joshua," said Mr. Maydig. "Why not? Stop it."

Mr. Fotheringay looked at the moon.

"That's a bit tall," he said after a pause.

"Why not?" said Mr. Maydig. "Of course it doesn't stop. You stop the rotation of the earth, you know. Time stops. It isn't as if we were doing harm."

"H'm!" said Mr. Fotheringay. "Well." He sighed. "I'll try. Here—"

He buttoned up his jacket and addressed himself to the habitable globe, with as good an assumption of confidence as lay in his power. "Jest stop rotating, will you?" said Mr. Fotheringay.

Incontinently he was flying head over heels through the air at the rate of dozens of miles a minute. In spite of the innumerable circles he was describing per second, he thought; for thought is wonderful—sometimes as sluggish as flowing pitch, sometimes as instantaneous as light. He thought in a second, and willed. "Let me come down safe and sound. Whatever else happens, let me down safe and sound."

He willed it only just in time, for his clothes, heated by his rapid flight through the air, were already beginning to singe. He came down with a forcible but by no means injurious bump in what appeared to be a mound of fresh-turned earth. A large mass of metal and masonry, extraordinarily like the clock tower in the middle of the market-square, hit the earth near him, ricochetted over him, and flew into stonework, bricks, and masonry, like a bursting bomb. A hurtling cow hit one of the larger blocks and smashed like an egg. There was a crash that made all the most violent crashes of his past life seem like the sound of falling dust, and this was followed by a descending series of lesser crashes. A vast wind roared throughout earth and heaven, so that he could scarcely lift his head to look. For a while he was too breathless and astonished even to see where he was or what had happened. And his first movement was to feel his head and reassure himself that his streaming hair was still his own.

"Lord!" gasped Mr. Fotheringay, scarce able to speak for the gale, "I've had a squeak! What's gone wrong? Storms and thunder. And only a minute ago a fine night. It's Maydig set me on to this sort of thing. *What* a wind! If I go on fooling in this way I'm bound to have a thundering accident! . . .

"Where's Maydig?

"What a confounded mess everything's in!"

He looked about him so far as his flapping jacket would permit. The appearance of things was really extremely strange. "The sky's all right anyhow," said Mr. Fotheringay. "And that's about all that is all right. And even there it looks like a terrific gale coming up. But there's the moon overhead. Just as it was just now. Bright as midday. But as for the rest—Where's the village? Where's—where's anything? And what on earth set this wind a-blowing? *I* didn't order no wind."

Mr. Fotheringay struggled to get to his feet in vain, and after one failure, remained on all fours, holding on. He surveyed the moonlit world to leeward, with the tails of his jacket streaming over his head. "There's something seriously wrong," said Mr. Fotheringay. "And what it is—goodness knows."

Far and wide nothing was visible in the white glare through the haze of dust that drove before a screaming gale but tumbled masses of earth and heaps of inchoate ruins, no trees, no houses, no familiar shapes, only a wilderness of disorder vanishing at last into the darkness beneath the whirling columns and streamers, the lightnings and thunderings of a swiftly rising storm. Near him in the livid glare was something that might once have been an elm tree, a smashed mass of splinters, shivered from boughs to base, and further a twisted mass of iron girders—only too evidently the viaduct—rose out of the piled confusion.

You see, when Mr. Fotheringay had arrested the rotation of the solid globe, he had made no stipulation concerning the trifling movables upon its surface. And the earth spins so fast that the surface at its equator is travelling at rather more than a thousand miles an hour, and in these latitudes at more than half that pace. So that the village, and Mr. Maydig, and Mr. Fotheringay, and everybody and everything had been jerked violently forward at about nine miles per second—that is to say, much more violently than if they had been fired out of a cannon. And every human being, every living creature, every house, and every tree—all the world as we know it—had been so jerked and smashed and utterly destroyed. That was all.

These things Mr. Fotheringay did not, of course, fully appreciate. But he perceived that his miracle had miscarried, and with that a great disgust of miracles came upon him. He was in darkness now, for the clouds had swept together and blotted out his momentary glimpse of the moon, and the air was full of fitful struggling tortured wraiths of hail. A great roaring of wind and waters filled earth and sky, and, peering under his hand through the dust and sleet to windward, he saw by the play of the lightnings a vast wall of water pouring toward him.

"Maydig!" screamed Mr. Fotheringay's feeble voice amid the elemental uproar. "Here!—Maydig!"

"Stop!" cried Mr. Fotheringay to the advancing water. "Oh, for goodness' sake, stop!

"Just a moment," said Mr. Fotheringay to the lightnings and thunder. "Stop jest a moment while I collect my thoughts . . . And now what shall I do?" he said. "What *shall* I do? Lord! I wish Maydig was about.

"I know," said Mr. Fotheringay. "And for goodness' sake let's have it right *this* time."

He remained on all fours, leaning against the wind, very intent to have everything right.

"Ah!" he said. "Let nothing what I'm going to order happen until I say 'Off!' . . . Lord! I wish I'd thought of that before!"

He lifted his little voice against the whirlwind, shouting louder and louder in the vain desire to hear himself speak. "Now then!—here goes! Mind about that what I said just now. In the first place, when all I've got to say is done, let me lose my miraculous power, let my will become just like anybody else's will, and all these dangerous miracles be stopped. I don't like them. I'd rather I didn't work 'em. Ever so much. That's the first thing. And the second is—let me be back just before the miracles begin; let everything be just as it was before that blessed lamp turned up. It's a big job, but it's the last. Have you got it? No more miracles, everything as it was—me back in the Long Dragon just before I drank my half-pint. That's it! Yes."

He dug his fingers into the mould, closed his eyes, and said "Off!"

Everything became perfectly still. He perceived that he was standing erect.

"So *you* say," said a voice.

He opened his eyes. He was in the bar of the Long Dragon, arguing about miracles with Toddy Beamish. He had a vague sense of some great thing forgotten that instantaneously passed. You see, except for the loss of his miraculous powers, everything was back as it had been; his mind and memory therefore were now just as they had been at the time when this story began. So that he knew absolutely nothing of all that is told here, knows nothing of all that is told here to this day. And among other things, of course, he still did not believe in miracles.

"I tell you that miracles, properly speaking, can't possibly happen," he said, "whatever you like to hold. And I'm prepared to prove it up to the hilt."

"That's what *you* think," said Toddy Beamish, and "Prove it if you can."

"Looky here, Mr. Beamish," said Mr. Fotheringay. "Let us clearly understand what a miracle is. It's something contrariwise to the course of nature done by power of Will. . . ."